ELLIE K. WILDE

The No-Judgment Zone

Copyright © 2023 by Ellie K. Wilde

All rights reserved. No part of this publication may be reproduced, stored or transmitted in any form or by any means, electronic, mechanical, photocopying, recording, scanning, or otherwise without written permission from the publisher. It is illegal to copy this book, post it to a website, or distribute it by any other means without permission.

This novel is entirely a work of fiction. The names, characters and incidents portrayed in it are the work of the author's imagination. Any resemblance to actual persons, living or dead, events or localities is entirely coincidental.

Ellie K. Wilde asserts the moral right to be identified as the author of this work.

Designations used by companies to distinguish their products are often claimed as trademarks. All brand names and product names used in this book and on its cover are trade names, service marks, trademarks and registered trademarks of their respective owners. The publishers and the book are not associated with any product or vendor mentioned in this book. None of the companies referenced within the book have endorsed the book.

First edition

Cover art by Ashley Santoro
Editing by Jennifer Herrington

This book was professionally typeset on Reedsy.
Find out more at reedsy.com

Ellie K. Wilde

THE No-Judgment ZONE

Chapter 1

Jenna

People are predictable.

I first learned this at my seventh birthday party, when I ditched the private piano concert in my parents' living room to strip down to my skivvies and splash around in the pool. My uptight mother was so mortified she gifted me the silent treatment for a good three days.

I learned it again at twenty-seven, when I followed the sounds of skin-on-skin to find my shameless flirt of a live-in boyfriend screwing another girl in my bed.

These days, *predictable* is a daily reality every time I leave the hotel rooms I've existed out of during my last eight months of travel. When you've got a head of pink hair, you can pretty much expect one of three reactions:

1. The blatant staring. Either judgmental, perplexed, or horrified.
2. The *don't look, honey, just keep walking*. Often uttered to small children, usually girls, who stare in awe as they pass me in the street.
3. The *you must be wild in the sack*. Shouted at me by drunk frat boys at the bar, who instantly disqualify themselves from ever learning the truth of that statement.

Half the time I'm convinced they put something in the pink dye to help eat away at your shame. Keep you coming back whenever your roots start growing in.

I tug my hair from the ponytail on top of my head, using the mirrored elevator wall to fluff it into place around my shoulders. It's a fruitless exercise. I'm not trying to impress anyone—not yet anyway—but the fact is that I'm damn proud of my hair and how it announces to the world the flimsy number of shits I give about what it thinks about me. It's kind of a by-product of living the first quarter of my life in a heavy-on-the-judgment, light-on-the-personality world.

My entire body tingles in anticipation the second the elevator opens. By the time I make it across the private lobby and knock on the door at its other end, suitcase trailing behind me, I'm actually bouncing. *Bouncing* from excitement, because about three whole seasons have passed since the last time I saw her—

Also predictable: the high-pitched yelp I cut off when I throw myself at my best friend Jude, launching us into her apartment to smash into the console table on the opposite wall.

"You're here!" she cries. "I can't believe it—did you come straight from the airport?"

I pick her up around the waist and spin her around, made easy by my God-given long legs and completely un-earned, natural strength.

"Had to make one tiny stop on the way. My hair was in dire need of maintenance."

Jude grabs my overstuffed luggage and starts hauling it down the hall ahead of me. "You look amazing. Exactly the same," she says over her shoulder.

"What were you expecting, a face transplant?"

"I don't know! I spent the better part of a year obsessively refreshing social media, and those pictures only get you so far. You could have grown a third eye for all I knew."

I hurry forward to give her a healthy smack on the ass. Because I'm over the moon excited to see her, but also loving the lightness in her step that had been missing for years. That I'd worked hard to help her get back until I could leave it in her boyfriend's very capable, if slightly grumpy hands.

We emerge into the open living-room-kitchen and I whistle, taking in the space. The high penthouse ceilings, the wall of windows framing a perfect view of the city skyline. "This is one hell of an apartment upgrade, Juju. How's cohabitation treating you?"

Jude stashes my suitcase against a wall and leads me to the deep leather sofa—definitely picked out by her boyfriend, pre-cohabitation—accessorized with plushy cushions and linen throw blankets—definitely purchased post-cohabitation.

"Well, it's only been a month. But it feels like I've always lived here. I know it probably seems fast, moving in after less than a year together but..."

"Who cares how it seems?" I say, taking her in. "You look so happy."

She flushes. "I really am. And even happier now that you're back. Tell me everything. How was your flight home?"

"You wouldn't believe how bad it was," I tell her, slumping against her and letting her wrap her arms around my neck. "The guy next to me wouldn't stop commenting on the movie he had on like I was watching it with him. And then he finally zonked out and snored in my ear the rest of the flight. I swear I can still hear it when the room's too quiet."

"You didn't fly business class?"

I wrinkle my nose. "God no. I'd take an overeager seatmate over business class any day of the week."

With a little smile, Jude reaches for a blanket to cover us both. She's possibly the one person with any sympathy for me in this department.

And look, I get it. Poor little rich girl, rebelling against her family's generational wealth and the sickening dollar figure in her trust-slash-bribery-fund.

I'm not a total saint, obviously. I let my dad buy me a penthouse when I turned twenty-five, didn't fight him all that hard when he insisted I keep the profit after I sold it before my trip. And I've been living off the bribery fund since the day I quit my job to travel. But I was the first Carling-born girl in two generations to take on a job after college, and I stuck with it for a good four years, sitting behind a reception desk and talking Jude into unnecessary coffee breaks throughout the day. Eventually, though, the Carling gene won out. I couldn't have withstood that swivel chair another minute.

"When do the family festivities start, by the way?" Jude asks gently.

All the gentleness in the world couldn't prevent me from throwing back my head and letting out a helpless groan. "The actual wedding isn't until the end of the summer. But we shop for bridesmaid dresses tomorrow, and in true Carling fashion there are precisely two-thousand pre-wedding events to attend."

"And nobody thinks it's at all weird that you're not maid of honor? She's known you since birth."

"Ah, but she's known her best friend Portia for a full six months," I say with a wink. "Besides, you've been to enough Carling gatherings to know what a silly statement that is. I'm shocked Ronnie's acknowledging me as a sibling at all."

The fact that Ronnie, my pearl-clutcher of an older sister, chose a virtual stranger to headline her bridal party should tell you everything you need to know about our relationship. And the fact that I call her Ronnie instead Veronica, like she's angrily insisted since I picked up the habit at thirteen? Well, it should tell you just as much as the fact that she insists on calling me Genevieve, even though I've expressly gone by Jenna for as long as I remember. I was so eager to distance myself from the family name and the expectations behind it that I went so far as to swap the G for a J.

Sue me.

"But enough about *those* nuptials. Where's my favorite bite of cherry pie? I thought he decided to close his restaurants on Sundays and Mondays?"

I pretend to look around the open apartment for Theo, her total grump of a boyfriend who's so staggeringly eager and sweet for her, he earned himself the nickname about the third time I met him. Sweet and tart as cherry pie. I take Jude's hand.

"And how is it possible there's no ring on his finger yet? I lost my bet, you know. You both cost me five hundred bucks."

"They're closed on Mondays and Tuesdays," Jude says, blushing as she takes back her hand. "You're making bets on us?"

CHAPTER 1

"I bet you'd get engaged within six months and elope by the one-year mark. Guess I can still pin my hopes on that second one."

"Who are you making bets with?"

I pick a piece of fluff off my leggings, waiting for it to connect.

Suddenly she jolts. "*Finn?*" she says it so loudly I lose the ability to hear from my left ear.

"Take it easy, jumpy," I mutter, tugging at my ear. "We came up with the bet after you and Cherry Pie left us to our own devices, the time we bumped into them at the bar."

"You're telling me you haven't spoken a word to him since that one single time, almost a year ago?"

"Correct."

"Okay, what the hell is going on here?" Jude moves so that she sits facing me cross-legged, with her arms tightly wound across her chest and a look so stern my chest seizes for a second, until I remember I am not sitting with my mother. "You had one whirlwind night, in which you supposedly *didn't* sleep together—"

"We did not sleep together," I confirm for the umpteenth time.

"Didn't even kiss—"

"Definitely didn't kiss."

"And yet here you are making *bets* on us—"

I lay a scandalized hand on my chest. "*Bets?* Surely not!"

She switches tracks, suddenly giving me a pleading look. "Look, nobody's on board with this union more than I am. He's one of Theo's best friends and I love you both very much. Please don't hold out on me—let me bask in your budding love."

"There will be no *unioning*," I say tartly. "No budding and *definitely* none of that... L-word stuff. I've got a flight back to Europe booked for after the wedding."

I ignore her pout. God, I hate it when she pouts. She knows exactly what those wide, round eyes do to me.

"You're really going to pretend you don't have a thing for him?" she asks innocently. "Not even a tiny little crush?"

"Nope." I make a popping sound on the *P* for emphasis.

"Not even when you picture his baby blue eyes? The way his skin tans a little gold when he spends time in the sun?"

Damn her.

Damn her and the way her words instantly have Finn's face flashing in my mind and my lungs constricting. He was tanned when I met him. Skin so golden it brought out the blue of his eyes and the pink in his mouth. How lethal he looked when he just casually licked his lips... He's sexy without even trying. And when he does turn on the charm? Well—

"No," I say firmly. "Not even then."

"Not the way his hair sometimes just falls into his face? That sandy color, how soft it looks even though it's always kind of disheveled or under a baseball cap?"

I've felt his hair, as it happens. I stripped off the backwards baseball cap in question in the cab we'd been riding on the way to hook up at his place before we got stranded in the countryside. It *was* soft, wasn't it? The way you just want to grab a fistful on top and—

"He goes running with Theo sometimes. Did I mention that? I've seen him without a shirt on and—"

Suddenly my skin feels about six sizes too snug.

"Fine. *Fine.* You want to know what the deal is with Finn?" Jude's eyes widen eagerly. I let out a great sigh, dramatically sinking into the sofa cushions. "He's the one that got away."

Jude squeaks. Actually *squeaks*. "I *knew* it. I knew you were perfect together."

I nod, combing my fingers through the lengths of my hair, staring dreamily at the ceiling. "Finn Palmer. That pesky little almost-one-night-stand I couldn't close the deal on before my trip."

I snort, dissolving into silent laughter. Jude's smile fades into a scowl so deep it's clear how much Theo has rubbed off on her. And not in the good way.

"But you got along so well," she says, shoulders slumping. "Come on, don't tell me this is just a sex thing."

CHAPTER 1

"It's exactly a sex thing. In fact, we agreed on it the last time we saw each other, before the night went totally sideways: we're two people with the hots for each other, who just need to fuck and move on. Nothing more to it." I come out from under the throw blanket to stand. "Speaking of which. I think it's about time I head out."

"Hang on, are you not staying with us? I was banking on having you here until you went back to Europe."

I focus on a spot on the far wall. Avoiding the pout.

"Don't worry, little one, I'll be back later tonight." I try to pat her blindly on the head but end up smacking her in the face. She swats away my hand. "I just need to take care of some long overdue business. But first, I need an outfit change."

Chapter 2

Finn

On all counts, Bianca Astley is a good-looking girl.

More than good-looking, if I'm being fair, and I've made it my business to be fair with any of the women I've dated. And the women I haven't dated because I use the term *dating* loosely, anyway.

So, yeah. If I'm being fair, Bianca Astley is volcanic kind of hot. Tall, the kind of curves that demand you sink your teeth into them. Sexy chin length hair, all messy around her face. Freckles spattered over her button nose.

So why—*why* in the ever-living hell—can't I dial up the charm, here?

At this point in my life, this shouldn't be a struggle.

Smile. Not too big so she thinks I'm overeager, but she's gotta know I'm interested.

Drop my voice, just casually. The kind of tone that signals intimacy, requires us to stand just a little closer together.

If—and only if—she's giving off clear signals, lightly brush her hand, her arm. I don't play games. I make my attraction clear.

Let her take the lead. And if she suggests going out, lay it out clearly for her so there's no chance for misunderstandings or hurt feelings. I don't date, haven't been out with the same woman more than once in a decade. I'm a one-night-only kinda guy, and I like it that way. If she's on the same page, I'd be happy as a clam to take her to drinks, dinner, whatever she wants. And

CHAPTER 2

if I still get an invite back to her place afterward, all the better.

Maybe it sounds a little cringe-worthy, having the this-is-just-sex talk upfront. But I don't make a habit of messing with people's heads and, these days, I barely have to get the words out, anyway. The servers at work all talk, and when any of the new girls come to me it's because they've heard all about the bimbo head chef manning the kitchen.

It's almost scary, how fast word can spread that way.

But if it's just a casual lay she's looking for, better me than the other guy who'll toy with her emotions just for the egotistical gratification of it. You come to Finn Palmer for one thing and one thing only. And you leave a happy camper.

So. Bianca Astley. Curvy, funny, total sex-bomb new server at Sunset Landing, the restaurant I was brought to almost a year ago. Standing here in front of me by the swinging doors to the kitchen, basically employing all my moves on *me* as she describes her recent trip to Europe and all the nude beaches she explored.

Done deal, right?

"I've never been to Europe. Haven't traveled much lately in general, actually. I've got this pet turtle—Eddie, short for Edison, because the pattern on his shell looks weirdly like a light bulb and... Where was I going with this? Oh yeah, it hurts my heart a little, leaving him for too long."

Huh?

It's the word that pops into my head the second I stop blabbering, and it's written all over Bianca's face, too.

She looks off to the side, gaze clashing with the wall as though she's waiting for someone to fill her in on the prank she's clearly been subjected to. Because whatever she was expecting to hear when she came over to talk, it wasn't about Eddie.

Which is a real shame because I love that little guy.

After a second, she wipes the little frown off her face and feeds me the kind of grin that, objectively, looks like an open invitation to bed.

"What are your plans tonight?"

"Cold pizza and that new documentary on fish farming that's streaming now. Have you heard of it? It's an inside look at the fish farms all along the Pacific, and man, that stuff gets real depressing. It's why I jumped at the opportunity when Theo asked me to join the kitchen here. Sustainable sourcing and all that. It's one of the things that makes this place so unique, you know."

What? *Why?*

Why did I dive straight into my Sunset Landing sales pitch? Forget the fact that she already knows the sales pitch because she—you know—*works here.* This is just *bad.*

"That's... nice?" Her frown is back.

Abort mission.

I start casting around for a way to head off further conversation. Maybe I can claim I need to go clean the kitchen now that it's closed, and pray she doesn't know it's not strictly part of my job description.

But Bianca, poor, sweet Bianca Astley is right there with me, it seems. "Anyway, I need to go clock out. See you around. I guess."

The *I guess* sounded a lot like an *I hope not.*

"What the hell are you doing?" I mutter to myself, dragging a hand down my face after she leaves me to wallow in shame.

"By the looks of it, you're making a damn good fool of yourself, that's what."

Behind me, Nina leans her shoulder against the wall, unbuttoning the white chef's jacket that's still pristine other than a couple drops of tomato sauce on her sleeve. I've always been impressed with chefs who, like my sous chef, go for the white jacket and escape a whole cook with barely a stain. I don't bother pretending I can manage that, even as far back as culinary school—well, the couple months I was there before dropping out. I go straight for the black jacket when it's offered.

I've known Nina since my last gig at Brookwood, where we both started out as line cooks and moved up the ranks for a few years. I was a groomsman in her wedding and Nina regularly wing-womaned for me back when I still had any semblance of game. When I was offered this job I couldn't think of a better person to bring here with me.

CHAPTER 2

Nina reaches up to shake free the long, platinum blonde hair she had coiled on top of her head. "I thought it was bad when you told Sarah Harvey about the weird rash you got after petting that stray dog a couple months ago. You're really giving yourself a run for your money."

I groan into my elbow. "Please, don't remind me about that. It was bad enough in real time."

"Worse than the time you told Jessie Bates she reminded you of your Great Aunt Sue?"

She's right. This malady has been afflicting me longer than I want to admit. It's not like I haven't noticed. I haven't been on a date in months, and my right hand hasn't seen this rigorous a workout since I was somewhere around thirteen.

"Nina, I'm scared. What's wrong with me?" I shuffle closer, bending my knees to bring us at eye level. "Feel my forehead. Do you think I'm dying?"

She snorts and shoves me in the shoulder. "You're not *dying*."

"You sure?" I plant a hand on the wall above her head. Tilt my head, drop my voice a little. "You look great tonight, by the way."

She recoils into the wall, looking completely disgusted except for the definite twitch in her cheek. "Nope. I'm still gay, you idiot."

I hang my head, hiding my laugh. "Figures."

"You know, I was talking to Maddie about it—"

I stuff my hands in my pockets. "God, what is this? Are my misfortunes marital gossip fodder now?"

"Oh, shut up. You know how much we care about you," she tells me. "We're worried. This is such a far cry from the sexual frenzy you stirred up at Brookwood. But then Maddie had this idea that maybe this is your brain telling you to lay off sex."

I'm so horrified by the statement that I almost trip over my feet in an effort to move away. "That can't be true. Why would it want that?"

Nina shrugs. "Then maybe it's a sign from your body. When was the last time you got checked?"

I throw up my hands to shield my face from the slap of those words. "I'm *clean*. I get checked regularly."

"Then maybe the Tin Man has a heart, after all?"

"*Tin Man*—I'm a good person." I feel the color drain from my face. "*Aren't I?*"

"You are," she concedes, sucking in her cheeks to stop from laughing. "But I'm loving the prepubescent pitch your voice goes to when you panic."

That little brat. She huffs out a laugh when I get her in a headlock and muss her hair.

"All right, is it all cleaned up in there?" I nod to the kitchen, dropping my arm around her shoulder. "Yeah? Then let's get the hell out of here. I've got day-old pizza in the fridge with my name on it."

Chapter 3

Finn

You know what? Who needs sex.

Putting on a pair of sweats, swapping my contact lenses for glasses, wolfing down last night's veggie delight pizza. Isn't this what life's really about?

Contrary to what people seem to believe about me, I can survive without sex. I may have taken an extra few minutes in the shower to take the edge off. But everyone does that.

Settling into the sofa, I listen to the soothing narration from the documentary on TV. Just as I start stuffing pizza into my mouth there's a knock at the door.

I groan into the living room. "For the thousandth time, Mrs. Jenkins," I call at the door as I stand. "It doesn't matter that I live alone. I'm still allowed to talk to myself, and it's not my fault they built this place with paper thin walls."

I stick the piece of pizza into my mouth, letting it hang there as I wipe greasy fingers on my sweats before wrenching open the door.

Holy. Fucking. Shit.

I choke on the slice of pizza. It falls out of my mouth and I scramble to catch it with a Charlie Chaplin kind of juggling act, struggling to catch my breath. I'd pay every single cent in my bank account to undo that failure of an entrance, because *holy fuck*.

Jenna Carling is standing in front of me, looking so delicious this bite of pizza becomes dry cardboard in my mouth. Tiny skirt over those killer long legs, shiny, pouty mouth, the heels that bring her to eye-level with me, at a solid six-foot-two. And the pink hair that might be my favorite part about her if I were brave enough to say so. Because choosing your favorite feature on this girl is worse than Sophie's choice. So impossible I wouldn't dare even give it a shot.

"Hey, kid."

Haven't heard that husky voice of hers in just about a year. Tonight, she feels like my first breath out of the womb. I cross my arms and lean my shoulder on the doorjamb. "Well, well. Suddenly my night's looking up."

"Bit presumptuous, but I'll allow it."

Jenna cocks her head, giving me a sweeping up and down. I quickly become aware of my lack of a shirt and how low my sweats are sitting on my hips. But loving—*loving*—her eyes on me like this.

"See anything you like?" I ask her.

"Actually, yes." And she snatches the half-eaten slice of pizza from my hand, taking a bite.

I throw my head back in a laugh. "Is this how you found me? You tracked this slice all the way across the Atlantic?"

"Didn't need to." Those big blue eyes shine with a smile as she demolishes my pizza. "Fourteen-eighty-one Rockney Road, not Lane. How could I forget after the last time?"

"And what brings you here tonight?"

She grins. "I've come as a representative of Mrs. Jenkins, who asks that you *please*, for the love of God, stop singing *My Heart Will Go On* at the top of your voice."

I rest my head on the doorjamb. "And you can tell Mrs. Jenkins that, while I *very* much appreciate the view, this new thing where she flies in doe-eyed flirts with nefarious motives to come talk to me just isn't gonna work. Nothing will ever trump my commitment to Celine."

She licks her mouth, biting down on her lower lip to hold in a laugh. "And what are these nefarious motives, Finn?"

"The kind that have you showing up here past midnight."

She hums. "I can certainly see why that would seem suspicious."

"Am I wrong?"

With a little smile, a tuck of her chin and the kind of eye contact that sends a bolt of lightning down my spine, Jenna shakes her head.

I've never—not once—resented my well-earned reputation as a bona fide man-whore. Frankly, I find it hot as all hell that she isn't too shy to ask for what she wants. Jenna's come here to finish what we started the night we met. And… yeah. I believe the only word worthy of this miraculous scenario is *absofuckinglutely.*

"You're leaving me hanging, Finn. Are you going to make me beg?"

"How'd you know that?"

"Know what?"

I flick my eyebrows. "Girls in skirts like yours begging for it is kinda my kink, sweet thing."

Jenna pushes those perfect pink lips out in a little pout. "What's wrong with my skirt?"

She turns slowly on the spot, and the woman knows exactly what she's doing because she arches her back to pop out that incredible ass of hers and good grief. She's got the kind of body that must leave a trail of carnage behind, just by existing.

"There's not a damn thing wrong, Jenna."

"I'd ask you to twirl for me too, but you're not leaving much to the imagination," she tells me, gaze dipping again, teeth grazing her lower lip. "Do I get to come in now?"

Do not fuck this up. I repeat: do not fuck this up, Palmer.

I straighten and she brushes past me closer than she needs to. I stay rooted to the spot, taking in the way she smells. Like the fresh roses my mom used to cut from the garden, but with a hint of heat, musk. I bite into my lip, trying to get it together. To keep my cool, slap on the grin that's always seemed to reduce people to puddles since I was young and get this one over the finish line. To focus on the way her ass moves in that skirt and *not* on trying to pinpoint exactly which type of rose her perfume is made from—

"Finn?"

Jenna has dropped into the spot on the sofa I just vacated, throwing me a look over her shoulder. She kicks off her heels and tucks her feet underneath her, skirt hitching in the process.

I'm still standing by the wide-open door. I nudge it shut.

"Want a drink or something?" I ask, pivoting to the open kitchen when she nods and ducking into the fridge. "I have beer, and... more beer. Mind giving a guy the heads-up next time? I might've done a few things differently."

"Like what?"

"Got some of that Cabernet Sauvignon you like. Put a shirt on."

Not gone almost a year without fucking someone so I had a chance in hell of not bursting to pieces the second you put a hand on me.

"Beer's good, and the shirtless thing just saves time." Her eyes linger on me. "You remember which wine I drink from that one night?"

So much for playing it cool.

After muttering a stream of curses at the tub of ketchup in the depths of my fridge, I round the island with the beer bottles behind my back.

"You're telling me that you set foot in here without remembering my beer of choice? How dare you?"

Her lips twitch. "Smithson's Pale Ale. You had a couple before switching to a strawberry daiquiri."

I grin, twisting off the top to one of the Smithson's and handing it to her. "Excuse me. It was a *cosmo*. I like to think only a secure man would have the balls to order that in front of a woman he was trying to sleep with. Plus, they're delicious."

"Hey, no justification needed. It was kind of the perfect move. A total nice guy drink to lull me into a sense of security before you tried to kidnap me."

It's a relief, knowing I'm not the only one who keeps that night on replay. But what's more than a little worrisome is that it's the little details of it that come to mind for me. That first smile she gave me when she and Jude approached the table where I sat with Theo, pure confidence though she didn't know either one of us. The way the passing streetlights fell across her

CHAPTER 3

face in the back of the cab we thought was taking us back to my place, and not out in the middle of the country where it stranded us. How soft she felt when I passed out spooning her, both dressed from head to toe, too exhausted to act on the flirtation after hitching a ride back into the city.

She's existed in my memory like a mythical force, who stormed into my life to unsettle me for a night before disappearing into thin air.

Jenna takes a long sip of her beer, eyes on mine as I sink down on the other end of the sofa. "So, what's new, Jenna? How was the trip?"

She watches me fiddle with the label on my bottle. I make myself stop. "It was amazing. I've never traveled alone before, but there's really something to it. Definitely tops sitting behind a reception desk all day."

I let out a low whistle. "Wish I coulda witnessed the damage you did. Jenna Bear out in the wild."

She grins around the lip of her bottle at the silly nickname I came up with the last time I saw her. *Like a sexy mama bear*, I told her of the way she protected her friend, when Theo had been a predictable headcase that night.

"I picked up a few new friends here and there, so half the time it turned into a girls' trip. Honestly, it's kind of nice to be home."

"Are you staying put for a while, then?"

She gives me a knowing smile. "I'm only here for my sister's wedding. A couple months and I fly back, straight to Portugal."

This is it: my white whale. No need even for the this-is-just-sex conversation because she pre-empts it with a clear declaration of her own.

So... what was that uncomfortable twinge in the pit of my stomach?

I shake myself mentally. There's a stunning, playful, ready and willing woman sitting on my sofa, in my apartment. If I screw *this* one up? I'll check myself into a monastery for the rest of eternity.

"Where are you staying in the meantime?"

"With Jude and Theo. What are you watching?"

I glance at the TV just as a net full of thrashing fish rises from the ocean on screen.

Shit.

"Nothing, I..." I grapple for the remote sitting between us, but Jenna snatches it up first and flicks up the sound. Stomach sinking, I clear my throat and nudge my glasses a fraction up my nose. "It's a documentary on fish farms along—"

"The Pacific Ocean," she finishes with unmistakable enthusiasm, turning in her seat to face the TV. "I watched it on the flight home. I never knew I could develop such strong feelings about tilapia."

"Does anyone have strong feelings about tilapia? It's the plain white bread of the ocean. Zero flavor and kind of unpleasant unless it's toasted and slathered in jam."

She frowns laughingly. "Jam? Really?"

I settle into the sofa cushion, taking a deep drink from my beer. "Preferably apricot."

"*Apricot?*" She's really laughing now. "God, I need to get out of here. Who knew you were such a freak—"

Jenna makes to get up from the sofa but I lunge for her, taking hold of her waist and tugging her down on my lap.

"Not so fast," I mutter in her ear, and with a breathy giggle that does something wicked to the lower half of my body, she sinks back into my chest. "I don't like watching scary movies alone. Stay and hold my hand a little."

"Scary movies?"

"You don't find the systematic destruction of the earth's bodies of water scary?"

She throws me a funny look over her shoulder. "When you put it like that..."

I lean back against the sofa, spreading my arms across the back and letting her slide off my thighs so that she sits with her legs draped over my lap. They're sun tanned and unbelievably smooth, and I think my first order of business when I get her in bed will be to run my tongue over every inch of them.

I watch Jenna wince at the TV. I wouldn't have pegged her as someone who'd willingly watch something like this, let alone on a long flight home. Then again, I'm sure Bianca Astley woulda said the same about me.

Feeling like a little bit of an ass, I clink the bottom of her bottle with mine.

CHAPTER 3

We've both drained our drinks in record time, mine going down quick to tamp down the nerves. I wonder what her excuse is. "Want another?"

She nods, tipping her beer to her lips and dropping it empty on the coffee table as she heads to the fridge. So at ease, like she lives here with me and has done it a thousand times. Something prickles deep in my chest, spreading heat as it goes. Some kind of weird heartburn, probably from drinking on a near-empty stomach. I rub at it absently, trying to dissipate it. Now's really not the time.

"I find these docs really hard to watch sometimes," she says over the sounds of bottles clinking together from the fridge. "Did you see the one about bees last year? How they're basically being wiped from existence? I never thought my heart would break for bees, of all things. But here we are."

She hands me a fresh beer, flashing me a quick smile. God, she's pretty. So edgy with the hair, the little skirt. And then she melts you with the stunning blue of her eyes and the way her cheeks round when she grins.

"Thanks." I take a deep drink and feel it rush straight to my head. "I know what you mean. I hate 'em. The documentaries, not bees obviously."

"Why do you watch?"

I shrug. "I've always felt a bit of a responsibility to it. Learning this stuff, reading the research. I make a living off animals being consumed, which doesn't feel all that great considering I don't like to eat them myself. It's only right that I'd at least try to understand the bigger impact. What I could do to help."

I feel myself start to launch into the Sunset Landing pitch and clamp my mouth shut. Jenna studies me with a small furrow building in her brow.

"Sorry. I'm boring you."

She shakes her head. "You're not. I don't think I knew you wore glasses."

Out of habit, I nudge the frames up my nose. "That's because I never wear them out, and the last time you were here you passed out cold by the time I took out my contacts."

"You'd think someone like you could have come up with a creative way to wake me."

I rear in mock-insult. "Someone like me? What are you implying, Jenna?"

"I've heard stories about you."

"I've heard stories about *you*," I counter. "And I'm willing to bet they're all true."

She perks up. "Really? Enlighten me."

I grin at her obvious delight. "You launched your cheating ex's belongings off your penthouse balcony when you walked in on him with another woman, a few years back. He wailed like a baby in the background."

Jenna tips her bottle in my direction. "True. The revenge and the wailing. I don't regret either."

"You threw the girl's clothes outside too, and she had to walk a few floors down to her place butt-naked."

"*That* I feel bad about. She knew he'd been cheating, but away from the initial blind rage I think it made me as bad as she was."

"I respect the self-reflection but I still think she's a teensy bit worse," I say around the mouth of my beer. "The story goes that after that, you... chose to forgo monogamy."

"That's a very sweet way of saying I started spreading my legs all over town."

"Nothing wrong with that."

"See?" Jenna winks. "It's what makes us so perfect for each other, Finn."

I pick up her legs and drop them back into my lap. "You're saying we're soulmates?"

She laughs, a deep, breathy sound that pairs immaculately with the low tone of her voice, and it incites a painful, confusing spasm in my stomach. Between this and that weird burning thing earlier... I really need to get some food in me.

"What have you heard about me?" I ask her, smoothing a damp palm down the side of my sweats, and hoping she doesn't notice.

"I've heard you do the man version of spreading your legs all over town."

"What *is* the man version of that, by the way? Thrusting my way across the city?"

"Sticking your dick in anything that moves?"

"Playing hide the sausage like it's my job?"

CHAPTER 3

"That's a good one, actually."

"Not bad, huh? Alright, I can't deny any of that. I like sex and I don't do relationships. But for the record, I don't stick my dick in *anything* that moves. I like to think I have standards."

"I heard you were batting at a hundred percent with the single servers at the last restaurant where you worked."

"They each had their merits. How is that my fault?"

"Who said anything about fault? I'm in no position to judge," she says. "Is it true there was a scorecard where the girls compared where and how you fucked them? I heard it turned into quite the competition."

I groan. "Okay, I had *nothing* to do with that. Nor do I have any evidence of it existing, but I heard the same rumor after I left there, and I'm not exactly... I don't know. I hope that's not true."

"There's definitely an ick factor to it." Jenna watches me carefully. "I'm sorry. I thought you were in on it."

I shrug. "I brought it onto myself. If I'm gonna stick my dick in anything that moves, people laughing about it or turning it into some kind of game is probably fair—"

"No, it isn't," Jenna cuts in. "Not unless it was a game to you, too."

"It wasn't." I rub absently at the back of my neck. "I thought we were just having a good time."

My gaze catches on the TV screen, but I'm not really seeing it. There's a weird prickle of realization crawling up my spine. I never spent much time dwelling on it, this hypothetical scorecard, because I thought it was fair game that they'd use me for sex if I was doing the same. My reputation is my own doing.

Except... I put a lot of effort into making sure I wasn't hurting anyone in the process.

"For the record," Jenna says delicately, drawing my eyes. She pulls her legs off my lap and curls them underneath her, smoothing her skirt as far down her thighs as it allows. "I'm interested, and there's no scorecard involved."

A goddamn *scorecard*?

My skin starts to crawl. I'd never have embarrassed them like that, and

I'd *never* have gone after any of them just for the competitive thrill. What the hell did I ever do to these people?

It occurs to me at this moment that maybe I should've put on a shirt.

"What I'm saying is," Jenna continues solemnly. "My reasons for wanting to jump your bones are completely innocent."

I drag my gaze back to her face. All traces of playfulness are gone. She eyes me like she's feeling it too. That heaviness in my chest. The humiliation. How did this conversation take such a sad turn?

Get it together, Palmer. She didn't come here to see you mope.

I run a rough hand through my hair, shoving it off my face. Trying to unclench my shoulders. "What are your reasons?"

My voice doesn't come out as light as I wanted. Jenna gives me a long look.

"Well, here's the thing, Finn. I'm only going to tell you if you want it."

"The reasons or the sex?"

She gives me a small smile. "Either one. I'm not shy about why I came here tonight. But it'll only be good for me if you want it just as much. If we're exactly on the same page, going into it with the same expectations. We'd both be in it to feel good and make each other feel good. No games, no scorecards. And if you decide you don't want it, if you tell me no, I'll thank you for the beer and walk right out of here, no questions asked."

How'd she do that?

She just turned a proposition for emotionless, no-strings-attached sex into something almost tender. Like we'd be in it together, like I have a choice. I can never claim to have gone into sex under coercion. But realizing I'd been blindly going into it as a game to be played, and having someone acknowledge that I was allowed to feel bad about it… In the wake of this uncomfortable revelation, it feels like she just offered me sturdy ground to stand on.

Where'd this girl come from, exactly?

Jenna smoothes down her skirt as it starts to hitch up. No games in sight. She's just a woman asking a man for gratification. I want to do that for her. To give her what she needs, to make her feel as good as she wants to feel.

"I want it."

CHAPTER 3

Jenna lifts a delicate eyebrow.

"Both. I want both. The reasons and the sex."

With a lingering look like she's double checking my math, that I really mean what I'm saying as though it matters that much to her, Jenna moves to kneel at my side.

She lifts an index finger. "Number one," she says, and that husky voice of hers somehow drops another octave. "You're unbelievably gorgeous."

She twists her wrist and crooks that single finger at me. I inch toward her like she's got me on a string, and with my face a mere foot away from hers, she lifts that hand. Slow, like she's got all the time in the world, so slow my throat has enough time to dry, goose bumps have enough time to cover my skin. Her fingers run through my hair, pushing it back off my face and fuck, I should probably be embarrassed by the groan that leaks out from my throat, but the way she looks at me like I've just sung her the sweetest note makes it hard to care.

"Number two, we seem to get along." Jenna's hand finishes its trajectory through my hair and runs down the nape of my neck. She curls her fingertips into my skin just for a second as though she means to pull me in, pull me closer to those sweet, plump lips. But she doesn't move me at all. She only looks at me with those perfect eyes, long lashes hitting the skin below her eyebrows. I feel my entire upper body hollow out, heart pumping furiously to refill my veins as it all rushes down, leaving me heavy and throbbing below the waist. What's she doing to me?

"Three, I'm in need of a real good lay. And I've got a good feeling about your ability to deliver, no strings attached. Am I wrong, Finn?"

Without losing my skin for a second the hand at the back of my neck moves, trails forward and up until all she's doing is brushing the tips of her index and middle fingers over my mouth, and it parts involuntarily under her touch so that she drags her skin along the wet edges of my lips. What is breathing? I couldn't tell you. My lungs couldn't either.

"Finn," she prompts me with a little raise of her brows. "Am I wrong?"

"No," I swallow, in a trance. "You're not wrong."

"You'll make me feel good?"

I nod. This tiny, jerky, frantic movement. "Yeah."

"I'll make it really good for you, too, Finn."

"Fuck," I breathe. I'm not going to last. This will be the best and worst night of my life.

Goddamn I completely forgot about that dimple. The single, tiny dimple that pops up by her chin, whenever she smiles big. Her smile grows, eyes go bright and playful, and she tucks both her palms between her knees. I find myself leaning forward, already missing her touch.

"Number four…" Jenna's gaze falls to my lap. "I need to send flowers to whoever invented grey sweatpants."

Just like that the tension snaps. A laugh bursts out of me and her shoulders shake in the sweetest giggle as she watches me sag into the sofa.

"Jesus. You're something else," I say, shedding my glasses to rub up and down my face, half-chuckling, half-shivering from the intensity of those thirty seconds. This girl is dangerous. Lethal. She turned me into a damn puddle with a single finger and a handful of words. I shove my glasses back on. "Don't take this the wrong way, but there's a real chance you're my dream girl."

"Because I'm just as horny as you are?"

"Because you just psychoanalyzed the shit out of me and picked up my mood off the floor a second later. The horny thing is a bonus."

"It really doesn't bother you? My total lack of chastity?"

"Does mine bother you?"

She shakes her head.

I flick a strand of hair behind her shoulder. "You like sex, I like sex. I don't see the problem."

I swear for a moment I see something shift in her. A little twinge of satisfaction, a barely-there loosening of her shoulders. Maybe that confidence isn't as much of a given as I thought it was, and I find the idea more than a little disturbing. What's a girl like this have to be self-conscious about? I haven't found a single thing wrong with her.

I'm about to ask when Jenna's gaze cuts to the TV.

"This part really got to me," she says, sweeping the remote off the coffee table and turning up the sound. "Listen to what this guy says here—if anyone deserves to be gnawed at by a thousand fish, it's him. Do fish have teeth?"

"They do."

"Lethal ones?" She settles back into the sofa, resting her head on the cushion behind her.

"Maybe if there's a thousand of them gnawing at you. Kind of a harsh death to wish on someone, Jenna Bear."

She shushes me. "You'll rethink that statement in three, two, one..."

Yeah, she was right. This guy's a monster.

We don't say much for a while. After a few minutes I let my arm drop over her shoulders and she shuffles into my side, and we watch the documentary play itself out with nothing but the sounds of her reactions to what's on screen.

I start to feel a weird little buzz in my extremities, and I think it's probably because of all the beer until I remember I've only had a drink and a half, and I'm usually a lot better at holding my liquor. But the feeling thickens with every one of her little hums of sympathy and grumbles of disgust as she watches the movie.

And I become aware of how... *aware* I am of her. She shifts in her seat, and I give her a little room to stretch her legs. Tugs at her skirt when it rides up, and then gives me a grateful smile when I place a cushion on her lap.

It all feels good, *really* good, but also off in a way I can't place. I'm insanely attracted to this woman. I've pictured sleeping with her more times than I should ever admit. I'm turned on, I miss sex, and she wants it bad, too. And yet...

I swallow, sliding my arm off her shoulders and moving away, pretending to stretch my limbs, suddenly needing to touch as little of her as possible. Because... Hell. She stormed into this apartment in that killer outfit, looking for the same thing as the women before her, yet slipped so naturally into the solo night I had planned for myself. She carved my chest open without even trying, took a quick look inside and started bandaging up all the open sores she found.

This is too close for comfort. This is too... real.

By the time the credits start rolling, I'm still trying to make sense of it all. Jenna looks completely steady, though, stretching her arms over her head with her eyes fixed on the screen.

"Well," she says, arching her back into the stretch. "What now?"

I clear my throat, trying to buy myself some time. Because I have a pretty good idea of what she expects me to do next, and there's panic building in my stomach instead. I flick off the TV.

"Now that we're good and depressed, you mean? That wasn't exactly uplifting."

She pouts playfully. "Poor thing. How can we cheer you up?"

What a loaded question.

Especially when my next thought is that I'd really like to bundle us up under a warm blanket and watch *Seinfeld* until we doze off on this sofa.

Goddamnit. I can't do it, can I? I can't sleep with her.

I don't do relationships. I *couldn't*. Not after seeing what's become of Dad. With that look she's giving me, I should have a hand up her skirt by now. Not wanting to fall into something so… domestic. I'm honest about my intentions with women to protect their feelings. Refusing to sleep with a woman I could actually be interested in is how I protect mine.

Jenna shifts beside me, and for a second I think she's reading me, that she's taking mercy on my tortured soul and grieving dick and giving me some space. But she then moves onto her knees, shuffling closer. She leans in and rests her palm on my thigh for balance.

"If you're out of ideas, I have a few that might interest you," she says, voice dripping with all the dirty things I've ever wanted to do with her. Winding me up so bad I have to tamp down a shudder.

From the way she's leaning toward me, I can see the curve of her breasts in the low neckline of her shirt. And God, it would be so easy, so good just to hook a finger and tug that shirt down, because I couldn't waste a second stripping it off before getting my mouth on her.

It takes Jenna's gaze dipping to my lap to realize I have a raging hard-on under my sweats.

"Maybe we can finish what we started the last time." That voice. That sexy, low rasp gets me harder in an instant.

And the panic sets in. I need to stop this. Now. Right now.

Turn her off. I'm an expert at it now, aren't I? Exhibit A took place only a few hours ago.

Think. *Think.*

Documentary. Cold pizza—

"Do you want to see my turtle?" I blurt, standing abruptly.

She laughs uncertainly. "Is that, like... a euphemism? I've heard better but okay, I'll play. Yes, Finn, I want to see your turtle."

"No, it's..."

Jesus Christ. Why isn't any of this working?

I put out a hand and after a second she takes it, letting me help her off the sofa. I mean to move away the second she's upright, but Jenna threads her fingers between mine and raises her brows expectantly when I don't immediately start leading the way.

Presumably to my bedroom so that she can *see my turtle* which is now a euphemism for my dick, what the actual hell has my life become?

I steer us down the hall and into the spare bedroom across from mine, flicking on the lights. Jenna takes in the room, wide-eyed, until she affixes on the large glass tank on the wall opposite the bed.

"Oh my God. You actually meant a turtle." She turns to me, mouth a little ajar. "Like a real-life turtle?"

I follow her to the tank. "A real-life turtle."

She bends to peer through the glass. "I swear I thought you were about to drop your pants."

I chuckle. "Sorry to disappoint."

She lightly taps at the glass. "It's okay, we'll get there." Damn. It. "Who's this?"

"This is Eddie. One of my housemates in school had him. After he graduated he got it in his head that he'd set Eddie free in the wild. A domestic turtle, of all things. Eddie's never had to work for food once in his life. It didn't sit right, so I took him over."

I bend next to Jenna. Eddie's lounging on a rock at the back of his tank, totally retracted into his palm-sized shell.

"He's tiny," Jenna says, and bumps me playfully with her hip. "Do you cuddle with him? Can you even cuddle with turtles?"

"He's been known to enjoy a little neck scratch from time to time."

There. I'm now the weird guy cuddling with his pet turtle. No one ever wants to fuck the weird guy who cuddles with his pet turtle—

"That's really sweet, Finn." She straightens slowly, bestowing me that dimple and you must be joking. "What's with this room?"

"What do you mean?"

She gestures vaguely around us. "The walls are black. Is it, like, a secret sex dungeon where you stash your voyeuristic turtle? Which is definitely *not* code for your cock."

Her smile grows playfully when I give a choking sound on the word *cock* and God. Damn. It. She is so damn sexy it's painful.

I plant my hands on my hips. "You know what? No. Laugh all you want at my sex dungeon, but you leave Eddie out of this."

She laughs, moving closer. "So, you're admitting to the sex dungeon? Poor little Eddie. The things he must have seen." She tips down her chin and gazes at me through her eyelashes. Playing me like a goddamn fiddle, this girl. "Is it really a sex dungeon?"

I shake my head, hesitating before sweeping her hair off her shoulder, holding the base of her head. Letting my thumb graze her jaw. Heart pounding so hard it's probably fracturing my rib cage, one beat at a time. Her skin is so soft and a wicked tremor runs along my arm, shoulder to pinky, when that little dimple appears not an inch away from my thumb. I want to feel it, to see if it'll pass on some of her sweetness through the touch.

I should be moving away. I can't, though. I can't. Not when she looks at me like that.

"The room was like this when I moved in. Never painted it."

"I think I like the dungeon story better."

I smirk. "Bet you do."

She knows she's got me right where she wants me, and she loves it this way. Hell, I love it this way. She walks backwards until the back of her knees hit the foot of the bed and sits. Patting the spot beside her.

Don't sleep with her. Don't sleep with her, don't sleep with her.

Think. *Think.* Something better than the turtle thing, because somehow even that struck a chord.

I mean, how could it not, though? Eddie's adorable.

But damn it, she looks good on this bed. Crossing her legs at the knees, hitching up her skirt to get comfortable.

Goddamn it. *Think.*

"You should stay here," I say suddenly.

Wait. No... *What?*

She frowns. "Okay, if my signals aren't clear enough, let me lay this out for you. Finn, I'm *trying* to stay here tonight. I'm offering you sex. Hot, *naked*, headboard-punching-through-the-wall kind of sex. And I don't know about you, but I've pictured us together more than a few times since the last time I was here."

"Motherfuck," I mutter under my breath.

"Finn, what's going on?" she hesitates. "If you're not interested you just have to say so—"

"No," I say quickly. And maybe the answer should have been to agree, to take the out, but just the thought of her thinking this is a matter of whether I want her makes me a little queasy. "I'm *definitely* interested. I mean, you're pretty fantastic."

"Then what? Are you seeing someone?"

"No, I—"

"Then should I start stripping or something? Would that help?"

"No!" I practically shout when she stands, reaching for the hem of her shirt. "No, don't—don't do that. I meant that you should live here with me this summer. Until your sister's wedding."

Jenna freezes. "*What?*"

I... like this girl. She makes me laugh, will sit through a documentary with me. She'll talk about my body count without looking at me like I'm something to fix. Tonight was nice. Great, actually. I've lived alone for three years and still, I hate it.

Maybe liking her means I can't sleep with her. I know myself—the second I get a hand on her, I'll be in it. I'll want more, and that just can't happen. There's a reason I keep sex to women I barely know.

But suddenly, Jenna staying here with me feels imperative. Like there's no other option but to wake up to her rooting around the kitchen or fogging up the bathroom with some flower-scented showers. It barely makes a lick of sense. And yet...

Who says we can't be friends?

"Yeah, you should stay here. You know, Jude and Theo are still in their honeymoon phase. Forget Eddie. Think of the things *you'd* see, staying with them."

"I'm sure they can manage to keep their clothes on around me." She laughs uncertainly. Her gaze drifts to Eddie's tank. For a moment she's silent. "Although..."

I seize on the word. "*Although?*"

She nods slowly, brows gently pushing together. "Think of the things I'd *hear*."

"Yes. *Yes*, exactly. I have this perfectly good spare room, and—"

"And I guess I'd rather hear you through the walls than listen to my best friend and her boyfriend."

"Wha—oh. Oh, no..." I shake my head. "Nope. I don't bring people back here. Never do."

Jenna gives me a funny look. "You brought *me* back here. The last time we met."

I... How is this the first time that's occurred to me? I stare at her, lost for words.

Jenna takes pity on me. "Anyways, it's a smart move. If you go to their place, you decide when the night ends. I do the same, but it's also so they can't come back and murder me one day."

"Why do I get the feeling you're only half joking about that?"

"Because I am only half joking. Being a woman sucks, sometimes." Jenna crosses the room. I force my gaze away from her hips, entranced by the way they sway when she walks. "I really do like your glasses, by the way. Between that, Eddie, and the documentaries, you're kind of the hottest nerd I've ever met."

"Kind of? You're breaking my heart."

"You'd definitely be the hottest roommate I've ever had." She squints. "Are you sure about this? It's kind of a crazy offer."

"Not any crazier than you actually considering it. Why *are* you considering it, by the way? Just out of curiosity."

She pauses. "I don't know. This summer was about to be a total wash, with the wedding from hell around the corner. This could be fun. I'm always up for a little misadventure, hot, unexpected roomies included."

"So, you're in? Just like that?"

"Just like that."

The sirens in my head are wailing so loud I'm surprised she can't hear them. *Alert, alert. This is a terrible idea. You really think you can keep things platonic with this girl?*

Right on cue, Jenna rests her hands on my hips, toying with the waistband of my sweats. Her fingers are flames licking my bare skin.

I swallow. "We should call it a night. It's been a big day. Surprise visits, new roommates... I'm gassed."

"Your turtle seems to disagree."

Sure enough, my dick is shamelessly swelling against the thin fabric of my pants. Straining to bridge the distance between us.

Traitor.

I can't blame him, though. Everything about this woman pulls me in. Even without her heels on she's tall, maybe five-foot-ten or eleven, and it would barely take a tilt of my chin to press my mouth to hers.

I take a long, calming breath that doesn't help one bit. These are uncharted waters. Actively trying *not* to sleep with a woman, while simultaneously trying to keep her around when she's only come to me for sex in the first place... It feels like the tallest order.

And I'm not entirely sure it's doable. I'm the sex guy, full-stop. There's a scorecard out there to prove it. So, how do I talk her into becoming my friend? To look past the sex part, stick around because she digs me as a person?

"You're zoning out again, Finn," Jenna says, pulling me back into the present. She's still holding me, stroking my hips with her thumbs.

Friends. Totally platonic roommates with the woman now looking at me like she knows a secret I'm not privy to. Who's tipping her head to one side and absolutely *not* trying to entice me with the smooth curve of her neck.

I need to get out of this room, stat.

Gripping her by the waist, I walk her backwards. Letting my hands trail down her sides, feeling her soft, warm skin through her shirt. I realize the zipper for her skirt sits on the side, right under my fingertips. It feels wrong, completely criminal not to tug it down, and let that little strip of fabric drop around her ankles. But I walk her back until she hits the bed instead, and push her down onto the mattress.

Jenna drops onto her elbows, chest heaving as she watches me lean over her. Dropping her head back, giving me full, perfect access to her lips. Letting her hair sweep over the white comforter.

I can totally pull this off. I can get Jenna Carling to like me for me. I can go a full summer without sleeping with her. Totally can.

Twirling a strand of pink hair around my finger, I throw her my most winning grin.

"'Night, roomie."

Chapter 4

Jenna

"I much prefer to wear clothing that leaves things to the imagination. Some things are meant to stay between you and the shower walls, don't you think?"

Ronnie's voice weaves through my brain, followed by a smattering of giggles. I hear each of her words in isolation but they don't manage to land in a way that makes sense. Which will probably come back to bite me because I'm almost certain I'm the one she was speaking to, and nothing sets my sister off like having to repeat herself.

The problem is, my mind is a little busy trying to figure out what the hell happened last night.

Because I agreed to live with Finn Palmer. All summer.

I barely know the guy. That should be enough to make the entire thing a terrible idea. But what really takes the cake is that this entire acquaintance was built on exactly two things: we were going to sleep together, and then we'd never see each other again.

Living together definitely puts a wrinkle in the whole avoiding each other post-sex thing.

I finger the bridal veil hanging by the wall I'm leaning on. What the hell was he thinking, asking me to live there? And why... Why didn't he sleep with me?

Since the day I lost my virginity, men being interested in me for my body has been as certain as the moon rising at night.

And Finn told me he wanted to sleep with me, multiple times, point blank. Which probably goes to show just how rusty I've become at the whole flirting thing, after that self-imposed sex break during my trip. As tempting as they were, European men just weren't doing it for me. A strange phenomenon. But I choose not to dwell.

"Earth to Genevieve. Why would she bother coming all the way here, just to stand there catching flies with her mouth all morning?"

That last part was muttered under Ronnie's breath, as though the only people who could hear her were the other six women making up her wedding party, all standing right next to me. Plus, the bridal shop assistant hovering awkwardly behind her, carrying an enormous load of sample bridesmaid dresses.

Hastily, I stop fiddling with the veil and slap on a smile. Today, I am a good little sister to Ronnie. Today, we get along. I will work to fit in with her and her friends. I will make her forget all the reasons she can't stand me, all the ways we're different. I will gush about her bridal beauty and smile when she tells me how pretty I look in all the dresses we're here to try on.

That last one is wishful thinking.

"I'm sorry. What were you saying?" I ask, taking care to make my tone just the right side of upbeat.

"I *said*, 'I was really hoping for you girls to wear pink gowns—that color there, the light pink? I've had my heart set on it since I was a little girl, you know.'" She smiles sweetly at the women surrounding her. "But I suppose we won't be able to manage it since it will match your hair, Genevieve. You'll look like *My Little Pony*, that is if Pinkie Pie woke up and decided to wear the world's shortest skirt to a bridal boutique."

Seven pairs of eyes convey their disdain for me. I catch sight of myself in the floor-length mirror behind Ronnie. Where my beautiful sister wears a polka-dotted, soft green sundress with her blonde hair pulled into an immaculate low bun, I'm still wearing last night's to-catch-a-man miniskirt, borderline stripper heels, and my hair a disheveled mess

CHAPTER 4

around me. I hadn't had time to swing by Jude's to change before this early appointment.

It's a walk of shame without the sex.

For the twentieth time since I caught my sister staring, I comb my fingers through my hair, fruitlessly willing the ends to lie in the same direction.

"Don't change your dream color scheme on my account," I say, smiling encouragingly. "I'll make it work, Ronnie. Besides, I don't mind looking like a sexed-up pony."

I don't know whether her mouth twists in disgust over the nickname, or the fact that I just sexualized a child's cartoon character. This isn't my finest hour.

"*Veronica*," she corrects, laying to rest my debate. She turns on her heel, beckoning us to follow her to the dressing rooms.

The young boutique assistant trails behind us, weighed down with so many dresses the girls have thrown at her that she damn near trips along the way.

"Here, let me," I tell her, reaching for some of the gowns she's trying to carry.

"Thanks," she says gratefully, picking up a dress at her feet. "You'd think I'd be better at this after three months of working here."

"Don't beat yourself up," I tell her as we follow the trail of bridesmaids through the bright, pastel-dotted showroom. "I've been sisters with Ronnie for twenty-nine years and I'm still not any good at it. What's your name?"

"Quinn. The world's most flustered shop assistant."

"Nice to meet you. I'm Jenna, owner of the world's shortest skirt."

Quinn laughs, eyeing my lower half over her handful of bridesmaid gowns. "It's really not that short, you know," she says with a shrug. "I'd wear it. And your legs look amazing in it."

"*Thank* you. I really hoped it would help me score last night, but the guy didn't go for it."

"Blind?"

She gets a laugh out of me. "That has to be it, right?"

My smile falters when I see Ronnie standing in front of the row of mirrored dressing rooms, tapping her foot impatiently.

"Sorry," I mumble to her, rushing to help Quinn deposit dresses into each of our dressing rooms, which seems to irritate Ronnie even worse.

"That is the *worker's job*, Genevieve," she hisses as I pass her. "Could you at least *try* to act like you remember your last name?"

My stomach drops. She's anything but subtle. I throw Quinn a quick look of apology. Her cheeks flame as she stares at my sister.

I stand by the last remaining changing room and throw a tentative smile at the bridesmaid next to mine. She turns away without returning it. Suddenly I'm fourteen again, trying to keep up with Ronnie and her friends after failing miserably to make some of my own at boarding school. I was the weird girl who laughed too loud, slept with too many boys and, after being unable to find a ballgown I liked, showed up to cotillion in a knee-length dress, much to my mother's disgust.

"Okay..." My sister claps, regarding us all poised by our dressing rooms. Suddenly I feel like a racehorse at the Kentucky Derby, ready to spring through the starting gate. "Let's get started, ladies!"

It's the WASP version of a starting pistol. The girls twirl on the spot and disappear one by one into their dressing rooms.

"Hey—Quinn," I mutter, catching her by the arm as she rushes by. "For the record, I think you're doing great. It's a tough crowd. Hang in there."

My words seem to make her day more than they should. As I twirl into my own dressing room and shed last night's outfit, I hope that she fairs better than I ever did, when it comes to hanging with this crowd.

~

"Peanut!"

I hear him before I catch sight of my dad settled comfortably in a linen and rattan chair across the restaurant patio. The sight is so typically Dad. Totally at ease like he owns the joint, even though it's only his membership that gets us into the Hubbart Marina Supper Club. He's dressed like the wealthy, white-haired retiree he is, with his loafers, and white collared shirt, and straw fedora. And of course, he scored us the best table in the place, the corner spot by the glass railing overlooking the water.

He should be everything I hate about this world, which so brutally chewed

CHAPTER 4

me up and spit me out more than once over my childhood. But growing up, Dad was the only one who's ever consistently been in my corner. Even now, he's my quiet cheerleader whenever my mother's back is turned. Proud of me for breaking the mold and working a job for four years, and even for dropping everything to travel the world. I could never resent him for the discreet approval, anyway. My mother's cold stare and ruthless words know no bounds.

"Hi, Dad."

He rises to wrap his arms around me, holding me to him long enough to let me appreciate his familiar peppermint scent before leaning away to get a proper look. "Look at you, Peanut. Tanned and fresh from adventure."

"Speaking of tans." I poke his forearm, watching the white imprint of my finger darken to match the rest of him. "You've been spending a lot of time on the boat, I'm guessing."

We sit and a waiter immediately appears to place a wine glass in front of me.

"Mom insisted we spend the past couple of months at the beach house. Not that I blame her. We'll be stuck in the city for the next two months, working up to Veronica's big day. She's just over the moon about it all."

I nod into my drink, taking an extra-long sip to avoid coming up with an answer. My mother and Ronnie have always been particularly close.

Dad notices my silence, watching me as he helps himself to a slice of thick sourdough bread and slathers it with butter. "How was the dress shopping?"

I blow out a long breath, letting it rattle through my lips like a dejected horse.

"Same old thing," I tell him. "We ended up with these pink dresses I liked just fine before she told me it made me look like a slutty *My Little Pony*. It always just comes back to the hair with her. You'd think I was forcing her into the same dye job."

"Language, Peanut." Reflexively, he glances at the top of my head. He'd never say it outright, but Dad hates the pink color as much as any of them. "Your sister means well—"

"*Dad.*"

"Alright, it may not be the most obvious thing. But I know she cares for you very much."

"Yeah, well. She's got a funny way of showing it."

Dad doesn't know the half of what it felt like to grow up with Ronnie. The day she realized I stopped idolizing her as a kid, that I was veering down a path totally different from hers, she decided she'd drill her dissatisfaction into my bones. Backhanded comments, pointed insults. And it was never enough that she was letting me have it for not fitting in. She needed everyone else to remind me, too. I never feel as badly about myself as I do when I'm around Ronnie, her friends, my mother, or anyone in the world where I grew up.

"Where are you staying this summer?" Dad asks abruptly. "Should I get Anne to air out your bedroom?"

The waiter chooses this very ideal moment to reappear, taking our food orders and buying me time to utterly fail at coming up with a good enough cover story.

"Peanut?" Dad prompts after we're alone again. "Are you staying with us?"

I blow out a breath. "No, actually. I'm staying with a friend."

"Jude?"

"No, it's... someone else. A friend."

He regards me sternly. "Jenna, tell me you're not staying with one of those toy boys you seem to have amassed in recent years." He hesitates. "Is it toy boys, what they're called?"

"Boy toys," I mumble, running a hand over my face. "I haven't amassed anything, Dad. I'm single."

"That's not how Veronica tells it."

Immediately, my cheeks flood with color. Of course, Ronnie would blab about the sleeping around. Honestly, I don't even know how she managed to figure it out. It's not like we talk.

"I have friends who aren't Jude, you know."

"Genevieve, don't you skirt around the issue."

I slump back in my chair. "Fine, okay? It's a guy I met last summer. But

CHAPTER 4

he's nice."

"He's not unemployed, is he? Not like this last boyfriend you moved into your apartment? That one had far too much free time on his hands."

Read: free time he used to sleep with another woman.

Unsurprising, my sister's voice filters into my brain uninvited. *Men don't like to settle.*

"He's very employed, Dad. But we're not in a relationship." Dad looks at me, presumably waiting for me to say something that makes sense. "We're... friendly," I supply. When his expression doesn't change, I add: "We're sleeping in separate bedrooms."

It doesn't work. "I don't like it, Peanut. You staying with a stranger. I understand why you might prefer not to stay at home with your mom and me, but at least look into getting your own place again now that you're back."

This conversation is swirling straight into the gutter.

"Well, I'm not *really* back," I say delicately. "I fly out the week after Ronnie's wedding. I've still got a whole half a continent to explore."

"And how long do you plan to keep exploring said continent?"

"I'm giving myself another six months, and then I'll figure out what I want to do with the rest of my life. Hopefully put that marketing degree to good use."

"Your filet, Mr. Carling, medium-rare." The waiter reappears with our lunch and places the first plate in front of my dad with a flourish. "And the cous-cous stuffed pepper for Miss Carling, with the soy-based gravy."

"Thank you," I tell the waiter, as Dad immediately starts aggressively shaking salt onto his meat. Probably picturing his interpretation of Finn's face on the receiving end.

"Text me this man's full name, home address, and workplace. God forbid anything happens to you, but I'd at least like to know who to murder and where to find him."

"You, murder? At least admit you'd hire someone to do it."

"I won't admit to anything," he says, drawing his steak knife and slicing through his lunch. "Peanut, it all seems a little reckless. What are you hoping to gain, exactly, by living with this man? Are you looking for a relationship?"

"No, it's not like that. It's a zero-attachment situation."

Dad's eyes flick up, and I realize I've just validated Ronnie's interpretation of my dating antics. "He's not trying to rope you into one of these benefits for friends situations, is he?"

"Of course n—" I freeze, fork poised over my plate, feeling the metal click, the cogs connect, the gears start turning.

That's it, isn't it?

I stare at Dad, who raises his brows expectantly. Except, I have no intention of clueing him in on this epiphany. Because I think I figured it out: the reason Finn asked me to stay with him.

We get along. I need a place to stay. We've both been known to be good in bed. Why settle for a one-night stand of exceptional sex, when you could have a temporary, live-in fuck buddy?

Why didn't I see this before? Of course, it's what he's thinking.

Except... what the hell is he thinking? This isn't what we do.

"Peanut?" Dad prompts me.

Hastily, I busy myself with my stuffed pepper, picking through it for bits of mushroom to nibble on. "Don't worry about me, Dad. I won't be roped into anything I don't want."

"Still, Peanut. I don't like it," he says, with a lingering look before he tucks into his plate. "Especially if you'll be living together. It sounds like a disaster waiting to happen."

Yes. *Yes* exactly. Thank you, Dad.

There's a reason we don't do this. We said it from the start: we'd sleep together and remember it fondly from afar. Not from the bedroom across the hall.

The second I shake off enough of this rust to get him into bed, we'll both be cursing ourselves over this misguided living arrangement. The awkward morning after.

Dad sighs when I've been quiet too long. "That imbecile really did a number on you, didn't he?"

"It has nothing to do with my ex," I tell him. I'm not lying, either. Maybe my last boyfriend ignited this particular scandalous phase of my life, but I

CHAPTER 4

haven't put much stock in sex since I was fifteen.

My sister saw to that.

I watch Dad shovel mouthful after mouthful of his lunch, but I'm suddenly not the least bit hungry.

What *am* I looking to gain from living with Finn? I'd be doing us both a favor by telling him no.

~

By most accounts—other than my mother's or Ronnie's, obviously—I have decent enough manners.

Which is why, even though I end up thoroughly convincing myself that living with Finn is, in fact, a terrible idea, I'm standing at his door. Declining his offer for a place to stay would best be done in person. It's the polite thing to do, after all.

Inside, the Smashing Pumpkins blare around me, totally muffling the sound of his spare key hitting the kitchen counter as I follow the music toward what I assume is his bedroom. But it's the sight inside the spare room that has me stopping in my tracks.

Every piece of furniture is gathered in the middle of the space and covered in a giant white sheet. The ghastly black walls are gone. Finn is standing high up a ladder with his back to me, carefully running a paintbrush along the pale green tape protecting the ceiling, the room now painted a soft, dreamy blue. It's like he's standing in the middle of the open sky.

That should be reason enough to incite the odd, tingling sensation snaking its way through my body. But what tops it all off—the total sprinkles on top of this sweet gesture—is that Finn's wearing nothing more than a pair of black gym shorts, just fitted enough to show hints of an ass good enough to take a bite out of, and a backwards hat I suspect he's using as a makeshift headband to keep the hair off his face as he works.

And I mean, come *on*.

I've seen him without a shirt on. But watching him *move around* without a shirt on? Well, that's a whole other ballgame. And there's just no other thing to be done but to watch the way the muscles ripple over his shoulder blades as he runs the paint brush across the wall. How tanned his skin is, so golden and somehow completely devoid of tan lines. The man must live without a shirt. And why the hell not, if this is what he looks like?

I'm tempted to holler at him over the music just to get a good view from the front, but I'm afraid he'll die falling off this ladder if I startle him.

Also, I should probably stop ogling him. Just an idea.

I tiptoe into the room and flick at the volume key on his portable speaker.

"What the…" Finn turns, confused until he finds me standing behind him. "Oh, shit."

"As far as unconventional greetings go, I tend to prefer a good *wowzah* or even a *hey, kitty-cat* if you're feeling saucy."

He breaks into that signature grin. Wide, tucked up higher on the right and lights up his face all the way to his eyes. Finn grins as easily as any man I've ever met, and it's as contagious as anything. Between that, the scruff, the perfect, strong line of his jaw and the subtle bump on the bridge of his nose, he looks like the kind of guy who'd patiently help your grandmother cross the street one minute and fuck you dirty on the floor the next.

I can only imagine the type of trouble he gets into when he cracks that smile.

And I was right. The view from the front is even better. He has a little paint smudged on his forehead just under the strap-back of his hat, and if paint wasn't toxic I'd probably go lick it off.

"Trust me, it was a good *oh shit*." Finn comes down the ladder, using a rag slung over the top rung to wipe off his hands. "I thought I had more time to wrap this up before you got home, that's all. I still have to touch up the baseboards."

I eye said baseboards. They already look immaculate.

"I was gonna paint it all white," Finn starts uncertainly, and I realize he's been watching me eyeball the space. "I guess it's what's trendy right now, according to all those Architectural Digests Jude reads. But…"

"But she talked you into the blue?"

"She doesn't know about this." His gaze drifts to the wall behind me, and he rubs the back of his neck. "I don't know. This color felt more like you."

Baby cherry bombs go off in the pit of my stomach, igniting little fires that spread a pleasant warmth through my extremities. Three times. I've met this guy three times and he already seems to have me pegged. And I'm supposed to tell him thanks but no thanks?

Come on, I coach myself. *Say the words. I can't live with you.*

"I like it," I say instead.

"Okay, great," he says, with renewed enthusiasm. "I moved Eddie out into the living room. And there's some space now in the bathroom vanity."

Shit.

"Do you need help getting your luggage in here? Is it by the door?"

Double shit.

I have no luggage to speak of. I only swung by Jude's after lunch to change out of last night's clothes.

Apparently silence does speak volumes because comprehension seems to dawn. Finn gives me a tight smile, tipping his head to the side. "You came to tell me you're not staying here, didn't you?"

Why does that suddenly sound like the last thing I want to do? Borderline stranger or not, he seems like a nice guy. He painted part of his home for me just for a two-month stay, for crying out loud.

There's a pink flush building up his neck now, flooding his cheeks. With his hands deep in his pockets, Finn shrugs. "Hey, don't worry about it. It was about time I got rid of that black paint, anyway. Eddie will love you for it. And anything that makes Eddie happy is good by me."

He says it nonchalantly, except that he looks almost... resigned to the idea that I wouldn't stay. Maybe I'm imagining it, but he seems to deflate a little. And when he offers me a smile, it's nothing like the other one. The Finn smile. This one barely hits the mid-point of his cheeks, barely crinkles his eyes. My stomach pinches uncomfortably.

I could live with Finn, couldn't I? We can totally figure out how to co-exist while we sleep together. Assuming I haven't already done something to give him the ick, given how bad I struck out last night. Seriously, I need to shake off these cobwebs.

I walk up to Finn and pluck the paintbrush from his hand. "Sorry, kid, you're not getting rid of me that easy." I climb up the ladder to help finish the job. "I do need to hitch a ride with you to pick up my stuff after we're done painting, though."

Finn plants his hands on either side of the ladder, holding it steady. "You sure about this, Jenna Bear?"

It gets me every time. That this mind-numbingly gorgeous man calls me something so wholesome. I love that ridiculous nickname.

I dip a finger into the bucket of paint perched on top of the ladder and dab a blue smudge on the tip of his nose.

"Sure. We can live together. What's the worst that can happen?"

Chapter 5

Finn

"Hey, Pa? You here?"

Dad's house is dead quiet when I come in, dim and not a single light turned on. I haven't been over in a few days, and it shows. When I step into the kitchen there's a tall stack of empty takeout cartons on the counter, and a tower of water glasses in the sink. Under the counter the garbage is spilling over. The fridge is clean, at least, but it's only because there's not a single thing in here but a pitcher of water and condiments I should probably check aren't expired.

I leave the mess for later and cross to the sliding doors to the yard. It's like a different world out here. Bright from the setting sun, airy, Mom's rose garden thriving over on the right, leaves dripping water from being recently watered.

I find Dad in his usual spot. Sitting on the wooden bench across from the roses, staring wistfully like they're telling him a story.

"Dad?" I say quietly, forcing my gaze away from a drooping peach-colored rose.

Dad jumps out of his trance, fixing dazed eyes on me a long second before standing up. "Finley," he says hoarsely. He clears his throat. "Is it six-thirty already?"

"Seven. I was running late."

"I forgot to order us dinner."

"I got it, Dad. Stopped for some groceries on the way." I glance at the roses behind him. "Why don't you come inside while I fix us something."

He follows me in. Quietly, meekly, the baseline emotion he rarely budges from since the day Mom died.

Unloading the three paper bags of groceries, I try to remember the exact time I realized Dad hadn't been getting better. Granted, it took me more time than my little sister Hayley to recover, whatever recovery means. I avoided the therapy thing even though she swore by it, but after a while I started to feel more and more myself. At this point, the only thing that really sets me off is the anniversary of her death.

So, when Dad still lagged a couple of years later, I chalked it up to moving at his own pace. There's no single roadmap for grief, right?

But ten years in, and we're still at square one. He feeds himself, goes to work. Tends to Mom's garden in the spring and summer, watches their favorite movies over the fall and winter. Rinse and repeat.

He stopped acknowledging their friends, our extended family, everyone but Hayls and me. Barely reacted when she announced she and her husband were expecting a baby this year. And as the designated single sibling, and also the one who lives close by, it's come to me to check in on Dad once a week, twice when I can bring myself to spend another night drenched in misery. I'd resent Hayls for not pulling more weight around here if I didn't feel guilty over letting Dad get this bad, for this long. Even though I wouldn't know how to start putting him back together.

They say love conquers all.

What conquers this, then? What gets you out of the dark hole you fall into when you inevitably lose the woman you love? Is it even possible?

I'm not willing to find out. I just hope Dad figures it out.

I lay out four slices of bread and check the expiration date on the mayo in the fridge. Good until the end of the month.

"So, what's new, Dad?"

Dumb question, and I regret it instantly. I keep my attention on the sandwiches, laying pieces of lettuce on top of the mayo as Dad eases into a

CHAPTER 5

stool across me at the island, grunting quietly as though his joints protest every bend in his body. I can't remember the last time I made him a doctor's appointment. I'll need to give them a call.

"Ah, you know. Trimmed the rose bushes after work today." He taps his fingers on the granite counter and I avert my eyes from the gold wedding band reflecting the light. The thing could probably use a good wash. I can't remember a time I saw it off him. "I haven't seen you the last couple days."

"I've been a little caught up with some stuff," I say lightly. I pull a knife out of the drawer and start slicing through a tomato. "I have a new roommate."

"That right?"

"Uh-huh." I press more bread over layers of ham for Dad and veggies for me, and slice the sandwiches in half. Crosswise, because I'm not a monster. "Here, have this. There's extra everything in the fridge for you, enough until I can come back next week."

He sighs over his plate. "You take good care of me, Finn. Should be the other way around—"

"Everything's fine, Dad. You don't need to feel bad."

He nods slowly. "How's everything going at work?" he asks with a mouthful of sandwich. "I'll get myself down there for dinner one of these days."

Not likely, even though I'd get a damn good kick out of seeing him at Sunset Landing, the way he used to be. The lasagna-cooking, home run-hitting, loud-laughing Vince Palmer of old. With his borderline inappropriate jokes and the constant hearts in his eyes whenever he'd set them on my mom. Buying a round of shots for the serving staff and shutting the place down. I round the counter to sit in the stool next to his.

"It's alright. Our seabass got ranked one of the top seafood dishes in the city the other day, so that felt pretty good."

"You don't say. Hey, that's great. Did you come up with it?"

"I came up with the hibiscus sauce, yeah."

"That's great," he says again. He brings a half-sandwich up to his mouth and pauses. "You said something about a roommate? You need some extra cash?"

"No. Just a friend who needed a place to crash."

"The one who helped train you after the hiccup at school?"

Sometimes it blows me away how much Dad retains despite the lack of eye contact and quiet responses. The so-called hiccup at culinary school happened right in the thick of our grief. Just a year after my self-implosion at school, I managed to land a job as a line cook mostly thanks to Theo's benevolence and the fact that he was already something of a rising star where we were working.

My entire apartment could fit into the main floor of his.

"Nah, this is a newer friend. You've never met her."

Dad frowns down at his plate. "Her? This is a roommate?"

"Yep." I take a big bite of my sandwich to keep my mouth occupied long enough for him to give up this line of inquiry. Bringing Jenna into this feels intensely wrong. This home isn't a place worthy of her energy anymore.

The sun continues to move across the sky, casting a cool, blueish hue around the room. Without the lights on, it's starting to get dark in here. But I know Dad prefers it that way, keeping it to the floor lamps out in the hall and in the living room. He shut down pretty bad, the one and only time I turned on a ceiling light after Mom died.

"Your sister says she's bringing dessert to the anniversary dinner in a few weeks," Dad says suddenly. "You'll come too?"

I push away my plate and rub both hands over my face. "Yeah, I'll be there."

"Good, good."

I'm heading for the sink with both our plates when he clears his throat. "You know, your mom and I lived with a roommate, once."

There's a large, whale-sized ice cube running down my spine, chilling me to the bone. We don't talk about her. Don't talk about Mom unless we can help it.

"Yeah?" I turn on the tap all the way, letting the water splash loudly off the glasses in the sink.

"It was a complete stranger. We were short on money, so your mom put an ad in the classifieds. I spent the weeks leading up to her move-in date planting weapons around the house just in case we ended up with a killer across the hall. A crowbar, hammer, anything we had. Mom thought I was insane, of course."

"Uh-huh." I fiddle with the stack of glasses, letting the clinking sounds bounce around the kitchen.

"And in the end, in moves this tiny lady and her little yappy dog—"

The plate I'm washing clangs loudly off the side of the stainless-steel sink. "Hey, how are the guys at work doing, by the way? Haven't heard about them in a while. Did Terry's wife have the baby?"

After a long pause, Dad picks up his cue. "They're doing alright. Baby was born last week."

"Good. That's great."

And we lapse back into silence.

Chapter 6

Finn

"Hey, Jenna?"

I follow the sounds of humming toward her bedroom, getting pummeled by the smell of her shampoo as I pass the steaming bathroom. It's some kind of rosy, floral scent—

Who the hell am I kidding?

It's roses and honey. And I may have inhaled the hell out of it straight from the bottle during my shower this morning. Thing is, it smells like her. Not in the way you'd come to associate a perfume to someone, or the way the smell of olives or lemons makes me think of a kitchen.

It smells like *her*. The heady self-confidence, the persona. The pink hair, the easy flirtation. And then she moves in just the right way and you catch it in the light: a tiny sliver in her skin showing you something sweet on the inside. And it's weird, definitely odd that I've come up with this kind of assessment considering I barely know her. But...

"Jenna?" I call again.

She doesn't seem to hear me. Jenna goes on humming on the other side of her half-open door. After a split-second's hesitation in which I convince myself that said door wouldn't be open if she wasn't already fully dressed, I stick my head into her room.

And, yeah.

CHAPTER 6

I seem to have lost sight of one key little detail.

Which is that my new roommate is trying to kill me.

Jenna stands in front of her fully stocked closet. Wet beads of shower water glistening on her shoulders, pink, wet waves cascading down her back. It seems her hair goes a little darker when it's soaked through, and I'd probably spend more time admiring its effect if I wasn't immediately incapacitated by the sight of her body wrapped in a fluffy white towel.

A tiny, fluffy white towel.

Have I always owned such tiny towels? Where did I buy them from, exactly?

She has a deep tilt to her head staring into this closet, like it's spewing out pages from *War and Peace* she's trying very hard to keep up with. Beyond her, I catch sight of an impressive collection of skirts along the lines of the ones she wore the night she showed up here, and what's incredible is that I want to see her wear them just as bad as I want that towel to drop to her ankles. Or to watch the way the cotton rides up as she leans forward, arches her back a little, the towel slipping a fraction as she reaches for something on a high shelf in her closet—

"I could use some help here, Finn. Unless you'd rather keep watching?" Jenna bestows me that dimple from over her shoulder, so casual it's clear she knows I've been standing there the whole time.

Shit.

I clear my throat for no reason whatsoever. "Sorry. Didn't mean to..."

She lifts and drops a single, bare shoulder. "I really don't mind if you wanna watch."

And with that she turns back to her closet, lifting onto her toes to reach for a pink shirt folded up on a shelf—and fuck me. I could watch her wriggle like that until my eyes fell out and it would be well worth the loss of eyesight.

It starts up in my brain. The mantra playing on loop since the moment I decided I wanted her to like me for me: *I will not fuck my roommate. I will not fuck my—*

Her towel slips another fraction, revealing more of her back, and immediately my legs propel me forward. She's cast a rod across the room, caught me with a tiny little hook and a line reinforced with everything I like about her. That dimple. The way she snorts when she laughs. The way she loses her mind at the injustices inflicted on the world's oceans.

There's a good chance I've made her up. We'll be out one day and I'll be getting all kinds of weird looks from passersby, who'll watch me talk away as though a stunning girl with pink hair was there listening.

"Here. I got it," I say, reaching past her outstretched arm and handing her the shirt.

"Thank you," she says softly. She hugs the pink fabric to her chest. Her gaze stuck to mine, eyebrows curving so sweetly as she lowers her chin. "I don't know how I managed to get it up there in the first place."

I reach for the single wet wave falling across her cheek, unable to resist twisting it around my finger. "Hey, what are roommates for? You know, other than once again sincerely apologizing for this morning's toilet incident."

Her eyes narrow playfully. "And once again, you are unforgiven. At least until the memory of splashing into the bowl fades from my brain. It'll take a lot more than an apology to bump your ranking on my all-time list of roommates."

"You're saying I'm worse than the one who outed you for watching the same episode of *Gilmore Girls* every day for a month?"

"I agree that wasn't very nice." Her eyes round as though remembering a painful memory, and instantly I want to tuck her into my chest and kiss away that crinkle in her brow.

Jenna lets her teeth graze her full bottom lip, leaving it all shiny and so goddamn plump looking. And that shampoo really does smell incredible—

Shit.

I move back so fast I smash into the open closet door, banging my elbow and sending a flash of pain shooting up my arm. "*Fuck*, you're good."

Surprise eclipses the doe eyes. But the little minx lets her eyebrows pinch just a touch. "What do you mean?"

"I know what you're doing." I cross my arms and try to fight off the grin that threatens to betray the stern look I'm shooting for. I nod at her. "The towel. The pretending you can't reach this shelf even though we're damn

CHAPTER 6

near the same height. The way you left your shoulders just a little bit wet." I swipe at her skin, collecting moisture, and hold the evidence up for her to see. "It's expertly done, Jenna, but you forgot who you're dealing with. I can smell a seduction from a mile away."

Her mouth drops indignantly. "I'm not trying to *seduce* you—"

"Oh yeah?" I jab a finger at her torso. "Where'd this towel come from, then? Did you go out and buy it strictly for this?"

She looks down at herself. "This is *your* towel, Finn. I got it from your linen closet."

"I don't *have* a linen closet."

Jenna's mouth opens over a word, one long second until it snaps shut again. She purses her lips instead, fighting off the same laugh I'm trying hard to kill. We end up in a staring contest that's half-glare, half-silent giggle. Out in the living room, I hear Eddie splash around in his tank.

"Okay, *fine*!" Jenna blurts out, breaking first. She throws out her arms in defeat. "I went out and bought this towel to seduce you. Are you happy now?"

"I *knew* it!"

"You're telling me this did *nothing* for you?" She gestures down her body. "Nothing at all?"

The towel in question starts to slide, the knot at the front coming undone, and with a choking sound I dive to hold it in place. "Goddamn it. Get that shirt on before I shove it over your head myself."

"Why? Let yourself be seduced, Finn. I'm told I can put on quite the show."

The obvious answer is telling her we have to nix the sex thing. That I need to keep it platonic. But frankly, I have my doubts she'd stick around if I do. She came to me for sex, and if I make it clear it's not a possibility, then what keeps her here?

Jenna twists out of my grip and if I had worse reflexes, I'd be treated to the sight of the cotton fluttering down her body as it drops. But I manage to slap my hands over my eyes in the nick of time.

"*Are you trying to kill me?*"

She releases a frustrated sigh, and I listen to the sounds of fabric stretching as she gets dressed. "*No.* I'm trying to get you hard," she enunciates. "And then give you what I'm fairly confident will be the best sex of your life. But I can let you be the judge of that."

"Jesus Christ—"

She wrenches my hands from my face and I peek through my lashes, making sure she's dressed. The woman has no mercy. Turns out I handed her *half* a t-shirt. The fabric cuts off at her waist, leaving smooth, tanned skin between it and the waistband of the ridiculous spandex shorts she chose to wear. God help me, but I can't help reaching out to run the back of my finger along the curve of her waist. Just to see what it feels like.

She's properly frowning now. "If you're concerned with my ability to handle casual sex, let me put that to rest for you: I am an expert at emotional detachment. We have this in common, Finn."

Seems we don't have that in common. Not when it comes to her, anyway. I know myself. I'll be done for the second I touch her.

"So," I say, sidestepping her proclamation. "I'm thinking we should come up with some ground rules. You know, for successful cohabitation."

She pulls a face. "What, like a cleaning schedule? I guess that makes sense..."

"Sure, a cleaning schedule. But also, maybe you start changing with your door closed. And I'll announce myself more loudly when I stop by your room."

"You're saying you *don't* want to see me naked?"

Of course I want to see her naked. *Obviously* I want to see her naked.

"Next rule: this towel is hereby banned from our apartment." I sweep it off the floor. "In fact, I'll get rid of it right now."

She laughs, grabbing for it as I make to walk away. "It's brand new. And extremely soft. You could give it a whirl, if you want."

"Nice try. Now, about this half-a-t-shirt—"

She pops a hip. "You don't like it?"

I let my eyes drop down the length of her body. Big mistake. "Fine. The half-a-t-shirt stays."

She chuckles. "I promise you that I can handle casual, Finn."

CHAPTER 6

"Doesn't matter. I'm immune to seduction. As recently demonstrated."

She stares at me a long moment. "*Oh*, I get it now." She nods along with her own train of thought. "This is about your begging kink, isn't it? Look, I'm not too proud to beg, but it's a lot more fun to get you to cave first. I give you one week. I'll even start limbering up. Make sure I'm nice and bendy for you."

She demonstrates, bending at the waist and touching her toes, wet hair spilling forward to tickle the ground.

Goddamn it.

"Stop that." I grab her by the shoulders and wrench her upright. She's struggling very hard not to laugh, and a traitorous chuckle trickles out of my own mouth. I cross my arms. "I. Am. Immune."

Jenna doesn't say a word. Instead, she lets her gaze drop. Doesn't take me long to figure out she's not-so-subtly pointing out the not-so-subtle half-erection I'm working with.

I am obviously not immune.

But she doesn't have to know that, nor do I have to readily admit it.

"Ignore it."

"If you insist."

She turns toward her bed, tossing the towel over her shoulder. It lands over my head, immediately dousing me in her scent, and the front of my jeans get a little snugger.

"*Anyway*, I came here to tell you I'm heading out for a bit," I tell her, ripping the towel off my head. "Do you need anything?"

She hops to sit on the end of her bed, bouncing a bit on the mattress. "Where are you going?"

"Gonna go pick up a few groceries before work tomorrow. I don't usually get home until about midnight, so I stock up for the week. Want anything?"

"What are you getting?"

I shrug. "Whatever takes no effort. Cooking's the last thing I wanna do when I get home."

"So, like, Bagel Bites and corn dogs?"

"I hope for your sake you're not about to disparage Bagel Bites. That's a punishable offense in this apartment."

She tilts her head, suddenly looking very grave. "You're not threatening to spank me, are you? You should probably know that turns me on."

I choke on my inhale and she gets such a kick out of it that her dimple comes out.

"Kidding. Sort of," she says as I gather myself, and now I'm definitely picturing her bent over my lap— "I'll come with you, I was hoping to get a few things. I can be ready in a minute."

She reaches for a hairbrush on her nightstand and starts running it through the lengths of pink. There's something a little cathartic about watching her do it. Soothing. The way she tips her head to one side, then the other, sending the strands this way and that way. It's oddly mesmerizing—

"Do you want to help?" She blinks innocently, holding out her hairbrush.

Fuck. She's lethal and she knows it. And it's hard not to get a little kick out of it myself. I wipe the growing grin off my face and offer her a stern look instead.

"I'll be at the door."

~

"Promise me I get to drive the next time we go out!"

Jenna grapples with the strands of hair catching in the wind and cycloning around her head as the Wrangler picks up speed. She begged me to take the top off the car, even with the rain starting to come down.

There's something about her that unhinges me, like I'd happily agree to swim with sharks if she asked me to. But the thought of her driving this car, tearing down the freeway the way I am now without any experience behind this particular wheel?

"Not a chance in hell," I shout over the wind whipping around us. I flip the brim of my hat forward, trying to get some coverage from the rain. "I'm not trying to get you killed."

We're going exactly in the opposite direction of the grocery store. The rain is really falling now, and I can see the weird looks we're getting from cars we're passing but I don't have it in me to feel self-conscious about that. Not with the way she's laughing next to me. Not with the sight of her hair starting to clump together in little waves again.

She looks like the kind of woman you only ever meet in a dream. Except she's real, and by some wild stroke of luck I definitely don't deserve, she's sitting right beside me.

"I'll have you know I've only ever crashed one car in my lifetime."

I throw her a grin over my shoulder. "And that's supposed to win me over?"

"It is if you let me finish: I've only ever crashed one car in my lifetime, and out of fairness to myself, I gifted that car to my ex. So I was the only one losing money there. Plus, he turned out to be a cheating ass anyway. I like to think it was my intuition trying to tell me something."

"You gifted your boyfriend a car? Didn't you work behind a reception desk?"

She pokes me in the ribs. "I thought we didn't judge."

"We *don't* judge. It was a serious question," I tell her, switching into a quieter lane to pick up speed. Her grin grows wider as the rain hits her face. She tips her head back and closes her eyes blissfully, letting it wash over her.

"Then in the spirit of no-judgment, I'll confess that I used my bribery fund to buy it. I knew he wanted the car, and it felt nice to give it to him."

"Bribery fund?"

"My parents are well off," she says, looking suddenly serious. Not a single trace of that bliss left over. "And they've very generously made sure my sister and I are comfortable."

"You're a rich kid?"

"You look surprised."

"Nothing about the way you carry yourself screams *rich kid*."

She heaves a sigh. "Yeah, I get that a lot."

"And that's a bad thing?"

"Depends who you ask. I haven't historically been good at modeling what it means to be a Carling. Part of the strings tied to our trust funds—well, *my* trust fund—was that I'd fall a little more in line with the family if I wanted to get it."

Jenna tucks her chin against the onslaught of rain that had thrilled her just a minute ago. She wipes her face, a pretty pointless exercise given she gets hit with another twenty drops at two second intervals. I pluck the hat off my head and drop it on hers. It's way too big, falling over her ears and eyes, and she nudges the brim higher up her forehead to give me a little smile.

I return it, merging onto the next off ramp to set us back on course for the grocery store. "So, this bribery fund. Your parents didn't expect the same from your sister? It was just a standard trust fund for her?"

"Just a standard trust fund. Ronnie wasn't the problem child. There wasn't a doubt in their minds she'd end up exactly how they wanted when she turned twenty-one. The age we'd get the money."

There's a full-on dam in my brain, trying hard to hold back the onslaught of questions I'm dying to ask. But she's staring grimly out the windshield now, and I get it. We have a lot in common, and there's no denying a natural intimacy between us. But it all makes it easy to forget that even though we met close to a year ago, we barely know each other. Talking about similar sexual histories is one thing. Sharing deep dark family secrets is completely another.

"Sorry. You don't wanna talk about this, do you?"

Jenna throws me a smile over her shoulder, and that thing is fake-as-hell. Hell, *I've* faked that smile, more than anyone knows.

"It's definitely not the kind of touchy-feely I thought we'd be doing if I ever saw you again."

I chuckle. "You and me both. You won't hear me complain about it, though. You're surprising, Jenna. I like trying to figure you out."

That lackluster smile slips, and Jenna studies me with a lot more skepticism than I'd like to see. "I'm *surprising*? That sounds like the equivalent of my ex telling me my big feet give me character."

"What's wrong with that?"

"Well, he said it totally out of the blue. I never once felt self-conscious about my feet until he brought it up. It was kind of par for the course for him, in hindsight."

I make a face. "Sounds like a real nice guy."

"Is that what you are, Finn? A nice guy?"

I glance at her, long enough to catch the way she squints at me. "You don't think so?"

"I don't know yet," she tells me, and without looking I know she's still watching me. "I guess I'm trying to figure you out, too."

"Would you say you find me *surprising*?"

She laughs. "Yeah. I guess you are."

We make it to the grocery store. Cursing this damn car for not having an automatic roof, we zip the covers on the Jeep, and run inside like we aren't already dripping wet. Jenna drifts toward the produce section while I wheel a cart to the freezers.

My addiction to take-out and pre-made meals has nothing to do with being sick of cooking after work. Cooking for myself never has the same appeal as making something for others to enjoy. Not that I do much of that these days anyway, between the basic cooking I do for Dad, and the fact that I barely lift a toothpick at work. It's what they don't tell you at school. The higher up you get in the restaurant food chain, the less cooking you actually do.

"You look like you're having an existential crisis," Jenna says, dumping an armful of fresh produce into our shopping cart. "What are you debating?"

"Whether this lasagna tastes as good as my dad used to make, and if I can get away with sneaking a box of Bagel Bites into the apartment without your merciless ribbing."

My hat sits a little askew on her head and I settle it into place. Jenna gives me a funny look.

"Probably not, and *definitely* not. Lasagnas freeze really well, though. You could get your dad to make you a couple to keep."

I know this. Before everything happened, Dad would turn the kitchen into a full-on lasagna conveyor belt, recruiting Mom, Hayley, and me to help assemble about a dozen of them he'd then throw in the freezer.

"He doesn't..." I run a rough hand through my hair, dislodging rainwater that drips down my neck. "My dad doesn't cook much anymore."

"Oh," she says quietly. "Is he..."

"No," I say, annoyed with myself for turning the conversation in this direction. "He's alive and... Yeah. He's alive, I guess."

"Is he sick?"

"In a way," I say, and instantly I hate how short I'm being with her. The way she's looking at me, the concerned frown, and the way her eyes have gone soft with sympathy, tells me this isn't callous curiosity. I sigh. "He's... not well."

Letting anything remotely like this out of my mouth is a bit of a new concept. I've carved out a very specific path for myself as the easy going, good time guy since Mom died when I was twenty. This type of thing is meant to stay buried in the box at the back of my closet. Not coming up in conversation with a woman I was trying to sleep with a couple days ago.

Is this what it'll take to get her to like me? I'm not sure I can hack it.

"What's in his lasagna?" Jenna asks abruptly, turning back to the freezer. "I'm sure if anyone can recreate it, it's you. And I could help. I spent tons of time hiding out in my parents' kitchen when I was younger. I picked up a few tricks from our chef."

It's completely transparent, but I'm grateful for the change of subject.

"You have a chef?"

She reaches into the freezer and pulls out two boxes of Bagel Bites, throwing them into the cart. "My parents have a chef. Their staff turned into my best friends growing up. I was a loner as a kid."

"How is that possible?"

"There's a weird girl at every school, isn't there? No? Just ours? Well, you happen to be in the highly esteemed presence of Rotham Academy's resident weirdo, class of 2012."

"I can't picture you as the resident weirdo."

"Meanwhile, I can totally picture you as the lascivious cool kid who sat in the back of the class and refused to strip off his backwards hat, even when the teachers scolded you." She appraises me. "Let's see... You're tall. Athletic. What were you, the star quarterback?"

"Star pitcher," I correct with an eyebrow wiggle, and she groans. "And I would definitely have been the little shit in the back of the class, if they could ever get me to *go* to class."

CHAPTER 6

"Hooking up under the bleachers?"

"Nah, snuck them into the boys' changing room."

She laughs. "Ah, to be a man. I turned into the school pariah the very first time I had sex."

"*What?*"

"Excuse me."

Jenna tucks into my side, making room for a man trying to reach into the freezer. I should really just move to give her some space, but I can't bring myself to. For a long time, I've suspected Jenna operates her own gravitational pull.

She hikes up the brim of my hat as she takes a step away from me. "Anyway, it was a small class, as I'm sure you can imagine at a private boarding school, so word really got around. Someone overheard the guy bragging about it and decided to tell just about everyone else. I was the first girl in my class to lose my virginity, or the first one to cop to it. And only the boys would give me the time of day after that."

"Jenna, that's..." Words start whizzing in my head. Fucked up. Devastating. But most of all: "That's really unfair. I'm sorry that happened that you."

She tips her head as if considering me. Sizing me up. Maybe deciding whether I'm worthy of her next few words. "It was my sister. The one who overheard. She ratted me out."

The sputtering sound I make is somewhere between shock and disgust. "How does this story keep getting worse?"

She gives me a wry smile. "Not what you bargained for when you let me tag along, was it? I know it's not really grocery-shopping-with-a-new-friend material." She crosses her arms tight across her chest, and suddenly she looks more uncertain than I've ever seen her. Nothing like the woman I'm used to. "I've been told I can be a little intense. Over the top."

I run a hand down my face. "Jenna, there are so many things wrong with what you just said, I don't even know where to start. I *like* how intense you are. And that's the wrong word anyway, because it makes it sound like a bad thing." It's there again. That skepticism as she looks at me. "Why does it feel like you were just testing me?"

Her lips quirk. "Because I was."

"And? Did I pass?"

Say yes.

Jenna gives me a long look before nodding at the freezer. "Do you want to try it? The lasagna?"

I slide open the glass door and grab a box. "Are you gonna answer the question?"

"No, I'm not. This whole thing has already reached peak levels of weird. One second we're on the verge of a one-night stand, the next I'm wheeling your groceries around," she says, moving our cart down the pasta aisle. "A scarlet woman and a himbo out on a totally platonic domestic chore. There's definitely a joke built in there somewhere."

"What the hell is a himbo?" I drop a family-sized bag of dry pasta noodles into our cart.

"You know, like the dude version of a bimbo," Jenna says, pointing at herself. "An airhead you want to sneak into the boys' change room."

"You aren't an airhead."

"But you *thought* I was an airhead when we first met." She clocks my frown. "It's okay, you can say so. People usually take in the flirting and the pink hair, and act like I don't have two brain cells to rub together. I get the sense people think the same about you."

I think back to the night we met, the easy way she owned the conversation even though she'd never met half of us at the table. She was a flirt right off the bat, sure. But she had also been funny, and clearly protective of her friend.

"I thought you were probably the one person on earth who liked sex as much as I did and wasn't afraid to admit it. But I never thought you were an airhead."

That little dimple dents her cheek.

"Did you think I was an airhead when we first met?" I ask, even though I already know the answer. It's how most people tend to think of me, and fair or not, it's a by-product of my reputation and propensity for rambling.

Jenna gives me a small, contrite smile. Bumps me with her shoulder. "I

CHAPTER 6

was really wrong to think so."

Chapter 7

Jenna

"Girl stuff is so damn *weird*."

He doesn't mean for me to hear that.

Finn says the words under his breath just as I come out of the bathroom. I didn't hear him come home, and really; I didn't expect him back so soon. It's only been a couple of hours since he interrupted my call with Ronnie to quietly tell me he was stepping out.

Either way, I'm glad he's back. A week into this living arrangement and I already feel a distinct void when Finn isn't home. He's constantly talkative even when I'm not in the room. He thinks out loud, rambling about whatever he's doing or reading. I've absorbed an incredible amount of knowledge just listening to him mutter to himself about whichever National Geographic article he's on that day.

Fascinated, I tip-toe into the living room to see what's caught his attention this time. My bet is on the little vase of dried eucalyptus stems I put out on the coffee table while he was out. Or maybe it's the oversized candle sitting on his bookshelf, a *cereal bowl* scent I bought out of pure curiosity and blew out the second I realized it was making the place smell like the inside of a Play-Doh container.

I'm wrong on both counts. I find Finn with his back to me, standing over the little side table next to Eddie's tank with a bag of turtle pellets in his

CHAPTER 7

hand. He pokes gingerly at something, like he expects it to lunge out and bite him, before carefully bending to sniff it.

"I see something's struck your fancy."

"Fuck!" He starts so hard at the sound of my voice the pellet bag rattles in his hand. "Either learn some CPR, Jenna Bear, or stop doing that. Swear one day my heart's gonna stop."

I watch him straighten his glasses. There's something so irresistible about him when he wears them. It takes the perfect amount of edge off his near-intimidating sex appeal, making him just approachable enough to think you might have a shot with him.

Or maybe that's just the story I'm telling myself. A week in and still, no short shorts or half-shirts have done a thing to sway him. The only thing that's kept me from losing faith in myself completely are those slack-jawed stares he gives me when he thinks I'm not looking.

It's strange. For reasons unbeknownst to me, all Finn seems to want to do is talk to me.

Talk.

What's that about?

"You'd think I've lived here long enough that you'd be desensitized by now," I say, bouncing onto the sofa. "What were you grumbling to yourself about?"

He tosses Eddie's food onto the coffee table and points an accusatory finger at the side table. "*That.* What the hell is it?"

I crane my neck to see around him. "Oh, that. It's a Himalayan salt lamp."

"What the damn hell is a salt lamp?"

I rise. "Well, for one, it's a lamp." I bend to flick a switch at its base, casting a pink glow on the wall behind it.

"And for two?"

I turn just in time to catch his gaze dart away from where they wandered on my ass. "Saw that," I say, poking him in the chest. His attention drops to the offending hand. "For two, it's supposed to have all these soothing properties."

He blinks. "Help me out here, Jenna."

"As in, it gives you better sleep, puts you in a better mood. Cleans the air. That kind of thing."

"*This* thing?" He flicks the lamp off and on. Takes it in both hands and shakes it tentatively, looking so affronted a warm laugh starts bubbling up my throat. "You're telling me this is supposed to *clean the air*?"

"The benefits of pink Himalayan salt are well documented—"

He grimaces. "I can tell you with total certainty that's a load of crap. Where the hell did you hear that?"

"The Planet Network ran a documentary."

He groans, dropping the lamp where he found it. "The Planet Network? They once aired a special defending the flat earth movement."

I shrug, working to keep a straight face. I love riling him up over nonsense. "You have to admit it's plausible. If the earth were round, wouldn't we just drive off the end?"

"That... doesn't even make sense."

"Doesn't it, though?"

He narrows his eyes. "Don't be coming in here with your conspiracy theories, Jenna. It's bad enough you're putting salty lamps and fuzzy blankets everywhere—"

"*One* fuzzy blanket. And if you actually bothered to watch the special about how the earth is flat—"

The next sound out of me is a squeak. Finn tosses me on the sofa, coming down on top of me and smothering my snort of laughter under his palm.

"One more word about it," he growls. "I dare you."

I mumble into the hand covering my mouth, and with a little smirk it drops away. "Got something to say, sweet thing?"

I blink innocently. "Only that I think you should spend a bit more time with that lamp. It really seems to be working for you." I sigh, wriggling comfortably underneath him. "This is a lot more like it."

"A lot more like what?"

I hook a finger into the waistband of his jeans and give a little tug. "Like how I thought we'd be spending our summer together."

He takes in the way he hovers over me like he's only just realized he's

CHAPTER 7

doing it. "Still? I thought you'd give up after the bathtub incident. If *that* didn't prove my immunity—"

"You mean yesterday, when you watched me take a bath?"

Finn's eyes saucer, and he sputters as he tries to form a sentence. He is *adorable* when he's flustered. And a lot easier to fluster than I'd ever have imagined. "I did not *watch you take a bath*—"

"Then what exactly do you call what happened?"

"You weren't making a sound and the door was unlocked. I had *no idea* you'd be in there, all... All—"

"Naked?"

His entire face flushes. It's so unintentionally charming I want to kiss every inch of those cheeks. He squeezes his eyes shut, like he's forcing away the memory. "There were bubbles. There were still a few bubbles—"

"You didn't see anything?"

"I..." He gives a full body shiver.

Honestly? Whether he sleeps with me or not, this little game of ours is worth it just for the sake of seeing him blush. It's almost as fun as getting him going over a good conspiracy theory.

Besides, the bath thing really was an accident. I was quiet because I'd dozed off for a minute, and I swear I thought I'd locked the door.

"You can see me naked, Finn," I say, gripping the front of his shirt. "In fact, I sincerely encourage it."

With narrowed eyes, he pries away my hands and tugs them over my head. "You're evil. I let a demon in a tiny pink skirt move into this apartment—"

I snort. "A *demon*?"

"A demon. Hiding her horns under all this hair. That's why it's pink isn't it? Smoke and mirrors so that poor fuckers like me get all turned around, and the second we drop our defenses you sink your teeth in and—"

"See, that's where you've got me all wrong, Finn; you'd have to *ask* for teeth. If I'm on my knees, I'm doing it right. I promise to give it to you how you like it."

Finn's face crumbles. He closes his eyes and starts to silently mouth something.

"What are you doing?"

"Praying."

"To who?"

"Literally anyone who will listen. Please, if someone out there can hear me, give me the strength to resist the sex demon that's taken residence in my spare bedroom—" A laugh bursts out of me and Finn peeks through his lashes, mouth twitching. "She's beautiful and so, *so* fucking tempting and I am in serious, excruciating pain but—"

"Tell them about how good I look underneath you," I stage whisper.

His gaze travels down, pausing at the strip of skin between my shirt and shorts. "Yeah. It's the last thing I should be saying, but she does look fucking good underneath me."

"Wanna see something even better?"

"No," he says morosely. A second ticks by. He gives a resigned sigh. "Yes."

I grab fistfuls of his shirt, tug him into me and lurch us sideways so that we topple off the sofa. Finn lands on his back with a hard grunt as I fall on top of him, reversing our positions. Feeling hard muscles under my palms as I spread my hands over his chest.

Finn blinks rapidly, a little winded from the fall and the weight of my body landing on his. "Jesus, Jenna," he says, when the fog clears.

He gives me a groan when I curve my fingers and sink my nails into his chest. "Well? Better or worse?"

He clenches his jaw, and the way he raises his eyebrow is almost scathing. He grips me and slides me down and to the left. Bumping my thigh into his swelling cock. "What do you think?"

A hot flash goes off in the pit of my stomach, echoing down my legs. *Hell yeah.*

I back into it again. Just a nudge. "I can do a lot more for you than look pretty. If you want it."

It's a silent game of chicken. It feels like we're sussing each other out. Where this is going. Which one of us makes the first move. Finn holds me in a firm grip, looking a lot like he wants to know what it is I can give him. He licks his lips, rubs them together, and runs his hands up and down my

CHAPTER 7

thighs, never taking his eyes off me. Slowly, I move my hands to either sides of his head. Lean down, staring at the way his lips part like he's waiting for mine to land.

I think we're doing this. I think we're actually, *finally*—

In one smooth movement Finn lifts me off him, dropping me carefully back onto the sofa like I'm heavy as a stuffed bear. "You're gonna be the end of me."

"But—"

What? What the hell just happened? Do I need a shower, or something? Subtly, I pinch the end of my ponytail and bring it to my nose.

Finn gets to his feet, nonchalant like the last minute only happened in my head. I'm stuck somewhere between frustration and hurt as I watch him cross over to the kitchen, walking stiffly.

He's... He's really not into me, is he?

That'll teach me for opening my mouth about Ronnie. About making myself seem so pathetic with all that stuff from school. It feels like I've been sliced open, exposed for him to see. He decided he didn't like what he saw.

I comb through my ponytail with my fingers, willing away the stinging in my eyes.

One day, you'll meet a man who won't care for that thing you have between your legs. And you won't have a thing to offer him.

Ronnie warned me.

"I almost forgot. I got you something." Finn clears his throat from the kitchen. I fist my hands, letting my pink fingernails dig into my skin. He gestures to a sunshine yellow box on the counter. "Are these the ones?"

I squint in his direction, trying to make out what he means. And then I recognize the box.

"Oh, *Finn*," I gasp, moving quickly to meet him. "This is where you went earlier?"

"Well... yeah," he says, like it's the most obvious thing in the world.

He watches me flip open the box to reveal six perfect cupcakes—fluffy white frosting swirling inches high with bits of crispy caramel sprinkled on top. I've been raving about these for days. Before I went away, they were the ultimate pick-me-up whenever I'd come home from a visit with my parents or crossed paths with Ronnie.

"You drove all the way across town during rush hour just to get these for me?"

He rubs the back of his neck, a pale flush creeping up his neck. "Yeah, I... I overheard your phone call earlier. You sounded really down. Seriously, what the hell is your sister's problem?"

"Now that's a mystery worthy of a Planet Network special."

Truly. Somehow, an offer to help book the limo for Ronnie's bachelorette party turned into an hour-long lecture about an outfit I hadn't even decided to wear to it.

I stare at Finn, trying to understand.

I don't think a man has ever caught me more off-guard. He's... considerate. Attentive and... Respectful. Definitely different from what I've become used to in recent years. Even my ex never did this kind of thing for me, and we'd been together for ages.

It's weird.

I don't understand why Finn's trying so hard. I already agreed to sleep with him.

What's your game, Finn Palmer?

"Are they the right ones?" Finn looks so suddenly anxious my heart pinches. I force my confusion aside.

"Definitely the right ones. I can't believe you did this."

He dips his chin. Without the typical backwards hat on, sandy strands fall into his face. Finn reaches for a cupcake and carefully hands it to me. "How'd you find this place?"

"I lived in the condo building next door. The nutritional value of my diet plummeted after I discovered these ones in particular." I groan into a massive, messy bite that gets frosting all over my mouth. "There's no way to eat these gracefully, by the way. It's part of their magic."

The frosting is all over my face, covering my top lip and clumping over my chin. I hand Finn the cupcake, freeing myself up to wipe my chin, the tip of my nose. I lick at the smear of vanilla on my mouth. In my peripheral vision, I see the cupcake go down on the counter, still in Finn's hand but compressing strangely so that the small tower of frosting starts to lean to one side. And suddenly the entire cupcake bursts, cake and frosting pooling over his entire closed fist.

When I look up, he's staring at me with such intensity his jaw pulses, eyes so hard he almost looks furious. I lick off the corner of my mouth, about to ask him what gives, when I realize it. He's staring at the way I'm licking my lips.

"You know, your signals are more mixed than a tape in the nineties."

He doesn't seem to hear me.

Is this all I needed? A little vanilla and caramel to make myself appealing?

With my thumb, I brush the edge of my lower lip and lick off the icing I collected with the flat of my tongue. He runs his tongue along the outline of his own lip as though wishing for traces of vanilla.

Relief pools in my chest. He *does* want me. He does.

His hand still holds the destroyed cupcake in a death grip. I take his fist, pry the cake free and lift his hand. Take a finger in my mouth, letting the velvety frosting coat my tongue as I slide it out. I do it again with his next finger. And the one after that.

Finn's mouth has popped open. It tastes so good, that creamy and caramel flavor mixing with his, and I crave more of it. I place an open kiss on the last, tiny fleck of icing on his skin.

Finn shifts on his feet, moving his hips to try to give himself breathing room in the front of his jeans. He looks like he's on the verge of snapping. The Finn I know, all smiles and bright eyes and upbeat diatribes, he's gone. I've never encountered this version before but God, I'm glad to meet him.

He looks like trouble. The good kind of trouble.

The leave a beard rash on the insides of my thighs kind of trouble.

"You doing okay?" I ask him, letting my voice dip, go breathy. His jaw pulses, pissed off and a little bit desperate.

In a flash Finn whirls me around to face the counter. Steps behind me, enclosing me. Grips my jaw with a hard hand, turning my head over my shoulder.

Oh my God.

His lips meet my ear. "You wanna play this game, sweet thing? Let's play."

Fuck.

I've never heard him like this. All traces of the affable man gone, replaced by something a little rough and teasing. Finn hovers behind me, just out of reach of my skin. He releases my face and his hands come down on the counter on either side of me. His breath hits the back of my neck when he gives a long, steadying exhale. For a while that's all I feel, that and the heat rolling off his body. For so long it starts to feel unbearable, anticipating his touch or whatever it is he has in store for me. I wait so long my muscles begin to bunch, tensing to the point of a shiver that peaks between my thighs. Painful goose bumps cover my skin.

And then I feel it. I almost jump out of my skin at the press of his fingertips just above my right hip. Just for a second, before disappearing. The breath I'd been holding expels from my lungs.

"What's wrong, Jenna?" His lips graze down my neck in just a single, languid pass. "Did you forget who you were toying with?"

Finn drops his fingertips along the edge of my shoulder, sweeping the skin so lightly it's a breath. His fingers trail along my back—down, *down*—until they roam back-and-forth along the waistband of my shorts. He weighs down my limbs, winds up my muscles so that they sit taught underneath my skin, waiting to see what happens next.

"Relax, sweet thing," he says into my shoulder. "This won't hurt. Much."

Hurt?

God, yes. It's been so long since I've been touched like this. I'm dying to have him keep this up. Get a little rough with me.

"Finn?"

He grazes the skin under my ear with his teeth and I whimper. "Yeah, babe?"

"I want you," I tell him, gripping the counter, desperately trying to steady my legs. "Rough, soft, however you want. Hang me from the fucking ceiling for all I care. I'll take it."

I'm begging. I've played right into his hands and I don't even care.

CHAPTER 7

He gives a low laugh behind me. The sound is so husky it almost sends me into a tailspin. And then Finn reaches around my hip, aims down, and a tight cry escapes me when he cups my pussy through my spandex shorts.

Yes. Please. My clit throbs painfully against his palm, and the way he's shoved the seam of my shorts up into me. It's been so long for me that I've already soaked all the way through my shorts. I know it—he knows it.

"Got yourself this wet trying to get me hard, Jenna?" he says against my ear. "Was that part of the plan? Or is it just an occupational hazard for a hot little tease like you?"

My reply cuts off as he moves his hand over me, rubbing me through my shorts. So gently, with such little pressure the sensation lands somewhere between a sweet tickle and a painful burn. With a moan, I sink back into him. My entire body flushes.

"*God*, Finn," I mumble. I feel his cock against my ass, but when I press into it he inches away.

"No. None of that," Finn says quietly, still running his hand along my pussy. "Here's what's gonna happen, Jenna. I'm gonna keep touching you. Gonna make you squirm and need and beg for me. And then just as I get you close, right when you're about to come on my hand, I'm gonna stop. You're gonna go tuck yourself into bed high and dry, and we'll do it all again tomorrow."

"Why would you do that?" My voice trembles.

He nips my neck. "So that you know how it feels. To see you in that little towel. To have you touch me and tease me, knowing it won't go anywhere."

His fingers hone in on my clit, rubbing quick little circles, building pressure, and it's so good my legs are shaking. *Shaking.*

"It *can* go somewhere. You can fuck me right now—"

Finn lets out a frustrated breath that tickles my skin, going at me harder, faster, like he fucking means it. Like he's hellbent on getting me closer. Like it's punishment for my words. His other arm wraps around my waist, holding me steady. I moan, head falling back onto his shoulder. Wondering if he's really serious about edging me, because if he stops this before I come I might actually cry—

"I'm not gonna fuck you," he says, grinding his thumb across my clit so perfectly firm I'm properly panting now. I close my eyes. "What I'm gonna do is make you crave me so bad you'll be screaming my name in your dreams. So bad all the little toys I'm sure you have tucked in that nightstand won't ever measure up to what you'll fantasize I'd give you if we ever fucked. You'll go out every night of the week trying to fuck other men to a level of satisfaction you'll never reach because in the back of your mind you'll know it's my cock you want to soak. Is that what you want all summer?"

Fuck. I'm so close. *So* close—

I grit my teeth. "I could do the same to you."

"I know you could. What I propose instead is that we put a pin in this thing, before neither of us can manage another decent orgasm. That would be the true tragedy in all this."

I muffle my sounds, try to steady my body. Try to hide how close he's getting me in case he's serious about stopping. His fingers move relentlessly over me and—God—oh *fuck* I'm—

"I meant what I said, Jenna. High and dry."

"*No—*"

A half-whimper, half-slurred attempt at his name comes out of me as he withdraws his hand. Finn grabs my wrists when I move to finish myself off, and I hang my head on a dry sob.

I'm in agony.

Fucking *agony*. The searing pain between my legs. The beginnings of ecstasy, so close I almost tasted it, now ebbing away. The fact that, despite the state I'm now in, there's something so incredibly hot about what he just did. He's gone and made it all worse. This side of him only makes me want him more.

A hell of a lot more than he wants me, I guess.

"Tell me you get it now," Finn says against my ear. "Tell me you're done with this. No more come-ons. No more flirting."

"You really don't want me?" The words come out more delicate than I ever wanted them to and I hate myself for it. This isn't the time, or the place, or the person.

CHAPTER 7

In a blink Finn's got me facing him again. I can barely make sense of his expression. His body is tense, and he's got a light sheen of sweat at his temples, like all the touching was working him up too. But there's an odd twist to his brows, and a downturn to his lips as he stares at me.

Finn nudges my chin, forcing up my gaze when it drops. "She really did a number on you, huh?"

"Who?"

"That sister of yours."

I feel the heat rise in my cheeks, mortified that I've made myself seem so pitiful. It doesn't exactly mesh with the me that he knows. Jenna Carling, the sex kitten.

"It's not that bad," I tell him. "I'm being over the top."

His mouth pinches into a tight smile. I don't think he buys it. "Let's be clear about something, Jenna. I've been dreaming about fucking you since the second we met. In a way that already bordered on unhealthy, even before you moved in. And now that you're here looking the way you do, being the way you are, I can't get through a single damn thing without feeling the agonizing need to have you underneath me. On top of me. Your mouth around my cock, my tongue inside you—I've already played it all out in my mind about a thousand times. But we're roommates, and it's a bad idea. Let's end this game, for our sake." He reaches for me again, slides his hand to the nape of my neck, gently stroking my skin with his thumb. "You can do that for me, can't you? Tell me yes."

His thumb moves along my jaw and I melt into his touch, feeling the fight leave my body with every stroke. I give him a jerky nod.

Finn brings me closer and presses a kiss on my cheek. "Good girl."

My legs give a violent shake at the words, and I let the counter behind me carry my weight. Finn's eyes narrow at the sudden slack in my body. Brows twitching when understanding dawns.

"We'd be a dream in bed together," he says, shaking his head regretfully. "But this stops now, okay? Let's make it to the end of summer in one piece. As friends."

He backs into the fridge as though to prove he means it.

Friends, huh?

I've never had a platonic male friend. Not since puberty hit and I, in my attention-starved, friendless way, realized how much the boys around school liked me when I weaponized my body. I've never gone without flirting. As a fallback, but also as a first line of offense, whenever I meet a man. A little flirting goes a long way in getting people to like me. But with sex and flirtation firmly outlawed, that leaves...

What does that leave?

"Okay," I say at last. "Okay, Finn. I can't pretend to fully understand because if ever there were two people suited for a casual fling, it's us. But I can respect your prerogative to take sex off the table if that's what you want. So... no more come-ons, no more flirting. We're platonic roommates from here on out. Scout's honor."

I salute him. Place my left hand over my heart and lift the other. Then flash him the live long and prosper hand signal. "I don't actually know how to punctuate a Scout's honor, but I swear my intentions are pure."

I expect him to give me that smile now that he's getting his way. The big one. The Finn smile. But only a single corner of his mouth ticks up. He gives me a lingering look before turning to the fridge. "Good. Great."

Chapter 8

Finn

I follow the smell of cumin and cheese into the kitchen to find Jenna seated on the counter, grinning down at her phone. Her forever-long legs are folded underneath her, neat and delicate in a way I could never pull off even though she's pretty much as tall as I am.

And I know it's not right to stare, that I have no *right* to stare when I've asked her for platonic. But her hair is a little wild around her shoulders tonight, falling in every direction, and there's something so endearing in the way her neck curves to the side as she thinks. In the way her shoulders shudder as she laughs silently to herself.

We haven't been avoiding each other, not exactly. I slept in this morning, and she left me a note saying she was meeting Jude for lunch, and then I went out for a run and…

I clear my throat. "Hey."

Jenna does a double take, almost fumbling her phone. She gives me a tentative smile. "Hey."

She crosses an arm over her stomach to clasp her other elbow, and something's different. With her, but with me, too. Things have shifted since last night's Scout's honor. It's a little delicate. As though we're only just meeting now.

I'm nervous, I realize. Even after deciding I wouldn't sleep with her, the idea of it was still *there*. A possibility. We mesh when we flirt. What does this—what do *we*—look like without sex and overt flirtation?

Pink stains her cheeks. "Okay. I think we've been staring at each other longer than normal."

My chuckle is half-laugh, half the expulsion of a breath I didn't realize I've been holding. I nod to her phone and move to sort through the cupboard over the fridge for a fresh bag of turtle pellets. "You looked like you were plotting someone's untimely demise. And may I casually remind you that I pay the rent in this place, so it better not be mine."

"I'm a trust fund baby, remember?" She laughs. "You're definitely not off the hook. But I will once again thank you for covering my half of the rent and remind you that you can change your mind about that at any time. Seriously, I feel the feminism seep out of me every time I think about it."

"I'm not taking your money. But I will put you to work if you want me to." I jiggle the bag of turtle pellets and tip my head toward the living room. "Wanna help me feed Eddie?"

Oh.

I've seen this girl smile and smirk and laugh her head off, but *that* look? The way her entire body seems to brighten, light up from within at the suggestion of feeding my pet turtle?

It's pure magic.

"I get to feed him?" she says, bouncing off the kitchen counter and following close behind me as we cross the space to the tank on the far wall.

"Get to? You're telling me you've been harboring a secret turtle caretaking fetish this whole time? Why didn't you say anything?"

"I don't know," she says with a laugh. "I saw you passed out together on the sofa last night. He's your baby. It felt kind of like asking to wear a prizefighter's belt, or something."

I throw her a grin over my shoulder. "I'm big on cuddles, what can I say? They don't come around often when you live alone."

I catch it. The way she opens her mouth and snaps it shut. If I ever learn she was about to offer up cuddles, I'm gonna hate myself for this platonic thing.

CHAPTER 8

Jenna sidles up to me and together we peer into Eddie's tank. The turtle is completely unconcerned with us. He lounges on a rock in the corner of his tank, neck stretched out towards the water like he's contemplating his next move.

"So all he eats are these pellets?" she asks, tentatively reaching down to run the back of her finger along Eddie's shell.

"Well, turtles are omnivores—" I cut myself off. I'm on the verge of waxing poetic on the dietary preferences of turtles and if Nina were here she'd give me that snarky look she does whenever I get too National Geographic on her.

Jenna dips her finger into the water, as though checking its temperature. "Meaning you feed Eddie pellets with a side of filet mignon and broccoli?"

"He tends to prefer collard greens. Worms, if he's been a good boy."

"Well, you must get a *ton* of worms then, don't you, Eddie?"

Her voice goes all soft and cooey, and fuck—something searing hot blows up in my chest. She wasn't faking being into the pet turtle thing the night she showed up.

Where did this woman come from, exactly?

Jenna does a double take in my direction, and only then do I realize I've been intently staring at her profile. The way laugh lines carve near her eye as she smiles down at Eddie. Immediately her cheeks flush the sweetest shade of pink, her mouth pinches in a bashful smile. It's nothing like the deliberate doe eyes she gives when she's trying to get a rise out of me. This is real, and something uncomfortable lodges itself in my throat.

"Do you think we can take him out for a bit? So I can hold him?"

Marry me.

What?

I clear my throat, thoroughly disturbed by my own brain. "'Course we can. Here." I push the coffee table into the sofa, giving us more room on the floor. "Sit. I'll cut up some greens for you."

Jenna settles on the hardwood and I airlift Eddie between her outstretched legs, heading back to the kitchen to tear up some collard greens. I return to see Jenna leaning back on her hands, watching Eddie move around between her legs like she's having an out of body experience.

"You know, this is the first pet I've ever had. Not that... He's obviously not mine, or anything," she says, as I settle across her. I stretch out my legs, feet touching hers, and together we form a diamond-shaped playpen for Eddie.

"Eddie is a turtle of the people. He's yours if you want him to be." I hand over a leafy stem. "So, no pets in the Carling household? Not even a hamster?"

"Nope. None. My mom ran a tight ship."

Eddie lumbers toward the greens I'm holding. I pass it to Jenna and turn him around so he aims for her. "Meanwhile, if I take a deep enough breath in my childhood home, I can catch whiffs of Tammy the Cockapoo."

"How long have your parents had her?" She waves a fist full of greens at Eddie.

"Oh, Tammy died fifteen years ago. But it's nice to know you can leave that kind of mark on the world, you know? We also grew up with a gerbil and a parrot."

"A *parrot*?"

"Yeah, Peter was my doing. My parents got so annoyed with him they eventually moved him into my room. I think it's how I got like this," I say, gesturing to myself. "I've been told I can't shut up to save my life. Which I probably should have advertised before letting you move in here, unawares."

Eddie reaches her at last, chomping on her offerings, and I want to taste that dimple of hers. "The talking is nice," she says. "I'm going to sound like I'm bragging when I say this, but the houses I grew up in were so big you could go hours without running into someone."

I make a retching sound. "I'd never have survived."

She laughs. "I barely did. I like it here. I mean, yeah, you're slowly turning me into a neat freak, which I very much resent. But it's already to the point where I have to put music on when you're at work, just to fill the silence. This place doesn't feel like it's meant to stay quiet."

"Yeah? What does it feel like?"

"I don't know." She drops her gaze, and that flush in her cheeks is back. She knows. She's just deciding whether to admit it. And then she shrugs, like she's telling herself *why the hell not?* "It feels easy. Like I don't have to remind myself to sit up straight or cross my legs at the ankles. Even in my own place I didn't feel like that, and in hindsight I think it had to do with my ex. Here... it's like I could snort-laugh as much as I want and talk about the stupidest thing I've ever done and it wouldn't matter. I could lick vanilla frosting off my roommate's fingers, basically throw myself at him for days, and he wouldn't think any less of me. It's a no-judgment zone."

My chest feels like a glass of champagne. Bubbling, fizzing aggressively, on the verge of spilling over the edge. She doesn't just like it here. Somehow, a week and a bit in, she feels at *home* here. With me.

With *me*?

I wish I knew what my face looks like, and why, after a quick glance, Jenna drops her gaze again. It takes her a couple of tries to tuck her hair behind her ear, and I reach for one of the socked feet pressed against mine. I don't know what I intended to do with it, exactly, but I end up just holding her toes in my hand. Giving them a little squeeze.

What's happening here?

Why does touching her foot feel bigger than it's ever felt to touch a woman anywhere else?

Jenna wiggles her toes under my grip. I don't think she's asking me to let go. The funny look she's giving her own foot is the physical manifestation of my thought process. She's wiggling her toes like she's testing a theory.

What is this? I hope she clues me in once she figures it out.

I clear my throat, let go of her foot, coaching my heart to settle down. "You can pet him, you know. Eddie. He likes his chin scratched."

"Like this? Oops." Whatever she does definitely doesn't hit the mark. Eddie darts partially into his shell, and I might be reading too much into it but I swear he gives me a look that says *what the hell, man? Who is this chick?*

Great question, Eddie.

"It's okay, Edison. We like her." I reach for the top of his head and give it a rub until he comes all the way out again.

"Suddenly I'm understanding the long line of women clamoring to get with you," Jenna says, shaking her head. "You have to know how insanely adorable this is, right?"

"You'd be surprised how often I've struck out talking about Eddie."

"I find that highly disturbing," she says, pulling a face. Jenna folds her legs and shimmies closer to where Eddie's wandered. "Help me get this chin scratch right. I need him to like me."

"On second thought, I think we should cover the basics first. Let's master the head scratch." I move so we sit side by side. "You'll wanna go at him slow so you don't startle him, and then make sure you stay away from his eyes and nose."

"That... gives me no room to work with," she says with a laugh. "Look at the size of him! How am I supposed to do that when his head is basically made of up eyes and nostrils?"

"Carefully and without the defeatist attitude." I take her hand and jiggle her index finger until she relaxes it in my grip. "Like this. You want to do this kind of crooking motion but with the pad of your finger. Try not to knick him with your nails." Jenna demonstrates the move. "Yeah, exactly. Go for it."

She moves slowly this time, reaching for Eddie, but with a little squeal she retracts her hand before it's even within a foot of his head. "I can't. I can't do it."

"He won't bite you—"

"I'm not afraid of *biting*. I have a major fear of rejection. This visceral, totally pathetic need for people to like me."

I scoff. "Who the hell doesn't like you?"

"Well, most importantly—" She points between us.

"Eddie's a *turtle*. I think you can take it easy on yourself, Jenna Bear."

"First of all, I don't appreciate you minimizing Eddie like that. He's much more than a turtle. Aren't you, little buddy?"

She pouts down at Eddie, and fuck, she's sweet.

"Sorry, Eddie. Pretend you didn't hear that." I pat the turtle's shell. "And what's the second of all?"

"The second is I've already struck out with him once. I can't put my heart on the line like that again. You'll have to go out for more cupcakes."

"You *won't* strike out. But if you do, I promise I'll get you as many cupcakes as you need to recover."

"Yes, but will you also swaddle me in my fuzzy blanket and sing me to sleep as I cry my eyes out?"

"My voice isn't lulling anyone to sleep, but I'll put you in a damn good swaddle if that's what you need."

"Tight like a burrito?"

"Tighter. I'll have to leave you an emergency whistle so you can call me to unwrap you."

Jenna hums. "And once you unwrap me you'll let me take the Wrangler on a joyride?"

I bump her shoulder. "Keep dreaming. I will personally take you on a joyride and belt out the song of your choice."

"*Whiskey In The Jar?* The Metallica version."

"You want me to belt out *Metallica* on a feel-good joyride?"

She gives me an exaggerated smile. "Hearing you growl out Metallica would fill me with oh-so-much joy."

I poke her dimple and her smile grows. "All this over Eddie? You're telling me you've never given a good head scratch before?"

"People don't tend to come to me for head scratches. Why, what's that look? Are you some kind of head scratch connoisseur?"

"Head scratches are my *favorite*." Jenna's gaze cuts to the top of my head. I sigh dramatically, lying all the way down and lacing my fingers behind my head. "You're tempted aren't you? You wanna prove you can give a good head scratch, and you wanna do it on me. Well, don't even try. I've got a high bar and won't accept anything but a very long, very thorough head scratch where you spend extra time on the spot behind my right ear—"

She fights a smile. "Are you seriously trying to reverse-psychology me into giving you a head scratch?"

"Is it working?" She gives a breathy laugh, eyeing my head again like she's actually considering it. "It is, isn't it? I don't blame you. Look at all this hair. So much to play with." I rub the top of my head, sending my hair onto my forehead. "Alright, then. I can't deny you such a simple joy. Go for it."

I settle into my spot on the ground, blinking up expectantly as she suppresses a smile. "You're kind of a weirdo, you know that?"

"I do know that. And I think you've got a little weird in you, too." I am *addicted* to that dimple. It has to be unhealthy. "I'm also in dire need of a head scratch, so…" I take her hand and guide it to the top of my head, closing my eyes. "Don't leave me hanging."

She doesn't. Jenna's fingers rake through my hair, pushing it back, gently scraping her nails along my scalp and fuck me, I let out a stuttering groan.

Her laugh sounds like she's got her lips pressed tight together. "Is it okay?"

"You're gonna have to roll me into my room." It's so good I give a full-body shudder. "My mom used to call me a tomcat and claimed I even purred if the head scratch was good enough. I never heard evidence of that, though. I think she was just trying to make me look bad."

She scratches at the crown of my head. "I don't think that's possible."

"The purring thing?"

"The making you look bad thing."

My eyes snap open. Jenna's wincing at the ceiling like she can't believe she just let the words out. She quickly forms blinders around her eyes with her hands. "Are you looking at me right now?"

"No. I'm not looking at you."

Jenna peers down, meeting my eye. Eddie nudges my hip like he's trying to tell me something.

"You're going to pretend you didn't hear me say something so cheesy," she says quietly. "Okay?"

She's blushing again. Goddamn. This girl is just so… I like Jenna the flirt. The one that keeps me on my toes. But *this* Jenna? The soft one? She's crippling. Something strange starts happening in my throat. This thick, burning feeling as I stare up at her.

"Are you flirting with me, Jenna Carling?"

She makes a face, so sweetly embarrassed. "No. *No*, of course not. That would be against the rules. And I…"

I sit up, wiping damp palms on my jeans, struggling to take my eyes off her. Struggling to tamp down this grin, and we're just smiling at each other now, kind of like we're sharing a secret. This girl is doing something to me, and I really need to figure out how to make it stop before I can't go back.

"What's the end of that sentence?"

Jenna lifts and drops a single shoulder. "I follow the rules." She chuckles when I tilt my head. "I follow *these* rules. I want to be your friend, Finn. I think... I'd really like that. I've never had a guy friend before."

"And I've never had a friend who's a girl before."

"You have Jude," she points out.

"A girl friend who's single."

She rolls her lip between her teeth, and it's the strangest thing. I want to snatch that lip between mine, sure. But what I really want to do is tuck her into my chest. Touch her dimple. Hold her toes.

Do friends do that?

A high-pitched beeping breaks the silence.

With a little jolt, Jenna blinks around the room, like she'd completely lost sight of her surroundings. I understand the feeling. There's this thing my vision's started doing, in the last ten minutes. Everything's gone a little grey around the edges, lines and colors blurring and dulling around Jenna like she's drawing the light out of everything around us.

That can't be good. I'll have to call the doctor about it.

Jenna rises and leaves me to drop Eddie back into his tank as she heads for the beeping oven. "You're off work tonight, right?" She bends to peer into the oven and, satisfied with whatever she sees, turns off the heat. "I'm going to head out for a run before dinner, but I saw the new Hunter Williams documentary just came out. We could watch when I'm back?"

"Ah..."

Guilt and want twist around my insides. But it's Monday night and I'm already gravely late for meeting Dad.

Jenna turns with her back a little stiff, giving my hesitation a small, pinched smile. "It's okay, Finn, we don't have to. It was just an idea."

She clasps an oven mitt tightly between her hands. She looks... What is that look, exactly?

It's as though someone's stuffed embarrassment, resignation, and a dash of hurt into a mason jar, and shook it up until it emulsified into this heavy, self-conscious look that's painful to see. It's so damn close to the look I caught on her last night, after we called off the flirting. How hard she was taking the rejection. I couldn't stomach it then, and I sure as hell can't now.

"You just dangled two of my favorite things in the world in front of me," I tell her. "Documentaries and you in those spandex shorts. That'll teach me for making plans."

Her body expels its tension, and her eyes go back to the way they should always be—bright and playful. "Tomorrow then?"

"Hell, yeah."

With a nod and an even bigger smile, she turns to lift her dish out of the oven. "Where are you going?"

"I..." I know I can't muster up the right kind of enthusiasm to say that I'm visiting my dad, and I don't want her to ask about him again. If I can't fuck my way into her good graces, the least I can do is keep things light and fun enough to tempt her into a real friendship.

Good Time Finn. People love him.

She gives me a curious look over her shoulder. "Oh. You're going on a date."

"What? What makes you say that?"

"You aren't wearing your glasses tonight." It's true that I've worn them around more often in the past week and a half. Had no idea she noticed. "And I've been wondering since... Well, I noticed you haven't been going out lately. I figured it was only a matter of time. Where are you taking her?" she asks nonchalantly, but she shoves things around in a drawer with enough force to seem upset.

"Hang on a minute," I say, rounding the counter. "Jenna—"

She turns, knife and fork in hand, and there's nothing like the intense relief I feel at seeing the lack of pink in her eyes. She pauses when she sees my expression. "What?"

"I... Are you alright?"

Her gaze drifts slowly to the side. "What do you mean?"

She isn't upset.

CHAPTER 8

Of course, she isn't. She's made it clear she can handle casual, and we agreed on platonic, anyway. This is what I wanted. To distance myself from the trap of romantic emotion. So… why does this feel like pulling a soufflé out of the oven, only to watch it collapse?

"Finn?" she prompts me.

"Nothing. Forget about it," I say, clearing my throat. "You're going for a run, you said?"

"Yup, just a short one. Don't let me keep you." She gathers up her hair and ties it on top of her head. "I'll even save you a veggie enchilada. A post-hook up snack to regain your strength."

She thinks I'm going out to fuck another girl and she's teasing me about it. She doesn't care, and it's a soggy, droopy mess of a soufflé.

"Actually," I say, shoving the hair off my face. "That documentary sounds good."

"We can watch when you get back?" she asks, oblivious to the mindfuck tearing through my system. "I'll wait up for you if you ask nicely. Just promise me you'll shower first."

This is what I wanted. This is what I wanted—

"Finn?"

"No." I clear my throat again. I really need to stop doing that. "Don't worry about it. You can watch it if you want. I'll catch up on it later."

"Okay…" She shrugs. "Have fun."

This is what I wanted—

I zombie-walk my way to the front door.

"Oh, Finn?" I turn to see Jenna give me a full-watt grin from the kitchen, dimple, and all. "For the record? The glasses are sexy as hell. You should use them to your advantage."

I'm in hell.

Chapter 9

Jenna

It wasn't one of my most successful runs for several reasons, the most glaring of which involved my overall lack of physical fitness. It shouldn't be a surprise that I was only able to keep up a sustained pace for four minutes at a time, puffing like I've just crossed the finish line of a double triathlon.

I let the hot shower water run over my head, needing it to help unclench my muscles. I deeply inhale my shampoo, willing the smell to help soothe me. And willing myself to stop picturing Finn and this woman he's with—

But I'm not thinking about Finn's date. I'm not. He's not looking for a clingy roommate or even a hookup with me, and I proudly fly my flag of emotional detachment when it comes to men, anyway. I shouldn't care about this date.

At all.

It's just, the things he says sometimes... It's like he's got a clear sight line into my brain. He's so good at easing me into this idea that... Maybe I'm alright. Maybe, when I'm outside the circles inhabited by the likes of Ronnie, people can like me just fine. Even without all the sex.

Are you sure about that, Genevieve?

I wonder who this girl is that Finn's taking out tonight. What's she like?

I groan. "Get him the hell out of your head, woman. You're friends.

CHAPTER 9

Platonic roommates."

I flip off the tap and wring the water out of my hair with so much force it's like I'm hoping it'll wring him out too.

Music blasts from my room, and it's deafening now that the water's off. I can't even hear the *shit* I mutter when I realize I left my towel on the bed. A quick peek in the cupboard under the sink confirms my suspicion that Finn only actually owns two towels.

I shake myself out over the bath mat as best as I can and sprint to my bedroom. I doubt he'd be back this early from a hookup, but just in case—

My attention is on my feet, which is why, when I slam into something solid in the doorway of my room, it catches me off guard.

I scream, bouncing off the shape in front of me, and slip on the water I'd been dripping at my feet. Stumbling backwards, I try desperately not to concuss myself on the wall behind me as I realize that *holy shit*, it's Finn in my doorway. Finn yelping a startled *fuck* when he sees me.

It's Finn lurching to catch me and slipping on the same puddle on the floor.

It happens fast. He falls forward, taking me down with him, somehow managing to get an arm under my head to cushion the impact as I hit the ground, and compressing the air out of my lungs as he lands flat on top of me.

The music is still blaring. I think it's what makes me come to the realization a little slowly, that *oh my God*, I'm completely wet and naked on the floor with a fully clothed Finn on top of me. Hard muscles bearing down on me, all warm and molding my skin to fill every one of his ridges.

Oh my God.

Oh my God.

"Oh my God!" The music is so loud I have to shout it. "What happened to announcing yourself?"

Finn lifts his head from where it landed in the crook of my neck, blinking rapidly as he takes in my face.

"Why the hell is the music so loud?" he shouts. "I was yelling your name—"

"Obviously I couldn't hear you—"

"Yeah, because you're hell-bent on bursting our eardrums!"

"You were supposed to be out on a date!"

"I wasn't *on* a damn date, Jenna—" His brows furrow. He moves his hand out from behind my head and looks down at his palm. "Why the hell are you wet?"

"I forgot my towel on the bed!"

Finn freezes. And even in the dim light, I can see a flush building in his face as he slowly realizes—

"Holy fuck." His tone is low, inaudible over the music but I read his lips just fine.

He lifts onto his elbows and after a moment's hesitation he lets his gaze drift. Down my face, neck. His mouth popping open when he takes in my breasts, torso. The way his hips are pressed into mine, the parts of me he's pushing against.

"Jenna," he mouths. He settles on my face again and he looks in physical pain now. Like he's been hit over the head, bleary-eyed, breath picking up to a light pant. "Fuck."

And then I feel it. I've never been so happy about my height, the long legs and torso that align us perfectly. His dick swells against the most blissful spot. Applying incredible, unintentional pressure, and when he shifts to bury his face in my neck again, the friction it causes releases a moan.

"Holy fuck," he says again, and I hear it this time against my ear. "Jenna—fuck, just give me—one second and I'll move—"

His body tremors against mine and there's no help for it. I feel my nipples harden, the shiver in my legs building upwards until a hot, sharp ache blooms between them.

Finn shakes his head into my neck, over and over like the act of it will help him survive this.

Because it's pure survival-mode now, if he's feeling anything like I am. I'm moving with his breathing, loving the way his weight presses me into the floor, the feel of soft cotton and denim against my bare skin.

"Finn—"

"Shh," he says into my ear. "Stay quiet a minute. Let me get a handle on

CHAPTER 9

this."

He sounds desperate, like he knows his arms couldn't carry him off me if he tried. I don't want him to try. I'm so keyed up, have pictured us this way so many times I think I could easily come like this. If he rocked his hips into me, just there—

"Fuck," he says again. And with two harsh, bracing breaths into my shoulder he plants his hands and pushes off the ground. He hovers over me on hands and knees and winces as he tries to adjust himself in his pants.

We stare at each other. I'm on full display for him now, panting, but I have no desire to move. I love his eyes on me. When I don't try to cover myself his gaze drifts again to see more of me. His shoulders slump—they actually *slump* as he takes me in.

And I wonder if, like me, he's regretting the deal we made. Taking sex off the table.

I don't get the chance to ask. With another deep breath he stands, locking his gaze on my face as he helps me up. Jumping like I've electrocuted him when the momentum drives me up and into him. He turns immediately and slams his bedroom door behind him.

Shit.

I slip into my room, slapping at the speaker by the door and leaving the apartment in deafening silence.

Shit. What was I thinking, running around naked? He must be livid.

And I... I have never needed someone this badly.

Truly *needed*, and the punishing throb between my thighs is in a league of its own now. It's acute, painful, and as I lean against this bedroom door, chest heaving, relief no longer becomes a choice. I squeeze my eyes shut. Press my back against the wooden surface for stability, and when my hand trails down my stomach I pretend the palm is bigger, fingers thicker and calloused and scarred from various knife injuries the way his are. When my middle finger slips over my clit, I pretend my closed-mouthed sob comes out into his shoulder. Sturdy and smelling so good, so *Finn*.

I imagine how he'd sound as he touches me, and maybe touches himself. Uninhibited, feral, letting me know exactly what I do to him, even when I'm just standing nearby. He'd sound like—

Like *that*.

I freeze. Fingers stop moving, holding my breath, straining my ears because I swear, I just heard—

A groan, thick with relief, on the other side of the door.

Oh God. Oh *God*. He's in his room touching himself. He is, isn't he?

Another quiet groan, deep and stretched out and followed by a rattling bang, maybe a fist or his body coming into contact with his door.

My legs move before I even realize I've decided to go. To open my door, take the two steps across the hall, to lay a palm on his door and feel the way it rattles in its hinges, because Finn's definitely there, leaning against it. His sounds and curse words more audible, even more breathtaking from here. A sweet, gentle stroking sound I'd give anything to see in person. And just when I think it can't get any better—

"Jenna."

I clamp my mouth against a gasp. He isn't talking to me. He moaned it. He *moaned* it.

God.

I turn to lean my back against his door. This is wrong. So wrong and yet nothing has ever felt this good. I clamp my teeth in my lip. Stifle a moan when I start rubbing my pussy again, his sounds helping me along, and after a second I'm totally lost in it. I slip a finger inside me and—

"Jenna?"

Shit.

It wasn't a moan this time. There's silence on his side of the door, and I must have made some sort of noise because I can feel him there, straining to hear me again. And really, I should stop this. I should take my hand away and run back into my room but God, I can't. I just can't, I—

"J-Jenna?"

"Finn." My voice is breathy, desperate. "Finn, I can't stop. Just let me finish—please, just let me—"

"*Jenna*. Are you—"

He sounds panicked. Keyed up and I keep pumping into myself, letting out

CHAPTER 9

a broken sob into the hall.

Another bang against the door. His fist. "*Jenna.*" It's a growl this time. "Let me open this door. Jesus Christ, Jenna. Let me open it."

"I can't move—"

Another bang. "Is that a yes?"

Oh God. I add another finger. "Yes. It's a yes."

In a second I'm falling backwards. And then I'm not. I'm pressed into bare skin, into his hard, defined chest. An arm comes around my waist to hold me tight to him. The momentum breaks my focus and my fingers come out of me and I'm now glaringly aware of this new, perfect sensation. The zipper of his jeans, slung low on his hips, scraping my skin. And thick, hard flesh digging against my ass. I press back into it.

"*Fuck*," Finn growls into my neck. He's panting hard, shaking his head where my neck meets my shoulder. "Fuck, fuck, fuck."

"That sounds like a plan."

His grip doubles around my waist. "Don't talk. Don't move. Don't say a fucking word, Jenna." His tone leaves no room for argument, and oh my God, that's hot. I *love* this side of him. "We're supposed to be friends. We're supposed to be roommates, and we're *not* supposed to be fucking. But now this, and *motherfuck*. What am I supposed to do, here?"

"Eighty-six the no fucking rule?"

His arm pulses around me. "Not another word, or so help me God. The fuck am I gonna do with you?"

A second ticks.

And then another.

"Let me watch you."

I gasp. And thank God he's got an arm around me because my legs falter.

I'm not shy about sex. And when you spend a couple years fucking your way through the city's male population, you lose all sense of shame, too. But what's there to be ashamed of, anyway? The way he's carrying my weight, panting against my skin, the way his dick presses into me. There could never be something shameful in being desired like this.

"*Jenna.* Yes or no?"

"*Yes.*"

In a flash we're moving. Backwards into his bedroom, the walls are a blur around me until he hikes me up on the bed with him. He shifts me so my head hits a pillow smelling dangerously like him. Moves onto his knees beside me, and I get a proper look at him. His face is hard, tense, jaw pulsing and visibly grinding. Tanned, broad shoulders. Abs flexing with every harsh breath, and his cock—

My toes curl. "Fuck, Finn. You look so good."

"Fuck, yourself." His gaze glides down my body, every inch of me. He shudders. A real, visible-to-the-naked-eye shudder laced with need. "Goddamn, Jenna. You're so beautiful."

He looks at me with so much awe that I flush. Feel a little flustered for a second. I force it aside and shoot up, reaching for him, but his reflexes are faster. He catches my hands, pushing me back down and tugging my fists over my head.

"*Don't.* Don't go there or you better fucking believe I'll end up doing something we'll both regret in the morning."

"I want you. I would never regret it—"

"Stop. *Talking.*"

I can see them. The threads of his control, fraying at the edges as he looks down at me, hovering inches above my face. He takes a few harsh, steadying breaths. Leaves my hands over my head and sits back on his heels. He starts tucking himself back into his pants.

"No," I say urgently. "I get to watch you, too."

I'm bluffing. Totally bluffing because hell or highwater couldn't stop me from fingering myself under that gaze. But it does the job. He drops his hands from his waistband. Closes his eyes, just for a moment, as though saying a silent, desperate prayer for the survival of his restraint. When they open again, he's got a fist around his cock.

"Touch yourself."

It's the easiest request ever dropped in my lap. I make my movements slow, purposeful. Lift my hands from over my head and cup my breasts. Squeezing for him, pinching my nipples for him. His tongue draws a line over his bottom lip and I can almost feel it on me. How he'd tease me with it. It sends a tremor up my legs, delicate at first and scorching by the time it reaches my center.

And maybe I'm moving too slow, or maybe he saw my pussy clench because Finn shifts around and oh my God. He grips my ankles, slides his hands up to my knees, bends them, parts my legs. He hangs his head, throwing his hair forward over his face and it's a look of pure defeat.

"Goddamn it, Jenna. Look at you. Fucking dying to know what this pussy tastes like."

I reach up and run my fingers through his hair, pushing it back so that I can see him. His eyes are squeezed shut.

"I want you to know."

He grits his teeth. "What did I say about talking?"

"Do I strike you as someone who listens?"

The word *fuck* blows out with his next exhale. His hands trail along my legs and I cry out when his thumbs, light as air, barely there, caress the creases where my legs meet my body. So lovingly before he spreads me open wider.

"Get your hand down here."

And God, when my fingers land, when they meet that perfect spot again, he moans with me. Licks his lips, sinks his teeth in so hard the skin goes white around them.

"Finn. You're allowed to."

"*Jenna.*"

"I want you to."

He groans, lowering his head, and I think I'm finally going to feel his tongue on me, finally going to know if it feels the way I've imagined for almost a year. Instead, his forehead meets my belly button.

"Torture. This is fucking torture, you know that?"

"It's self-inflicted. If it were up to me, you'd already be deep—"

"Be *quiet.*"

He nips at my stomach and I squirm underneath him. Apply more pressure with my fingers and moan to the ceiling. He swears again, watching my fingers work small, fast circles over my clit. His tongue slides across the wet edge of his lip.

"One taste," I hear him say. His voice is so low I don't even think he's talking to me. I think he's coaching himself, giving himself this allowance. He meets my eye. "Just one. Okay?"

"Please."

And he moans. Actually *moans* at the supplication.

"That mouth. It's gonna get us in trouble one day," he mutters to my stomach. Finn moves between my legs. The anticipation of it, the promise of his warm mouth on me has me shaking now. "Make room for me."

I part my fingers. And holy shit, I don't know what's better. The sight of this man coming down to kiss me there. Or the way his mouth clamps around me, the gentle, perfect suction on my clit, just for a second. Or how his tongue drags lower, dips inside me, swirls around, just once. How he gently kisses the skin on the lower swell of my ass, where I can feel myself dripping.

It's all of it.

All of it has me trembling, shaking like a leaf, whimpering into the room, sobbing in frustration when he keeps his promise and sits back up. Shakes his head at me, looking almost angry. Like I have him completely unhinged, and it turns me on even more.

"Sweet enough for you?" I manage.

"It's so fucking good."

I can't help it. I giggle. This low, breathy one where nothing is funny except for how badly I need him. I watch him stroke himself a moment, long and slow, lips parted as he looks at me. And I sit up. Gently, inch by inch so that I don't startle him, break this moment. He doesn't move away, though. Just drops his gaze from my mouth to my neck, to my breasts and back up again when I smile at him.

"My turn," I tell him. He flinches. "One taste. Okay?"

Two more strokes, up and down his length. And he drops his hand. "Fuck it."

I drop onto my hands. Dart out my tongue, getting my first taste. Wrap my lips around the tip of his cock and his head falls forward. Suck a little,

CHAPTER 9

then a little more when he groans, until I hollow out my cheeks, taste a little salt on my tongue. He lets out a low growl.

"Fuck, that's good."

And it's probably as much as I can let myself do before taking it too far. I start pulling away but in a second his fingers thread my hair, keeping me there.

"Jenna." He breathes in, and out. "Once?"

It takes me only a second to realize where he's going with it. What he's asking for. And when I nod, his hips surge forward, gentle but possessive, sliding his cock over my tongue, throwing his head back on a groan, abs tensing. Just once, before pulling right out.

He runs a hand to the nape of my neck and brings me back up, gazing at me under heavy lids and running a thumb over my mouth. "That was probably a mistake."

I know what he means. I can still feel the ghost of his tongue on me. "I don't regret it," I tell him, so he knows. "And thank you for the spank bank material."

The tension in his face breaks. He laughs, eyes lighting up, shoulders shaking. "Back at ya."

I smile, laying back down with my head on his pillow. "I've got a bit more in me, if you want it."

And suddenly he's serious again, coming over to me on hands and knees. Touching his forehead to mine, teasing my lips with his as if he's about to do it... actually about to kiss me. I can play this game too. My tongue touches his lower lip. A slow, careful lick, the same kind of attention I just gave his cock. Finn grins against my mouth. That sexy, crooked one that gets me hot just looking at it. Turns out, it gets me wetter just feeling it.

"Show me how you make yourself come," he whispers.

I tug at his waistband. "You too."

He nods, watching me bring my hand down, finding my clit again. He groans and shifts his weight to free a hand and stroke himself. These long, perfect drags as he watches me, and after a minute I reach lower, pushing my fingers inside me. I match his pace, crying out and writhing underneath him as I fuck myself. Feeling the heat from his body, feeding off the desperation in his eyes. Moaning louder when he comes down on an elbow to mutter in my ear.

"Did you do this last night? Did you play with yourself after I touched you?"

I nod almost frantically.

"Say it."

"I played with myself."

"Did you picture me?"

"I pictured you, Finn," I moan. "Do you ever picture me?"

"I've had you in my head every single time I've come since the day we met." I whimper. Finn looks down, watching my fingers work. "Do you understand how fucking bad I wish it was my cock coming in and out of you like that?"

"Not too late," I say, running my fingers through his sandy hair. "It would feel so good."

But he shakes his head. "Can't, baby. We're too good the way we are. You don't want to fuck this up, do you?"

The logic is flawed. Because maybe we aren't fucking, but we're pretty damn close. I shake my head anyway and he kisses my shoulder, pleased with my answer. His satisfaction with me sinks into my skin, coating my bones.

"Good girl. Keep going. Keep fucking yourself the way I wish I could. Make yourself come so hard I can feel it from out here."

I do what he says. I push my fingers in and out until my thighs tense. My neck starts to arch off the mattress. I watch him touch himself above me, the way I wish I could do for him too. He makes these low, deep sounds from his throat as he watches me. And they sound so pure I feel them down inside me, pleasuring me alongside my fingers.

"I'm close. I'm gonna come," I whisper.

"Give it to me. Loud and drawn out, baby. Don't hold back. Make it ring in my ear. Make it so I can't ever forget how you sound."

Another easy request, even easier than the last. Because the sight of him above me—his face twisting in pleasure, the way his eyes devour me, how he pumps into his fist with harsh snaps as though he were fucking me, I couldn't be anything but loud.

"Finn—oh, God, God, *Finn*—"

Finn watches me come, *sighs* as he watches me ride it out. He buries his face in my neck again to mutter a string of words I can't make out because I might as well be underwater. The world has gone dark and quiet around me as I tremble on his sheets. But the way his lips move against my skin tells me they're soft words, gentle, praising. Rewarding me for giving this to him.

After a moment I feel his chest tense against me. His hips pick up their pace, moving a little sloppy now, and I know he's not far behind. He starts to shift away, but I get a grip on his waistband before he gets too far.

"On me."

"*Jenna.*"

But I just called out his name as I came, used the four letters to help me cling to reality. I've made myself vulnerable and I need him like this, need him to give me another piece of himself tonight.

"Finn, please."

Finn opens his mouth like he's about to protest again. But his body has other ideas. His orgasm catches him off guard. I watch the shock flash across his face, hear his startled groan. His wide eyes lower to watch as he paints my skin. Finally he falls into my neck, panting into me as the tension wrings its way through his body. I run gentle fingernails up and down his back.

It's true what they say.

Finn Palmer is a hero in bed. His eyes did more for me than a man's hands ever have. His words pushed me to complete abandon, so sweet and delectably dirty at the same time.

"Goddamn it, Jenna." He sounds angry again. But when he pulls away his eyes are gentle, smile soft, and he lays a single kiss on my forehead. "Stay put. You can at least listen to *that* for me, can't you?"

He's himself again, that easy, affable Finn, and it's a relief to know we can get back there after this. At least I don't have to pack up and hightail it out of here. Offer Jude some shifty excuse when I show up at her doorstep needing room and board.

Finn crawls off the bed and crosses the hall into the bathroom, returning quickly with his pants back on and a cloth in his hand. I expect him to hand it to me. Without hesitation he runs it over me instead. It's so gentle it tickles my skin, and when he finishes he tosses it into a hamper across the room. He turns to rustle around in his dresser. I sit up at last, stretching comfortably, feeling light, loose, and satisfied, though he barely laid a hand on me. I wiggle my toes, making sure I'm able to stand before touching down on the hardwood.

"Where are you going?"

Finn eyes me with a grey t-shirt in his fist. Looking... confused. Confused at the sight of me sitting on the edge of the bed.

"To my room."

His brows pull together. "Why?"

Now I'm confused. "You don't have to do this. I'm a big girl. You won't hurt my feelings if you send me off like anyone else."

He rears a little like he's dodging a slap to the face. "I'm not... I'm not sending you off, Jenna."

"It's totally fine—"

"Jenna," he says heavily. He hands me the t-shirt. "Put this on and get back in bed, please."

"Why?" I stare at the fabric. "Unless you're trying to tell me you changed your mind about sex?"

"No. It's not about sex." He goes back to the dresser and pulls out a pair of sweats and a t-shirt, getting dressed. When he sees I haven't moved, he takes back his t-shirt. "Arms up, Jenna Bear."

"Why are you doing all this?" I murmur, but I do what he says. He threads my arms into his shirt and tugs it gently over my head, brushing the loose hair off my face.

"Just go with it, okay?" He hooks an arm around my waist and pulls me back down onto the bed with him, drawing the covers and tucking me into his side.

I don't get what I'm doing here, why he's tucked me in with him. He

CHAPTER 9

doesn't do this and I never once expected him to if we ever hooked up.

Finn stares at the ceiling, brows drawn together, contemplating something very hard. His muscles are tense under my head. Even though he's got an arm holding me to him, absent-mindedly running his thumb up and down me, I start to worry that he *is* angry after all.

Maybe he really doesn't think I can handle it. Playing it cool. Sex for the sake of sex. Maybe he feels like he has to baby me through this. But I *can* handle it. I handled all the one-night stands just fine before this one.

"Wow," I say against his chest, infusing as much playfulness into my voice as possible. I stretch into him, throwing an arm over his waist. "Is this the white-glove Finn Palmer service? You should really charge extra for this. Definitely worth a second orgasm, at least."

Finn looks down at me, frowning sternly but with traces of that signature playfulness.

"Quiet, you," he says pleasantly.

He plants another kiss on my forehead and kills the light.

Chapter 10

Finn

I was right.

Hooking up with Jenna was a mistake. It was Pandora's box, releasing all the pent up want, *need*, I've had for this woman since the second I laid my eyes on her. Letting out into the open this stifling crush that started developing with the first words she ever said to me.

So, you're Finn. The one who never called me.

Her tone rings in my head like I heard the words just yesterday. She was calling me out for never reaching out after Jude tried to set us up. She wasn't mad, wasn't trying to back me into a corner. She was teasing me, working to build us common ground. Already sweeping me into her orbit the way that she does.

I'm not one for substances beyond the occasional drink. But I suspect that last night, watching her body move, taking in her skin and the pleading look as she neared her orgasm, like I was the one who would give it to her... It's gotta rival the strongest high anyone's ever experienced. The whole thing felt like it was happening through a glistening fog. My limbs felt heavy and like they weighed nothing. My mind felt too big for my head, everything moved at a crawl.

And here's the thing about Pandora's box: once it's open, you can't take it back.

CHAPTER 10

So that's exactly why I'm now laying here, staring at the strip of morning sun hitting the ceiling over my bed, silently panicking.

I turn, eyeing the other end of the bed. She was supposed to be there. I was supposed to wake up to her. Instead, there's a grey t-shirt neatly folded up on the pillow that was supposed to be hers. The sheets are cold and empty. I shouldn't care. I've woken up alone enough times that it shouldn't matter. Whatever this ache is in my throat, it shouldn't be there.

Fuck.

I reach for the shirt and stare at it in my fist like it's got sins against me to atone for. What was she thinking? Why did she go?

Does it smell like... Hating myself, I bring the fabric to my face.

Roses and honey.

I'd be willing to bet she wore it barely a few minutes. Still, she managed to soak into the threads. She's got that kind of magic, doesn't she? The kind that soaks into you. I can feel it happening to me in real time, as I lay here. This warm, painful feeling under my skin. Bones calcifying with roses and honey.

How do I get her out?

Was she in it last night for the same reasons as the others? For Good Time Finn. Sex and nothing else. Was that it?

I've been listening to Jenna bang around the kitchen for the last half hour, making way more racket than necessary. I hear a sizzle of fat in a pan now and within seconds the smell of eggs and cinnamon wafts under my door.

I'm starving. Completely starving but I don't have it in me to go out there just yet. Besides, I doubt she's making any extras this morning. No one cooks breakfast for Good Time Finn. That's the whole point of him. You fuck, and life goes on.

Suddenly, I hate that about myself.

I hear her gentle footsteps come down the hall, expecting her to go into her room and damn near jumping out of my skin when she knocks lightly at my door.

"Finn," she says quietly. "Are you up?"

This would be the ideal time for words to come out of my mouth.

Any second now.

Any. Second.

"Finn?"

"Hey," I call at last, clearing my throat of its rasp. "Yeah, I'm up. What's up?"

"I made breakfast," she says, sounding perfectly cheerful. "French toast. Want some?"

That's it?

We live through this life-altering thing last night and all I get is an offer for French toast?

I press my palms into my eyes. "Yeah, that sounds good. I'll be out in a minute."

I don't move until I hear her rattle a pan back in the kitchen, and I trudge into the bathroom to freshen up. In the kitchen, Jenna's standing over the stove wearing a pair of black spandex shorts and a loose t-shirt, hair tied up in a ponytail on top of her head, so long and smooth that it slides around all over the place as she moves, like a pink brush over her shoulders.

I hover awkwardly by the edge of the island. Wishing for my eyes to suddenly develop x-ray vision so I can get another look at her body under those clothes. To confirm that her skin has those little flecks of shimmer throughout it. That it really glows the way I remember it did last night.

"Hey." She beams at me over her shoulder, dimple and all.

Meanwhile, I feel like a ghost of myself. Like my soul has leaked out of my body and latched onto hers.

I clear my throat. "That smells good. What's the occasion?"

Mind-blowing masturbation?

Admitting this thing between us is bigger than casual?

"I always make breakfast," she says with her eyes on the pan. "This is just the first morning I decided not to hog it all." She pries a slice of toast from the pan and stacks it carefully onto a plate with another four perfectly golden pieces.

Swallowing, I round the counter and hoist myself up on a stool across from her, taking in the sweet way her nose upturns at the tip, just a little. How she presses her lips together when she's focusing.

Jenna catches me staring. "What?"

"Did you sleep in my bed last night?"

That didn't sound bitter. At all.

"I got up after a few minutes. I have to say, Finn, I'm very impressed by how fast you fall asleep. I've never seen anything like it."

Seen anything like it, implying there have been plenty of people—*men*—she's watched fall asleep, and motherfucker I envy them all.

She places the last steaming slice of bread onto the serving plate and switches off the stove, reaching into a drawer for forks and knives. She hands me a set.

"Eat up."

I stare. On the list of things I want to eat up, which mostly consists of her body parts, French toast doesn't even make the cut. But I take the cutlery and she joins me in the stool next to mine, not making any effort to create an abnormal amount of distance between us.

So that's it, huh?

She's completely unfazed by last night. It really, *really* meant that little to her?

Meanwhile here I sit, feeling like my internal makeup has been rearranged from head to toe. Turned inside out so that all that's left of the sturdy, emotionless-sex armor I used to proudly wear is a sorry layer of flesh she's slowly flaying, with every nonchalant bite she takes out of that French toast.

Christ. When did I become so melodramatic?

I pride myself on clear and open communication when it comes to sex. Everyone knowing where they stand. Maybe I'm doing it backwards this time around, but a retroactive conversation is better than none, right?

"Hey, so," I say, clearing my throat again and hoping she hasn't noticed I've needed to do that far too many times since I got up. "Should we talk about last night?"

She pops another bite into her mouth and chews, watching me thoughtfully with those clear blue eyes. Torturing me slowly with her silence.

"Sure," she says, once she swallows.

She puts down her fork and after a long, quiet moment, I realize we're both waiting for the other to go first.

"I don't know about you—" I start.

"I should apologize—" she says at the same time.

"*Apologize?*"

Jenna twists in her stool to face me. "Yeah... In hindsight I might have been a little pushy with the whole going down on each other thing. I feel bad about it."

Every ounce of blood in my body screeches to a halt and immediately pivots in the direction of my dick. I'll be on my deathbed one day and still fantasize about the way she looked with her mouth on me.

"I have no regrets about that," I say quickly, echoing her words from last night. "I mean, yeah, we probably took it too far. But I loved every second."

She nods, shifting slowly in her seat. "Okay, good. And look, I meant it when I said you don't have to worry about me. I get how this goes. It was just sex. *Kind of* sex."

She grins so easily something in my chest shrivels away. It was just sex. It was just sex.

Goddamn it, what is *wrong* with me? I've said those words more than enough times myself. They should roll off my back like water.

I pick up my knife and cut into my toast, lathering it with syrup in an afterthought like it'll soften my tone. My vocal cords are dangerously close to bursting out into a frustrated growl. "Yeah, exactly. We're good, then?"

Jenna chews another bite of her breakfast and swallows hard. "No harm, no foul."

"No harm, no foul," I echo.

"Okay. Great." She shifts uncomfortably in her stool, still staring down at her plate. Out of nowhere she jumps off her seat and makes a sudden beeline for her bedroom. "I'll be back to clean up in a minute," she calls over her shoulder.

I swear her voice is tight and her walk just a little unsteady. She locks herself in the bathroom and a moment later goes straight into her bedroom, definitely dragging her feet. And I know that it's wrong, I know it is, but the

CHAPTER 10

relief pooling in my chest feels so damn good. She's bluffing. We're both bluffing and I'm on my feet so fast you'd think my chair was on fire, heading straight to her room. We can talk this through, figure out what this is and how to get it under control.

"Hey, Jenna—"

I stop so abruptly I sway on my heels, grabbing the doorframe to steady myself. The sight in front of me completely shatters me. Jenna is curled up in the middle of her bed, on top of the covers. Eyes squeezed shut, arms wrapped around her middle. She doesn't look upset. She looks like she's in pain.

"Hey, what's wrong?" I come up to the bed and scan her from head to foot, looking for signs of trauma. When I don't find any I hike a knee up on the mattress, leaning in closer. "Are you okay?"

Her eyes open and she fixes on me a little unsteadily.

"Jenna, what's wrong?" I ask urgently now, reaching out to brush a strand of hair off her forehead. My heart is trying to bust its way out of my chest. "You're scaring me."

Her face spasms. She curls her lips into her mouth, clamping down on them with her teeth. After a moment she releases a breath, giving me a bit of a sheepish look. "Can you grab me some painkillers? There's a bottle in the purple makeup bag in the bathroom."

I beeline for that motherfucking makeup bag, jogging into the kitchen for a glass of water on the way back. When I return, Jenna slowly heaves herself into a seated position on her bed, face looking a little like she's sucked on a lemon.

"One or two?"

"Two, please," she mumbles, accepting the pills I drop into her palm and downing them both with one sip of water.

I take back the glass and put it down on her nightstand, smoothing back her hair as she reaches for a pillow and hugs it around her middle. Her skin feels a bit clammy, and she's losing some color in her cheeks.

"What's going on, Jenna Bear? Are you getting sick?"

She shakes her head and her face twists painfully for a few seconds. "No,

I'm okay. The meds will kick in and I'll be good as new. Ignore the mess in the kitchen. I promise I'm not trying to get out of cleaning."

She's trying to hurry me out of her bedroom. But the thought of her struggling in here on her own... There isn't a chance in hell I'll be able to sit still in the other room. I take her in, the strands of hair starting to stick to the sheen of sweat building on her forehead. The way she's doubling over with her pillow on her stomach, swaying a little. How she was squirming in her barstool earlier...

"Is it cramps?"

She nods, giving me another sheepish look.

My relief is instant. Not because she has cramps—I've obviously never had any, but I've seen my sister suffer through her fair share and that shit doesn't seem like a fucking picnic, that's for damn sure. But cramps I can work with.

I reach behind her and prop her other pillow up on the bedframe. Go to my room and grab another two off my bed and add them to her stack.

"Does it always hurt this bad?"

Jenna shifts uncomfortably, pressing the pillow down harder on her stomach. "I can usually catch it early enough with painkillers so that it doesn't get to this point. But you insisted on distracting me with *the talk* this morning."

There's a smile in her voice, but her words come out tight, like she's partially holding her breath.

"Come here." I hook under her arms and pull her gently up the bed until she's reclining against the stack of pillows. I untangle her fuzzy blanket from the foot of her bed and lay it over her legs. "Comfy?"

"Finn. You don't have to do this."

"I'm gonna need you to stop saying that." I tuck the blanket around her feet.

I go sorting through a cabinet in the bathroom, and in the kitchen I fish a couple of chocolate bars from the back of the pantry. I always keep a stack of them in case of a sweet tooth emergency, and this seems as good as any.

"Here. Have this." She watches me wearily as I peel the foil off a chocolate bar and hand it to her. "I also have..." I touch the hot pad to my arm, checking the temperature before handing it to her. "I messed up my back at the gym a little while ago, so I have this. Got distracted coming out of a squat. Hopefully it works."

She accepts the pad, still looking at me suspiciously like I'm about to come up and cuddle her too. Which doesn't sound half bad. Finally, she gives in and tucks the hot pad under the pillow she's still holding to her middle.

"Were you checking out a girl?"

"Checking out a what?" I sit on the edge of the bed, tugging up her blanket. "A girl."

"Pretty sure you're the only woman here, Jenna Bear." I hold the back of my hand to her forehead. "Can you get delirious from cramps?"

She smirks and shoves my hand away. "At the gym, Finn. Did you throw out your back because you were checking out a girl?"

"Hey. I'm a bit more smooth than that."

She gives me a look that says *come on.*

I slump my shoulders. "Okay, *fine*. I threw out my back at the gym because, yes, I was checking out a girl mid-squat and could barely come out of it. Listen, I can't always be at the top of my game."

I haven't been at the top of my game in months. But I see no reason to share that particular detail. Jenna looks amused, at least, and there's only a little bit of a pained twist left to her eyebrows. She still hasn't taken a bite of the chocolate bar. I lean in, lifting her hand to my mouth and take a bite.

She smiles. "Thought this was for me."

I swallow with a dramatic smack to my lips. "You snooze, you lose, baby. This is the good stuff, too. There's little chunks of macadamia in there."

With a little giggle—an honest to God giggle that ignites a fire in my stomach—she takes a bite of the chocolate. "How'd you become such an expert at period cramps?"

I crawl over her legs to lay back against the headboard next to her. It's hard and uncomfortable but I don't have it in me to leave the room to grab a cushion from the sofa.

"My sister used to get them pretty bad when we were younger. I'd watch my mom fuss around her every month and picked up a few tricks, I guess. We kept chocolate pudding always stocked in the pantry, just for her. I'd have drawn you a hot bath, but…"

But I might have jumped in with you.

Jenna untucks a pillow from the stack behind her and taps my shoulder, a small smile playing at her lips like she knows exactly the end of that sentence.

"Lift up."

When I do, she places the pillow between me and the wooden headboard. I sink deeper into the bed, lying down with just my head propped up. After quickly telling my conscience to shut the hell up about boundaries, I thread an arm around her and pull her into me.

Jenna hesitates, giving me the same funny look she did last night after I practically begged her to sleep beside me.

"Give in," I tell her sternly. "Succumb to the cuddle, Jenna Bear. It's one of my specialties."

With a snort she melts into me, so warm and soft, and lays her head on my chest with an arm slung over my waist.

Goddamn, this feels good.

It's a mistake. But she feels good.

She rubs her cheek into my shirt. "You know, you're very lucky to have a mom who'd fuss over any one of her children. Mine just sent in the housekeeper to teach me how to use tampons the day I turned eleven."

"Wow. Happy birthday to you, huh?"

"I know, right? What's she like? Your mom?"

Something lodges itself in my throat. A thick, fat lump of pain, constricting my airway. It takes three attempts to swallow it clear.

Good Time Finn doesn't talk about this stuff. Not just with the girls I go out with, but with anyone. I'm nothing but flirtation, smiles, and cheesy quips, outside the walls of my dad's house. It's easier that way. Makes it easier not to think. Not to get my mood down. Other than the small handful of friends who know about my mom—Theo, Jude, Nina and her wife, and God knows they know better than to bring it up—this is one thing I keep to myself.

CHAPTER 10

But I can tell Jenna feels the heaviness in our silence, and when she moves to drape her throw blanket over me too, I'd bet she understands how the story goes. I don't want to talk about it. But this is her. She'd get it out of me eventually, no needling required. That's just the kind of power she has. Look at what she's already done to me. I'm trying to cuddle the period cramps out of her.

"You don't have to talk about it, Finn."

The words spill out, anyway. "It was a heart attack, ten years ago. Total freak accident. She rode her bike every day, all our lives, and for whatever reason she couldn't take it that day."

Don't say you're sorry. Don't say you're sorry.

Nothing makes my skin crawl more than hearing those words. There's something so performative about them. Generic. And my mom was anything but.

Jenna doesn't say them. She releases the chocolate bar she'd still been holding and extricates the pillow wedged against her stomach, shuffles her body flush against me instead.

And she takes my hand. Threads our fingers together and holy shit, that lump in my throat surges up with a vengeance. My hand twitches in hers, as though my skin can't comprehend this kind of touch, has no idea how to handle it. I don't think I've held hands with a woman like this since my last and final girlfriend, back in high school. Somehow, it feels even heavier than the way we're lying together.

Jenna senses the inner turmoil. She smiles at me, one that doesn't quite reach her eyes, and lets my hand go. Somehow, the loss of her confuses my skin even worse. My fingers start to shake a little and so I tuck them under my thigh.

"How's the pain?" I ask, voice barely more than a rasp.

She exhales. "Well, it no longer feels like my insides are slowly peeling. More like someone's giving me a good pinch every few seconds."

"Nothing like a sob story to take the edge off, huh? I told you I knew how to deal with cramps."

"It's not a sob story," she says carefully, picking at a loose thread on my shirt. "It's incredibly sad. But it's part of what makes you *you*. It means a lot that you'd share it with me."

It's not nearly the half of it, as far as the story goes. But it still feels like I've offered her a piece of me this morning, one of the jagged edges from the inside of my chest.

I wonder where she's keeping it.

I take a deep breath, inhaling until my lungs are stretched and full and can't take in anymore, and blow it all out. This girl's gonna be the end of me. I feel it down in my bone marrow.

"How'd you turn out like this?" I ask suddenly.

She lifts her head, fixing me with an amused look. "Like what? Funny, beautiful, capable of inciting incredible orgasms without even touching a man?"

I chuckle. "All that, yeah. But the rest of you too. The way you talk about your family, you should be an uptight WASP who wouldn't give someone like me the time of day because—*gasp!*—I work in the service industry."

"Well, first, being head chef's nothing to turn up your nose at. Maybe more of a patronizing smile." She demonstrates the move, offering me a smile that barely lifts the corners of her mouth.

An uneasy shudder racks my body. "Shit you're good at that. I just got goose bumps."

She finds the evidence on my arms and laughs into my chest. "Please, call my mom and tell her I'm not a total failure, after all." But she rubs at the goose bumps until they melt away. I force my eyes away from the way her hand sweeps across my skin, warm and like someone who cares. Before a completely different set of goose bumps show up.

"They teach that snob stuff in school where you're from?"

"Don't be silly. You're supposed to *arrive* at school that way."

"So, you arrived that way and what? Your sister stuck you with a scarlet letter and you snapped out of it?"

Jenna appraises me. "Referencing Nathaniel Hawthorne? You really are a hot nerd."

"My sister likes to throw it in my face whenever she asks about my social life. Something about no respectable woman wanting to end up with a guy who's slept with half the female population on earth. Her words, not mine."

"I don't believe that's true for a second."

"It's a moot point. I won't be ending up with anyone if I can help it."

She raises her eyebrows. "That's very finite."

I can sense the follow up questions lining up in her head. But I'm not in a place to discuss it, with her of all people. Mostly because I can't decide which reaction would kill me most: hurting her feelings or realizing there aren't any feelings to hurt.

"It's finite." I nod. "Tell me more about Jenna the snob. What was she like?"

She shakes her head, shuffling up a little so that her cheek rests in the crook of my neck. "I was never like that. I tried to be for a long time if I'm honest. And for a while I thought there was probably something seriously wrong with me, because it didn't come as naturally as for the kids around me. For my sister. Just... I don't even know how to describe it. Carrying this air about you. Following the generational roadmap of your family."

"The one with the bribery fund at the end?"

"The one and only," she starts counting off her fingers. "Excel at a hobby from childhood. And not just any hobby. Something musical or artistic as a girl. Sports if you're a boy. My parents had it in their heads that I'd become a concert pianist," she puts up another finger, "boarding school, straight A's, tasteful extracurriculars that would stand out on a college application, as if you'd have any trouble getting into college in the first place, because," she lifts a third finger, "you're going to the college where your parents met, of course. And they've been donating to the school since they graduated, so you're already a shoe-in. You'll go there, study something sensible like history, meet the love of your life—and he's only the love of your life if he comes from good stock, by the way. Or he's at least got to have a rich daddy too. Graduate with a degree you'll never use, because by the time you know it, you're married, supporting charities alongside your mom, and popping out a few kids of your own."

I think back to Hayley and I growing up, and all the trouble we got into as kids. The lackluster report cards I'd bring home and the repeated calls from my teachers, ratting me out for skipping classes whenever I felt like it.

We'd get in trouble, sure. A good talking to, maybe the silent treatment for a couple hours if I committed a particularly bad offense—the time I got caught between library shelves with Sandra Thompson's hand down my pants comes to mind. But I always got the sense that our parents were, on a deeper level, amused by our antics—library handjobs aside. Like they were a bit proud to see us rebel against molds and live a little wild. I couldn't imagine growing up with the kind of structure Jenna did.

"You must have made it pretty far down the roadmap," I say. "Since you got the trust fund."

"Not exactly. I blew off every piano lesson I could while my parents were busy or out of town, which was pretty much all the time. Became the school whore just one year in. Got an actual job out of school, manning a reception desk which my mom just *adored*. I *did* meet a guy at college I thought I could maybe marry, but then I walked in on him screwing another girl, a couple months after he moved in with me. Dyed my hair pink as a big *fuck you* to all of it, and eventually quit my life to travel." She gives me a wry smile. "How do you think I did?"

I pinch her chin. "You should add you moved in with a guy you barely knew for the summer."

She grimaces. "Hooked up with said guy just over a week in, ignoring his better judgment. You can see why my mother hates me."

"So, why'd they give you the money?"

"It was simple. My ex's family was filthy rich, and my mom couldn't stand the idea that they'd think we weren't just as well off. In the end, she needed me living in a swanky penthouse and driving shiny cars more than she cared to punish me for never living up to her expectations."

I stare at the ceiling, thinking about this ex-boyfriend with the rich daddy. What would she say if I ever brought her home to Dad's? We didn't grow up poor, but we weren't rolling in money either. My modest childhood home felt perfect, back before Mom went. Now, with its dark halls and peeling wallpaper...

She'd forgone every bit of that roadmap except the filthy rich boyfriend. Is that what it takes to be with her?

Not that it matters.

I shake myself mentally. It doesn't matter. I'd never put myself through a relationship. Mom's death made sure of that.

I sigh. "We can wipe that last life decision off the slate if it helps. I won't tell if you won't tell."

She shakes her head. "I think I'll keep that one."

The single sentence soothes a wound I didn't realize existed. "Good. I couldn't stop thinking about last night if I tried."

Her cheeks flush the sweetest shade of pink that tousles up my chest. Messes with my resolve. We haven't even scratched the surface of what it would be like, sleeping together, of what I like or what she's into but damn, there were clues last night. Good ones that'll probably haunt me until the day I find out for sure—not that I will. I won't. We're not going there, ever.

I bet she'd be an incredible kisser though. She's got the kind of full, wide mouth that makes her smile something spectacular.

Maybe she notices my eyes on her mouth or maybe she's thinking the same thing I am, because she lifts her chin, only a couple inches from mine. She lightly nibbles at the corner of her lip, and I lift my head and it's completely unintentional. A full-on compulsion. Because it feels so unfair that she'd be laying right there, biting that lip the way I want to be, parting her lips just gently like that, offering them up to me if I'm willing to take them.

My chest aches. I can't remember ever wanting something this badly.

"Thanks for looking after me," she whispers, eyes going all soft. And if it's just a move, those sweet, dreamy eyes, then the woman deserves a standing ovation. Because she makes it feel like I'm the only man on earth, the first man she's ever given them to. She blinks slowly, and the smell of roses and honey coils around my brain.

This is it, isn't it?

The moment I'll look back on one day with regret.

Because I've seen how this story goes. We'll kiss and it'll be the last nail in my coffin. I'll be all in with her, desperate to win her over and maybe one day I will. Maybe one day we fall in love. She'll become the center of my world until the rest of the universe decides I'm not allowed to be that happy. Until it sends something in to destroy us. A freak accident heart attack that rips us apart and sends me into a tailspin of grief I never recover from. Then I'm nothing more than a guy whose kid force feeds me sandwiches in a dark house. I'll spend my days staring at her rose garden like it'll somehow bring her back to me.

I think my hesitation is on full display. As quickly as she pulled me in with that look in her eyes, Jenna presses her cheek back into my shoulder with a deep breath she holds in her lungs for several seconds. I stare at the ceiling, feeling like the coward I am.

"To be fair," she says quietly, "my dad and I get along. And I'm very aware that I have luck pouring out of every orifice to even *have* these kinds of problems. I know people have it worse. My mom's roadmap leads to a nice enough life. But it never really felt like *mine,* you know?"

It takes me a second to catch up and realize she's circled us back to our conversation like there hadn't been a lapse in it. I rub my face, rougher than necessary.

"People having it worse doesn't mean you're not allowed to feel unhappy. And it doesn't make it okay to stay unhappy," I muster from behind my fingers. "Look, Jenna—"

She yelps at the sudden ringing from my pocket, startling so hard I move with her.

"Shit, that scared me." She presses a hand to her chest as I shift around to pull the phone out of my sweats.

"Fuck. It's Nina," I mutter, staring at the screen. I prop myself up on my elbows as Jenna sits up.

"*Nina?*" She stares. "Your sister doesn't happen to be named Nina, does she?"

I shake my head, lifting the phone to my ear. "Hey, Neens. Am I late?"

"Considering that's your opening line while I'm sitting in the car outside your building, then the answer's yes."

"Give me two minutes. I'll be right down."

CHAPTER 10

In the background I hear a car engine cut out. "You and I both know it takes more than two minutes to make you pretty."

"Shush, you," I say into the phone. I round the bed and tuck Jenna's throw blanket back over her, handing her the abandoned chocolate bar.

"Finn, stop," Jenna says quietly, looking suddenly guarded. She grabs me by the elbow, tugging my hand away. "Who is that?"

The phone slips from my ear. "What do you mean?"

She shrugs. "You said you didn't have friends who are women, and I... Are you dating someone? Is that why you won't sleep with me?"

"*What?*"

She narrows her eyes, losing patience. "Finn, please tell me I don't have to knee you in the balls and then apologize to a woman named Nina for going down on you last night."

She says it at full volume this time, and Nina's trumpet of a laugh sounds from the phone in my limp hand.

"Did he at least return the favor?" Nina shouts. Goddamn it. She'll never let me live this down.

I give Jenna a wry smile. "I assume that clears it up for you? Nina's a friend."

Jenna's eyelids drop in relief. "Well in that case, Nina," she says loudly, "I'd say he wasn't very nice to me at all."

"Men. I don't know why you girls bother," Nina answers, and from up here I can easily picture that head shake she does to send her blonde hair whipping around her head. "You and I are about to have a very serious conversation about reciprocity, Finn."

Jenna bites her lip hard, fighting back a laugh. That little twerp. I tip her head with fingers at her chin. "Way to make me look bad. Should I tell her about how *nicely* you whined my name last night?"

She pouts playfully, and it takes every single strand of self-control not to bite that lip. "That's just mean. I thought we were good. No harm, no foul."

I place a light kiss on her forehead. "We are good, Jenna Bear. That's why I'll keep that one to myself. I can't lie though. I'll be playing that whine over and over in my head, every time I have a hand around my—"

Nina's tinny voice sounds in the room. "You know I can hear every word of this, right?"

"Pipe down," I call into the phone. To Jenna, I add: "I have to go into work for a couple of hours. Are you gonna be okay? You want me to call Jude over, or something?"

She shakes her head when I comb a strand of hair off her face. "I feel better."

"Good girl."

She bites her lip. It's been agony not pressing that button since the second I figured out what those words do to her. I take her hand and bring the last bit of chocolate to my mouth. It's so easy to forget myself when we're like this, all playful, not over-thinking. I lick the melted chocolate off her thumb.

"Finley Palmer, you better not be putting moves on this person while I'm still on the phone."

I grin down at Jenna, and the way her lips part tells me it must have subconsciously come out. *That* smile. The one that gets me into trouble.

"Bye, Nina," I say into the phone, hanging up the call.

Jenna hasn't taken her eyes off me. "I thought this was your day off."

"It is. Just have a few things to take care of but I'll be home for dinner."

"You will? Should I pre-heat some Bagel Bites?"

I smile over my shoulder, reaching her door. "Quit the dirty talk or last night's gonna look like child's play."

"Hot, steaming Bagel Bites with gooey cheese that just melts in your mouth—"

"*La-la-la,*" I call from my room. "I can't hear a word you're saying."

Chapter 11

Jenna

"You can find a ride home can't you, Genevieve? Portia's car is full."

You have to be kidding me.

Through the passenger side window, I eye the inside of my sister's maid of honor's massive SUV. All six other bridesmaids apparently made the cut for a ride home after our dress fitting, even though I'm positive that two of them live in the opposite direction from Portia's apartment. Finn's place is on the way.

It's bad enough I was subjected to a morning of my sister's pointed remarks about the weight I've supposedly gained since being back in town. She's probably right. I've ingested an ungodly amount of pick-me-up cupcakes because of this wedding.

So, I eat my feelings. Sue me.

But I can't even get a ride home for my troubles?

The car peels away before I can pull together words of protest. So fast the tires screech.

"Oh, don't worry about me," I call after the car, digging out my phone to send Jude a text. "It's not like I'm your little sister or anything!"

A couple passing me on the sidewalk add feet of distance between us like they expect me to lunge at them. I give Jude a few seconds to answer my text, but I know it's wishful thinking. It's the middle of a work day and she happens to be gainfully employed.

"What kind of idiot sells her condo and car just for a couple years of travel?" I grumble under my breath, opening a ride-share app on my phone. "Me. I'm the idiot. I'm me."

"Talking to yourself in the nice part of town. And here I thought I was the weird one."

I wheel around. Finn saunters down the sidewalk, smile brighter than the summer sun above us. It's incredible how quickly that beam lifts my mood. How quickly the sting of a morning with Ronnie fades. I barely have a second to mumble a shocked *hey* before he reaches for my shopping bags and leans in to give me a kiss on the forehead.

Forehead kisses.

Freaking *forehead kisses*.

The sweet new habit he's developed since that night in his bed. The one that immediately incites a confusing spasm in my chest, and causes a pale flush to flood Finn's cheeks, every single time his lips hit my forehead. It's like he's just been caught giving in to an urge, or something. Still, it's become his signature greeting.

Forehead kisses. What the hell do I make of them?

Don't flatter yourself. He's only being nice so he doesn't hurt your feelings after the almost-sex. It's nothing to do with you.

Finn clears his throat, visibly flustered. He tucks the hand not carrying my bags into his pocket. "How was the fitting?"

"Oh, you know. I counted twelve veiled insults, seven *direct* insults, and a pair of painful bridesmaid shoes guaranteed to put me in crutches for a solid week after the wedding. Honestly, in the grand scheme of Ronnie and me, it's not so bad." Finn grimaces sympathetically. "So, is this you answering the SOS I sent Jude? You're pretty quick, I only just texted her."

"No, I… I got here a little while ago. Just wanted to make sure you're alright—I know how Ronnie can get. Hope that's okay."

I stare. "You… came here in case my sister upset me?"

His flush deepens. "Yeah. I know how much you've been dreading this fitting and I just thought… I don't know. Should I not have come?"

CHAPTER 11

Oh, Finn.

He looks so sheepish now, all pink in the cheeks and guilty eyes. My chest warms. I'm suddenly gripped with an overwhelming urge to tuck him under my fuzzy blanket and give him the kind of head scratch he covets.

"Finn, that's really... amazing of you. Thanks for doing that."

"Yeah, of course." His relief is palpable as he throws an arm over my shoulders and leads me to his car. "I also brought cupcakes. But you're only allowed to eat them if you're facing away from me or there's a good chance I'll crash this car. And I really wanna take you somewhere."

"The ride home is enough. You really don't—"

"Tell me one more time how I *don't have to do this.* I dare you."

"But you *don't*—"

Finn sighs like he's the most put-upon man in the world. In one swift movement he lifts and drops me into the passenger seat, straps on my seatbelt and deposits the yellow cupcake box into my lap, lid open.

"*Take it*, Jenna," he says sharply when I open my mouth to protest again. He pokes my shoulder. "And before you say it, this has shit all to do with the almost-sex thing from last week. Let me be nice to you. Let me do nice things for you without protesting or looking at me like I'm trying to get something out of it. *Take the nice.* You deserve it."

"But—"

"*Take it.*"

"But it's—"

Another poke. "*Take the goddamn nice,* Jenna Carling."

He points a threatening finger an inch from the tip of my nose so that my eyes cross when I stare at it. The corner of his mouth twitches.

"Alright. *Alright*, take it easy. I'll take the goddamn nice." I shove away his hand and he breaks into a satisfied smile. "Now where the hell are we going?"

Finn reaches into the back of the car and drops a baseball hat on my head, brim backwards.

"It's a surprise. But I did bring you a change of clothes." He eyes my miniskirt a second longer than decent. "Hope you don't mind getting a little sweaty."

~

"I have to warn you, these aren't the kind of balls I'm used to working with."

Finn chuckles without looking around. "That's alright. We're all about broadening our horizons these days."

It's intensely hot and sunny today, like the world decided to make up for the rainfall of the past week. Finn leans against the hood of the Wrangler, staring off at the deserted baseball diamond ahead. He's wearing a black, badly faded t-shirt with a high school logo on the sleeve and his last name across the back. A relic from his time as the school's star pitcher, no doubt.

He hasn't yet explained why he felt *sports* were the way to cheer me up after a morning of Ronnie. Yet here I am in the back of his car, changing into the half-a-t-shirt and pink spandex shorts he brought me. Finn's eyes are averted, giving me privacy like he hasn't already seen everything there is to see.

He's seriously adorable.

"Okay, I'm decent," I announce, hopping out of the car. "So, are you going to tell me why you brought me here to humiliate myself?"

As I crouch to slip on my shoes, he adjusts the hat on my head so that the brim faces forward. "Is Jenna Carling suddenly scared of a couple balls coming at her?"

I smack his chest. "*No.* I'm only pointing out that if you're looking for decent competition, you've come to the wrong girl."

"This isn't a competition; you and I are on the same team. Actually, I used to come to this park with my dad in high school, whenever I needed to get an extra practice in. Or if I got hit with a bad mood. Running bases is the best when you're having a shitty day."

"Is a bad mood possible for you? I don't think I've ever seen you a level past lackadaisical."

"It's definitely rare." With a gym bag and bat resting on his shoulder, Finn leads me to the baseball diamond.

"So, what does it take to put Finley Palmer in a bad mood? Other than the systematic destruction of the earth's bodies of water."

"That should put *everyone* in a bad mood."

"I'm not arguing with that. I've listened to you narrate enough articles to wake up in cold sweats over it all. But is that it?"

"Well... there's my mom passing away. That did a good number on me."

I eye his profile as we round the chain-link barrier between the diamond and a small set of metal bleachers. "You still have a hard time with it, huh?"

He glances at me from the corner of his eye. "I haven't played since she died." He points the bat at one of the bleachers. "That's where she'd sit with Hayley whenever I'd come practice with Dad. Mostly she just read a book while we were at it. But it was nice that she was there, you know?"

He still sounds like him. Upbeat. Positive. But there's a little tick in his jaw.

"Is it hard for you? Being here?"

He nods.

I reach for his shirt to hold him still. "Finn. We don't have to stay, if that's the case."

He shakes his head, offering me a small smile. "Nah, this is worth it. You're gonna love it."

We reach the home plate and Finn crouches to sort through his gym bag. My phone chimes from where I stuck it in the waistband of my shorts.

JUDE: *Why hello, stranger. Just came out of a meeting. Want to grab lunch? I'll come get you.*

ME: *Actually, Finn came to get me.*

JUDE: *One day he's going to get a talking to for hogging you. Not that I blame him.*

ME: *I know, I'm sorry. I've been a terrible friend.*

JUDE: *Don't be sorry. I remember the early days of a budding romance... One second you're pretending it's about sex, the next you can't stay away from each other. Classic stuff.*

JUDE: *Just admit I was right about you two being perfect for each other and I'll totally forgive your ghosting.*

ME: *Can't. There's been no romance, Juju.*

JUDE: *Admit it.*

ME: *We're friends.*

JUDE: *ADMIT IT.*

ME: *Okay, you've officially lost it. Let's grab dinner tonight. I need to check up on you.*

JUDE: *May I casually point out that you're suggesting dinner with me on a night where Finn is working?*

ME: *No. You may not.*

I toss my phone into Finn's bag, tugging up my socks as he stuffs the pockets of his shorts with baseballs. It's not like I haven't noticed that we spend all our free time together. But new friends can be inseparable, can't they? Besides, we're roommates. It's a matter of convenience.

Finn stands, sweeping the bat off the ground and knocking it on the toe of his shoe to dislodge the dirt now coating it. "Alright, how much do you know about baseball?"

"There are balls and bats. And men in tight pants, which you seem to have robbed me of. I take that personally, by the way," I say, nodding down at his shorts, which, despite the snark, fit the man like a fucking glove. "I thought you were trying to cheer me up."

"Little flirt." He flicks my ponytail and lets his hand rest on the nape of my neck, fingertips burning into my skin. Making my body hum. He's been so hard to resist since the night in his bed. *So* hard. Made even worse by the way I'll catch him looking at me sometimes. Drawing me in with a playful smirk, like now. Squinty, smoldering eyes like he's trying to glimpse inside me, and I think we might be the only two people left in this park. This city, for all I know.

And then it seems to dawn on him what he's doing. Finn clears his throat and drops his arm. "You seem plenty cheered up already."

I force a pout. "There's always a little room for improvement. How about some shirts versus skins action, huh? I volunteer for the shirts team."

He flicks the brim of my hat. "Same team, remember?"

"*Right.* You're so right." I strip my t-shirt, leaving behind a sports bra that he takes in with a strangled cough. "There. Over to you, kid. How far are you willing to go to put a smile on my face?"

"A fucking demon in pink," he mutters under his breath, yanking off his hat.

"Sorry? I didn't quite catch that."

Trying and failing to give me a stern look, Finn tugs his shirt over his head. "I'd go pretty fucking far for that smile, it seems."

My toes immediately curl inside my sneakers. This was... a truly terrible mistake. Any chance I had of hitting a single baseball today evaporated the second that shirt came off. This man is just... I blink and we're back in his bedroom, and he's hovering over me as he pumps into his fist—

Finn crosses his arms, biceps flexing deliciously. "Quit checking me out and let's see it."

"Hm?" The sound comes out several octaves higher than normal. I cough, trying to pull myself together. "See what?"

"You know what."

"Oh. This thing?" I bat my lashes, giving him a small close-mouthed smile.

"Nope, not gonna cut it. Bigger." I stretch my mouth another fraction and he shakes his head, poking me near my chin. "*Bigger.*"

I give him a wide smile this time, and there's nothing forced about it. Not when that crooked Finn smile takes over his face as his gaze dips to my chin. "Yeah. That's the stuff."

A very pleasant fluttering manifests deep in my stomach. Is he... Is it my dimple? That's what's making him smile so hard?

"Alright, enough funny business. Let's do this," Finn says with a breath. He takes me by the shoulders and positions me so that I face the side of the diamond, nudging my feet in a wider stance. With a soft cough, his palms land on my hips. "Bend over a little bit. Yeah, like that. And then move your weight forward, on the balls of your feet—exactly. Now, you're going to stand here and hit the ball I throw, and you're gonna picture Ronnie's face on it. I promise it'll feel incredible."

"Of all the nice things you've ever done for me, acting like I have a shot in hell of hitting a ball might be the nicest."

He pinches my chin. "Don't sweat it. You'll be great." I grip the bat as Finn jogs out to the middle of the diamond.

"If I hit this, do I get to drive the Wrangler home?"

"Not a chance in hell, babe," he calls back.

Finn moves so deftly even someone like me—a certified anti-athlete—can tell there's serious skill behind it. The ball comes at me in a soft, underhanded throw that's more of a toss than anything else. I swing, missing it by a wide margin.

Finn tosses another one. It's not even close. I miss his next pitch, and every single one until his pockets are depleted of balls.

"That's it. I'm officially blaming the pitching," I call, sinking to the ground cross-legged. I fan myself against the heat from the sun. "There's no way I'm actually this bad."

Finn joins me at the home plate. "You *aren't* bad. You just need a little practice, that's all."

"What I need is to give my bruised ego a breather. Sit." I tug his wrist until he drops next to me.

He adjusts my hat even though it didn't feel particularly crooked. "This idea was a bust, huh?"

"No, I like that you brought me here. Even if this was all just a transparent excuse to make sure we'd be together at one o'clock. You're really not that subtle, Finn."

His jaw drops in mock-outrage. "Excuse me. I don't appreciate you accusing me of—"

I pull my phone from his gym bag, waving the screen in his face. "Would you look at that: one o'clock on the dot. Almost like you planned it."

"You know what? I resent that. I came because your sister is a nutbar, but if this is the attitude you're giving me—"

Finn makes like he's about to get up, but I grip his arm with a huff. "Do you want to do this or not?"

"Do I want to participate in *cuddle o'clock*? Is that even a question?" He throws an arm around my shoulders and crushes me to him, lurching us back so that we land softly onto the ground. The brims of our hats shield our

CHAPTER 11

eyes from the sun.

"We're not calling this *cuddle o'clock*, by the way. That's almost as bad as *six-hundred seconds of snuggles*, which was objectively terrible."

Finn settles in, tucking me under his arm. "I don't hear you trying to come up with anything better."

I've never been a fan of spooning or cuddling, not even with my ex. But since the morning he looked after me and my cramps, Finn has slyly chipped away at the aversion.

He got me good.

It started out with just a couple of head scratches. Nothing crazy. Just a little something to help him get to sleep, after watching some particularly depressing documentaries a couple nights in a row. Next thing I know, the tyrant invokes a daily *cuddle o'clock*, which basically means that we drop everything for a ten-minute snuggle on the sofa the second the clock strikes one.

I'd hoped it was a blatant excuse to cop a feel. No such luck. The man seems to have roped me into some kind of friends-with-cuddle-benefits situation.

I try to burrow my face into his chest but it's so solid that I shimmy into the crook of his neck instead, adjusting my hat out of the way.

"You've come a long way, Jenna Bear. I'm proud of you," he says, tightening his hold on me without opening his eyes.

"I don't know what you're talking about." I throw a leg over his hip, and he immediately grips it with a satisfied hum.

"Say I converted you to cuddles."

"Never." Finn starts to shuffle away, but I push him back into place. "Fine. *Fine*. You converted me, okay? I like to cuddle. Now, sit still."

"You know that was the wrong answer."

"I like cuddling with *you*, Finn. Happy now?"

"Extremely," he says, settling back into the ground with his eyes closed and an immensely content smile.

I take a deep breath, inhaling the scent of soap off his skin, the way it mixes with the smell of my shampoo. This is nice. "You know, I've never met a man so addicted to physical touch. I have no idea how you ever survived living alone."

"It was a dark, terrible period in my life I'd like to forget. But the touchy thing would be my mom's doing. She could barely go a conversation without taking my hand or ruffling my hair. She was the same with Hayley."

I lift my chin to watch him stare at the sky. "You were close with her, huh?"

Finn nods. "I miss her a lot."

I can't begin to explain the sense of privilege I feel whenever he speaks about his mom now. It doesn't happen often, and most of the time he'll immediately change the subject. Sometimes, though, when he's in just the right mood, she'll slip in and out of conversation almost easily.

I love the way he speaks about her like she was one of his closest friends. Part of me feels incredibly jealous that he'd had a mom so different from mine. But I'm also relieved to know he'd been cared for like that. He's so different than I thought he'd be—sweet and soft in a way that makes me want to fret over him. Tuck him into bed and rock him to sleep.

I reach for his hat and slip it off, running my fingers through his hair. He gives a small shudder. "Are you close with your dad, too?"

Finn gives a half-shrug, half-nod.

"That's where you go Monday nights, isn't it? To see him?"

"Yeah. He needs a little looking after these days. For the last little while, actually." He pauses. "I'm sorry—I don't mean to go all secretive over him. I don't like to talk about it with anyone."

I prop myself on his chest to get a good look at him. "Don't apologize. But just so you know, I'm here if you ever want to... You know. Smash some dinner plates. Scream into the ether. Succumb to a bad mood, from time-to-time."

"'kay." He brushes my arm with the back of his fingers. "How long do we have left?"

I reach for my phone. "I'll tell you what: I'll throw in a bonus minute for your chivalry today and make it an even three."

Finn gently pushes me onto my back and settles on top of me with his head resting on my ribcage. I scratch at his head, ignoring the familiar,

CHAPTER 11

inconvenient pang of want I feel in the pit of my stomach every time he arranges us like this. It's his favorite cuddle position.

Secretly, it's my favorite too.

He gives a happy sigh. "You're the best friend a guy could ask for, you know that?"

"I know."

"Jenna."

"Mhm?"

"You're supposed to say it back."

I chuckle. "You're the best friend a girl could ask for, Finn." He lifts his head just enough to peek at me over the rise of my breasts. "What?"

But he only shakes his head. Moves to press a kiss to my forehead, and melts back into me so comfortably that warmth floods my chest. I stare at the sky, still in utter disbelief that he actually showed up for me. I've never been looked after like this. Like I'm worth the trouble. The closest was our nanny growing up, and she got paid to do it.

It feels incredible. In a way, it makes me resent my upbringing even more, knowing I could have felt this all along. But I'm so grateful to have it now, from someone as good as Finn.

Three minutes and forty-two seconds later, Finn sits us up, adjusting both our hats so that the brims face backwards. There's no good reason for the flurry of butterflies now aggressively raging in my stomach. All he did was flip my hat the same way he wears his. But they're there, and get even worse as I watch him idly pick at the sole of his sneaker.

Don't do it, I tell myself. *Do not fucking do it, Jenna Grace Carling.*

He's not looking for a clingy roommate. And I'm not looking to make a fool of myself, pining for a commitment-phobe. It would truly be cruel and unusual comeuppance for all the sleeping around.

Do not fall for this guy.

Finn gets to his feet, holding out a hand to help me up. I study the ground, suddenly needing to look anywhere but at him. "Alright, Jenna. Let's do this. We're not leaving here until you hit a ball."

He sweeps my arm, my shoulder, nonchalantly brushing off the dirt sticking to me.

Do not. Do it.

I unnecessarily clear my throat. "Don't you have to go into work in a couple hours?"

"Yes, which is why you're gonna hit this next one. Now, look at it," Finn says, holding up a ball. "What do you see?"

"Ronnie's face?"

"Exactly. Send that face across the fucking park. You've got this."

It's not exactly across the fucking park. But somehow, someway, that ball knocks into the bat I'm holding, and it skitters across the diamond like a stone skipping water. Finn pivots on the spot to watch it travel past his feet.

"Did that just—" I stare at him with my jaw dropped. "Did I just—"

With a loud *fuck, yeah!* Finn races toward me, bending at the last second to throw me over his shoulder with a loud whooping sound.

"Aren't I supposed to run the bases?" I laugh as he hitches me up his shoulder, locking his arm around my thighs to secure me.

"We *are* running the bases. You fucking *smashed* that thing."

I really didn't.

But Finn takes off around the diamond like I did, running the bases with me hiked up on his shoulder, hollering like I've just placed on a podium.

Chapter 12

Finn

"Compliments to the chef from table eleven!"

Bianca Astley gives me a tight smile through the open pass from the dining room as she grabs the two plates I've just put out for her.

"Tell 'em thank you," I call as she walks off. "I'll never turn down compliments—*ow*!"

Nina whips me in the thigh with the towel she keeps slung over her shoulder, and the snap echoes so loud a couple of customers sitting closest to the kitchen look over in alarm.

"Compliments for what exactly? You haven't lifted a finger today," she accuses, placing two plates in front of me with towering fish burgers and heaping piles of fries, and doubling back for a third. "All you've done is mope around—"

"Oh, that's just mean," I say. I pluck a soggy arugula leaf from one of the burgers and brandish it between us. "If I weren't standing here cleaning up your messes, we'd be sending out limp lettuce all over the place. Nobody compliments *limp lettuce*, Neens. Nobody."

I slide the plates underneath the heat lamps as they wait to get picked up and turn to face the kitchen. Almost a year in and the place runs like a well-oiled machine. The two massive workstations dotting the middle of the room are alive with line cooks darting between stove tops, with towers of smoke rising from the burning pans and the most incredible smells wafting around us. It's true that I've been reduced to barely more than a figurehead at this point, unless I'm creating a new dish for the menu. But there are very few things that bring me to life like the bustling of a commercial kitchen.

One of the other things happens to be out at a bachelorette party tonight, probably wearing the world's most incredible dress, over the world's most incredible body.

I turn to Nina. "I resent that, by the way. I, Finn Palmer, do not mope. They don't call me Good Time Finn for nothing. It's part of my charm." I give her a wide, winning grin.

Nina returns a deadpan stare. "The Finn Palmer I know would tell me everything. And *this* person," she flaps a hand in my face, "has decided to go secretive right when it counts. Give me something good!"

"There's nothing good to give!"

"You seem to forget I was privy to a very disturbing conversation over the phone a couple weeks ago—"

"Oh, *that*?" I wave away her words. "She's my roommate. We have fun. Nothing to it."

She blinks, I blink. I'm lying. She knows it, I know it.

Nina adjusts her hairnet. "Finn, you're the biggest over-sharer I know. You're saying you're fine with me knowing all about the time you pulled off a three-way with those redhead servers from Brookwood, but you won't tell me about the girl holed up in your apartment right now?"

"That was an accidental three-way!" I say hotly. "The second one caught us in the parking lot and joined in uninvited. Besides, I *didn't* tell you about that. One of them must have said something."

It was part of the scorecard, wasn't it?

The thought pops into my head uninvited, and immediately I feel the sting of humiliation. I want to ask her about it. But saying the word *scorecard* out loud, here... I have no interest in bringing past promiscuity to the surface, even with Nina. No one here would get it. Not like Jenna does.

Nina squints at me. "Why are you getting defensive over a two-year-old

CHAPTER 12

hookup? Who is this girl?"

I choose to ignore her. The digital clock above the pass tells me it's coming up on nine o'clock. Another hour and we can start cleaning up for the night. The hours in the kitchen are brutal, but it's the bar staff I really feel bad for. We get to shut down a precious two hours before they do. Tonight though, with Jenna out with her sister, the thrill of finishing up just isn't there.

"*Oh*," Nina says suddenly. And even without looking at her I know she's finally connecting the dots. "It's the girl from last summer. Isn't it?"

I hike up my glasses. "Her name is—"

"Jenna. I remember now. I'm shocked I forgot about her, given you wouldn't shut up about meeting her. She's back from Europe, then? And staying with you? How'd that happen?"

"I'm sensing you have a lot of questions about this," I say, wiping off the edge of a fresh plate of food.

Nina gives a low, gurgling laugh. "Oh, this is amazing. I never thought I'd see the day. Finn Palmer, owner of romantic feelings. I have to say I am seriously tickled pink about this."

"Very funny." I roll my eyes. "It's just a little crush. Totally innocent. But let's all laugh at my problems like I don't cut your checks."

"You *don't* cut my checks. So, what is this then? A friends with benefits thing?"

The contents of my stomach turn sour. I've never decked anyone before, but if ever a guy suggested a friends with benefits thing with Jenna, I'd be inclined to give it a try. She's worth better. She *is* the benefit.

"I told you we're not sleeping together. I don't... I don't know what's wrong with me, Neens. I just need to get a grip. It's nothing. A crush. It'll pass. We're just friends."

"Is it the kind of nothing that's had you turning me down for after-work drinks for a month now?"

It's true that I've spent a lot of time with Jenna lately. Scratching at a fresh splatter of sauce on the front of my shirt, I try to remember the last time we hung out separately. Surely, we have.

Ah! I don't bring her with me to Dad's.

There.

"If this is just your way of telling me you miss me, Neens—"

"Tell me about her," Nina interrupts. "If it's nothing, then talk about her. Tell me what she's like."

It's a trap.

The way her eyebrows have innocently gone up confirms it. But out of the corner of my eye I see that the line cooks at the workstation closest to us have gone suspiciously quiet. Leaning forward, just casually. Moving slowly.

Great. Witnesses to the mess I've dug for myself. I need to salvage this, before they get the idea I've become some sappy, love-drunk idiot.

"She's..." I rip off my hat, shoving my fingers through the hair that immediately springs onto my face. "She's... kind of this..."

Giving up on words, I gesture around us. Nina raises her eyebrows, waiting for me to make sense, but I barely know what I'm trying to articulate. Goddamn it. What has this girl done to me? Rambling is one of my specialties. Theo tells me so all the time, and I take great pride in how bad it annoys him.

I try again. "She's... kind of this *force*, you know? I met her once and never got her out of my head."

Fuck. Those were definitely the wrong words. Nina looks at me smugly. One of the line cooks pouts down at her cutting board.

"Is she the kind of force that had you subconsciously self-sabotaging every time you tried to flirt with someone who wasn't her this past year?"

My mouth pops open. "Can't be. That's insane."

Besides, if talking about Eddie is self-sabotage, they weren't someone I should have been flirting with in the first place. I don't know when it is I decided that, but it's the fucking truth.

I'm the guy with a pet turtle. Take it or leave it.

Plus, Jenna loves Eddie. I watched her give him a nice neck scratch last night. It was the sweetest thing I've ever—damn it.

"It'll pass," I say again. I grab a rag and start vigorously scrubbing at a crusty patch of aioli on the counter. "What are you doing after work? Wanna get a drink or something?"

"Yeah, that sounds good. Maddie's away for work."

"Perfect. Drinks it is."

There. We spend plenty of time apart.

Anyway, she's out with her sister tonight. Against my own wishes, my gaze drags up to the clock. I'd have heard from her by now if things weren't going well. She was so nervous waiting for her cab that I had her cancel it to drop her off myself. She didn't let me walk her up to where the party was, though. Something about there being no need to be over-protective?

I don't know. I wasn't being protective.

I just wanted to scope it out a little, that's all. See what these girls were like. Whether I could trust them to behave—

My phone goes off in my back pocket, and I leap for it, grateful for the distraction.

HAYLEY: *What are you bringing to Mom's anniversary dinner? I'll cover dessert. Dad says he'll make a lasagna.*

My stomach sinks. The answer to her question, so far, is nothing. For several reasons, many of which I'm about to live through in a couple of weeks, the anniversary of my mom's death is the one day of the year I work hard at blocking from my mind.

ME: *That's what he said last year. I had to make a last-minute stop for pizza.*

"You okay?" Nina says quietly, frowning at whatever's on my face. She angles herself to give her back to the kitchen.

I pocket my phone, clearing my throat. *Not the time. Not the place, Palmer.* I force a smile. "'Course I am. So, where'd you wanna go tonight?"

The chiming from my pocket cuts off whatever Nina opens her mouth to say. I pull my phone back out, expecting another text from Hayley.

It's from Jenna.

And I take off running.

Chapter 13

Jenna

I'm an idiot.

Tonight was bound to be a disaster. I've been dreading my sister's bachelorette party for weeks. Did everything I could to try to smooth my ride—took her calls, let her tell me all the ways she was worried I'd humiliate her. I let her buy me an outfit which included a knee-length, black flowy cocktail dress. Flat shoes. It didn't matter that it was so far from what I like to wear. This was her night. So, I put it all on. I smiled, made small talk whenever the girls bothered to give me the time of day. I clinked champagne glasses; I captured all the group photos.

And somehow, I still ended up here.

Sitting on the curb in front of this skyscraper hotel, home of the rooftop lounge where they left me. I'd only been in the washroom for a few minutes. But they cleared out fast enough to be halfway across town already, back at Ronnie's place which she decked out as an at-home spa for the second part of our night.

It was an innocent mistake, she'd texted, when I asked where they all went. They didn't even realize I wasn't with them.

At a point, it becomes time to reflect on the fact that you *might be the problem, if you can't seem to form connections with others.*

I wipe my nose with the back of my hand, ignoring the hushed words of

CHAPTER 13

passersby wondering what it is I'm doing crying alone on the pavement in the nice part of town. If there's one thing this dress is good for, it's providing coverage for my crotch as I hug my knees to my chest, resting my chin on top of them.

How will I survive this wedding? I couldn't even make it through this.

Suddenly, my surroundings come alive with the screeching of tires. My heart leaps into my throat. Across the street, four lanes away from the curb where I'm sitting, Finn's forest green Wrangler stops, rousing a proper brass band of car horns behind him. I only have a second to wonder whether he means for me to cross the street over to him before the opposite lanes clear up and he hits the gas, swinging the car around, tires burning up on the asphalt to come to a halt on this side of the road.

He wrenches open his door and slams it shut behind him like he wants to see the window shatter. When he rounds the car, beelining for me, I barely recognize him.

Overall, he doesn't look much different. There's the open chef's jacket over a dark shirt, the backwards hat, the sandy hair tickling the skin behind his ears where it's been pushed back. But his face is a whole new Finn. Harder than I've ever seen it. Unforgiving. Even from where I sit, I can see the heavy pulsing at his jaw, grinding so hard it looks on the verge of popping off his face entirely. His entire body looks rigid, hands in tight fists at his sides.

Immediately, I feel guilty and a little stupid. I've turned him into a raging bull, and for what? Just because my sister left me behind at her own bachelorette party? It's her night, anyway. She's perfectly entitled to spend it with whoever she wants. I'm making it about myself.

"Get up," Finn tells me when he's within a couple of feet. His voice is firm, hard, and my stomach sinks. I've annoyed him. Of course, I have. I made him leave work early because I was being silly—

He reaches me and crouches, taking hold of my elbows, and his grip is a lot softer than I'd have expected from him in this state. The fury in his face stutters as he takes me in properly. The mascara that must be streaking my cheeks, the snot I probably haven't managed to wipe off completely. I'm sure I look an awful, unappealing mess.

"Baby, get up. Come here." The words come out gently this time. He helps me to my feet and immediately grips my face, wiping at my cheeks with his thumbs.

"I'm okay," I say, sniffing quietly. I mean to pull myself together. But the way his eyes sweep my face, fingers move like he's hell-bent on ridding me of every tear, makes a fresh wave of them appear. "Finn, I'm okay."

"What part of this is okay?" he says, shaking his head in disbelief. "You're the last person who belongs alone on the fucking curb."

"I know I should have called a cab, but—"

"Jenna, don't ever not call me. Ever. Do you hear me? Day or night, no matter—no matter where we are twenty years from now. No matter what you need. Call."

From somewhere behind me, I hear a passing laugh. "—I'm watching this girl sob in the middle of the street. Probably a sad drunk—"

Smile, Genevieve. You're making a spectacle of yourself. Is this how you were raised?

"What the hell is wrong with you?" Finn snaps, head whipping around to find the passerby over my shoulder. "Keep walking." He glares until he's satisfied the offender has given us a wide enough berth.

"I'm sorry," I tell him. I'm not really sure why. "I haven't had much to drink, I swear."

"Believe me, your sister will be the one who's sorry," he mutters darkly, catching a tear I feel dangling precariously along my chin. "Take me to her."

He's serious. And I know it's insane, that there's no way Finn, sweet Finn, could stomp on an ant, let alone a gaggle of mean girls. But knowing he's in my corner, validating my hurt and humiliation, it means everything.

"I don't want to see them right now," I whisper.

His jaw pulses. He's livid. And somehow, he's not. Finn still hasn't let go of my face. The way he drags his thumb along my forehead to smooth out my brows, how the back of his finger strokes my jaw, my mouth. The way he brushes the wisps of hair off my forehead to make room for the kiss he puts there instead. My heart aches. *Aches.* A second ago I was huddled on the pavement. Now, I'm being looked at like I matter. A thick sob escapes me.

CHAPTER 13

"Hey—*hey*. Jenna, I've got you. You aren't alone. Okay? I have you." I nod and Finn touches his forehead to mine. "Tell me what happened."

For a moment I hesitate, embarrassed all over again, feeling so stupid for letting it get to me this badly. But this is him. Finn. It doesn't matter if I'm caught up in breathless laughter or drowning in tears. He always feels safe.

"They left without me after dinner. Ronnie swore it was an accident, but how do you not realize that the girl with the wacky hair is missing from the limo?"

Finn lets a breath hiss through clenched teeth. He reaches behind me to gently finger the tight bun I've made of my hair. Gets a grip on the elastic band, twists my hair free, letting it cascade around my shoulders. He combs through the lengths with his fingers.

"Your hair isn't wacky, Jenna. I *love* your hair."

"I'm so stupid, Finn. I begged them to come back for me. Ronnie had me on speakerphone and I could hear someone laughing in the background. I think they left so they wouldn't have to spend the rest of the night with me."

Finn's face breaks free of its anger, leaving behind something so much worse. He looks like he's in excruciating pain. "You didn't deserve any of that. This petty high school bullshit." He releases a frustrated breath. "And what I can't stand—the most *infuriating* part of this—is the thought of you internalizing their shitty behavior. Thinking it's somehow a reflection of you, and you couldn't be more wrong about that. Because shit, Jenna, you... I can't get enough of you. I've been moping all night, so bad everyone could see it. All I could think about was showing up at home tonight, and not having you there."

He doesn't wait for me to react. Finn tugs me into him in a near-death grip, like he's trying to squeeze the pain out of me. I release another sob into his shoulder, basking in the accelerated *thump thump thump* of his heart against my chest, sinking my fingers into his back.

I shouldn't be gripping onto him so tight. I shouldn't be reading into his words, hoping to find something deeper than those of a friend. A man who plans to end up alone. But it's hard not to, when he's squeezing me so hard my heels lift off the ground.

Don't do it, Jenna.

I pry myself away with extra effort against the resistance from his arms, like he isn't done having me against him. Brows crinkled, he watches me run my ring fingers under my eyes, wiping away any smudged makeup. Slapping on as much of a smile as I can muster.

He doesn't return it. Finn lets his gaze drop down the length of me, like he's taking me in for the first time. By the time he reaches my feet, his teeth are grinding again.

"You're wearing flat shoes."

"What?"

"You don't wear flat shoes. You never wear flat shoes."

I look down at my feet, as though I wasn't perfectly aware of the silk-covered flats with large square brooches on the tops. Finn lets out a great sigh.

"Come on." He takes my hand, laces our fingers. "I know where we need to be."

~

"We'll take them all."

Finn stands in front of the display counter of Hanna's Bake Shoppe, staring down at the rainbow of cupcakes through the glass, hands planted on his hips as though to signal that he truly means business.

The shop assistant stands frozen in front of him, looking like she can't decide whether she's the subject of some bizarre prank. Tucked a little behind him, I can't help but giggle at the scene. He peeks over his shoulder at the sound, flashing me a grin.

"You... want to buy all the cupcakes? All of them?" the shop assistant asks.

"All of them," Finn confirms, waving along the counter. "Every single one. And we'll eat them there." He jabs a thumb over his shoulder, indicating a booth along the back wall of the pastel-colored shop.

"But..." The young girl stares down at the display. "There has to be, like, fifty cupcakes here."

"Seems like a nice number. And why don't we throw in a chocolate éclair while we're at it. Do you like éclairs, Jenna Bear?"

CHAPTER 13

"I love éclairs."

"Two chocolate éclairs, please."

The shop assistant's gaze slides over to meet mine, as though to verify that she isn't dealing with a madman. I'm not entirely sure I can accurately answer that question, as it stands. Finn's mood seems to have veered into an unprecedented level of enthusiasm on the car ride over. To be fair, mine has managed to pull in that direction, too. We took a long detour along the freeway with the top down on the way here, and my reflection in the glass display shows me just how insane my hair is right now.

Apparently, the shop assistant decides it's probably safest to just give the nutter his fifty cupcakes and two éclairs. Finn nods at the purple nylon-covered booth behind us and follows me in, balancing five cupcake boxes and a paper plate of éclairs the size of my head. He lays it all out on the table between us, our overzealous sugar feast, opening all the boxes as though he really expects us to gorge on all this in one sitting.

He hands me an éclair and bumps it with the one he's holding. "Cheers."

And he smothers the thing into his mouth with so much force, the custard squirts out of the other end so heartily I dodge the stream with a squeak.

"Fuck, that's good stuff," he says, mouth so full I'm not exactly sure how he manages the words, or how I manage to make out the garbled syllables. "Dig in, Jenna Bear, or I'm coming for yours next."

You know what's hard? Eating while you're smiling.

So hard that a little dribble of custard leaks out of the corner of my mouth as I chew the pastry. Finn keeps his eyes on me, returning my smile until I manage to swallow. Satisfied, he pulls a cupcake out of one of the boxes laid out between us and smashes the remaining half of his éclair down onto the icing.

"Now this?" he says, lifting his concoction, icing oozing onto his fingers. "This might be my best creation yet. To hell with my award-winning dishes. Frankencake beats them all."

A couple walks past our table, and the woman's head turns at the declaration. She eyes his Frankencake dubiously.

"Give me that," I say, grabbing for it. I have to open my mouth as wide as it will go to get it in, and when I do, the combination of vanilla frosting and chocolate and custard dribbles over my chin.

"Well?"

"Yeah." I nod, swallowing the soft mess of vanilla and pastry. "Honestly, it's so gross it's kind of amazing."

"God, I'm good. Make a note to tell Theo he owes me a raise. He doesn't know how lucky he is to have me." He reaches over the table to dislodge frosting off my chin with his thumb, licking off what he collects. My gaze snags on the tiny fleck of icing he leaves behind on his bottom lip.

"You have…" I reach for it without thinking, lifting the frosting off his soft, pillowy lower lip. I lick it off my own thumb.

I'll make you crave me so bad you'll be screaming my name in your dreams.

It's a lot more pleasant than that usual voice in my head. That hot discomfort between my thighs resurfaces every time that line hits, since the moment Finn whispered it in my ear weeks ago.

I've never ached for someone this badly. And what's funny is… the more of Finn I get to know, the worse it gets.

At this point, I make myself come to the thought of him every single night. And still, I've woken up mid-orgasm enough times to wonder if it's possible he hasn't heard me in my sleep by now. I can't remember the last wet dream I had before moving in with him.

"Don't." Finn looks like he's descended deep into the same ocean of lust where I find myself, all hard eyes and stiff shoulders as he stares across the table. "Jenna, please. Don't do that."

I realize I'm licking my lips again. I make myself stop. "I swear that was an accident," I tell him, grabbing a napkin. "I've been trying really hard to be good."

"I know, I… Me, too." Finn rips his gaze away from me and sags in his seat, giving the ceiling a frustrated growl from the back of his throat. "What do they put in these damn cupcakes?"

I laugh and despite the frustrated eyes Finn chuckles with me. "Do you ever wish I never moved in?"

"What the hell would make you say something like that?"

I wipe my fingers on a napkin. "The *no sex with a roommate* thing. We'd probably be a lot less frustrated. One-and-done, and onto the next."

He shakes his head. "That's the problem, isn't it? I don't think it would be one-and-done with us. I couldn't have you just once."

My stomach spasms. I think I've been holding my breath since the second my question leaked out.

Finn pins me with a look. Heated. Hopeful, and a little bit careful. "Could you do it? One-and-done with me?"

I can't look away. "No. I don't think I could."

I think he might have been holding his breath too. He deflates as though relieved by my answer, and after a quiet beat we break into simultaneous wide grins, like we've just confessed to twin crimes, knowing we're in it together now. Finn dips his chin, rubbing the back of his neck so bashfully I feel a hot flush spread over my cheeks. He looks so sweetly shy about it all I have to drop my eyes before I get any crazy ideas. This doesn't mean anything. He plans to end up alone, and I'd do well to remember that.

"The answer's no, by the way," he says without looking up. "I've never wished you didn't move in. Not once."

I watch a flush rise over the neckline of his shirt, and I melt into the bench. God, I'm in trouble.

Finn drops his head into his palms and rubs his face so hard he has to catch his glasses before they fall into a box of cupcakes. "I once got a nasty rash from petting a stray dog," he says suddenly.

The pronouncement is so random I laugh. When he surfaces from his palms, he looks oddly determined.

"That sounds about right for you," I tell him. "What's the story?"

"I was on a run one day by the river and saw this little brown Terrier up the path. No leash, nothing, just moseying around by some bushes. And then as I was passing it, I realized it wasn't brown. His fur was actually white. He was filthy, and skinnier than I've ever seen a Terrier, and... yeah. I waited around a while to see if anyone would come claim him, then I brought him to a rescue when no one did. I don't know what he ended up having, but I earned a gnarly rash up both arms for my effort. I had to go on meds."

Who made this man?

It's the single thought that pops into my mind after he pushes out the story in one single, breathless rush. It seems impossible that he turned out this way without specific design. He's downright gorgeous, a blast to be around. Capable of lifting me out of the dumps within minutes of finding me there.

Finn sits back in his seat, arms crossed, gazing at me almost… expectantly. I let my eyes skate over him. This face I've looked at for weeks now, that I've had in the back of my mind for a year. This face used to rouse something hungry in me, wanting badly to see it buried between my legs.

When did I start looking at it with this much affection? That's the face that brings me cupcakes when I'm upset. That listens to me talk about my body count without even flinching.

"How are you so wholesome?"

He blinks. "You think that was wholesome?"

I shift a box of cupcakes to press my elbows on the table. "You think a story about you rescuing a stray dog isn't wholesome?"

He gazes at me, eyes narrowing incrementally. He looks confused now, stripping off his hat to run an uncertain hand through his hair. "The last time this story came out of me, I sent a girl running on the word *rash*. I have a habit of saying too much. Not knowing when to quit rambling. Nina still laughs about it."

I make a face. "What kind of girls were you going after, exactly?"

He gives a wry smile. "Honestly? I've started to wonder. I guess the answer is that I was going after the kind who'd make a scorecard out of me. I can't decide who that says more about."

My heart pinches. He looks suddenly so vulnerable I want to crawl into a hole and wither away. A world in which someone as sweet as Finn Palmer is made to feel that way isn't a world I particularly want to be part of.

"It says more about them, Finn," I say, gazing at him. "Is that what you were doing? Trying to send me running?"

Finn looks away, and I know the answer is *yes*. I'm dying to understand, to ask any of the hundred questions in my head. About this, the story. The forehead kisses. But he looks so uncomfortable that I can't bring myself to.

CHAPTER 13

It's funny. I've never met a person more attuned to my moods. My feelings. While being so willing to skate over their own.

I shuffle off the bench. "Scoot over."

He moves slowly, giving me enough room to plop down beside him. Tentatively, I reach for his hand under the table. He'd held mine earlier, out in the street, despite the way he clammed up when I took his hand the morning he looked after me and my cramps. And if he only wants to hold hands on his terms that's okay. As long as he knows how grateful I am for him. How hard I'd work to bring up his mood, too.

Finn drops his chin. He stares at our fingers as they interconnect, swallowing heavily, shoulders reaching for his ears. Lower lashes brushing the skin under his eyes. The bell chimes over the bake shop door, from somewhere to our left.

"Jenna."

It's all he says, voice barely above a whisper. Brows crinkled like he doesn't even know the end of his own sentence. His eyes close.

And then he lets go of my hand, moving so swiftly I barely have a moment to feel the pang of disappointment before he runs his arm behind me, snaking it around my waist, and tucks me into his side. He squeezes until I sink into him, cheek hitting his warm shoulder. He smells like he does every night after work. Fresh laundry and a concoction of delicious spices from standing in the kitchen. I breathe him in.

"Want another story?" His voice is soft. He fixes his gaze on the leftover Frankencake sitting on its side in the lid of one of the pastry boxes.

"Yeah. I want another story."

My chest feels heavy. It's painful, like I'm seconds away from a sob. But it's also kind of warm. This feeling like I've got a laugh trapped at the base of my throat that can't decide whether to come out.

"Did I ever tell you about the one and only time I tried using a fake ID?"

"Tell me."

He lets his head rest against the back of the bench. "I was sixteen and a total shit-head—"

"Shocker."

A grin breaks over his face, dislodging the discomfort there. "Seriously. My parents were saints, between the hell Hayley and I would put them through. I went through a phase where I would sneak out the window in my room at night. And on this night in question, I was going to meet up with my buddies to try out our new fake IDs. And so I've got one leg out of my window, ready to climb down, when my bedroom door blows open with my mom on the other side."

"Oops."

"Oops," he agrees with a nod. "So, we sit there in this stand-off. Staring at each other, not saying a word. And I could tell she was steaming on the inside—she was white-knuckling my doorknob, you know? I could see it from where I was, hanging out of the window. But after a minute she gives me this funny look. Backs out of the room and shuts the door. And I think... Shit. She's really letting me off the hook? And I start feeling guilty about it, but then the guys pull up in their car and I head out anyway."

I sink deeper into his body as he speaks, comforted by the sound of his voice. Just loving the way he connects dots within a story.

"And I'm a total idiot at that age—did I say that already? Yeah, I think I did. So obviously I get drunk even before we make it out to the bar. And these IDs, they were so bad. I don't know what we were thinking. The whole blond hair, blue eyes thing I have going on made me look about five years younger than I was back then, too. Obviously, the bartender doesn't buy it for a second. And so security starts walking me out, and I trip on the threshold leaving the bar. Fall flat on my face and smash my nose up. Blood everywhere."

I give a shocked laugh. "This started off so upbeat."

Finn's crooked smile takes over his entire face. "It'll come back around, don't worry." He points at the subtle bump on the bridge of his nose. "See that? They could never really set it properly. But I'm getting ahead of myself. So, I'm panicking, refuse to go to the hospital, right? And I make it back home and when my damn nose still won't stop bleeding, I wake up my parents." His whole body stills in that moment, gaze drifting in a faraway stare. A little wistful, like he's back there in his parents' bedroom. He swallows heavily, collecting himself. "My dad starts flying off the handle when he sees me.

But Mom puts a hand on his arm. Tells him to stop, to go back to bed. And then... she gives me this kiss on my forehead. Gets me in the car and takes me to the hospital. Never yelled. Never asked what I'd been up to, nothing. Just got me fixed up and took me back home."

I curl my lips into my mouth and bite down. It has to be a little sick. That I envy him for a mother he no longer has, instead of feeling that way about the mother I still have around.

"I never really understood why she didn't give me grief over it. But I never snuck out again."

"She got you good, huh?"

He gives a low laugh, and every single note of it sinks into my skin. It was just a small dose. A tiny high. Instantly, I crave more of it.

"She got me good. Parental guilt is a hell of a thing," he agrees. After a small pause he adds: "It's almost the anniversary. Of the day she died."

"Finn..."

Before I can finish, Finn plasters a wide smile on his face that doesn't quite reach his eyes. "Sorry. I'm killing the mood. Probably not what you needed from me, huh? After the night you've had."

Sweet Finn.

"You didn't kill the mood. This is what it is to get close to someone. You share, and it gets heavy sometimes."

"It feels weird," he mutters, looking out over the other side of our booth at the purple wall framing the front windows of the shop.

"What, you never had pillow talk with any of your girls?"

"That's not the kind of talking I do in bed."

"I'm aware. And I like both."

Finn dips his chin. The way he looks at me now, the way the faint lines around his eyes have softened, it fills my lungs with sugar and velvet.

In a second we're back in my bed again, the morning he looked after me, staring at each other like the very same thought was passing through our minds. Like we were really about to do it, kiss for the first time. I saw the naked hunger in his eyes, he saw mine. His eyes trail down my face to my mouth and they stay there one long, quivering second.

I watch it happen in real time. His expression morphing minutely, a tic in his jaw one second, twitch of his brow the other, a tiny pinch of his mouth the next. He loses the fight. Talks himself out of it. Just like that morning in my bed, I watch a veil drop behind his eyes.

Finn lifts his chin and places a lingering kiss on my forehead instead. To my intense relief, he doesn't let go of me. We go on like that, listening to chime above the door every few minutes, the way the shop assistant hums as she wipes down the display. After a while my eyelids grow heavy, lulled into luscious comfort by the warmth of his arm, the way he's started to stroke my waist with his thumb as he holds me.

Thank you for coming for me, I want to tell him. *I don't know what I'd do without you.*

I'm so tired it's all I can do to not fall asleep. I don't want to suggest we leave, though. I don't want that space between our seats in the car. Don't want a hallway's worth of distance between where we lie in bed.

These are the wrong thoughts to have about my platonic friend, my roommate, a man who plans to end up alone. I blame the weakened state of my brain as sleep comes for me.

"I've got you," Finn says softly, when I make a last feeble attempt to wrench open my lids. "Close your eyes. I'll get you home, Jenna Bear."

And the very last thought I have before letting go of the day is this:

I am in so, *so* much trouble.

Chapter 14

Jenna

"Don't hate me, but I feel like I need to say this: if I'm not maid of honor at your wedding, this friendship is over."

Jude's right. I do hate her for saying it.

She flicks on the windshield wipers as we glide to a stop at a red light. Beyond her, I see a guy in the next car look over. I can't tell whether he's checking us out or admiring this sleek blue thing she drives now.

I kick off my wedge sandals and tuck my legs underneath me. "How did we go from forehead kisses to weddings? Your mind works in fascinating ways, Jujube."

"The forehead kisses are freaking adorable, that's how. And you know what's even *more* adorable? The fact that it's Finn Palmer doing it. Honestly, I'm still not entirely sure whether I'm dreaming this conversation."

"Yeah, it's all adorable until the next minute, when he sits two full seat cushions away from me on the sofa. *Two* seat cushions, Jude. We practically have to shout through a conversation. This is what I get for going all needy on him. One second we have this totally PG-13 sexual incident, the next I'm making him rescue me from the sidewalk—"

Jude snorts. "Jenna, I love you dearly but there was nothing PG-13 about that *sexual incident*. You masturbated to each other."

I lay a hand on my chest in mock outrage. "Excuse me, Jude Holland. Are you judging me? Your sexual incident was way worse than mine. You let a client you hated fondle you."

"And said client I hated is now my live-in boyfriend." She glances at me. "Why are you stressing over all this, anyway? You want to talk him into another sexual incident?"

I stare down at my upturned palms.

"Jenna."

"Mhm?"

"If Finn wanted to be together, as in *together*, together…"

I give her a look. "Let's not play this game. He isn't interested like that. The man doesn't *do* relationships. He told me point blank he plans to end up alone."

"But if he did want to," Jude insists. "Would you?"

"Did I tell you we haven't even kissed? *Ever*? We got close a couple of times but he always calls it off one way or another. I mean, he's obviously allowed to decide not to kiss me—"

"You're dodging the question."

I sigh. "Look, it's kind of hard to wrap my head around a what-if scenario I know won't ever happen."

"And yet you both seem to have veered into old married couple territory."

"And we don't even have the years of hot sex to show for it! It's total crap, Jude. I don't know how I got roped into this. This is *me* we're talking about. You know how I get when I go too long without sex. Soon my hair will start falling out, I'll get all shriveled and wrinkled—"

"Jenna."

"*What*? What's that tone for?"

"It's for calling you out for pretending this is about sex. You like him. You *like* him, like him. Don't you?"

"He's made it clear on multiple occasions he isn't interested in anything other than platonic."

"I didn't hear a *no* in there."

I knew she'd have a field day with this.

With mischief over every bit of her face, Jude swings us into the next lane

CHAPTER 14

and takes such an abrupt right-hand turn down a side street that I slide around in the leather seat.

"Jesus, Jujube." I pull away the hair that's become stuck to my lip gloss. "What kind of sexual incident did it take to con Theo into giving you this car? You shouldn't be allowed to operate a vehicle like this. Wait..." I peer through the window and see us heading for the Hubbart Bridge connecting the two sides of the city. "Where are we going? Finn's apartment is back that way."

"We aren't going to his apartment."

"And where are we going?"

Jude wags her brows at me over her shoulder. "We're going to get you some answers, *Jenna Bear*."

~

The last time I set foot inside Sunset Landing, I'd been wearing sneakers of all things, having been recruited by Jude to help put the finishing touches on the place before it opened.

And even though Finn's now seen me dressed down and makeup-free for several weeks, I'm infinitely thankful I put on a little dress and heels for my impromptu dinner-date with Jude. This thing with Finn won't ever amount to anything. But it doesn't hurt to show him what he's missing from time to time.

Sunset Landing is a gorgeous restaurant, speaking totally objectively, and not at all because my best friend designed it and her boyfriend owns it. The interior is all sexy mood lighting, intrigue, and mystery. Intimate like you're about to turn a corner and meet the love of your life.

We breeze past reception where a girl wearing a black outfit waves enthusiastically at Jude, who gives her a timid smile back. Trust Jude not to let her almost-restaurant-ownership go to her head. She leads me through the lounge with its handful of occupants. It's late, coming up on the time where Finn would call to let me know he'd be home soon. It's a new habit he's developed, though I can't figure out whether he does it to be sweet or to avoid another naked surprise.

"Doesn't Finn work in the kitchen? Why aren't we going there?"

"I don't trust Finn not to deflect his way through a conversation about you, especially to your face. We're going to hear this from the next best source."

"Who, Nina?"

Jude snorts, leading me down a hallway past the bar. "No, those two are like siblings. She wouldn't let out so much as a peep if Finn murdered her own mother in cold blood."

We reach the end of the hall and Jude pushes open a door into the office. It's a small room, lined with filing cabinets and a large window at the back overlooking the rushing Hubbart River.

The desk in the middle of the room is occupied by what I can only describe as the most bored-to-tears man in the world. Theo sits reclined in his chair with his feet propped up on the desk, fingers threading through the dark curls falling over his face and a phone to his ear. As we tiptoe in, he gives a few noncommittal *yeah*s and *mhm*s, until finally he catches sight of us. Rather, he catches sight of Jude, and nothing on this planet will ever make me happier than seeing the way his face transforms as he lays eyes on my best friend. Instantly he's standing, smiling so big you'd think he hasn't seen her in years.

"Hey, Erica, I have to go. That all sounds fine. Just... Keep it up. All the good work, and whatnot."

He tosses his phone onto the desk and gets Jude into a crushing hug, sweeping her off the floor and stamping her shoulder with about a dozen kisses.

"You almost stuck the landing on the whole praising your team thing." Jude laughs. "Until the *whatnot* part."

That insane smile still hasn't come off his face. "Guess I'm still a work in progress." He sets Jude down and throws an arm around my shoulders, bringing me in next. "Hey, Jenna Bear."

"Hey, Cherry Pie. Does everyone know about my nickname?" I give him a hearty squeeze around the middle.

"Everyone," he confirms with a smirk. "I heard the kitchen crew rib him over it just the other day. They caught on to Nina teasing him about it. It's been worth it coming to work just to listen to him stutter through those

CHAPTER 14

conversations."

Jude gives me a gleeful look and hops up to sit on the desk. "Told you we came to the right place."

She pats a spot next to her and I jump up so that we're both facing Theo. He looks between us, and it seems he's slowly coming to understand what he's in for. He leans back onto the wall and crosses his arms tight over his chest, shaking his head at Jude who stifles a laugh.

I whistle. "Lay off the weights, Jordan. You're about to Hulk right out of that shirt."

He rolls his eyes, but there's no hiding the way the tips of his ears turn pink. "If you think flattery's going to get a word out of me—"

Jude tisks. "He's right. We need to do better than that if we're going to get him to talk."

"There won't be any talking. He's my friend."

"So am I..." Jude smiles sweetly.

"And me," I add, batting my lashes. "You wouldn't disappoint us like that, would you, Theo?"

I wind my arms around Jude and we pout up at him like a pair of sad puppies begging for a treat.

Theo blinks. "I love you both but that act is so bad, it's embarrassing."

"Oh, come on!" I throw my head back. "Help me out, here. You have no idea what kind of mindfuck the last few weeks have been. He says he's not interested in relationships one second, and the next he's cuddling me in a bakery."

"After running to rescue her," Jude adds, with an earnest raise of her brows.

"Go to *him*," Theo says, unmoved. "I don't see what good it'll do to talk to me about this."

"Theo," Jude says lightly. "You know that thing we did in the backseat of your car a couple months ago? If you tell us—"

"He talks about you constantly," Theo blurts, staring at Jude all wide-eyed. "I heard the servers comparing notes the other day. They know his reputation and it sounds like he hasn't taken any of them out. I'm talking since the restaurant opened. It used to be his thing, dating the serving staff. If you can even call it dating."

My chest goes all warm and tight. He talks about me constantly. *Constantly*.

I turn to Jude who grins at me wide as a Cheshire cat. "You little minx. I'm going to need a detailed description of that *thing* you did in the backseat. A full play-by-play with drawn diagrams should suffice."

She laughs. "To use on Finn?"

I sigh dramatically. "That would require him to sleep with me."

"You aren't sleeping together?" Theo frowns. "That's new."

I chuckle. "New for me or new for him?"

"Both of you, I guess." He stares at me a while, chewing on the inside of his cheek.

"*Spill*, Theo," Jude says suddenly, jabbing an accusing finger in his direction. "You're doing the cheek thing! What are you hiding from us?"

Theo gives a defeated groan, resting his head back against the wall. "I'm not hiding anything. Look, I feel like an ass even saying this out loud and I'd much rather you get this out of him directly... Do you know anything about what happened with his mom?"

I nod and watch him exchange a meaningful look with Jude. "What? What's that look about?"

"I'm surprised, that's all. He doesn't talk about her. Ever," Theo explains. "I'm sure you noticed this act he likes to pull?"

"Which act?"

"Theo calls him a happy leprechaun. How he's chipper ninety-nine percent of the time."

"That's not an act, though."

"You're right. It isn't," Theo concedes. "He genuinely *is* that happy, for the most part. But then there's the one percent. Has he told you about his dad, at all?"

"I know there's something wrong there, but he never gave me specifics." They eye each other again. I turn to Jude. "Do you know about it?"

She winces apologetically. "We met him for drinks after a visit with his dad one day. It kind of spilled out."

CHAPTER 14

My stomach sinks. "I feel like an idiot."

"Don't take it personally," Theo says kindly. "If there's one thing he talks about less than his mom, it's this."

I stare down at my wedge heels, letting them dangle from my toes. "Honestly, it's not even that he hasn't told me—that's his choice to make. I'm annoyed I let myself make more of this than it really is. Built it up in my head into something it's not." I turn to Jude. "Where have you been? You're supposed to be my Jiminy Cricket in all this!"

"I don't think you're making more of it than it is. Finn doesn't just go around cuddling women and dealing out forehead kisses."

"Yeah?" Theo pipes in. "He kisses you on the forehead?"

I groan. "Enough about the forehead kisses. I may as well be his kid sister!"

"He also gave you a nickname."

"Yes, *Jujube*, that simply must mean he's in love with me."

She raises her brows. "He took one look at you naked and locked himself in his room to jerk off—"

Theo chokes on a breath, looking suddenly distraught. "Fucking hell, Jude—"

"And then he dragged you into his room to watch you—"

"I don't need to hear any of this!" Theo cuts in loudly, glaring at the ceiling like it just started hurling insults at him. "Look, Jenna. I'd tell you about his dad if you asked because you're a sister to Jude. But I think it's worth waiting to hear it from him. If he's already talking about his mom, I doubt this is too far behind. He must be into you."

I stare at Theo, considering. If one of Finn's closest friends seems to think he's into me... I shake my head abruptly. This is Finn we're talking about. Certified commitment-phobe. Accredited perma-bachelor. Licensed for emotional detachment.

"Oh, what do *you* know?" I grumble at Theo, only half-kidding. To Jude I add: "He's seen a lot of people naked."

"So have you," she counters without missing a beat. "And still, you have feelings for him. And you'd date him if he wanted to."

I flush. Consider denying it. Theo gives me a single brow raise and a half shrug that says, *well?*

These last few weeks... the forehead kisses, the way he beelines for my favorite bakery every time Ronnie calls since he did it the first time. It only confirmed my suspicions: that Finn Palmer would be someone I'd give up my own commitment-free existence for. He makes me feel like I'm more than a body made for a man's attention. That I'm good enough for the sweet parts, too.

I let my next breath balloon my cheeks before blowing it all the way out. "How do I pull this off? How do I get someone with no interest in relationships to decide he wants to be with me like that?"

Only a proper lady would attract a good man—

"Patience," Theo says, cutting off Ronnie's voice. "Just being there for them. Accepting that maybe all it'll ever be is friendship, and that it's good enough in its own right."

I wrinkle my nose at him. "Who invited Gandhi over here?"

Jude gives a closed-mouthed laugh, but the hearts in her eyes could serve as target practice for a cherub.

"Yeah, let's all laugh at me," Theo says, pushing his fingers through the abundance of curls on top of his head. "It's not like I got a woman *who hated my guts* to change her mind about me or anything. Just ignore me. I'll keep sitting here, pining away."

"Pine quietly, won't you?" I stick out my tongue at him. "Besides, this is me we're talking about. We're going to need to think big. Like... Nineties teen romcom makeovers kind of big. Maybe I'll dye my hair back to my natural color."

Jude stares thoughtfully at the wall. "You could try to make him jealous? Oh—you could get a fake boyfriend!"

I wave away the suggestion. "That never works. They always end up staying in their fake relationship."

"*Well*, if you were to find yourself a better match in the process..."

"I wouldn't," I say dismissively. "This is going to require some major trickery. He saw me coming from a mile away when I tried to get him to sleep with me. Convincing him to *date* me... I'm going to have to pull out all the stops. Use every bit of game I have."

"What are you thinking?"

I move my ponytail off my shoulder, pondering hard. "The jealousy thing is definitely good, but it's not enough. He knows about my past and isn't fazed by it at all. I already swore I'd stop trying to seduce him into sex, so that's out." I nibble on my thumb, staring at Jude without really seeing her. There are numbers flashing across my sightline, and I'm scrambling to catch them all, do the math. "I need to take this all the way somehow. I need to make him fall in love with me. In a head over heels, there's no other option but to be with me sort of way."

"And how do you do that?"

Immediately, the question takes the wind out of my sails. They flutter uselessly around me.

"I... I don't know. I can't remember the last time I was shooting for love," I say, deflating. "I mean, has *anyone* loved me? Even with my ex, I can't be sure. Would he have cheated if he loved me?"

The realization is a punch in the gut. Has... Has Ronnie been right this whole time?

Am I too much?

Not serious enough? Too promiscuous? Do I really look like a sexed-up pony?

I pinch a strand of hair from my ponytail, staring at the pink lock.

"Jenna," Theo starts. His shoulders have capsized, watching me spiral. "Don't do that to yourself."

"I love you," Jude says softly, taking my hand.

"Right. Right." I nod. There are people who like me this way. There are. I release the breath I've been holding and shake out my shoulders. "Whew. Okay, that got dark for a second." I jerk my head in Theo's direction. "How'd you get this one so obsessed with you?"

"Honestly, I was kind of short with him at the start..."

I hum appreciatively. "Playing hard to get. That's certainly an option."

Theo drags a hand down his face, muttering something that sounds a whole lot like *for fuck's sake, these two.*

"Got anything to add there, sweetums?"

Theo turns a pair of highly exasperated eyes in my direction. "I won't entertain this bullshit. I'm telling you that you don't need to trick him into anything because he's *already into you.*"

"Okay, let's pretend for a second that's true. How do I get him to *act* on being into me? And don't tell me to tell him how I feel. I could lay it all out for him tonight and he'd give me a very polite thank you, lock himself in his room and refuse to come out until I leave in September, because he's too nice to kick me out. You know it's true."

I've got him there. He crosses his arms and stares at the ground.

I stand from the desk, shaking my hair out of its ponytail and massaging my temples. Suddenly I have a pounding headache. I've never had a problem getting my way with a man. Then again, I've never had an opponent like Finn.

This new plan, the one where I try to win him over, decide he wants to be with me despite the commitment issues... It'll be the hardest battle I've ever fought.

He's worth it. He makes me feel like I'm worth it, too.

But where do I start?

How do I talk Finn Palmer into falling in love with me?

"Thanks guys," I say wryly. "Came here for answers and left with even more questions. You two really are terrible matchmakers."

"Oh, I know!" Jude says brightly, jumping to her feet and gathering Theo's things off the desk. "Why don't we all go out for drinks Friday night? We can watch you in action and suss him out for you. Can you let Finn off the clock?"

"We can work that out," Theo says.

He takes his laptop from her and shoves his phone in the back pocket of his jeans. He drops a gentle hand on my shoulder when I make for the door behind Jude. "Hey. I know... I've lived through how hard it is, wanting someone who doesn't seem to want you back. I get how soul crushing it can get. But I want to make sure that *you're* sure—the all-in kind of sure, before jumping into anything with Finn. He's got an armor like no other, and I've heard of what happens when he takes a hit without it on. It's not pretty. Don't let him drop his guard unless you mean it."

I swallow. Pretty or not, Finn hurting isn't a sight I ever want to witness. "I'm sure. Theo, I really…" I gesture helplessly at my chest.

"Okay." He nods. "For the record, I think you'd be great together. If you can't pull this off with him, I don't think anyone ever will."

I flush. "Alright, alright, I get it: you're a nice guy, Theo. You've officially got my blessing to marry our girl. But do it within the next month, won't you? And have you considered eloping?"

"Enough about this bet," Jude groans. She takes Theo's hand, tugging him and his incredibly baffled expression out of the office. "Ignore her. She's so lovesick she doesn't know what she's saying."

I rush behind them and give Jude a playful slap on the ass. "I'm not in love."

"*Yet*," she throws over her shoulder.

As we near the swinging doors that lead into the kitchen, I hear Finn's loud, deep laugh go off inside. I adore his laugh. Every single time, he sounds like he's just been told the funniest joke he's ever heard. He laughs with total abandon, like he's trying to absorb the joy out of every little moment and give it back to you even bigger, in the form of that laugh.

As though my thoughts conjured him up, the doors open and I stop dead in my tracks as Finn backs out of the kitchen. "You're on solo cleaning duty tomorrow if I see you come in late again—" He backs right into me so hard I have to catch myself on a nearby chair.

"Watch where you're going, kid," I say, smoothing down my hair. "I didn't dress like this to get trampled."

Finn pivots around so quickly I catch the laugh fade off his face. His expression veers from surprise right into his signature grin. The lopsided one I can't get enough of.

"Woah. You're here. I was just about to call you." He shows me his phone with my contact pulled up. His gaze trails behind me, presumably finding Jude and Theo hovering nearby. "Everything okay?"

"We came to wrangle Theo from the back office," I tell him. "He was sending SOS signals through ESP."

"Oh. He should have joined us in the kitchen. We just finished a round of *Never Have I Ever*." Finn sends an innocent look over my shoulder, and chuckles at what I can only assume is a thoroughly unamused expression from Theo.

"Are you done, too?" I ask him.

"Yeah, you're right on time. Want a ride home?"

Home. I don't know exactly when it happened, him switching from *my place* to *home*, but I like it a lot more than I should. I *feel* it more than I should. Like it makes perfect sense for me to be there.

I can feel Jude's eyes burning holes into my back. "Finn, I'm about to become your... second favorite person."

He flashes her a quick smile over my shoulder. "Ah, you're selling yourself short, honey."

"Am I?" she says loftily, and I refuse to turn around to see exactly why Finn's mouth hardens into a line. "Anyway, I just got you out of work Friday night. We're all going for drinks."

Finn's eyes meet mine. "And why does it feel like I'm being stalked by a Jude-shaped shark?"

He's dropped his voice like he's only talking to me, and takes a little, conspiratorial step towards me. Like whatever game Jude's playing, he and I are in it together. I take a tiny step forward too.

"Just go with it. Her wide-eyed, sweet and innocent thing is a total act. Apparently, she did this really filthy thing to Theo in the backseat of his car—"

"Watch it," Theo says sharply from behind me.

I snort. "And he refuses to let her tell me what it was."

Theo wheels a cackling Jude toward the exit, grumbling about driving them straight to a deserted parking lot to collect his dues.

"See you Friday night, boss," Finn calls after them, waving them off with just enough enthusiasm to get a rise out of Theo. As soon as they're out of sight, he touches a hand to my hip, bringing his lips to my forehead. "We'll get him to spill. Just wait and see."

CHAPTER 14

He leads me out behind them, and a single thought pops into my mind as we meet the warm summer night:

I'll get you to love me. Just wait and see.

Chapter 15

Finn

I know a recon mission when I see one.

And that's exactly the feeling I get before I even catch sight of the three of them huddled in a booth by the bar. Jude and Theo sitting close together on one side, leaning in to speak to Jenna across the table, who's fiddling with the stem of a glass of red wine.

This place isn't exactly my scene. It's a little too dark, backlit in trendy neon colors and playing the kind of radio-friendly music that'll get stuck in my head until I finally crack and scream into my pillow tonight. The place is crawling with guys looking for an easy lay. Hanging around the bar, chatting up any pretty girl within earshot. Can't judge. I was one of them, not too long ago.

And I should probably maybe at some point perhaps start thinking about possibly getting back on that horse, sometime in the eventual future. Down the line. Eventually. Maybe.

The Scooby Gang haven't noticed me yet and so I sneak over to the bar to get a drink. Also, because I need to figure out how I'm going to get through a night trying to stay immune to those doe eyes Jude does when she wants to get something out of you, and worse, Jenna's entire existence, which I already know I'm prone to succumbing to.

It's all fair game. I haven't exactly been consistent with the whole platonic roommates thing. Half the time I don't even realize what I'm doing. The other half...

Fuck. Everything's just better when she's around.

This little crush is starting to get out of hand. So, I drove myself here with a new plan: no touching. No staring. No feeling lightheaded when Jenna laughs so hard she snorts and try not to get so loopy whenever that adorable dimple shows up near her chin. And don't, under any circumstance, get drunk enough to follow her into bed when we get home.

It's all just an occupational hazard of living with a woman I'm not related to, for the first time in my life. That's all. Stick to the plan, and it'll pass.

"Hey, how're you doing?" I nod at the bartender. "A Cabernet Sauvignon and double whiskey on the rocks."

From the bar, I watch Jenna's shoulders shudder as she laughs, and she's so goddamn stunning it makes me almost sick to my stomach.

The bartender drops the drinks in front of me and I down half of mine in one go, watching that dimple disappear as she says something to Theo. Instantly, I'm annoyed. That dimple should be on constant display. It should be out until she complains her cheeks are sore, until the only muscle memory she's got is the one that plumps up her cheeks, crinkles her eyes, stretches that mouth wide.

That's how she deserves to live her life. In constant ecstasy.

And anything that gets in the way of that, her mom, her sister, the fucking doorframe she stubbed her toe on this morning, it deserves to be set on fire.

Hell, I'll light the match myself.

"Need a napkin?"

I wrench my eyes away from Jenna and the bartender looks at me like I've lost my damn mind. I think I have. I'm standing here with the glass half-tipped at my mouth, distracted out of a sip, and the entire damn thing has dribbled down my front.

Fuck it.

I sweep her drink off the bar and head straight for the sinking ship known as my self-control. Jenna catches sight of me first, and with a meaningful look in Jude's direction the table goes silent.

She breaks into a smile when I reach her. "You're probably wondering if we were talking about you."

"Don't be silly," I say, sliding in beside her and putting the wine down by her near-empty glass. "You couldn't have been any more obvious."

It's a damn reflex at this point.

I don't remember how it started. But it's a reflex, and the second my lips hit her forehead, the second I pull back to absolute *crickets* at the table, I know I messed up. Committed a fatal error. It's inevitable now, the onslaught of questions from the two hyenas across the table, Jude and Theo, watching the whole thing unfold with their eyebrows trying to climb the stairway to heaven.

I'm in deep shit already, and so I round it out to the fullest. "Hey, Jenna Bear," I say under my breath.

"Hey, kid," she murmurs back.

Jude and Theo stare at me like they're seeing a solar eclipse.

I clear my throat. "I was actually wondering why I was promised a Friday night off from work only to end up working half my shift, anyway." I cross my eyes in Theo's direction, hoping it does enough to diffuse the tension.

"I've heard all about this work you do," Jenna says, sucking down the last of her wine and thumbing the rim of the glass I brought her. "Don't you spend half your day shooting the shit with your team?"

"Accurate," says Theo.

I nudge her. "Whose side are you on, huh?" I snatch back the new glass of wine and take a drink.

"That depends." She steals it back, takes her own sip. "Will you split some cauliflower wings with me? These two freaks *ate before they came*."

"Sure, I'll do that," I say. I lean around her for a menu tucked by her elbow, and I'm immediately immersed in the smell of her shampoo. God, I love that stuff. Fucking *love* it. I pause there, letting myself have just another second of it. Jenna's eyes lock with mine. We're so close there's barely space for air between our noses, and I'm immediately floating in the sky blue of her eyes. "You smell really nice tonight. I mean, you always smell amazing, but…"

"Thank you," she says softly. My lungs are broken.

CHAPTER 15

Kiss her, you idiot.

What?

Before I can dissect that irrational thought, Theo coughs from the other side of the table. I turn to see Jude's look of utter glee.

Shit. What the hell am I doing?

I clear my throat, shoving my fingers through my hair and Jenna shifts in her seat. "Which cauliflower flavors do you want? Honey parm?"

"And maple chipotle?" Her voice comes out a little weak.

I snap the menu shut. "Done."

Immediately I regret putting the menu away. It's a lot nicer to look at than the smug as all hell look Theo's giving me across the table.

"Maple chipotle, huh?" Jude says loudly, trying to move us past the awkward like the angel she is. "Whatever happened to straight up barbecue? Buffalo sauce? A tasteful dry rub?"

"Hey, don't look at me. I'm a fan of the classics," I tell her. "You can blame people like your fancy-pants boytoy."

Theo rolls his eyes. "We can't all be content eating the same veggie delight, from the same pizza chain, every single Saturday night."

"And leftovers on Sunday," Jenna pipes in.

I make a face at her. "I don't hear you complaining."

A server appears at my elbow and Jenna puts in our order. Once he walks off, she leans forward, smirking between Theo and me. "So, if it came down to it, which one of you could make the best chicken wings?"

"Me," Theo and I say in unison. I laugh, he scowls. Typical of our relationship.

"Oh, I like this game." Jude drums her hands on the table. She and Jenna exchange a look without even trying to hide the fact that they're about to stir up some drama. "Who makes the best burger?"

"What kind?" we ask together.

"Bacon," Jenna supplies.

I put up a hand. Theo hesitates a second before sitting back with another eye roll. "Who likes bacon burgers, anyway?"

"That would be *everyone*, Sherlock," Jenna says.

"Spoken like a true vegetarian."

She shrugs. "I'm a vegetarian, not delusional. I'll never pretend that faux bacon is anywhere near as good as the real deal."

"*Faux* bacon?" I laugh, nudging her with my knee under the table. "You're letting your rich girl show."

Jenna performs an over the top gasp. "You take that back. Before I ask which one of you makes the best barbecue ribs."

"I can say with total confidence that I make the better ribs, even though I've never eaten any."

"Then how can you be sure?"

"Because *he*," I jerk my head at Theo, "is a classically trained French chef and only dabbles in the fancy stuff. Go to him for your run of the mill scallop-caviar with a marinière sauce. Come to me for the juicy, saucy stuff you want to lick off your fingers."

At that Jenna's gaze lowers, and it takes me a moment to realize she's eyeing my fingers sitting on the table. And even though I didn't mean it suggestively—not consciously, at least—knowing I get Jenna Carling hot like this feels so damn good. Looking down with those sweet, puffy lips lightly parted, heavy eyelids, the thoughts simmering in her mind probably not too far off from mine: what I'd love to do to her with these fingers. How I'd put them everywhere she'd let me. The way we'd fuck changes every time I've fantasized about it. Hard, slow, from behind, on top. Behind closed doors and out in the open. I want it all with her.

I want Jenna Carling day after day, with no end in sight. And that's what makes her so dangerous. Off limits.

Anyway, it'll pass. It has to.

"Should we excuse ourselves?"

It takes a second for the words to penetrate. For me to realize that it isn't Jenna who's said them. There are two other nosy, meddling people sitting at this table with us, and an entire bar around us.

I sink down in my seat, trying to give my swelling cock coverage under this table.

Jenna sets her wine glass down carefully with a fleeting look at Jude. "So,

CHAPTER 15

what kind of chef are you, then? A classically trained saucy stuff chef?"

I rub a hand over my face. "I'm a classically trained Theo Jordan chef, with a healthy side of rebellion."

"What do you mean?"

"I mean following rules was never my strong suit, babe."

I don't know how to stop this. The flirting thing. It's a compulsion, for someone like me.

And yet, it's not. It's a Jenna Carling thing.

An I-want-her-to-want-me thing.

Theo sets down his pint with more force than necessary. "You know, I'm really proud of you, buddy. The first step is admitting you have a problem. Next thing you know, you'll actually manage to get through a day without starting a game of *Would You Rather* with the team during dinner service."

I shrug. "You lead with fear, I lead with fun."

"Fucking hell, I failed you."

"The prowling and scowling part of the curriculum really didn't stick, boss."

Jenna looks between us. "Wait, he really *did* train you? How does that work? Is culinary school optional?"

The table goes quiet. It's nothing but the pounding background music and laughter from tables around us.

"Why does it feel like I just put my foot in my mouth?" Jenna asks, looking around and settling her attention on Jude, who gives her a not-so-discreet wince.

I watch her realize we're dancing around some backstory of mine, knowing that everyone is in on it but her. And man. Her disappointment just *crushes* me.

I've already allowed this woman in deeper than anyone else. But I'm so desperate to slow down this train speeding straight to somewhere I never wanted to find myself, that I'm pulling on the brakes whenever I've got enough awareness about me. This subject, losing my mom and the subsequent destruction of my father, has been an easy, familiar roadblock to erect.

I run a hand over the back of my neck. "I had all the best intentions. But I dropped out of the program a semester in, a little after... I had a crisis in class after my mom died."

There's warmth in the way she looks at me now. "It's okay," she mouths.

She's so good at that. Flipping the mood on a dime, making me feel desired one second, and understood the next. She doesn't resent me when I pull up short. I slide my foot to the right, until we're touching from the knee down. It's an I'm sorry and a thank you.

Also, it just feels good.

Theo steps in to save us. "It's not an easy path, having to learn it all as you go. But it can work out if you've got enough drive and natural talent."

"Aw, boss. When'd you turn so sweet?"

Theo rolls his eyes. "I forgot the most important part: you've got to be a real pest, too. Finn worked as a dish washer at one of my earlier gigs—"

"Back when Theo was nothing but a nobody, he'd hang around the kitchen after everyone else packed it in. Cleaned it single-handedly every night so that he could have the space to himself after the shift ended. I'd watch him test out the gnarliest recipes from where I was washing dishes." I make a face. "The looks of one still haunts me—"

"If I could go back and warn myself that I'd never be able to get rid of you one day—"

"All soggy, and the *smell*. I don't know how you got where you are, boss, but the *me* from back then? He'd call it a goddamn miracle." Our server comes by to drop two heaping baskets of cauliflower wings at the table, and I hand Jenna a napkin. "So one night it's just the two of us in the kitchen. And I watch him dump out recipe after recipe of this sauce. And because he's a bit of a prick, he adds the dirty mixing bowls to my stack of dishes every time he goes for a new one. So finally I think, okay, I gotta try this stuff—curiosity got the best of my instinct to avoid food poisoning, you know? And immediately—"

"It wasn't *immediate*."

"Immediately, I realize what he's missing is tarragon. So I bring it over to him, and he looks at me like I'm a total idiot. You know, that look he's perfected?" I wink at Jude. "And he argues with me for a solid eternity until finally I deke around him and dump a bit of it into his bowl. And the rest is history. The restaurant put his dish on the menu. He goes on to become some big shot chef without so much as thanking me for personally getting him there. How dare you?"

I fix him with a look and shake my head mournfully. Trying badly not to laugh at the way he looks like he wants to throttle me.

"I *did* give you credit for the tarragon. Then I proceeded to clean the kitchen single-handedly every night just so I could teach you, as a thank you. And how is it, exactly, that you ended up head chef at one of my restaurants?"

I give him a wide, obnoxious grin. "My charm and good looks?"

With a laugh, Jenna lifts a honey parmesan floret from its basket and squeezes the stem, releasing juices onto her fingers. She licks it off and it sends me into a silent tailspin.

In an alternate world, I'd beeline us home and lock us in her bedroom until my body gave out, and then spoon her so tight hers would go numb.

But we're not in that alternate world, and it'll pass.

"I'm going to go fight this crowd at the bar for another drink. Anyone want one?" Jenna nudges me to let her out of the booth. I slide off the bench and she shuffles down, taking the hand I offer to help her up with a smile.

Jude and Theo decline drinks, and I put in an order for a beer. What I thought was a tank top she was wearing is actually a dress, in this pink color just darker than her hair, and it hugs every bit of her in the most mouth-watering way. What I'd give to lick a path up her legs. To get another taste of her—

As if sensing my eyes on her, or maybe knowing I'd be staring at her in a dress like that, Jenna glances back. Her shoulders shake in a delicate giggle. She knows exactly what she's doing, the little tease. And I fucking love it.

"Okay, Finn," I hear Jude say across the table. "Now's the part where you give us some freaking answers."

I sigh, toying with the stem of Jenna's empty glass. "I was wondering when you'd get around to this. You two have been sitting there champing at the bit like a pair of snapping turtles."

"Do you blame us?" Theo takes a long drink from his beer, and I know how much it's costing him to have this conversation. He'd rather be getting a whole new set of teeth than talk about relationships, unless you're a pretty brunette named Jude. "You're pulling out moves I've never seen before."

I smirk. "The fact that you even recognize my moves—"

"Believe me, I've already called my therapist for an emergency intervention."

Jude lets out a laugh, and the man looks so pleased with himself at the sound of it.

"Speaking as a totally neutral third-party," Jude says. "And not as someone who's been shipping you with Jenna since the day we met—"

"Doesn't that automatically make you *not* neutral?"

"What's the deal, here, Finn?" Theo cuts in, already at the end of his rope. He looks at me with hard eyes, and the kind of scowl he normally reserves for people who badly disappoint him. "Are you in with her, or are you out?"

I stab a fork at a piece of cauliflower. "It's that simple, huh?"

"With someone like Jenna? Yes, it is that simple," Jude tells me. "Speaking as a totally neutral third-party, of course."

"Of course."

Jude studies me. "You do realize you have feelings for her, right? This isn't one of those situations where you don't recognize that thumping in your chest whenever she's around, is it?"

"There's no thumping, Jude. Look, I can admit I have a little crush, but that's all this is. What's the big deal? The crush will pass."

"*This* is how you are when it's just a crush? Finn, the way you keep showing up for her whenever she's hurting... That's bigger than a crush."

Is it?

I frown at Jude.

No. Can't be.

It's a crush, that's all.

"I'd do all that for you too, and you know it," I say, stuffing a piece of cauliflower into my mouth.

"I do know that," Jude says with a nod. "But it wouldn't be the same and *you* know it."

I clamp my mouth shut when I can't come up with anything. Theo raises his eyebrows, and I can't tell whether it's because I'm passively agreeing with Jude, or because I'm for once lost for words.

"We're friends," I say slowly.

"You're attached at the hip."

"*Best* friends, then." I eye Jenna, who's leaning over the bar to speak to the bartender. I drum my fingers on the table. "What's taking her so long?"

Theo follows my gaze to the bar. He doesn't bother to hide the pure amusement in his voice when he says: "She's been gone thirty seconds, bud."

Thirty seconds too long. But she doesn't seem too concerned about it.

Jenna's hair slips forward, grazing the bar as she says something to the bartender. Her shoulders are shaking, and from here I can tell she's told him something funny.

My eyes narrow. What the hell does he think he's doing, just staring at her—

Finally, he returns a laugh.

Yeah. He'd better laugh at her jokes.

She jokes, you laugh. It's not a hard concept. I roll my shoulders back, relaxing into my seat.

"Finn, all I'm getting at is," Jude says now. "You're just friends until one of you wants more."

"I don't want more," I say absently. What are the odds I can talk her into another cuddle session when we get home? Is it pushing it asking for four in one day? She didn't seem to mind the other three.

Jude flicks my arm, drawing my attention away from Jenna. "You're not the only one involved, Finn."

My hearing peters out for a moment. It's just the whooshing sounds of blood rushing to my head, hollowing out the rest of my body.

"Don't do that."

"Don't do what?"

I shake my head, heart pounding uncomfortably fast now. It's not like

I haven't considered it before. How Jenna feels about me. Whether she's afflicted by this crush, too. But stopping those thoughts in their tracks, forbidding myself from fully entertaining the idea that Jenna Carling might feel something for me, it's the only way I've managed to keep my head straight these past few weeks. It's helped keep this crush manageable.

"Don't play with me like this," I tell Jude. "We're friends. Don't go giving this crush any crazy ideas." She exchanges a look with Theo as I sit back in my seat. "Yeah, it's easy to sit there judging from the ivory tower of your perfect relationship—"

"It's not perfect. I mean, don't get me wrong. It's..." She apparently is unable to come up with the words to describe said obnoxiously perfect relationship. Theo must forget I'm sitting here because he actually cracks a smile and Jude is immediately blushing.

What would it feel like, having something like this?

Theo reaches to tuck a strand of hair behind her ear and immediately I resent the tug of envy in my chest. He knew in a second he wanted to be with her and didn't give another thought to whether to pursue her. I wish I had it like that. I wish I was genetically predisposed to handle the pain of losing something like that when it were to end.

"We had a rough start," Jude says slowly, ripping her eyes off Theo who's still so blissed out he hasn't managed to get that smile off his face. "And even after we got together, it wasn't easy. I was a pariah at work for a couple of months, until people came around to the idea that I was dating a client."

Cue Theo's scowl.

"But it came back to there being no other option. We're in it together, no matter what." She eyes me grimly. "What's your plan, Finn? Live out the rest of the summer playing house until she flies back to Europe?"

I swallow. Damn it—and damn her for bringing that up. I don't let myself think about the expiration date on Jenna's presence at home. How could I, without going insane? That apartment feels like ours. She belongs there just as much as I do. And the thought of being there without her...

Whenever they filter into my mind uninvited, the thoughts of Jenna's departure attempt to form into a single, outlandish decision: that the only

CHAPTER 15

viable solution is to move out of that place the second she goes. To find somewhere she hasn't haunted, where I won't think of her every time I turn a corner.

That's insane, though. And it'll pass.

Jude reaches across the table to settle a gentle hand on my arm. "It won't work, Finn."

"What won't?" I ask, without looking at her.

"Fighting the way you feel. Pretending it isn't real. What's happened to your dad... It's awful. But to let it dictate your life like this..."

I meet the gentle way she watches me. "Please. I can't talk about that. Can you... Don't tell her about this crush thing, okay? I know it's asking a lot, I know how close you are. Just give me some time to figure out how to stop it."

"You better get stopping fast, buddy."

Theo tips his head toward the bar. I find Jenna surrounded now, but easily visible given her height and the extra boost from the heels that bring her solidly over six-feet tall. She's laughing big, dimple in full effect, looking so happy and beautiful, and that's probably why it takes me a while to figure out why Jude and Theo are looking at me like that, like I'm about to implode.

She's standing smack dab in the middle of a group of guys, probably around our age, all in varying degrees of drunkenness. Telling them a story of some kind, and every one of them has their attention glued right on her. She looks like a queen holding court.

As she should.

Jude watches me closely. Beside her, Theo shakes his head.

"That must make you crazy," he mutters darkly. "I don't know how you're not already over there, grabbing them all by the scruff."

I know he'd be doing exactly that. I stood too close to Jude once, before they started dating, and he looked about ready to set the earth on fire. But the tingling sensation running down my arms right now is a lot more pleasant than the kind that gets you dousing the place in kerosene and walking away from the wreckage.

I can't take my eyes off her.

The way she's smiling, how her eyes sweep over the crowd of fevered morons practically clawing at each other for her attention. That little laugh that seems to ignite their greed even more. The hand she touches to one of their shoulders as she speaks, just for a quick second. They're all completely riveted, spellbound by whatever she's saying, and it's so goddamn *Jenna* to waltz into a crowd of people and tug at the strings of their attention like she's the only other person in the room. She can make a total stranger feel like something real special.

She's incredible.

Maybe I should feel jealous. Probably should. But all I feel is a suffocating warmth in my chest, swelling it by about ten sizes. Pride, I realize. Awe. Satisfaction. Because this is Jenna. She deserves to be worshiped by every person fortunate enough to cross her path. Crowd of fevered morons included.

And then, for barely a moment, Jenna's gaze meets mine across this crowded bar.

What's there to be jealous about?

She might be gracing these privileged fuckers with dimpled smiles now. But—

"I'm the one who gets to have her at home."

"You do," Jude agrees. "But for how much longer, Finn?"

Chapter 16

Jenna

This is it: the perfect plan.

It took me a while to get here. After the total flop at the bar the other day, during which he sat perfectly unmoved by the sight of me surrounded by other men, I knew I needed to take Operation Finn in another direction. I don't know what I was thinking, anyway. Romantic feelings are kind of a prerequisite for jealousy. Of course, he didn't fall for it.

But my nanny didn't raise a quitter.

If you have to try this hard, Genevieve—

"Shut up," I mutter under my breath. "Just shut up. I'm trying this your way, for a change. You should be proud."

Silly me. Even imaginary Ronnie wouldn't be proud of me.

I hike up my pleated, knee-length skirt as I crouch to peer into the oven. The pastry is just starting to turn golden, and it's right on time. He'll be home any minute.

I smooth down the front of the sleeveless, high neck top I ran out to buy the second he left for work. I'm even wearing the pearl earrings my Grandma Georgia left me when she passed, and pulled my hair into a neat bun on top of my head. I am the picture of class and sophistication. I came very close to sending my mother photographic evidence, but she'd probably just accuse me of being high on drugs, or something.

I think I am, to be fair.

It's this new strain that's infiltrated my psyche, so that when I'm home alone I can't stop pacing. Putting on music at deafening levels just to fill the silence. Checking my phone more than necessary, just to try to get a tiny fix through the screen. The withdrawal hurts. But when the clock strikes eleven forty-five, when my phone chimes and it's Finn on the other end, calling to let me know he'll be home soon, I come alive again. And the second he plants that forehead kiss on me, in the way that makes me feel like I'm made of molten gold and blinding diamonds, mixed with a bit of fairy dust, I'm a goner. Floating high again, and nothing can bring me down.

I hear his key slide into the lock and mutter a curse I immediately scold myself for. I tiptoe around the island to light the tapered candles in the middle of the kitchen table. Also purchased today.

"Hey, Jenna Bear," Finn calls from the hall. I can hear him kick off his shoes. "Something smells good."

"Oh, you know. Just... cooking!"

What?

What was that? Of course, I'm cooking.

"I kinda figured," he says with a chuckle, as he makes it down the hall. "What's the occa—woah. What happened?"

Finn stops dead in his tracks in the doorway between the hall and kitchen, frown deepening as he takes me in.

I resist the urge to throw out my arms with a big *ta-da!*, instead settling for clasping my hands in a desperate attempt to stop them from shaking. I don't know why I'm suddenly so nervous. This is Finn. He's a warm hug, even from across the room.

Shoulders back, Genevieve.

"You act like I've never cooked for you before," I say, standing a little taller and crossing back to the oven. "I made us a vegetable Wellington with a side of asparagus." I peer into the pan on the burner. "Wilted asparagus. Fuc—fiddlesticks."

"*Fiddlesticks?*"

I brush some lint off my top without turning to look at him. "Yes. You

CHAPTER 16

know, as in fiddlesticks! This asparagus has become overcooked mush."

I don't actually know if that's the right application of the word, but I've committed to it now.

"Oh God. It's happening again, isn't it?"

I peek over my shoulder to see Finn with his face screwed up. "What is?"

He focuses on a point above my head, eyes going all foggy. "I used to have these night terrors where this primped-up headmistress would appear at the end of my bed. At first she'd just kind of stand there staring at me. But as the dream went on she'd pull out this stiff ruler and snap it at me like she was about to spank me. And I'd think: cool. This lady's kinky. She's not so bad after all—"

A snort slips out before I can stop it, and quickly I turn it into a delicate cough.

Do you have to sound like that when you laugh?

I rattle the pan in front of me, checking whether any of this asparagus can be salvaged. After a quiet moment, Finn wanders over to look over my shoulder.

"Aren't you gonna ask?"

He's standing so close his body heat permeates my clothes and I so badly want to sink back into him, savor the way he smells. God, I wish he wanted to kiss me.

I let out a shaky breath. "Ask what?"

His chin is inches away from mine. "Whether she ever spanked me."

Honestly? I'm not sure I can stand to know whether that's something he'd enjoy. No man has ever asked me to spank him before, but if the words ever came out of Finn I suspect I'd fall to my knees in gratitude.

I clear my throat, and it sounds a little like a dying animal. "That would be an improper thing to ask."

His grin gives way to a frown. "Since when?"

I force my eyes back on the pan. "Since I overcooked the asparagus."

With a lingering look and a little hum, Finn plucks a spear out of the pan and, blowing on it for a second, takes a bite.

"I'm not supposed to admit this, but I'm a damn big fan of overcooked asparagus. Don't tell my boss." He turns to the fridge and then rummages in a drawer for a knife. "Just needs a bit of lemon and you're golden."

He squeezes a lemon wedge over the pan and lifts a spear to my mouth, grinning as I chew. "Good, huh? So, what's this about, Jenna? You can't be trying to talk me into letting you drive the car, could you? Because you're gonna have to do a lot better than this Suzy Homemaker act."

"It's not an act," I say, lifting my chin. I fluff my skirt. "I'm an excellent cook, besides the asparagus. And I've become a lot tidier around the house with all your nagging."

"Uh-huh. Sure. What's with the…" He hooks a finger in the mock-turtleneck of my shirt and gives it a little tug.

I pat the collar back in place. "You don't like it?"

He gives a low laugh as he turns to peer into the oven, and I get the feeling that it's mostly to himself. "I think I'd like you in a clown suit, if that's what you wanted to wear."

Oh?

Should I have worn that tonight instead? I gaze down at my outfit. I know he likes the miniskirts and cropped tops, but this seemed like a good way to make him see me differently. As someone he could be with. Someone he might bring home to his dad one day.

Mercifully, the timer goes off and I busy myself looking for an oven mitt that Finn promptly plucks out of my hand.

"Fuck, that looks good. You nailed it, babe."

I stare anxiously at the golden dome of phyllo pastry he pulls from the oven. It seems to be coming apart near the bottom. "Do you think so? It was a little tricky to wrap…"

"Couldn't have done it better myself."

"You're a chef at an upscale restaurant."

"I said what I said."

Finn goes for a spatula and quickly I wave him away with a hand towel. "Let me do that. You're supposed to be sitting at the table, marveling at my culinary prowess."

"I'm marveling from here—"

CHAPTER 16

I jab him with the spatula. "Go. Sit."

He gives me a funny look. "If you think going all erratic is the way to get me to hand over the Wrangler, I've got news for you." He sheds his jacket on the way to the table, and I watch nervously as he eyes the candles, flames casting shadows over the wall. He sinks slowly in a chair.

I clear my throat, approaching the table with plates in hand and the most dignified smile I can muster, wishing there was a mirror somewhere in the room to make sure I'm doing it right.

Finn's eyes follow me as I take my seat. "Did Ronnie call or something?"

"What makes you say that?" I lay a napkin on my lap.

You are grace, and poise, and modesty.

"Oh, I don't know. Maybe the fact that you just sat down at the head of the table."

"I can't sit at the head of the table?"

"Sure, you can. Only, don't you think it's a tad strange that I'm also sitting at the head of the table? I can barely hear a word you're saying."

"You seem to be keeping up just fine. Besides, what's wrong with having a nice dinner from time to time? We can't always be eating off our laps, staining the sofa with hollandaise."

Finn tips his head, craning his ear towards me. "What was that? You're abstaining from soda over the holidays?"

I work hard to keep my mouth in its gentle smile, refusing to play into this comedy routine. Tonight's about showing Finn that I'm girlfriend material. That I can cook him amazing meals and engage him in thought-provoking conversation. I stand to pile food on his plate.

"Is this some weird attempt at practicing for your sister's wedding? It's definitely not the kind of role play I'm into, and the least you could have done was prep me on my character. At this point, the best I can do for you is Finnigan, the unwieldy wedding guest no one wanted to invite, except that I happen to be Aunt Henrietta's only kid and she'd have Ronnie's head on a spike if I weren't on the list."

"I don't have an Aunt Henrietta," I say, dropping back into my seat and cutting neatly through my slice of Wellington.

"Fortunately," he continues like he didn't hear me. "They've sat me in the corner and out of the way with our cousin Flavius, the failed politician who resigned in disgrace after confessing that he used your grandmother's inheritance to fund a mission to prove the earth was sucked into a black hole in 2012."

I blink. Finn blinks.

I'm trying not to laugh. He's waiting for me to lose that battle.

"According to Cousin Flavius," he goes on. "We've all been dead for eleven years. Only no one's noticed yet. Except him, of course."

The bite of Wellington hovers inches from my mouth. I curl my lips into my mouth and bite down hard to stifle my laugh.

"I like to think I would have noticed if I was dead," he says solemnly. He lets his eyes wander the length of the table between us. "Though I'm starting to think he might be onto something. This has to be some kind of weird death-dream, doesn't it? Jenna Carling in a turtleneck, sitting five feet away from me. Even if we aren't dead, I'm not quite sure I want to live in a world where Jenna Fucking Carling wears a strange turtleneck she felt the need to buy five minutes ago."

My stomach flips. He says *Jenna Fucking Carling* like he's talking about someone else. Some ancient mythical goddess, honored around the world with shrines and monuments.

I swallow, smoothing down the front of my shirt. "Jenna Fucking Carling has owned this turtleneck for years. Jenna Fucking Carling loves this turtleneck. It suits her."

"It's true. Everything suits Jenna Fucking Carling. But you have to admit it's reasonable that your sudden propensity for turtlenecks would raise a couple eyebrows."

"I've had this turtleneck for years."

He hums, contemplating me. "You won't mind it getting a little bit messy, then."

"Messy?"

With a slow blink and an innocent smile he slides a piece of phyllo dough off his plate and onto the table, and lines up his fingers behind it in a flicking

CHAPTER 16

position.

My eyes saucer. "You wouldn't."

He offers me the full breadth of his crooked smile. "Have you met me? Of course, I would. Now tell me what's going on with you, or this here piece of pastry will be the first in a long line of things making a mess of you tonight."

"Jenna Fucking Carling is impervious to mess—"

The piece of food hits me square in the chest in an explosion of crumbs. I stare down at myself, jaw dropping. "You wouldn't survive a second at a Carling family dinner—"

Splat.

This time, the piece of food carried a healthy serving of gravy that splatters all the way up to my chin.

"The day I survive a Carling family dinner is the day you'll know to check me into a wellness facility. And the day *you* survive one? Babe, that'll be the day I pack you up and ship us both to the other side of the world, until we've got enough time and miles between us and that insane family of yours for you to remember how much better off you are as the black sheep."

"Maybe I've decided I don't want to be the black sheep anymore." I go to flick my hair over my shoulder, only to brush away air as it sits in a tight bun on top of my head.

Finn watches the failed attempt with a tilt of his head. "Take that fucking hair tie out, or so help me God."

I lift my chin. "Or so help you God what, Finn?"

"Or so help me God, I'll take matters into my own hands." He gestures to the top of his head. "With the hair bun and that turtleneck. And don't even get me started on that damn skirt." He peers under the table and resurfaces, utterly scandalized. "Where have your legs gone?"

"Are you threatening to strip me down?"

That wasn't exactly lady-like. My mother would wither away if she ever heard me say something like that over dinner. But Finn's eyes flick to mine. And I watch it happen, watch the way heat cuts through play, the way his body stills. Like now that he thinks about it, now that I suggested it, there's nothing he'd rather do.

Finn rises with a slowly growing smile, so different than the playful ones he'd lobbed at me over the course of this disastrous dinner.

"Up," he says simply.

I've lost the ability to breathe. It might have something to do with the way my heart has picked up speed, inching up inside me so that it sits at the base of my throat.

"Make me."

His smile grows. It was the right answer.

"Tell me the truth," he says, voice low, gravelly as he stalks toward me. "Do you really want to be wearing this?"

I swallow. Shake my head.

"And you won't tell me why you put it on?"

I shake my head again.

Finn comes up behind me, dragging back my chair. "Get your arms up."

When I don't, he wrenches my arms over my head, and God, this night's completely gotten away from me because there sure as hell wasn't anything ladylike about that gasp. He leans over me, takes the hem of my shirt, and yanks it over my head.

Fuck. Cool air hits my body. He hasn't man-handled me like this since the night we touched ourselves in his bed. I missed it. I'm breathing so hard it's a little embarrassing, breasts rising and falling quickly.

Behind me, Finn takes a long breath like he's attempting to get a grip on himself. It doesn't seem to work. He circles me and crouches at my feet. Looks up at me with that look I love, the one he usually works hard to corral. The one that looks like he's a moment away from shoving me against a wall.

"Are you attached to this skirt, Jenna?"

My pussy clenches and it's painful. "Get rid of it."

He grips the bottom in two fists. And rips the silk from hem to waist.

Fuck.

With another hard yank, the waistband snaps. The skirt flutters down the sides of my chair, leaving me in a pale pink bra and panties that he takes in greedily, muscle in his jaw pulsing. I sink my teeth into my lip. He's already hard. His cock in an uncomfortable battle with the front of his jeans.

CHAPTER 16

I grip the sides of my chair, feeling like I'm seconds from toppling over. I don't know where this is going. I don't know what I'm allowed to do, with these boundaries in place. Finn looks at me like he's wondering the same thing. Whether he's really supposed to stop this now, even though I'm practically naked in front of him. My breasts heaving in his face, and the way the tiny triangle of pink folds a little into my pussy.

He lets a harsh breath hiss through his teeth. And he starts shaking his head. Over and over, without a word. His eyes still glued to mine like he's angry, accusing me of this, of making him do this, getting him here at my feet, making him rip my clothes off. My body vibrates, and the fingernails digging into the chair are no longer stopping me from falling. They're forcing me to stay put, to stop myself from lunging forward, tackling him to the ground. Grinding my pussy into that painful-looking bulge until we can't take it anymore.

And just as the silence starts to feel unbearable, just as I start losing my mind at the sound of our harsh breaths in the silent apartment, Finn moves. He reaches for my hair, fingers working to rid me of the elastic band.

"Don't ever pull this shit again," he tells me, hard eyes helping to deliver how much he means it. "The formal dinner. The fucking outfit. If it's for you, that's one thing. But this wasn't, so it sure as hell wasn't for me, either." My hair falls free from confinement, and I shake it out around my shoulders. "And when you doubt yourself again or forget who you are even for a second, you come to me. I'll remind you that you're Jenna Fucking Carling. Every. Single. Time."

The sweet words—the way they're delivered with a touch of frustration—punch a breathy whimper from my lungs. It fills the small space between our bodies. And before I can grasp onto that last fleeting thought about Scout's honors and friendships and boundaries, we pounce.

My hands lose their grip on the chair, his hands take me by the waist. In a second, Finn is flat on his back. He tugs me into his hips, and I shift around to find his erection, grinding into it. He groans a loud, desperate sound that echoes around us. Immediately he clamps his jaws like he regrets letting me hear it. But it's too late. I heard it, felt the wicked heat in my pussy at the sound, felt it down in my soul, and I need it again. I sweep the mess of hair off his forehead, threading it through my fingers and giving it a tug that incites another one.

"Kiss me," I say, without holding back the desperation in my tone.

I'm almost embarrassed by my train of thought. Because I'm convinced—absolutely sure—that the second we kiss, the moment he feels our lips connect, the slip of our tongues, he could no longer deny what we have. But he needs to be the one to do it. To decide he wants it.

His gaze slides away from mine, and he stares at my mouth. Breathing hard, his brows twist like he's suffering some brutal torture. He raises a hand and after a quivering second his fingers touch my lower lip. So light, it's barely there. I'm holding my breath. I expect him to say no. To pin me with that look he gets whenever we've come close to kissing before. Reproach. Regret. Utter desire.

This time, he drops his hand and says: "Okay."

My stomach clenches. "Okay? Just like that?"

"Just like that." A corner of his mouth ticks up. "Where do you want to be kissed?"

It takes me a moment to register the question and the meaning behind it. Like there's a whole slew of options and he's willing to explore any one of them.

I force calm into my voice. "I get to pick? That's very generous."

He flicks my hair over my shoulder. "I'm a giving guy."

"I wouldn't know."

His brows twitch. "Are you taunting me, Jenna?"

"Is it working?"

"Yeah. It's fucking working."

With a wicked smirk he doubles his grip on me and in a second he's flipped us around. He flattens me on my back and lands softly above me, with his knees on either side of my thighs, and his hands planted by my head.

It all crashes instantly inside me. Want, need, excitement. Nerves. A delicious concoction of emotion swirling in my stomach, speeding up my pulse. Compressing my lungs so that I breathe short, tight breaths.

CHAPTER 16

"You were naked the last time we were like this," he says quietly. "I think I like that better."

Finn sits back on his heels, running his hands down my thighs. His eyes, dark and smoldering, roam my body like they're feasting, causing little fires to ignite along my skin. I sink my teeth into my lip to stifle a whimper but also because I desperately need something to ground me.

"Maybe I'll kiss you here," he muses, punctuating his words with a soft brush along my calves. "Your legs are a real mile long."

"I always got teased for it," I say breathlessly. "My ex wouldn't let me wear heels because we'd be the same height."

Displeasure clouds his features. "Your ex is an idiot."

He comes down on his elbows again, pressing his hips into mine, pinning me down with his torso. His lips run along my jaw, and he smiles when I whimper. I'm clenching. Throbbing from head to toe, egged on by his hard body and the way my panties are wedged tight against my pussy.

"Look how good we fit together," Finn whispers. He punches his hips, and his cock presses right where I need it. He rocks back and forth and wrenches a moan from my chest. "I could kiss you while we fuck, without even trying."

I swallow heavily. "Would you do that?"

"Sometimes."

He runs his thumb over my lips and lifts onto his knees again. The sudden whoosh of air into my lungs feels as bad as it does good. Because I love the feel of him on top of me. I crave it again, so badly my hands shake at my sides. He knows it too. It's in the way his mouth stretches into a playful smirk as he drops his glance, studying my body. So calm and assured and brazen. He's toying with me. Reducing me to a needy mess the way he promised he'd do.

He pushes the straps of my bra off my shoulders. Slowly, he tugs it down the swell of my breasts. Torturing me with his pace until my nipples feel cool air. Finn takes me in with a harsh breath, like it's the first time he's seeing me this way.

"Other times I'd be kissing you here."

He runs a soft thumb between my breasts, trailing down over my bra, along the strip of skin above my panties. My body is flint, his thumb the match, and I'm on fire now. Scorching all the way through.

"Other times?" he says, as he hooks his fingers into the waistband of my panties. "I'd be kissing you there."

And he tugs, sliding them just under my ass.

Oh my God. Oh my God, oh my God, oh my—

I squirm. "Finn?"

"Yeah, babe?"

"Do I still get to pick? Where you kiss me?"

He lets out a soft laugh, and his eyes are nothing but trouble. "No, Jenna. You don't get to pick anymore."

It's the answer I wanted.

With another twitch of his lips, he drops. No hesitation, no teasing movements, just the sure, downward momentum of his mouth until finally it lands on my skin, over my nipple, a gentle, sweet, almost chaste kiss. There's nothing chaste about my moan. It's laced with need. A desperation to feel more. Finn pulls back to grin before dipping down again to lick and shifts his weight to bring a hand to my other breast. He cups it firmly. Grazes my nipple with his thumb, mimicking the same light circles he draws on the other with his tongue. Pinching when he sinks his teeth. Squeezing when he sucks. I squirm underneath him. The sounds I'm making are blatantly obscene.

Because it's so good—really good—the kind of good this has never been before. I can't tell whether it's because of what he's doing or because it's him doing it. He flicks the tip of his tongue, licks me with the flat of it. The way every nip sends a wicked tingle shooting down my torso, right to my pussy, there's a real chance, an actual chance—

Finn looks up and maybe I should feel embarrassed by the kind of moan the eye contact gets out of me, but I don't.

"Can you come like this, Jenna?" he murmurs over my skin. He runs soft lips on the side of my breast, licking underneath it before moving to the other one.

"Not—" I swallow, trying to form the words. "Not usually. But Finn, I need you to—I really, really need—"

CHAPTER 16

"Tell me." His voice is thick. Suddenly urgent. Eyes greedy. "Tell me what you want, Jenna."

I trail my hand down between our bodies, showing him where I need him to be.

Blue eyes meet mine. "Say it. You have to say it. Because right now, my brain's screaming at me to quit before we cross another line. And I really need you to overrule it. Tell me what you want from me and I'll give it to you."

I pant. God, the things I want from him... But he has to be the one to choose to fuck me. I won't push him into it.

"Put your fingers in me. Touch me. Make me come."

His shoulders sag in relief. I let him pull my hand away from my pussy, push it into the hardwood in a non-verbal command, *keep it here*. His gaze flicks up to watch me as he slides his fingers over my clit.

"Like this?"

He just let me glimpse it. The reason women line up to have him. Finn doesn't touch me with arrogance, like he already knows exactly what I like, how to give it to me. He wants to give me what *I* want. How I like it, how I want to take it.

He trails wet kisses up my body—my chest, over my shoulder, along my neck. He hovers with his face over mine, and studies every shift in me as he makes perfect little circles with his fingers on my clit. Pushing down when I tell him *harder*, and speeding up when I tell him *more, I need more*. And then dialing it back just when it starts to feel too much, without hearing me say so.

"Please," the word bursts from my lips. "Please—Finn, please—"

I don't even know, exactly, what I'm begging for. But Finn seems to be about a hundred steps ahead of me because his fingers slide lower. He groans as he slips inside me, twisting his fingers, pushing down, adding a finger, filling me up.

"Fuck, Jenna," he says, teeth clenched, brows twisting. He drives his fingers in and out of me, tantalizingly slow. "You have no idea how long I've wanted you like this. You have no idea how good this feels."

"I'm not even… You're not even—" In the back of my mind I know I should be reaching for him. Doing *anything* to him. I give a feeble attempt at reaching for his cock, still buried in his jeans, but then his fingers hit me with more pressure as he drags them inside me and I— "There," I choke out, feeling almost delirious with pleasure. "Like that. Please, Finn. Please make me come—"

And now that he's figured it out, he doesn't stop. Pushing his fingers in and out of my pussy in slow, shallow strokes. Both my hands are tangled in his hair, and I feel it starting, that tremor deep inside. He must feel it around his fingers because he shifts back onto his heels and puts his other hand to work. Thumb grazing my clit in that perfect way, just like I asked, and everything blurs around me as pleasure rises my spine. My hips start moving and he lets me set the pace as I start fucking his hand.

"Ohmygodfinn." It comes out like a single, slurred word. "Feels so good."

"For me too." With heavy lids, he watches the way his fingers move over me, in me. "I love feeling you. I love your body. Those *sounds*, Jenna. Your fucking sounds—"

I moan. It's the way he's touching me, but it's the words too. It's *him*. "Come here. Come closer."

He leaves his fingers inside me, fucking me in the same rhythm my hips moved before they stilled underneath him. He reaches for one of my hands and brings it down to my clit, watching as I take over rubbing myself before planting his hand by my head so that he hovers over me.

I can't pinpoint the exact moment something heavy settles in my lungs. But it's there now as I gaze at him. I take in the hunger in his eyes and the soft smile he gives me like he's having a moment too as he touches me, even though I'm not touching him. Finn dips to kiss my forehead and gives a hum of encouragement against my skin when I let out a tight whimper, until finally I shatter. Burst into tiny fragments that land in a heaping, disheveled pile on the floor. He keeps up his effort all the way through my orgasm, letting me shake into his hand, clench around his fingers until finally I'm limp, made of nothing but skin and air.

"You look so fucking incredible when you come," he mutters, kissing my neck as I gasp desperately for air. He combs flyaway hairs back with his free hand, the other still fucking me but slowing down its strokes as I start to come together again, vision starts to come back into focus. "I'd give up everything to do this for you every minute of the day. To make you feel this good and get those sweet little sounds out of you."

His fingers keep pumping into me, soft and soothing, giving me a point of focus as I try to regain myself. I'm still trying to take a single calm breath. My head is a jumbled mess of words, and all I can do is move between us, grappling with the waistband of his jeans.

Finn stops me, pulling my hands away. Still thrusting gently into me and I wonder now whether it's a tactic to keep me useless, boneless beneath him. I give a weak moan.

"Don't worry about me. I want you to come again, baby. Can you do that for me?"

I want to, badly. But there's one single thing I want more right now.

I want his body, yes. But more than anything I need to feel closer to him. To have him open himself up and stop holding back from me. Taking a deep, calming breath, I reach for his wrist and pull the length of his fingers out of my pussy. God, even that. Even that felt unbelievably good. So good I slide him back in, once, twice, whimpering desperately as I pull him right out. I push him upright by the shoulders, and meet him on his knees. He slips the fingers he'd just had inside me into his mouth as he watches me unclasp the bra he'd slid down, pull up the panties still around my thighs.

"If you tell me you don't want it, I will let this go in a second," I tell him, and he swallows heavily. "And it's not about returning favors or feeling like I owe you one. I want to touch you. To make you feel as good as you make me feel."

Finn closes his eyes, lets out a sharp breath. "What are you doing to me, Jenna?"

I don't think he's asking about *this*, what I'm offering him. But before I can probe him for more, he drops his hands to his waistband and unzips his pants. I shuffle forward, and he lets me take over. Reach into his pants, run my fingers along his cock. He's loud from the very first touch, groans echoing around us.

"Please, baby. Go easy on me. I'm only hanging on by a thread."

I feel them there, again. The words behind the words. With his head thrown forward he watches me stroke his cock, jimmying down his pants to his knees. I gather his shirt in my fists and he lets me tug it over his head. When he surfaces from underneath it his eyes are so open, almost vulnerable as he looks at me.

I've missed this. Not blowing a guy—though I've always had a bit of a thing for it, and most of the time I have sex I'd rather do it than not. I missed *him* like this. Like those minutes he gave me in his bed the night we touched ourselves, not a single wall in sight.

"Tell me you want it," I say.

He nods. This jerky, frantic one. "Yeah. I want you."

I want you.

I have no idea if he's said it on purpose, or if he even realizes those were the words that came out of him. It doesn't even matter. Finn looks at me desperately now, chest heaving. All I want is to make him feel wanted. To show him how much I care about him.

I drop down on one hand and feel his entire body melt as I stroke him again, slow, firm, feeling his harsh breaths like I'm breathing them myself. Finn leans forward and he's touching me everywhere. Stroking my cheek, my shoulder, fingertips brushing my spine. He reaches for a handful of my ass, groaning in relief like he's given himself permission to do something he's been thinking about a while. He cups my breasts from where he kneels, and I don't know if his sounds are from feeling my body or the way I'm pumping his cock with my fist, but it sounds so pure, so him, that I can't take another second of this.

I don't have it in me to tease him—to lick him. I dip the tip of his cock into my mouth and we give simultaneous moans. Finn leans back to watch, mouth ajar, head tilted, as I play with the tip of his cock, sliding it over my tongue. He murmurs a stream of deep *fucks* and *yeahs* and *babys* that make me so hot my hips squirm.

I want to keep watching him but he looks so perfect right now, dazed,

CHAPTER 16

delirious, eyes so dark, that it almost distracts me. And so I close my eyes and take him in deeper. Moving wetly over his cock, licking, drawing back, taking another inch on the way down, hitting my own fist as I stroke him.

"I wish you could see yourself right now," Finn grinds out. "You're so damn sexy it hurts. God, your mouth was made for this."

My entire body flushes at the words, and if I had any more hands I'd have one on myself, rubbing my pussy because God... The way he looks at me, those desperate groans, the stream of curses he lets out that melt seamlessly into my name, they do something so wicked to me. I'm aching for him again. I'm aching for him to get as much as he just gave me when I take my hand away. I grip his hips and ease my mouth down further and further until he taps the back of my throat, once, twice.

"Jesus fuck," he gasps. "Fuck Jenna, you're so good. So fucking good."

I'm a mess now. I can feel the wetness around my mouth, my chin, the strands of hair sticking to my face but a glance up shows me Finn's enjoying this view, eyes wide and hungry and I can feel how close he is—

"Jenna," he says urgently, combing back the hair sticking to my mouth. "What do you want me to do, baby? I'm about to come."

I stop. Slide him almost all the way out, toying with his tip and then freeing him so that he sits on the edge of my mouth. I look up silently and he already understands. He knows what I want, what I've been dying to give him since he asked me for a taste of it that night in his bed.

Finn lets out a shaky breath. "I'm not gonna last. I fuck this mouth and I'm not gonna be able to hold back."

"I can take it," I tell him, licking him.

"*Fuck*, you're so hot," he groans. He threads his fingers in my hair, bracing my head, and I drop my hands from his hips. "All the way in?"

I nod. "Every bit."

Finn surges forward, dragging his cock along my tongue, all the way, and it's a half-choke, half-groan he gives me now. If he keeps this up I might come just from his sounds. He pumps his cock in and out of my mouth, hitting me deep every time. Fingers clenching my hair, looking like he's in pain. My eyes start to water but fuck, it feels incredible, having him turn himself over to me like this. He keeps his promise. Another thrust, another groan, and he's coming inside me. I can't help but look at him as I swallow, take in the blissful torture on his face, loving the way his grip on me changes from firm to gentle, as he strokes soothingly through my hair.

I don't move until he's ready to leave my mouth, until he slips out and brings me up with fingers at my chin.

"Is there any part of you that isn't fucking perfect?" he asks ruefully, his gaze tracing over me. His fingers clean me up.

When he talks to me like that—when he looks at me like that, it doesn't feel like it. I do feel perfect. Like I was created in a collective effort by every god worshiped on earth.

Finn presses his lips to my forehead. And just like that the painful heat searing between my legs transforms into something light and fluttery. It rises through my stomach, lungs, and up my throat. I feel full in a way I can barely comprehend. In a way that makes it impossible to speak.

With a soft smile, Finn rises. Crosses to the living room where a basket of fresh laundry sits on the sofa. He roots around it as I watch, and it's funny. Once upon a time I'd look at him and catalog the way his ass looks in those jeans. The way his muscles ripple over his shoulders as he moves. The sun-tanned skin I crave a taste of, want to kiss all over.

I still see all that—except it's all through this rosy filter now. That's the backside of a man who's never let me down. Those are the shoulders of the person who lifts me up when I feel like I've crashed and burned.

That's the man I've fallen in love with, turning to hand me a large black t-shirt with a flush over his cheeks. His eyes watch me carefully as I take in what he's given me. It's his shirt, the one he wore at the baseball diamond with the name Palmer laid out across the back.

I lift my gaze. I can't tell which emotion I'm supposed to grasp out of the way he looks at me. Sheepish. Guarded. Possessive. I don't know which I'm supposed to focus on, and so I slip the shirt on instead, letting my hair pepper over my shoulders.

Finn stares down at me for a long moment, so still I don't think he's breathing. Then he fiddles with his glasses, pushing them up his nose.

CHAPTER 16

"Would you sleep in my bed tonight?"

There's something so vulnerable in the way he says it. A piece of my heart chips away.

"Okay," I tell him.

"All night this time?"

Another chip. I stand, comb my fingers through his hair. His eyelids drop, in the way a cat might sink into an embrace.

"All night this time."

Chapter 17

Finn

Mrs. Jenkins from apartment 511 gives me a look as she unlocks her door.

It takes me a second to realize why: I seem to be whistling what I determine to be a Metallica song, which isn't really whistling down the hall material. I also don't know when it is I became someone who whistles in the first place. At my door, I adjust my hat and scratch at a dried-up dribble of sauce on my shirt.

It's past midnight. I'm about to head into my own apartment, and there isn't a single good reason I should care how I look.

Inside, Jenna sings along with the Smashing Pumpkins so loud I can hear every single word from out here. Something searing hot rises in my throat, and I swallow it down. Weird.

"Hey, Jenna Bear," I call into the apartment, toeing off my sneakers.

The music is so loud she doesn't hear me, and when I emerge into the living room I'm greeted to the sight of her cross-legged on the floor. There's no nonsense from yesterday. She's herself again in the pink spandex shorts she likes to wear, hair down, brushing over the shirt with my last name splashed across the back.

I don't know what possessed me to give her that shirt. But it felt right, in the aftermath of what we did.

CHAPTER 17

God, last night.

It's strange. I've done a lot more, with a whole lot of women. But none of that felt the way it did last night. That? It wasn't fucking, or fingering, or whatever the hell someone might call it. It felt like coming into a whole new plane of existence. Where all that mattered was giving her what she needed. I just wanted her to feel good. Physically, but about herself too. And I know it was a mistake, letting her touch me. I know it'll make this crush that much harder to get over. But it wasn't in me to hold back.

"Jenna," I try again, only a little louder.

She still doesn't hear me, so I let myself soak her in openly. In an alternate world, I'd walk right into our living room, bring her to her feet, and sink into the kind of kiss that would levitate us to a layer of the atmosphere not yet known to mankind. I'd pull her onto that sofa and spoon her so tight she'd think I was nuts. And I'd be able to admit to her that I am a little nuts, at least when it comes to her. Whenever she gives me that single dimple I feel the sanity seep right out of me. But in that alternate universe Mom would be alive, Dad wouldn't be a broken man taped up with grief, and we'd be heading to see them for brunch in the morning.

As if sensing my attention Jenna turns, chin grazing her shoulder. And there it is. That dimple, beckoning me closer as she cuts the music.

"You're home," she says. She seems to be surrounded by a strange sea of tiny white boxes and ribbon I didn't notice until now, and she pushes it all out of the way to make room for me.

I cup her cheek and bring her in for a forehead kiss. "I'm home. What's all this?"

"These got delivered on your doorstep a couple hours ago, shortly followed by a phone call from Ronnie asking if I could help put together her wedding favors, as though I could easily figure out how to return all this stuff and say no."

I swear, I've developed PTSD from hearing her sister's name. Unfamiliar rage immediately starts boiling in my stomach whenever she says it. I sink to the ground and pick up what I realize is a piece of individually wrapped chocolate, with...

I squint down at the square. "Is that…"

Jenna drops some chocolate into a miniature white box. "My sister's face? Yes."

"And is that…"

She sticks a lid over the box and tops it with a neat little bow. "A much smaller version of my future brother-in-law's face? Yes."

I wrinkle my nose. "Why is it we're making these? Don't you all have enough money to have these done for you?"

She gives a little smile. "We do. The only reason I can come up with is that it's been a solid couple of weeks since Ronnie adequately tortured me. She didn't bother to explain, obviously."

I reach for a box, filling it with a piece of chocolate and mimicking the way she ties some ribbon around it, making a little bow on top. "And how many of these things are we making?"

"I'm trying to get to a hundred tonight. That's what the wine is for." She indicates a glass by her knee when I look at her, alarmed. "You'd be doing me a massive favor."

"Give me that." I take her glass and polish it off in two swallows flat, getting up to grab the whole bottle from the kitchen. "I don't mind doing you a solid, but this is such a sad way to spend our Saturday night."

"Sunday morning," she corrects.

That ache in my throat is back. I don't know why. She waits up for me every night. And still, every time I come home to her lounging on that sofa feels like being offered the sweetest treat after a long, listless day at work. Even better than how the Frankencake turned out.

"If I ever get married," Jenna says with her eyes on the bow she's tying. "Remind me to pay Ronnie back for this. She can pull loose petals for the flower girls one-by-one."

"Oh, I approve of this payback. She can single-handedly tear-down the room at the end of the night."

Jenna groans. "That happens to be one of my duties next week. Is it too much to hope for that she recruited the other bridesmaids, too?"

"Doubt she did," I say, pulling a face. "Give me a call when the wedding's over. I'll come dressed in my best busboy getup and help you."

With her chin tucked like that, the smile she gives me looks so sweet I want to pull her into my lap and tuck her under my chin and—

Get a grip, Palmer.

"Can I ask you something?" I ask instead, rubbing at the burning feeling in my throat. "It's been eating away at me for weeks."

"Of course, you can."

Jenna doesn't even look up from her box, like there isn't even a question that she'd tell me whatever it is I want to know, and the burning is downright uncomfortable now. I clear my throat, trying to loosen it.

"Why do you try so hard with Ronnie? She definitely hasn't earned it. And I have a hard time believing she'd lift a finger for you."

Jenna contemplates the finished favor in her hand, rattling the little chocolate inside. "You know, I've asked myself this about a hundred times since I came back into town."

"And what'd you come up with?"

"It's a little sad. And a lot pathetic."

I nudge her knee with mine. "You can tell me."

"I know," she says with a smile. "I think what it comes down to is misguided optimism. Maybe she and I don't get along. But she's family, and I *want* to get along with her, no matter how different we are. I never want it said that I didn't try hard enough to make things better between us. Working overtime on her wedding seems like a very opportune olive branch."

"Would be great if she put in the same effort. Or any effort."

"It would be," she nods, "but they're a different kind of people, she and my mom. It's never been in them to throw themselves at someone's feet like this. If I don't try, no one will."

I realize I'm crushing the white box in my hand, and work to smooth out the corners with a sigh. "Look, if getting along with her is important to you, you know I'm on board. I'll make as many of these tacky little boxes as you need me to, and I'll stuff down so many salted caramel cupcakes we'll soon be on the market for bigger pairs of pants. I'll do anything you need if you understand something, okay? You, of all people, don't need to try that hard to make someone love you. You're as good as it gets, Jenna. If someone, somehow, doesn't sink to their knees and beg to be part of your life, it's their loss. Not yours."

She breathes out this quick, mirthless chuckle.

"You think I'm wrong?"

She drops her eyes and something ugly rears its head inside me.

I need a list.

A list of every sorry person who doesn't fall in love with this woman within seconds of meeting her. I'll wrangle them all and drive them straight to the asylum. We can't have these kinds of people running rampant in the streets. It's bad for the rest of us.

Not that—I'm not in love with her or anything. It's… a metaphor. Or something.

I'm about to demand more information when she shrugs. "Anyway, you're right. Roles reversed, Ronnie would fill every one of these boxes with kitty litter. Remind me to seat her at the very back of my wedding. Maybe in a different room altogether."

That ache is just painful now. "You want to get married, then?"

"I do. I can only keep up the *men are only good for sex* angle for so long until the facade crumbles. At the end of day, I'm just like every other girl dreaming of a nice shiny ring, a hot stud, and white picket fence to come home to."

I hesitate. Don't even know why I'm asking any of this. "Kids?"

She coils some ribbon around her finger. "I could go either way."

I nod, picking compulsively at the corner of the finished box in my hand. Jenna Carling, married. To… some guy.

I've never been a jealous person. It's one thing to watch her harmlessly flirt with idiots at a bar. But her words inspire me to launch a one-man mission to ward away anyone who comes within spitting distance of her. I'm not above petty sabotage, apparently. Not when she's throwing around a concept like marriage.

"Are you grossed out by the thought of me playing the blushing bride? I thought we didn't judge." She pokes my cheek just as I mentally impale her

CHAPTER 17

would-be husband with a long, gleaming sword I definitely don't own. So much for petty sabotage.

I shake my head, shedding my glasses to rub my eyes. "I'm having a hard time picturing you married to someone."

The motherfucker gets to his feet, pulls my sword out of his chest, and tackles me to the ground.

"Because no one would want to wife-up a girl who wears skirts like I do?"

Huh?

I shove my glasses on with so much force I think it'll leave a bruise. I narrow my eyes, trying to make sense of what I'm seeing. Why Jenna's looking at a spot on the ground, blinking fast. Her shoulders deflate and I think this is it. I'm about to throw up the entire contents of my stomach right here, on Ronnie's wedding favors.

She thinks...

Jenna Carling—Jenna Fucking Carling thinks she lives in a world where people wouldn't line up around the length of the equator just for a sorry shot at being with her? It's so insane I'd laugh, if I wasn't so dangerously close to vomiting. And then I realize where this must be coming from.

"The day I meet your sister—actually, scratch that. Don't ever let me meet your sister. It would be a fucking catastrophe."

She gives a weak chuckle, same as the one from a few minutes ago. Busying her fingers with ribbon.

"Jenna, look at me." I shimmy closer. Close enough to catch this funny hitch in her breath when I sweep the hair off her shoulder. "Baby, look at me."

She won't and so I do it for her. I lift her chin and my entire body spasms painfully when I see how pink her eyes have become.

"Jenna, I have a hard time picturing you getting married because I wouldn't have you to myself anymore. And I have a hard time accepting that there's a guy out there who's worthy of my dream girl."

There. They're out there. The words I never meant to let out, except that this girl—my girl—*this* girl—seems to be deeply confused about who she is, and it's not acceptable.

I feel the heat in my cheeks. I see the heat in hers, darkening the longer she looks at me. Confused and hesitant. Skeptical in a way I can't stand.

"Finn. When you say things like that..." She loses steam. Strips the hair tie from her wrist and gathers up a ponytail high on her head. Grabs the wine bottle and takes a long swig, handing it to me when she finishes. I do the same.

"You don't believe in love?"

The question throws me off. I don't know where it's coming from, and so I'm fairly certain I stare at her like she's asked me to decode an equation so outlandish even Einstein would balk. Carefully, I set the wine bottle next to me.

"Of course, I believe in love. I absolutely believe in love."

"Then I don't understand. How are you so against everything that goes with it? I get not wanting to be married. It's not for everyone. But saying unequivocally you want to end up alone... I don't get it."

I rub a hand back and forth along my jaw, staring off at the wall. The question was bound to come at some point. Still, it takes me a while to line up the right words. This conversation is starting to feel unsteady. Already I'm saying things I shouldn't. I could easily come up with some line of bullshit about the merits of casual sex, of keeping yourself open, unattached.

But this is Jenna, and I don't bullshit with her.

"My parents had an incredible relationship. An incredible marriage. There wasn't a week that went by when we were kids that we didn't get shipped off to our grandparents for a night, so that they could get some time alone. They worked constantly at their relationship. And still, after all that... It's tomorrow. The anniversary of her death."

"Finn."

"It's okay," I say quietly, shaking my head when she makes a move toward me. She sits on her hands, like that's how bad the urge is to touch me. "I'm not telling you this for sympathy. It was... They were the best role models for love I could have asked for, you know? They fought a lot, don't get me wrong. I can't tell you how many times I watched them both screw up, say or do the wrong thing. But they always fought like they knew it didn't really matter. That their love was this ultimate, untouchable thing. And that no matter how bad they fucked up, it wouldn't change a thing between them. It was that way until my mom died."

"And you don't think you can find that?"

"That's the thing. Seeing everything that comes with it—the joy but the pain, too—it can make you realize it's not the right life for you."

I'm not sure any of that made sense. But Jenna looks at me like I've dropped all the answers in her lap, anyway. "You don't think you'll get lonely?"

Does she ever picture it? That alternate universe where we're something we're not? It's a nice one. I never feel lonely when I'm there.

"I do feel that way sometimes. *Did* feel that way. Until I got a roommate," I admit with a smile. "That's why I need you to find a guy who can stand having me around. Promise me I get vetting privileges. I'll find you that hot stud with enough money to buy you a nice big castle with a guest house that I'll beg you to live in, and you'll have to say yes because I'll have been the one to introduce you. It's my big master plan, see?"

Her mouth pinches into a tight smile. "Your big master plan is marrying me off to someone else?"

"You want to be married; I'll make it happen." The words feel like shattered glass coming out of my mouth. "That's how this works, Jenna Bear. Don't think I haven't noticed this leash you somehow managed to get on me." I pretend to tug at a collar around my neck.

The joke doesn't land. That lackluster smile fades off her face. "And what if that's not what I want?"

"You just said you wanted to be married—"

"What if I don't want someone else?"

The burning in my throat has reached unbearable levels. I take a second to try to swallow it down. And another second, when it doesn't work. Jenna's cheeks are flaming red and I think I might be missing something.

"I don't... I'm not sure where you're going with this."

"Aren't you?"

I shake my head. I don't even register that we're staring at each other until her expression starts to morph. It goes from soft to something hard.

Determined. There's a pep talk going on in her head, and I wish she'd voice the words so that I could help her with it, whatever she's working through.

Seems she doesn't need me. She moves to sit on her knees. Squares her shoulders. "I need to ask you about something."

There's a prickle at the back of my neck, and the hairs on my arms rise. Something's happening here, but I can't put my finger on it, so I say: "Anything."

Jenna sucks in a breath. "The forehead kisses. What are they about?"

"You don't like them?"

"I love them." She takes in the color in my cheeks. "What do they mean?"

My stomach drops. "It's a friendly greeting between friends."

Jenna contemplates me. "I don't believe you."

I stare back silently. Is this what it feels like? To have the gavel come down, declaring you guilty of all the sins you've ever tried to cover?

Jenna looks at me like she's seeing something I can't. Like it's something she's been searching for, and there it is. Finally.

"Jenna, I'm not sure what's going on—"

"I need to tell you something."

Suddenly I'm freezing cold. Whatever this is, it can't be good. Why else would she be looking at me like that, like she's expecting me to self-combust? I scan her from head to toe, looking for an answer. And just as the anticipation starts to kill me, she opens her mouth.

"Finn, I'm... I have feelings for you," she confesses in a rush.

Oh, thank God.

My relief is so intense I laugh, almost falling back flat on the hardwood. "Oh. *That*. You just scared the shit out of me, Jenna Bear. Honestly, thanks for bringing this up. This weird crush thing has been eating away at me for ages too, and I haven't been able to figure out how to squash it. But two heads are better than one, right? What are you thinking? How do we fix it?"

Her lips pop open, and a gust of air releases from her lungs. "You... *Ages*?"

I rub the back of my neck. "Yeah. Is that bad? It's bad, huh?"

"Finn. How long is ages?"

I frown, thinking. "A few weeks, at least. Maybe... A little after you moved in?"

"*Weeks*? That's not weeks, Finn. Summer's almost over," she says, aghast. She looks around the apartment, as though she'll find an audience to share in her disbelief.

"I swear, I've been meaning to work on it—"

"*Finn*," she says, eyes growing wider by the second. "I'm not trying to squash it. I'm telling you I have feelings for you, and that I want to be more than friends."

Oh… What is that?

Why does it feel like I'm both levitating and a second from throwing up? Why did everything go kind of blurry just now?

What's with this goddamn burning in my throat, and how do I make it stop?

"It's… It's frustration," I tell her, frowning. "I feel it too. We've been flirting and I've been touching you when I shouldn't. It's the hormones talking."

"It's not frustration." Jenna shuffles forward on her knees, grips my forearms. "I'm saying I have feelings for you, Finn. And maybe this thing with you started with sex, but it stopped being about that a while ago. I love how we are. I love who I am with you, and I love how you don't let me get away with hiding the parts of me I've been told over and over I should lose, before I never manage to find someone who'll love me back. I'm telling you that you make me feel good, way beyond the physical stuff."

I shake my head. Over and over like it'll help disperse her words from the air as they come for me, try to sink into my skin. Try to make me hope, believe there's a happily ever after at the end of this. She's wrong, anyway. She's letting a simple crush get the best of her.

"Is it…" I look around the room, feeling a sheen of sweat build at my temples. "It's kind of hot in here, right? Did you lower the A/C?"

"Finn."

"It's not me, Jenna," I tell her, heart pounding. "These people have fucked with your head so bad you'd feel this way about anyone who made you see how much you're worth."

"It is you. It's how playful you are, how unabashedly yourself you are with me. It's the way you back me unconditionally. The way you're my biggest cheerleader, even when I don't feel like I deserve one—and I hope you know I'm that for you too. Finn, it's how you put together stories in your head, and you don't bother trying to tame them or package them all pretty before letting them out—"

"I'm a rambler. I ramble. It's a fault. Everyone says so—"

"I love listening to you. So much."

My hands seem to be shaking. They also don't seem to belong to me. In fact, I can't seem to feel my body anymore. "It'll pass. Jenna, it'll pass. We've been spending all our time together. It's natural to get confused about our feelings."

Her face falls and I want to die. "You want it to pass?"

If only I could get a fucking breath into my lungs. I lift a hand to the base of my neck, trying to rub the lump away. "What's... There's something wrong with my throat. I think I'm coming down with something. There's something in there."

Her brows furrow, and her eyes skate over my face. "A... Like a lump in your throat?"

"Yeah. Do you have it, too? What do you think it is?"

She gives a shocked chuckle, and I watch a soft smile take over her face. "Tell me about it. When does it hurt?"

Yes. Thank you. She'll know what to do about this lump. She's Jenna. She can do anything.

"I think we need an air purifier. Something better than that pink salty lamp," I tell her, gesturing around the room. "It only happens at home. Like the other night, while we were watching *Seinfeld*. You said something, or... I think you laughed, actually. And it got pretty bad there for a second. I think it's contagious. Maybe you gave it to me by accident."

Her cheeks flush, and she closes her eyes a moment. "Maybe I did. When else does it happen?"

I clear my throat again, but it doesn't help any. "Sometimes... You do this slurping sound when you drink coffee that's too hot, but you can't wait to take a sip."

"Do I?" She presses her lips together, and at least one of us finds this funny. This could be fatal.

"Look, I think we need to get to a doctor," I tell her, and I'm on my feet before I realize I've decided to stand. "This is weird right? It shouldn't be happening."

She hasn't moved. She looks up at me like we're somewhere different. Like we're surrounded by fluffy, pastel clouds, and not talking about some disease running rampant in our apartment.

"I have it too," she says at last. "That lump in my throat. And I want to keep it."

I narrow my eyes. "You can't just live your life like this—"

"I can if you let me. That lump, Finn? It only happens when I'm with you. It's proof that what I feel for you isn't just some crush I can squash. It tells me that my feelings... They're big and they're not going away. And I think that's what your lump is trying to tell you about me."

I'm cold again. That's not...

Not possible.

It's just a crush. It's a crush. It's—

"*Fuck.*"

Something hopeful flares in her eyes. "What?"

I point a lightly trembling finger at her. "I didn't want to feel like this. I've spent my entire adult life making sure I don't feel this. And now look."

She goes still. "Look at what?"

I throw out my arms. "Isn't it obvious?"

She stares, and the fucking irony of my words isn't lost on me but I reach for my chest, curling my fingers as though to reach inside. "You're in here and I don't know what to do with it."

Why did I tell her that? Why did I let those words out?

Why does she look like she's melting, her entire body softening at my feet?

Maybe it's from the weight of the words, what I'm begging her for. To help me make sense of all this. To make it stop. To make me believe it could actually work, that I could live out the rest of my days with her, that I'd never lose her.

She stands slowly. "Don't do anything. Let me stay, Finn. Keep me there."

I make a choking sound, backing away from her. "You will stay. That's the problem, isn't it? I'm going to end up like him."

"Like your dad? Something happened to him after you lost your mom, didn't it?" She closes the gap between us, taking my hands again. "You don't have to go through tomorrow alone. Let me help."

Help? I've lived ten of these days. They should be a breeze by now.

So why does her help sound like the lifeline I didn't know I needed?

Why does the way her hair falls across her cheek make me want to weep? Why does that single freckle under her eye make me feel like I can scale a fucking mountain, no training required? Why does that crease in the center of her lower lip make me want to sink to my knees and beg her to cocoon me in bed with her?

Why can't I make sense of a single damn thing anymore?

"It's not a crush?" I ask her, just to be sure. She'd tell me the truth.

She gives me a soft smile. "I don't think so."

"The lump is a good thing?"

She touches my cheek. "Yeah. It's a good thing."

"Does yours hurt?"

"Mine feels really good."

"I don't... I'm sorry. I don't understand."

I don't even know what I'm referring to at this point. My mind is a hurricane.

It's not a crush.

Of course it's not a crush, you idiot. Everyone's been trying to tell you.

Am I... What does it feel like to be in love?

Suddenly, I'm exhausted. My body feels like it weighs more than I'm capable of carrying. I think she can tell. I don't realize I've backed into the wall until Jenna moves to pull me off it and leads me into my bedroom. She maneuvers me so that I sit on the edge of the bed, standing just out of reach.

Look at her. Of course it's not just a crush. How could it be?

She laid herself bare for me tonight and all I returned was an emotional

CHAPTER 17

meltdown. Still, she's not shuffling her feet, not clasping her hands together. She looks me right in the eye.

She's a badass.

She's a woman who maybe—fucking *finally*—understands how incredible she is. How capable she is. How much she deserves.

"I have feelings for you," Jenna tells me again. "What you said to me, Finn? What you feel when I laugh or… Or when I make that slurping sound I really wish you pointed out before now, because I had no idea I did that, and it's really kind of gross—" She breathes out a laugh and despite my catatonic state I hear one slip from my lips, too. "Maybe you're not ready to accept what that feeling is, or what it means. But I love the way we are, and I want it for real. I want the titles. I want the white picket fence with you. And I'm willing to wait until you're ready."

"What if I'm never ready?"

She smiles. Actually fucking *smiles*. This sweet one, free of accusation or resentment. "I'm going to choose to believe you will be. I'm going to choose to wait you out. You're worth it."

She takes my chin between her fingers, lifting my face, and I feel like an empty, starved man staring up at the god who can deliver me from this torment, waiting for salvation. And then she bends, puts a kiss on my forehead, and I'm fucking spiraling. A good kind of spiral. A bad kind of spiral. I don't know anymore.

Am I awake?

She turns to go and I lunge, catching her by the wrist. "Stay. Stay with me. Sleep here."

Without a word she finds herself a t-shirt in my dresser, and hands me a pair of sweats. We shed our clothes in silence without taking our eyes off each other. In a past life, I couldn't get through something like this without the urge to pin her underneath me, but I don't feel any of that. It doesn't feel empty, though. It feels like seeing each other for the first time. Acknowledging the stuff we've kept tucked deep.

She has feelings for me. Big ones that won't go away.

Mine won't pass. That's the truth, isn't it? They're here to stay. What do I do with them?

In the dark, I let my hand wander across the mattress until it finds hers.

"Jenna," I barely recognize my own voice.

She squeezes my hand. "Yeah?"

"You make it really hard, sometimes. Convincing myself I can live without you."

She doesn't say anything. She moves, shuffles around until she's tucked herself against me, her back to my chest. And sleep finds me in an instant.

Chapter 18

Finn

I squeeze my eyes against the morning light, willing myself to fall back asleep.

To pass out until tomorrow, skip this day in its entirety. To be able to stay like this, with Jenna. The small spoon to my big spoon, letting me squeeze her to me like I'm trying to absorb her into my body.

I want to turn her over and set my eyes on her sweet face. But I don't dare move. I want to keep her asleep, avoid that moment she'll inevitably have when her eyes open, and she remembers how bad I let her down last night. How much I must have hurt her. I'd deserve it if she tried to sneak out of here, thinking I'm asleep. I'd only have myself to blame if she packed up her room, moved out of our home, and never gave me the time of day again. I wouldn't blame her one bit.

I think I lost her last night. Never thought today could get any worse. Mom would have given me so much shit for leaving her hanging like that.

But Mom's not here, is she? I'm free to screw up my life however I damn well want. God, I need to fall back asleep. Just until tomorrow.

Jenna shifts and too soon she turns her head and peeks over her shoulder. She watches me carefully with those clear blue eyes, as open and inviting as the sky on a perfect summer's day. I hurt her last night, and there's not a single trace of resentment in that face.

My heart is in my throat. Somehow, I muster a smile. "Hey."

She doesn't return it. Instead, she shuffles around until she's facing me. "You don't have to pretend with me."

The sad attempt at a smile dies off my face. "Pretend what?"

Her fingers touch the corner of my mouth and lift my lips back into an approximate half-grin. "It's okay not to smile or laugh or act like everything is fine all the time. I'll still like you when you're angry. I'll still like you when you're miserable, or stressed, or when you just need a good cry, for no real reason. I'll still like you even if you show me how bad today hurts."

Fuck, I'm sick of myself.

I've known all along she's something bigger for me than any woman I've been with. Still, I've tried to treat her like one of them.

My Jenna deserves a lot better than that.

I swallow thickly. "My mom died eleven years ago today."

She already knows this. But she reaches under my pillow and slips her fingers between mine, our faces inches apart.

"Every year we have dinner together at my dad's. Me and my sister and her husband. As if this day can't be any worse."

Her thumb draws lines up and down my hand. Still, she doesn't speak. I can't be sure of why, but this is Jenna. We mesh on a level I've never felt before. I can sense what she needs without her saying, and she's the same with me. She's giving me the space to breathe. To pick through my words.

"He's still in bad shape, my dad. He doesn't talk. Doesn't do anything but obsess quietly over Mom. Mostly we eat in silence, trying not to look at each other. Waiting for enough time to pass so we can get up from the table and call it quits until next year."

Jenna pulls our hands out from under the pillow we're sharing. She brings them up to her mouth and places a kiss on mine.

"Come with me," I ask without thinking. "Come with me to my dad's."

I don't realize I'm crying until her free hand brushes the tears from my cheek.

~

"Pa? Hayls?"

CHAPTER 18

I pause so abruptly just inside the front door of dad's house that Jenna slams into my back.

"Oops, sorry."

I turn to see her gingerly adjust the box of cupcakes she insisted on bringing. "Why are you whispering?"

She shrugs. "Because you are."

"I am?"

I'm gripped with self-conscious nerves now, scanning the hallway we're standing in, trying to see it from her eyes. There's a healthy layer of dust covering the stair railing, and the dated wallpaper lining the walls is starting to peel around the ceiling.

Jenna comes around and, balancing the yellow box in one hand, snakes an arm around my waist to pull me in tight. My muscles sag against her.

"We don't need to whisper." I force my voice into its regular octave. It feels weird as hell. Loud in the otherwise silent house.

She gives me a healthy squeeze. I kiss her forehead. She feels more like home than the house we're standing in.

"Ready?" She's the one asking, like this goes the other way around. Like she knows exactly what she's in for, trying to brace me for the experience.

I take her hand and let her lead me through the house, past the empty living room and into the kitchen. I find them through the sliding glass doors to the yard. My dad, Hayley, and her husband Eric, sitting quietly on the wooden bench across from Mom's rose garden. Hayley's bump has grown twice its size since the last time I saw her. With a jolt in the pit of my stomach, I realize she's only three months out from her due date. She's chopped off most of her hair, blonde ends tickling her shoulders now like she's getting rid of all the frivolity while she waits for her baby.

"Should we go out there?" Jenna asks from beside me. She's dropped the box of cupcakes onto the table to hold my hand in a double grip.

I nod and she opens the door. If the silence hadn't been heavy out here before, it's downright deafening now as three heads turn to see us walking across the lawn, me trailing behind Jenna, tucking myself a little behind her like I need her for shelter. Like she's the one who knows them, my family, the one able to break the tension.

Jenna surreptitiously adjusts the hem of her skirt as we approach the bench, smoothing it down the back of her thigh. She asked me a dozen times if I was sure she shouldn't wear pants, or at least that black dress her sister bought her. I refused to let her. She drew the line at the half-t-shirts though.

"What the..." Hayley mutters, gaze clashing with Eric's before staring at Jenna with her mouth ready to catch flies. It falls all the way open when she hones in on our intertwined hands.

"You're probably wondering who I am," Jenna says, and they start as her voice breaks the stunned silence. "Finn very kindly took me in as a roommate after I did the whole *quit your job, sell your condo, forget to find a place to come home to after a year of travel* thing. I'm Jenna."

Dad fixes me with a frown.

"He *begged* me to let him give you all fair warning I was coming." Jenna grins at the three dumbstruck faces in front of us. "But I find I'm a lot more palatable with a touch of surprise. Plus, I brought cupcakes to soften the blow."

Actually, she'd asked me if I'd given them the heads up she was coming. I declined to, just in case they made it a big deal. Suddenly there was no way I'd show up here without her.

No one has moved. And I'm about to jump in and save her, or at least march us right back into the car and straight home, when she leans toward them and stage whispers: "They're really, *really* good cupcakes."

Another stunned silence. And Hayley lets out a single burst of laughter. The tension snaps. Eric rises from his seat and comes to clap me in the back, Hayley close behind him. Even Dad gives Jenna a small, uncertain smile as he stands.

"Sorry about that." Hayley lets herself get swept into the one-armed hug Jenna offers her. I still have her other hand in a deathgrip. "I thought for a second I was tripping on LSD again. And then I remembered I was pregnant."

"When the hell did you take LSD?" I frown at Hayley.

Jenna pats me on the shoulder. "Some things you just don't need to know about, kid."

CHAPTER 18

She turns to Eric, and Hayley raises her eyebrows. "I'm gonna need the full story, big brother," she mutters under her breath. "Don't be alarmed if I follow you into the bathroom when we're all inside."

"Add that to the list of things guaranteed to alarm me."

Simultaneously, we turn to watch Jenna hit her next hurdle. She gives Dad a careful smile when his gaze bounces from me to her. She touches a light hand to his forearm.

"I hope it's not too much trouble that I've come today," she tells him. "I don't mean to take away from your time as a family. Be a distraction."

Dad locks eyes with me one long moment before turning back to her. "I think a good distraction is just what we need."

~

Before Mom, Dad was a dynamo in the kitchen.

Not the way Theo is or anything, and even though Dad hasn't so much as boiled an egg for me in the last eleven years, I know over time I've grown better than him in that department. I think he'd say so too, if he ever came around to Sunset Landing or if I ever mustered up the will to cook him up something better than sandwiches, or soup, or something else he can throw into the freezer for later.

My most vivid memories growing up were of Mom sitting on that bar stool in the kitchen, watching Dad cook over piping hot spearmint tea.

Most days they'd talk all the way through, not saying much about anything. Who Mom bumped into at the store when she was shopping off Dad's grocery list, whether Dad thought they'd get any more peppers from the patch out in the garden that season.

Other times they'd sit in silence, and that's when we knew, Hayls and I, that they'd argued that day. They could have a full on blow out and still, at dinner time, Mom would sit herself down on that stool. Dad would cook. And maybe those family dinners weren't the fun variety where they'd let me get away with launching bits of bread across the table at Hayley just for the fun of it, but damn it if they didn't make us sit there as a family anyway.

Cooking for a living was a no brainer for me. Nothing brings people together like a good meal.

My hands are shaking. Barely, but just enough for me to fumble my chopsticks as I go for another helping of tofu dumplings. One chopstick clatters against the dining room table, and the room is so quiet it's like I fired off a shotgun.

Beside me, Jenna shifts in her chair. I've been hyper aware of her all evening, watching for signs of discomfort, whether I need to make an excuse and get us out of here. More than a little embarrassed by the state of the kitchen when we arrived, and the way after that first interaction, Dad hasn't spoken a word to any of us.

But she followed me back inside earlier to help with Dad's dirty dishes and emptied out the overflowing trash without being asked to. Ordered off the menu from that Chinese place around the block. Didn't seem at all offended when Dad only shrugged when she asked him what he wanted to order.

And she's been aware of me too.

She's watched me out of the corner of her eye all through our silent meal. Casually nudged the stir fry in my direction when I cleaned my plate, telling me without words or eye contact to go in for more. She's fussing over me and I can't tell if she knows that I've noticed.

I'm sure she's noticed the way Hayls stares at us throughout dinner, though. She isn't being subtle. I haven't let Jenna out of my sight long enough for her to corner me for answers, and she's getting antsy.

Dad pushes away his plate and leans back in his chair. He's done eating, and it's his signal that he's had just about enough of sitting at the table. I'm not about to pass up that opening. I shove the last dumpling into my mouth and I'm up before I'm even done chewing. Jenna lays her chopsticks across her plate.

Shit. She was still picking at her pile of food. I go to sit but she shakes her head and gets up too.

Hayley stacks our plates and follows me into the kitchen as Eric mumbles about going out to make a phone call.

"Here," Hayley says, handing me the dishes. I realize she's whispering.

We've been whispering for eleven years, haven't we?

Too late, I realize Jenna hasn't followed us. Through the archway to the dining room, I see her combining half-finished take-out containers with a pair of chopsticks.

Hayley steps into my path. "Nuh-uh. You're staying put. We need to talk, big brother." She peeks over her shoulder. Jenna doesn't seem to have heard. "What gives? Eleven years you've done this by yourself and out of nowhere, this. Her. And don't tell me she's just a friend."

I turn to the sink and she gingerly leans against the counter next to me, patting her bump. She runs the tap, even though we're whispering.

"She's not just a friend."

It's the first time I've said this out loud. Out of nowhere, my heart starts hammering in my chest. Not in a bad way. In a sort of vibrant way. The way it feels when you've been lying yourself into a circle, and then you finally tell the truth.

"I don't have much more to say than that," I add. "We're not together or anything."

"But you want to be," she says it like a statement and not a question.

I douse our plates with dish detergent and start scrubbing. "Remember that cabin we used to go up to in the summers before high school?"

"Sure," she answers patiently.

"You know that rope swing hanging over the lake? How you'd take it at a running jump and you'd always let go on your first swing over the water?"

"I remember. Then I'd tread water, screaming for you to jump in after me. You'd always take your time."

I nod, going a bit too hard with the sponge and wiping my forehead where I splashed myself. "I was never a fan of that water. How dark and murky it was. How you'd never really know whether your foot brushed over a weed or a fish."

"You'd make it in eventually, though. You'd jump."

She knows where I'm going with this. I'm taking the long way to my point, but she's letting me get through it.

"You always looked like you were having a blast in that water. And it got unbearably hot on land, after a while." I glance at my sister. Her face is heavy. Blue eyes, the same shade as mine, looking at me sadly. "I'm trying to decide, Hayls. Whether to jump."

She doesn't say anything. Just reaches over and ruffles my hair the way Mom used to. I work through the dishes and she sits there watching me in silence, rubbing her belly.

"I love this photo. Look how sweet the four of you are."

Hayley meets my eye the second I look for hers. Jenna's voice comes through clearly from the dining room. She isn't whispering.

"Where was it taken?"

I rack my brain trying to figure out which picture she's talking about, and who she's talking to. I can't see her through the archway anymore. She must be eyeing the frames by the window. Did Eric make it back into the dining room?

Hayley looks as confused as I am. And then we hear a reply.

"Up north. We rented that cabin every summer until the kids were too grown up to want to spend the break with their parents."

Dad. He's whispering. My stomach sinks. His silence is bad, but it's also safe. I know what to expect, what to prepare her for. What I'll need to explain to her later, when we're alone again.

"They look like they had a great time there. How old were they?"

Footsteps. "I think Finley was about ten there. He'd make a fuss every time Iris tried to get him in for a haircut that year. I think that's as long as it got."

I know the picture now. The four of us are sitting on the dock, backing the lake, waiting for the timer to go off on the camera Dad would prop up on a chair. My hair was shoulder length. I loved it.

"She would have us take this same picture at the end of every summer, right before we got into the car to head home."

It's subtle, but I catch it. Dad's voice rising a decibel or two.

"What the hell is happening?" Hayley mouths at me.

I shake my head. "No fucking idea."

"The way Finn speaks about her, she sounds like she was an incredible mother."

There's a long silence after that. Hayley bulges her eyes at me, and with a flash of dread, I turn to go in there and break this up. I don't even turn off the tap. She shouldn't have brought Mom up. There's a reason we don't bring her up around Dad. He's bad enough, doesn't need any setbacks—

Hayley grabs my arm and keeps me still.

There's the sound of wood clapping on wood. The picture frame coming down on the credenza.

"She was a great mother," Dad says.

"I never had that," Jenna says quietly, and my heart throbs for her.

"You didn't?" Dad's voice has grown a little louder.

"My mom wasn't involved. I wasn't hard done by or anything. But growing up was nothing how Finn describes it."

"He tells you about her?" Dad's question rings in my ears. Or rather, the tone of his voice does. It's heavy, forlorn. Envious.

Hayley's hand slips into mine. She's frowning.

"Sometimes," Jenna tells Dad, and her voice is soft. She can tell she's hit on something. "Sometimes on purpose. Other times it just slips out when he isn't thinking too hard."

"What does he say about her?"

"He tells me how nurturing she was. How she cared a lot that they were raised right, but gave them room to find a little trouble, too. There was one story, when she caught Finn sneaking out of his window—"

I rear like I've been punched straight in the gut. Because he just—

Dad just—

Hayley's hand squeezes mine, and when I turn to look, her eyes are brimming with tears. Dad just laughed. It was short, wheezy, rusty like he hasn't emitted that kind of sound in a while. Like his body is trying to remember how it goes.

I'm shaking. It's adrenaline, but something that feels pretty awful too.

"She'd never admit it to his face, but it was one of Iris's favorite stories," Dad's saying. "To this day I don't have the foggiest idea where the hell it is that boy went. But he showed up a couple hours later with a broken nose, face all bloodied up, asking for a ride to the hospital."

Jenna knows the full story, the parts Dad doesn't. She laughs, though, delighted by his retelling. I can see her dimple through the drywall.

"Iris never asked either, what it is he got up to. She was making a point. That he could come to us in a pinch without ever worrying he'd take crap for it." Dad pauses, and when he speaks again, there's something a little playful in his voice. "You know where he went, don't you?"

Jenna chuckles. "I've been sworn to secrecy. Did he really never get into trouble for it?"

"Oh, he was doing our dishes for a good month afterward. Not that he complained. He knew better. But the boy never snuck out again."

"That you know of," Jenna singsongs, and I picture her giving my dad that little conspiratorial nudge she does. The one that makes you feel like you're on the same team. Like you're someone important.

"That we know of," Dad agrees. "I still have the old photos, if you want to see them. The ones from the end of summer."

"*Please* tell me they include the year Iris gave Finn the bowl cut."

He does it again. Dad chuckles. "You heard about the bowl cut, huh? Well, you're in luck, young lady."

A moment later we watch them stream through the opposed archway into the living room. Jenna's got an arm threading through Dad's.

What—

"What the hell was that?" I turn to Hayls, searching her face for answers even though, if I can stop lying to myself for just one second, I know exactly what the hell that was.

"We screwed up big, didn't we?" Hayley says, putting her own pieces together. Admitting to her own lies. She isn't whispering. The tap's still running and they're in the other room now, but it still feels like something big.

I shove my glasses on top of my head, pressing my palms to my eyes. "I thought it would make it worse."

Did I? Because in this moment, it feels like I've been fooling myself. Keeping Mom out of my mouth *was* for Dad's sake. But also maybe for mine, and how bad it hurts to think about her sometimes, and how happy we were together in this home. So, I did the only thing I could think of: pretended she didn't exist, every time I came here.

Lying about my feelings. I'm really good at that, aren't I?

"We screwed up so fucking big, Hayls."

She wipes her eyes. "Where the hell did you find this girl?"

"Finding her wasn't the hard part."

I feel lost, and blown away, and confused, and a little bit mad at myself and how much time I've wasted. We could have had Dad back. He was sitting right there, aching to remember her.

Jenna's tinkling laugh floats from the other room. It feels like a life vest. I cling to it.

Hayls winds an arm around me, wrapping me in a tight hug. "Jump, big brother."

Chapter 19

Jenna

I think I screwed up.

The top of the Jeep is off, and we speed down the freeway in the direction of home. Metallica is blasting around us. It's like all our other joyrides of the past couple months. And yet, it's not.

Finn isn't singing along at the top of his voice, the way he usually does. Tonight, he stares fixedly through the windshield. He hasn't said a word since we left his dad's, and there's a real chance me and my stupid inability to just let things be made a hard day even worse.

After dinner, he sat quietly in an armchair watching Hayley and I huddle on the living room floor poring over old photo albums, his dad piping in every so often with a new anecdote about the kids growing up.

I'd meet his eye occasionally, but he only returned my tentative smiles with a barely-there lift to the corner of his mouth.

It didn't *feel* wrong, talking about Iris. Vince's eyes lit up the second I pointed out that photo in the dining room. And after only a few minutes, his face changed. Not just his expression, but the shape of it. His cheeks rose, eyes crinkled. I decided when I first saw him that Finn must favor his mom with his looks. But the second his father smiled, my Finn was there.

No. He's not your *Finn. That's the point, isn't it?*

I crossed a line. I'm not his girlfriend. I'm a friend to a man who's

CHAPTER 19

struggling to come to terms with his feelings for me. I forgot my place.

I reach for my hair, grabbing randomly at the strands blowing in the wind, trying to tame them as we approach Finn's apartment building. He winds us down the underground parking, and by the time he pulls into his spot and kills the engine, I'm a bundle of guilty nerves.

It's just a concrete wall ahead of us now. Still, it seems he'd rather stare at it than look at me.

"Finn—"

"Did I ever tell you one of my instructors at culinary school told me I was so bad I belonged behind the counter at a fast-food joint?"

He says it to the steering wheel, and it takes me a second to catch up with the unexpected direction of this conversation. He's gearing up for a Finn story, one of my favorite things in the world. They're the kind that seem random, out of the blue, until he finishes and you realize he's told you exactly what you needed to hear. Normally, I'd let go and enjoy the ride, see where he takes me. This time, I'm so nervous I wish I knew where we were going.

"That's only an insult within a certain context," I say slowly, without taking my eyes off his profile.

"Specifically, he told me I was going to be the kid with the saltshaker at the fry station."

I can't help it. A laugh bursts out of me, and finally—*finally*—Finn sets his eyes on me, a grin breaking over his face. My feet find solid ground again.

"D'you ever wish you could meet him again? Show him you made something of yourself?"

"Nope. That instructor had a front row seat to my meltdown after Mom died. I have no desire to see him again, and I'm sure he'd say the same."

My heart balloons about ten sizes. So this is where he's taking me. The story he's been holding onto. That barrier he's kept between us.

"What happened?"

The fluorescent garage lights beat down on us, casting shadows on his face, bringing out the sharpness of his jaw under that soft scruff. He moves around, pushing back his seat so that he can sit looking at me.

"It was the day after her funeral. He was pissed that I took the day off, missed his class the day before. Didn't have two shits to give that my mom just died." He tips his head thoughtfully. "In hindsight I know it had nothing to do with me and everything to do with how toxic this industry can be. Lots of people seem to think the only way to get ahead is to rip others to shreds on the way up. When you find a good kitchen to work in, you thank your lucky stars and you stick with it."

"Even in school? Doesn't it drive people away?"

Finn shrugs. "You're still naive enough at that point to accept it, hope it's an isolated incident. Keep your head down. Do whatever those assholes tell you."

"And this instructor was one of those asses?"

"Total ass. He started off class that day ranting about how I was lazy. Undedicated. Had no talent. We were taking apart chickens in that lesson. He knew I had a hard time with it, that I don't eat meat. Usually, I can suck it up pretty good, do the job without thinking about it too hard. But I was already feeling off because of Mom, and that asshole slammed whole chicken after whole chicken in front of me while everyone watched. I must have taken apart a dozen of them by the time I snapped." Finn's gaze drops to his lap. He's ashamed, and God, I hate that for him. "So he goes and puts another chicken down on my board. I grabbed a knife, sliced the thing in half so hard one piece flew off the bench and landed right at his feet. I told him to go fuck himself and walked out of class."

He starts fidgeting. Hiking up his leg on the seat, fiddling with the sole of his sneaker. It's instinct. I reach for his hands and clasp them between mine, squeezing hard. He stares at them a moment before linking our fingers.

"It was... I don't have to tell you how out of character that was for me. How *uncomfortable* it was. I'm a happy person, and people like me for it. Mom's death and the way my dad is, it's the one exception to that. And I've made sure to keep that side of me under wraps. To keep things light, simple. Easy. And I became pretty good at it. Until you."

My stomach flips. Over and over, and it's reassuring to know that if I passed out—because it really feels like I could—he would make sure I'd end up safely in my bed.

CHAPTER 19

"What you did tonight, Jenna? We could never give him what he needed, me and Hayley, for eleven years. And we're his damn kids. You brought him to life without even knowing him. How'd you do that?"

It's a sincere question, and I'm not sure how to answer it without making more of myself than I am. As we sat there over Chinese food, I watched Vince's eyes drift to that credenza about a dozen times. He wasn't exactly discreet. But Finn and Hayley seemed to make it their business to keep their eyes on their plates.

"You can't be that hard on yourself," I tell him. "He misses your mom so much—I know I don't need to tell you that. But he does, and tonight I think he felt like she was there. Not physically, but *there*. Talking about her made her real again. These things are easier to see from the outside. You and Hayley were hurting too."

"I don't know. It was pretty clear tonight how bad I've been lying to myself when it comes to Dad. I've been lying to myself about a lot, it turns out."

I feel like the undisturbed surface of a lake before the rain. Still. Delicate. Feeling that at any second, the downpour will start.

Finn watches me like he's trying to see into my brain. "I go over a decade without feeling a damn thing for a woman, and the second you sat down next to me in that bar, the first time you looked at me, I was done. I was just too stupid to realize it."

A drop of rain ripples my surface.

"You were done?"

"Yesterday you asked about the forehead kisses. What they meant. And I lied to you." His eyes tick up, meeting mine. "Ask me again."

I'm not breathing. "What do they mean?"

He gives me a little smile. "They mean I constantly crave the way you feel. They mean I can barely muster a thought about anything but you. They mean I wake up in cold sweats most nights, thinking about how much it would scare me to have you, and how bad it would hurt to lose you." My heart hammers and he looks at me earnestly. "Jenna, I'm so tired of pretending I don't have real feelings for you. Fighting the way I feel about you is *exhausting*. And I know I can't go without you. But I'm terrified I'll end up like Dad."

A tear hits his cheek. He doesn't move to wipe it. But he reaches over to wipe the one that's leaked onto mine.

"I don't know if that feeling ever goes away, after everything you've been through," I say slowly. "But I'm willing to help you work through it. Or to help you live with it, if it doesn't go away. And just so you know, Finn? I'm not afraid. This feels so right—we feel right. *You* feel right. I'm not afraid of this."

He gives a wet laugh. "That's because you're the badass in this relationship. I'm just the sorry guy trying to hang on for dear life."

It's that burning feeling in my throat. The good one. "Relationship?"

"I can't promise I'll always know what I'm doing, and I think you're gonna have to ease me into it. But I wanna give it a shot. My best shot." He runs his thumb along my palm. "And I'm already screwing it up. Because the very least I could have done is tell you all this *literally anywhere* other than an underground parking garage, but..." He shrugs helplessly.

I lean in, place a kiss on his cheek. "I wouldn't change it."

His chest swells at the words. "I wouldn't change *you*. Not a single thing. You know that?"

I melt in my seat like a swirl of soft-serve ice cream settling into itself, strawberry with a twist of ecstasy. For half a second I feel myself trying to play it cool. Casual. Giving him a moment to claw it all back if he wants to. But it doesn't stick. My face breaks and his does too, giving me that crooked grin I love, so big I wonder whether his cheeks hurt. We sit there smiling at each other like a pair of giddy kids, dumbstruck by our good fortune.

"I'm so sorry about last night," Finn tells me, smile not dropping an inch. "I think if delusion had a mascot, it would be me."

I laugh. "I think I might have you beat in that department. I don't even want to tell you what I thought I had to do to win you over."

The furrow in his brow only lasts a second. "*The turtleneck?*" His head falls back in a loud laugh when I nod. "Yeah, okay. You win. That was peak delusion. I took one look at you that night and thought I'd died and gone to hell."

"I *was* in hell. Do you know how itchy it was under there?"

CHAPTER 19

"That settles it. We're going up there to burn it." He brings up my hand to kiss it. "I'm sorry we spent our first date with my family. And that my idea for our second date isn't much better."

"What is it?"

"I want to come with you this Saturday. To your sister's wedding. I know it's a terrible faux pas, inviting myself to a stranger's wedding. But the thought of you there alone kind of makes me want to hurl up my tofu."

Can he hear that high-pitched squeal in my head? I wouldn't care if he did.

"I really want that. The wedding date, not the hurling. Just so we're clear."

The wattage from his smile could power an entire hemisphere. "Look at me go. Who says the over-sexualized himbo can't get the girl?"

I press my lips together, terrified the size of my smile will cause permanent muscle damage. "The same people who say the sexed-up pony can't get the guy."

"The sexed-up—"

"Trust me, you don't want to know," I say, and I reach to smooth the crinkle in his brow. "Should we go upstairs?"

With his gaze on me, Finn gives a slow nod. All my senses heighten. I don't know what upstairs means for us, after the things we did together the other night. After I spent last night in his bed.

God, I hope he kisses me tonight.

Upstairs, Finn watches as I dig my keys out of my purse. He's being uncharacteristically quiet, but he doesn't take his eyes off me either. Under that stare, every bit of me feels alive. Aware. Whatever he gives me when I open this door, I want it. Finn sweeps the hair off my shoulder and I fumble my keys.

I turn and he gives me a soft smile, taking in the burning in my cheeks. "See how good you are at this?" I tell him. "It's only the first date and I can barely keep my cool."

I finally get the lock open, but before I can open the door he tugs my hand. "Wait."

He's standing so close. So close his foot tucks in between mine, hand barely needs to pull at my hip to press me against him, turn my back into the door.

He's clenching his jaw, eyes heavy when he says: "I have a confession."

I shiver as the pad of his thumb strokes my waist. "What is it?"

Finn's gaze cuts to my mouth, and the way he licks his lips makes me squirm against the door. "I kiss on the first date."

I breathe out a startled laugh and he grins at the sound of it. I fist his shirt, pull him closer so that we're chest to chest. Pounding heart to pounding heart.

"I love that about you," I murmur.

Finn slides a hand around my waist, fingers spreading over my lower back, holding me tight to him.

He was right, the other night.

We fit together perfectly. His chin barely dips and his lips find mine. For a moment, Finn kisses me sweet. It's soft, the way he takes my lower lip, my top lip, gently sucking, grazing my tongue with his. The way his hand gently holds my face, fingers brush my cheek.

It feels like meeting for the first time. Like catching his eye across a crowded bar, and not being able to look away. Those butterflies, that flutter of anticipation as he approaches, that first smile. The first touch as he takes your hand. Not knowing how far this thing will go, or what you're meant to be to each other.

It's the kind of kiss you've been waiting to give someone, after months of wanting.

With a swipe of my cheek with his thumb, a last gentle kiss, Finn draws back. Presses his forehead to mine and he's smiling, so big and crooked I can't help but give it right back to him. I feel so lightheaded I let out a giddy giggle, and Finn swipes my mouth with his fingers.

"I've been dying to do that. *Dying* for it, Jenna."

He doesn't let me catch my breath. Finn crashes his mouth on mine again. Tilts his head, drops both hands to my hips, tightens his grip. And the kiss becomes the kind too obscene for public consumption.

I lick his tongue and he groans, loses his mind. Flattens me into the door, kisses me deep, hard, with my head braced against the surface behind me. My fingers find his hair. His slide down to my ass, grab two handfuls and tug me up and into him and I give a desperate whimper into his mouth. My skirt has bunched up in his palms, cool air hitting my ass, and he's hard, so hard and pushing his cock against me with a grunt. Like he's telling me *See? This is what you do to me. This is what you've always done to me.*

I come up for air and the low growling sound he makes tells me he isn't one bit happy about it. His face falls to my neck and he licks a path of skin under my ear. Oh my God. I think—are we about to—

"Finn—"

My lungs reject the renewed airflow and I think he senses that because he cuts it off, slicks his tongue on mine, draws away, nips my lip. Comes back in for more and my body rumbles with the force of his moan. Like this is so good, kissing me is *so good* it does it for him even more than it did to rub his cock into me. And it is good. It's so good, I need more. I need *him*—

"Finn." He blinks at me in rapid succession, like he's lost his sight, and I kiss along his jaw. "I have a confession, too."

"What?" The word comes out almost slurred, like he's drunk off my mouth.

"I fuck on the first date."

With a pained sound his forehead meets my shoulder. He's panting like he's just climbed ten flights of stairs, and he's gearing up for another ten. "I do too."

The words are barely out of his mouth before my hands fumble between us, finding his erection and stroking him hard through his jeans.

He moans, this deep, guttural sound, like this teeny tiny thing, the feel of my hand through denim, does it for him just as good as if he were sliding into me. He hikes my leg up around his hip. Runs a hand along my thigh, caressing the soft crease where my leg meets my body, before moving between us too. Our hands compete frantically for space, fighting over who gets to give and who gets to take. He wins. His thumb runs along my pussy, over the damp outside of my panties and he grunts into my shoulder.

"Fuck, I love how wet you get. Tell me it's just for me. Tell me all these fuckers who've had the God-given privilege of touching you didn't do it for you like I do. Tell me they had to work twice as hard to get you ready, that the way you're shaking right now only happens when it's my cock about to fuck you senseless against this door."

He doubles his grip around my waist when my legs give a violent shake that almost has me tipping over.

"It's you, Finn. It's you, it's you—"

It's not a lie, either. He doubles his pressure where he rubs me, and I'm sure that if he let go of me, if he stopped carrying my weight, I'd land face down in this carpeted hallway. I find his lips again, needing him to help stifle my moans. He toys with the edge of my panties.

And that's the exact moment at which the woman in apartment 511 sticks her head out of her door.

"Hey, buddy," she snaps, and with visible difficulty Finn turns to her, blinking rapidly in her direction as though trying to re-populate his line of sight. She's looking right at us, glaring at the jumble of limbs we've become against his front door. "Do us all a favor and screw her *inside* your apartment."

And she slams her door.

We stare in silent shock at the spot where her head disappeared. And then Finn swears under his breath and I burst into laughter against his neck.

Finn pulls back to look at me wryly. "I'm glad you find this funny."

"You have to admit she has a point."

But he looks stricken as he lowers my leg and extricates his fingers from where they'd just started pulling at my panties. He rubs the back of his neck, and with a loud exhale moves to plant his palms into his eyes, from under his glasses.

"Goddamn it."

"Hey, it's okay," I tell him. "We'll just take this inside. She'll get over it eventually."

"No, that's not—" He swallows heavily and lowers his hands. "I don't want to do this."

My stomach spasms. He's changed his mind. That easily?

With shaking hands, I smooth down my skirt.

His eyes widen at whatever he sees in mine. "Not about you," he amends quickly. "Not about us. Not about... Jenna, I want you so bad—I've *been* wanting you so bad, it has to be seriously unhealthy. At this point you only have to *breathe* in my direction and I'm losing my mind—"

"Hey." I grip his face and he fixes me with a frenzied look. "We're not doing anything you don't want."

"I *do* want it. Here and now, and that's kind of the point. I've done this more times than I'd care to admit. The front door make-out on the first date, stripping down as soon as we get inside... It's all the same bullshit, over and over again. But I want us to be different. I want us to last and I don't want to screw this up."

I smile. "Relationship, remember? It's already different, Finn."

But he looks over his shoulder again, at the door of apartment 511, and there's something else going on here. I want this, so badly, and his logic is shaky at best. But he asked me for slow out in the car, and it's excruciating but I'm not going to be the one to push him into anything he doesn't want, especially not when it comes to sex.

I stroke his cheek, drawing back his attention. "Can we still make out a little bit?"

There's relief over every bit of his face, like he's silently telling me *thank you*.

"First, I'm gonna take a cold as hell shower. And then yeah, Jenna Bear. We'll make out as much as you want."

Chapter 20

Finn

"Being with Jenna feels a lot like not being with Jenna."

"Sounds like a fantastic relationship." Nina smirks, running a cloth around the rim of the plate in front of her before putting it under the heat lamps.

I make a face at her, but the twerp isn't looking. She calls out a new order to the crew behind us, taking her time adjusting her hair net. I wait her out. Finally, she can't do a thing but look back and I grimace at her worse this time.

"What I *mean* you little jerk, is that beyond the added perks of making out and having her in my bed at night—"

"To cuddle?" Nina says, eyeing me carefully. "You're still just cuddling?"

The woman has no indoor voice. The two line cooks to my right exchange a look. I lean my hip against the counter.

"Yes, we're still just cuddling," I confirm, adjusting my glasses. "Why do you keep looking at me like that whenever I tell you this?"

"I'm not looking at you like anything." She turns to prep the two plates of sea bass in front of her. "It's just... You know. You're *Finn Palmer*. Whenever I thought about you getting your head out of your ass long enough to ask her to be with you—"

"How would you know I was going to do that? I only decided last night."

CHAPTER 20

She gives me a look that says *come on*. "Whenever I thought about you getting your head out of your ass long enough to ask her to be with you, I *also* thought you'd have her bedridden for a week. You've been celibate for a year—"

"*Woah.*" One of the line cooks looks at me with his jaw dropped.

"Quiet, you," I tell him. Turning back to Nina, I say: "It's not like I don't want to. Honestly, our water bill has gotten a little out of control with all the time I spend in the shower—"

"Why do I need to hear about that—"

"And the conclusion I've drawn is that I'm a victim of my reputation. It's a lot of pressure to deliver on, you know? She knows about... Well, she knows about everything. And I don't know how to live up to it."

"And what's her excuse? Why isn't she jumping your bones yet? Don't tell me you fell for a sweet, chaste virgin—"

"Don't," I cut in, jabbing a finger at her. "I don't see how that's any of your business."

She gives an acquiescing nod, taking the reproach on the chin. "You know, I'm proud of you, big guy. Finn Palmer, all grown up. I never thought I'd see the day."

Nine times out of ten, those brown eyes of hers help drive home whatever snark her mouth delivers. I've never seen them this soft.

"Thanks, Neens," I mumble, hooking an arm around her neck and pulling her in.

"God, you're such a softie." She pats my back. "Okay, speaking seriously now. You like this girl, right? She's different from anyone you've been with. So why are you trying to operate under the same expectations as with those other girls? The sex part can be different, too. You held off on being with her until it felt right. The sex thing, you'll know when it feels right."

"Yeah, but... It's kind of the only thing I know how to do. I have no idea how to be a boyfriend. Not that... I mean, technically we haven't talked about titles or anything. But you know what I'm saying."

Nina snorts. "Am I seriously the first person to break it to you that you've basically been in a relationship since she moved in? You spend all your free time with her. You hookup on occasion. You run off to save her from the clutches of her evil sister. Newsflash, Finn: *she got you months ago*. You don't need to sweat it because you've already proven your worth as a boyfriend. No titles needed."

I hum, all noncommittal. Except on the inside, I'm glowing. Neon sign in a pitch-black room kind of glowing. I grab a rag off the shelf above me and wipe at the counter. "You make an interesting point, Neens."

"Yes, I do. Now get your big boy pants on and fuck the girl alrea—oh. Well, this is interesting." I look up to see Nina's narrowed eyes have drifted over my shoulder. "You're telling me *that's* your type? I mean, don't get me wrong. She's cute and all that, but... she looks a little uptight, no?"

I'm suddenly aware that the kitchen has gone very quiet except for the sizzling pans and boiling pots. Even the kid washing dishes at the sinks has frozen in place, turning to look at something behind me.

"Finn Palmer in his natural habitat. You look really busy, kid."

My breath hitches and sucks my heart into my throat.

Yum.

Jenna leans against the counter by the swinging kitchen doors, and it's an instant serotonin release. Every single muscle in my body eases. I get a bit lightheaded. Nina chuckles behind me, and I can't be sure but I think it's because I let out a satisfied hum.

This woman is stunning. A dream. She belongs up there, in the clouds. We're blessed to have her among us. Don't deserve her one bit.

And then I get a good look at what she's wearing, and I'm instantly irritated. Because this look isn't her. Pink hair pulled back in a tight bun low on her head and a simple black dress with the hem around her knees. It's the same look she wore the night of her sister's bachelorette party, and immediately I know she's put herself together like this to please Ronnie.

Jenna beckons me over with that dimple, and I'm on her like a goddamn missile. In a second I've got arms hauling her up by the waist and squeezing her to me.

"You're wearing flats," I say into her shoulder.

She squeezes me back. "What kind of a hello is that?"

CHAPTER 20

I set her down, and hike up her chin with my fingers. Her eyes are all lit up and happy, and it melts the hell out of me that I've managed to put a look like that on her face.

"Hey, Jenna Bear."

Someone snickers behind me. I'm going to pay for this in spades later. Worth it.

Jenna peeks over my shoulder. "Finn? Why is everyone in this kitchen staring at us?"

"Ignore them. I'm kind of a celebrity around here."

Cue the forehead kiss. And the kitchen erupts.

"I *told* you he'd go for it the second she ever came to visit—"

"But you also bet he'd do it ten seconds in—I bet a minute fifty—"

"At least you bet he'd do it. I thought for sure he'd chicken out in front of everyone."

I groan. Jenna plants her palms to my chest and pulls back against my hold. "What the hell is going on?"

"There's a chance they're aware of the forehead kisses." I turn to see money exchanging hands across the kitchen. The dish washer walks over to hand a line cook a twenty, and the busser holds a fifty toward Nina.

"Traitor," I throw at her, but she chuckles heartily as she pockets her cash.

"Consider it payment for all your therapy sessions," she calls over the renewed bustling, swapping out her gloves for a fresh pair after handling the cash.

"Does everyone know about us?" Jenna asks, watching all this unfold. I take her hand and tug her out of the kitchen, away from the audience.

"Yup."

"You didn't waste any time."

I lead her down the quiet hall with the washrooms. "I just convinced a total rocket to be my girl. No way in hell I'm keeping that to myself."

"What'd you do? Call a team meeting?"

"I sent an email."

"You *didn't*."

"The subject line was 'Hands off, ladies. This himbo's off the market.'"

She snorts. "I know you're kidding but hear me out: send that email just for the sake of Theo's reaction."

Past the washrooms I turn her into the wall, and her dimple is the last thing I see. I've never been a noisy kisser. Not that I've noticed, anyway. But tasting Jenna feels too much like digging into my favorite pie at Thanksgiving, and I'm anything but quiet. I'm all moans when she licks at my tongue, grunts when she digs her nails into my back. I'm rock hard in a second.

There's nothing chaste about the way we kiss. Our lips pick up right where they left off this morning, the same hunger as when I got her underneath me on the couch and slid my hand into her panties. Before drawing on every ounce of self-control to pull back and take her hand instead.

I'm dying to fuck her. But I'm dead set on not fucking this up.

Her fingers skim my hairline and goddamn, it makes me wild when she plays with my hair. I rip the hat off my head, take her hands and move her fingers in deeper.

I'm addicted to her. Obsessed. Out of my motherfucking mind for her.

This burning thing in my throat is just something I live with now. And damn, it's started feeling real nice. I want it for good.

Jenna lets out the sweetest moan into my mouth and starts pulling back, but with a desperate sound I hold her still. I don't want to stop. I can't stop. Even the thought of stopping hurts.

"Finn," she mumbles against my lips. "You're at work."

Work?

I break away, blinking hard at our surroundings. Work.

I'm at work.

Work, this stupid, senseless concept that means I have to leave her at home. That I have to take my hands off her now.

I hate work. I hate everything but her.

I go back in for another kiss, and then another because one is never enough with Jenna. We've both got ridiculous grins on our faces. The loopy, happy kind. I wasted so much time fighting this.

"I thought you weren't dressing like this anymore," I say, smoothing back the strands of hair that came loose out of her bun. "Jenna Fucking Carling, remember?"

"Yes, but tonight I'm not Jenna." She wriggles until I free her and offers me a hand. She squares her shoulders. "Genevieve. Pleased to meet you."

I take her hand and instead of shaking it, she squeezes it lightly.

"Are people aware that Genevieve kisses dirty like that? I think she's got a little deviant in her."

She fluffs her dress innocently. "Genevieve has no idea what you're talking about." She picks up my hat and, after combing my hair back, places it on my head, brim backwards. This girl. This *girl*. It's a tiny, nothing thing, but she does it like she's been doing it for years and I think I'm floating.

"Is Genevieve sure she can't get me in as a plus one to this rehearsal dinner tonight? I hate the idea of you going alone."

"Genevieve already took a lot of crap for adding you to Saturday's guest list at the last minute. She didn't have the guts to ask for more. But it helps that she got to sneak over here to see you first."

Before I can get out more than a grunt, the door to the back-office swings open. "I think I missed the part where making out with funeral guests became part of your job."

I groan. "This guy again," I say loud enough for Theo to hear. I cross my eyes at Jenna. "Did I ever tell you about my stick-up-his-ass boss? He's a real—"

"Careful, Palmer. Your employment already hangs by a thread."

I turn to bestow him a wide, obnoxious grin. "It's *Chef* Palmer to you."

He rolls his eyes. "So, what fresh hell have the two of you come to drop on my lap? This can't be an innocent visit, Jenna."

Jenna flutters her lashes at him. "Sure it is. We're friends, aren't we? And I'll be maid of honor at your wedding, assuming you'll ever get off your ass and pop the question."

Theo blinks.

"Fine," she says with a sigh. "I'll settle for an elopement."

"Woah, woah," I jump in, digging my elbow into her ribs. "You've got a big family, boss. How cute would your sister's twins be, dropping petals down an aisle? These things, they take time to plan. Preferably another couple of months."

Jenna pinches my side and I give a loud yelp. She snorts, working to keep a straight face.

Theo looks between us, thoroughly unamused. "You do realize Jude told me about the bet, right?" Jenna swears under her breath and I see it: the teeny tiny little twitch in the corner of Theo's mouth. He catches me looking and immediately settles his face. "And you do realize how unimpressed I am that you'd go off making bets on our relationship, right?"

"I see how you could take it the wrong way," I tell him, nodding thoughtfully. "This suddenly seems like a bad time to ask for Saturday off."

"You have to be joking. That's tomorrow, Palmer."

"Come on, Cherry Pie. It's for my sister's wedding," Jenna pipes in, tone sweet and cajoling. "You always say he barely works, anyway."

I squint. "I'm not really sure who you zinged there, babe. But a well-made point, nonetheless."

"Thanks, honey." She blows me a kiss. Laying it on thick for Theo, and I fucking adore this woman.

"Fucking hell." He stares at us, deadpan. "You two must drive your neighbors crazy, talking all night. At least no one can claim you aren't meant for each other."

Jenna shrugs. "They'll get a reprieve soon enough. My flight back to Europe is next week."

I let out a burst of laughter. It dies in my throat the second she gives me a weird look. She's... not kidding.

What the fucking fuck?

Theo's gaze snaps to mine, eyebrows furrowing deeply when he sees my expression. He'd never admit it to my face, but I sense his concern even from where I'm standing.

"How long do you plan on being away this time?" Theo asks, ripping his gaze off me. "Jude won't be happy about this."

Jenna laughs. "I know the lengths you'd go to keep our girl happy, but I fear this particular thing is beyond your control. I don't have a return ticket booked yet."

CHAPTER 20

Is the ground moving? It feels like I'm riding a conveyor belt. I don't know how to get off, or how to make it stop.

I know we haven't exactly discussed the future, or what happens after this wedding, but... She's really got it in her head that she's leaving me in a few days, for an undetermined amount of time. My brain is short circuiting.

"I've been meaning to call you, actually," Theo is saying to her now. "There's this opening on my marketing team. That's what you studied, right?"

Yes. *Yes.* I bulge my eyes at Theo. My saint. My savior.

"Oh!" Jenna says, plucking a piece of lint off that ridiculous dress. "Actually, that would be awesome. Do you want me to interview? Can you wait a couple months for me to get back?"

A couple of *months*? What the motherfucking hell is this?

"Sorry, *Jenna Bear*. I have a business to run. If you want to interview after you're back from your trip, then by all means, I'll wait. As long as you keep it to four weeks away." Theo glances at me. I give a tiny shake of my head. "Three weeks," he amends. "Tops."

I clap my hands together. "She'll take the deal."

Jenna shoots me an amused look. "Okay, this whole thing is brimming with ulterior motives. But I guess I wouldn't mind working for you, Theo. Finn's said enough good things about you as a boss—"

I groan. "Come on, why'd you have to blow my cover like that? Look how smug he looks—"

She nudges me. "Three weeks. Okay. You've got yourself a deal, Cherry Pie."

Looking more amused than I've seen him over the course of this conversation, Theo takes her outstretched hand. "Alright, Jenna Bear. Deal."

I place my hand on top of theirs, making sure to brush my thumb up and down Theo's. "Deal. And I'm gonna need one of you to give me a nickname."

Jenna snorts, dissolving into laughter as Theo shakes off my hand and mutters something under his breath that sounds a lot like *you don't want to know the nicknames I've got for you.*

I don't have to try hard to make it out. He doesn't seem too concerned that

I hear it.

I give him a wide grin. "Well, now that that's settled I'll be heading home—"

"You're two hours into your day."

I throw an arm over Jenna's shoulders and give her a wink as we move back down the hall towards the lounge. "Alright, *alright*. I'll stay. But in return I'll take tomorrow off."

"I didn't agree to that," Theo drones behind us.

"What was that?" I call over my shoulder. "I can have Sunday off too? You are the *bestest boss ever—*"

"Do me a favor, Jenna? Friend to friend." Theo pauses with his hand on the washroom door.

"What is it?" She swats behind her when I go for a handful of her ass, shoulders shaking in a giggle.

Theo gives me that infamous scowl over her shoulder. "Take him with you to Europe."

Chapter 21

Jenna

"Jenna, we're gonna be late!"

Shit.

I fiddle with the strap of my bridesmaid dress, even though it's laying perfectly in place. In the mirror I dab at my lips, even though my lip gloss is clear and also immaculate. I brush my hair off my shoulders. Change my mind, and bring the strands back in front.

I can't believe I did this.

I've been avoiding Finn since the second I got back from the hair salon. Talking to him through my door, insisting I was busy getting ready and didn't want to spoil the reveal. The big ugly-duckling-turns-into-a-beautiful-swan moment. The part where I glide down the great staircase and reveal my exceptional beauty to my dumbstruck date.

Except, I think I've made a grave error. Finn will be dumbstruck alright, but not in a good way.

Last night's rehearsal dinner was a colossal disaster.

It was fine for a couple of hours. I practiced walking down that aisle all twenty-four times Ronnie requested, until I got the exact cadence she wanted. Until my smile was as perfect as she was looking for. Until the way I held my pretend bouquet was just right. That's all fair game. It's her wedding, her day, and I'll play along however she needs me to.

She wanted a photo of us bridesmaids at the dinner table. Actually included me in the shot instead of asking me to take the picture this time, which was very nice of her. But it was Mom who took the picture instead.

Mom who then sat there across from me for the remainder of dinner, telling me in as many different words as she could come up with how much it was a shame that I'd be ruining photos of Ronnie's special day with my hair.

I looked like a Troll Doll among sophisticated ladies, she said.

No amount of salted caramel cupcakes, or Cabernet Sauvignon, or cuddles with Eddie could really get me out of my funk last night. Finn had it all ready at home before he came to pick me up, accurately anticipating that I'd need it, and then I only felt guilty that he was trying so hard to cheer me up to no avail. He even offered to let me drive around in the Wrangler, but by that time I'd been too deep into the wine to take him up on it.

Then I woke up this morning and made a decision.

"Jenna," he calls again. I hear him tinkering with Eddie's tank out in the living room. "Need any help in there?"

"Is Finn Palmer offering to help get my clothes *on*?" I call back. I run my fingers through my hair, trying to make it look a little better but the way it's laying isn't the problem.

It's not that I look *bad*. The pale pink dresses Ronnie picked out really are stunning. They're floor length and flowy and flattering around the chest area which isn't always a given with the size of my breasts. It's even got a slit down the side, letting my leg peek out when I walk, which was a pleasant surprise.

Finn makes a retching sound from outside my room. "You're right. Don't open this door unless you want to get down to your skivvies."

"Does that mean if I open this door, we get to stay home?"

"Come on, Jenna Bear. This dress can't be that bad."

"It's not the dress."

With a deep breath, I swing open the door.

"Goddamn, Jenna." He *is* dumbstruck. Staring from his bedroom doorway with brows pulled together, mouth ajar.

CHAPTER 21

Oh God. He hates it. He liked me with the pink hair. Of course, this wouldn't do it for him. Of course, it wouldn't. What the hell was I thinking, doing this—

"Surprise!" I shrug, feeling so silly and small now that I almost can't fully appreciate what I'm seeing in front of me.

Almost. Because Finn Palmer, all done up?

Goddamn, indeed.

He's wearing a dark, inky blue suit and crisp white shirt and I almost need a double take to really process what I'm seeing, to reconcile looking at his face without the cursory jeans or sweats. He's foregone a tie, like he couldn't quite sell himself on all the formality, and it feels a lot more like him. His hair looks different too, pushed back and tamed except for a little strand breaching forward onto his forehead in defiant protest.

"God, Finn. You look amazing," I tell him. He mouths an inaudible word, still staring at me. I pinch a blonde strand of hair between my fingers. "Do you hate it? It's as close to my natural color as I could get."

Finn comes off the doorjamb and closes the distance between us like he's in a trance. "You look unbelievable."

My stomach sinks. "You hated the pink?"

"Jenna," he says, gently. "It's not the hair. You could shave your head, leave a single tuft up top and I'd gladly spend the rest of my life staring at you."

"Yeah?"

"Yeah." He sweeps the hair off my shoulder to toy with the thin strap of my dress. "I thought bridesmaids were supposed to get a raw deal. Big poofy dresses and all that."

"My sister might be an ass, but she's an ass with good taste."

"Are you gonna be okay tonight?"

"Probably not." I sigh. "Will *you* be okay? It's hard enough meeting my family under normal circumstances, but to do it surrounded by a few hundred people..."

"Nah. I'm excited."

I let out a startled laugh. "*Excited*? If that's true, I've done a terrible job of prepping you."

He tugs me out of my room and down the hall. "Are you kidding? I've got the most stunning woman in the world as my date. And I get to tell anyone who messes with her where they can shove it. Tonight's gonna be... Well, I'm not gonna lie to you, it's probably gonna be terrible. But it's you and me against the terrible." At the door, he gives me a lingering kiss on the forehead. "I've got your back, Jenna Bear. Promise."

~

The bride makes it down the aisle, the groom gives her a kiss, and they'll live happily ever after.

At their head table for two, Ronnie and Carl sit in quiet conversation, heads huddled together. My sister is all smiles, looking so happy that I feel an unfamiliar tug of affection for her. She nodded approvingly when she saw me arrive for the ceremony, minus the *My Little Pony* look. Maybe I can't stand looking at myself in the mirror but seeing her smile at her new husband that way might make my new, old look a little bit worth it.

The reception is gorgeous. Round tables under a sprawling gazebo set in the middle of a waterfront garden. The pianist plays over the trickling sounds of the Hubbart River, the setting sun casts a golden glow over the space, supplementing the twinkle lights hanging above the dancefloor.

Across the table, Mom tips her head to listen to whatever my Aunt Marian is saying to her. Dad digs into his plate of perfectly round and plump filet, roast vegetables, and delicate scalloped potatoes.

It's been a perfect day.

Under the table, Finn tugs my hand into his lap and draws soothing lines across my palm.

"I've got you," he mouths at me silently.

I return a tiny nod.

Mom has barely said a word to us all night. Growing up, her silence was even more nerve-inducing than her words. It was always a dead giveaway that I'd done something terribly wrong, and the fact that I never could figure out what was simmering in her head terrified the hell out of me. She was a ticking time bomb. Most of the time I'd be completely lost as to when she'd

CHAPTER 21

blow up, what exactly I did to earn it, or what I could do to diffuse it.

Tonight, her silence has me sitting so rod straight in my chair my neck muscles are starting to ache.

She delicately tosses her blown-out hair over her shoulder. When I was little, I used to covet her hair. She and Ronnie have the same bright blonde hue, so fresh and shiny and unlike my dull color. But I'm her spitting image in every other way. Our eyes the same pale blue, the little upturn of our noses. The ashy brows.

I used to love it. It was tangible, undeniable proof that I was hers, that even though we had our issues, I was still her daughter and that meant she had to love me. But as her love became less and less apparent, our resemblance felt more like a tight grip, keeping me in check. A chokehold making sure I toe the line. Because everywhere we went, people would immediately know I was Elodie Carling's daughter. And it was Elodie Carling I'd embarrass if I didn't act the part perfectly.

I miss my hair.

Mom lifts her brows. She doesn't look at me. Just raises her brows like she knows I'm tracking her expression. I've sagged a little in my chair, muscles fighting back against the unnatural posture.

Sit up straight, Genevieve. Haven't you learned anything?

I hitch myself back up, push my shoulders as far back as they can go. I only catch a glimpse of the grim look Finn gives me before a server leans between us. He places a vegetable medley in front of me, and a big hunk of meat in front of Finn.

Shit.

"Sorry," I touch a hand to the server's elbow. "He should have a vegetarian dish, too."

Every pair of eyes around the table turns to me, except Finn who stares politely at the plated steak in front of him. The server frowns, consulting the sheet on the round tray resting on a small serving table behind us.

"Yours is the only vegetarian I have here."

"That's alright," Finn says, squeezing my hand under the table. "Not a big deal."

"I made sure to tell Ronnie—"

"*Really* Genevieve," Mom says sharply from across the table. "This is your sister's wedding day. Can't you stop pointing fingers at her, today of all days? If you truly told her, there would be a vegetarian plate in front of this person. It's bad enough you threw him in as a last-minute guest."

Color rushes to my cheeks. Shit.

The eyes around the table turn disapproving. Aunt Marian purses her lips, Uncle John beside her shakes his head. Dad, trying to skirt confrontation as always, saws into his steak.

"I'm quite certain I told her—"

Mom tisks impatiently and turns back to my aunt, dismissing me altogether.

The server hovers awkwardly behind me. "Should I…"

"No," Finn says quickly, picking up his fork and stabbing at a roasted carrot. "I'm sure Ronnie had a lot going on these past couple days. It slipped through the cracks, that's all."

Mom's eyes narrow.

"So, Finn," Dad says loudly, between bites of scalloped potatoes. He pats his mouth with the napkin in his lap. "Jenna tells me you have a job. That's good."

Finn's thumb stutters as it strokes my hand. Out of the corner of my eye, I see him working very hard to suppress a laugh.

"Wow. It feels like you already know me so well."

Dad snorts. It's one of the few traits I inherited from him. But only he gets away with the sound in front of Mom.

"Don't take it to heart. She doesn't tell us much about anything, this one." He tips his chin in my direction, and gives me a smile that's half-affection, half-reproach. "What is it you do, then?"

"I'm a chef."

"Head chef," I add quickly. "At a very popular restaurant downtown."

Finn squeezes my hand and I shoot him a quick look of apology. It's not that he isn't good enough. It's that I'm terrified for him to feel the sting of those judgmental eyes next to Dad. I know how bad they cut.

CHAPTER 21

"A chef! Well, that's nice," Dad is saying cheerfully. "Isn't that nice, Elodie?"

My mom fixes her face with a smile. This delicate, polite one I've never been able to master. The kind that doesn't reach your eyes.

"How wonderful," she says thinly. She graces Finn with barely a look before focusing on her plate, where she cuts a small piece of meat. "Genevieve always quite enjoyed spending time with the staff."

Oh my God.

On Mom's other side, Aunt Marian smothers her laugh with a long sip of wine. Finn drops his gaze and picks around the large steak sitting in front of him. I move my plate over and sweep my veggies into his.

"You need to eat something, babe," he says. He speaks quietly, just to me, but immediately I notice Aunt Marian casually lean in to try to catch our conversation.

"I'm not really hungry."

He tucks my hair behind my ear with his free hand. "You haven't had a thing since breakfast. Have a couple bites and we'll stop for ice cream on the way home. And if you finish your broccoli, you can get extra sprinkles on your cone."

I snort, louder than I mean to, and Finn winks at me over the rim of his wine glass. Mom shoots me a searing look. Dad looks around the table cheerfully.

Aunt Marian clears her throat, now eyeing Finn with interest. "Finn, have you ever considered working as a private chef?"

"No, ma'am. I'm more of a commercial kitchen kind of guy."

He's awkwardly cutting a potato with the edge of his fork. I should give him back his other hand, but it's the only thing tethering me to my sanity. I might cry if he lets go. As though reading my mind, he doubles his grip.

My aunt smiles coyly. "What a shame. I would love to have a taste of what you can cook up."

Oh my *God*.

"Marian, for goodness' sake," Mom chides. "Your chef worked at a Michelin Star restaurant. I doubt there's much of a comparison."

"Yes, but this one is very pretty to look at," my aunt says with a shrug.

"Aren't you, sweetheart?"

"Jesus Christ," Finn mutters under his breath, somehow still managing a polite smile.

Beside my aunt, Uncle John fiddles obliviously with his phone.

"We have a full chef's kitchen off of our primary," Aunt Marian tells Finn. She leans closer, over her plate, and the long pearls at her neck swing dangerously close to the swirl of peppercorn sauce around the rim. "It's completely state of the art, of course. I'd love to show you around. John heads to Dubai for work in a week's time and I would much appreciate the company."

My nails dig into Finn's skin. Has a more painful dinner ever existed?

I want to crawl out of my skin and leave behind my soulless carcass as a decoy while I slink away with him to safer ground.

"Marian, John is sitting *right there*," Mom says sharply. "You might consider his feelings—"

"And I'm sitting *right here*," I mumble without thinking. "You might consider mine."

And that's when it all goes to hell.

"What was that, Genevieve? Enunciate your words."

"You'll cook me a little something, won't you, Finn?" Aunt Marian says, completely undeterred. She twirls her pearls around a finger.

Finn rubs the back of his neck. "Ah..."

"I said: I'm sitting right here," I say more loudly, staring at my mother. "Is that enunciated any better? Will you ask your sister to stop harassing my boyfriend now?"

"Babe, it's fine—"

"Genevieve! You will respect your aunt. Goodness, I don't know where I went wrong with you. You'd think we never paired you with an etiquette coach."

Dad scrapes his knife loudly against his plate.

"You want to talk about etiquette? She's propositioning the guy I'm dating—"

"Dating?" Aunt Marian chimes in, her eyes darting between Finn and me.

She pulls a face. "*Really*? I don't see it."

"Yes, *dating* speaks to a little more permanence than you're used to, doesn't it, Genevieve?"

"What did you think he was doing here, exactly?"

My aunt shrugs. "I've heard of these Making of a Wish charities—"

"Make a Wish, Marian. Come now, you helped me with their gala last year."

"Is that seriously what you took away from what she just said to me? Dad, a little help here—"

"Don't you dare try to turn your father against me—"

"Jenna, would you show me the way to the washrooms?"

Finn stands, carefully placing his napkin on the table. He puts out a hand for me and even though he looks completely even keeled, his voice leaves no room for argument. He doesn't look back at my parents once, not even at Aunt Marian who seems to find him even more appealing with that note of steel in his voice. She gives him bedroom eyes he doesn't notice as she sips her wine.

He takes off the moment I drop my hand in his. Past the head table where Ronnie and her husband pose for photos. Across the dance floor and down the short path leading to the main building of the estate.

"Are we leaving?" I ask hopefully.

"No, baby. We're not leaving." He leads us through a set of French doors, following behind a server balancing a tray loaded with dirty dishes. "I'm about to show you exactly how good you deserve to feel."

Chapter 22

Jenna

"Finn, where are we going?"

"I don't know yet."

We wind through quiet hallways, past the loud, steaming kitchen. *I'm about to show you exactly how good you deserve to feel.* Did that mean—

"Finn, are we... Are you looking for a place to hook up?"

We reach a deserted sitting room at the back of the estate, where the lights are low over two deep leather armchairs facing a large, unlit stone fireplace. From here, you can only hear the vague sounds of piano from out in the gazebo, and the clinking of glass and plates from the kitchen down the hall. Finn maneuvers me against the wall.

"I'm not fucking you here," he says into my neck. "These people don't deserve to hear the kind of show we'd put on with that dress around your ankles. Besides, we don't need sex to feel good."

I grip the sleeves of his dress shirt. "I'm so sorry about all that. I had no idea my aunt was so... God, I don't even know what that *was*—"

"Shh," he says, prying my hairs off his shirt and placing them around his neck. "I don't give a shit about all that. Tell me you're okay."

"I'm so embarrassed."

"They're the ones who should be embarrassed." He kisses my forehead and tucks me against him. "The whole thing explains so much."

CHAPTER 22

"About why I'm so messed up?"

"About why you're so goddamn perfect. All that wrong eventually has to make a right. It's the law of nature."

I chuckle into his shoulder. "Which documentary is that from? It sounds like something someone made up to feel better about their misdeeds."

"It's not," he says with a shrug. "It's how human life came to exist after the asteroid killed dinosaurs."

"You're comparing me to the death of dinosaurs?"

He pulls away to give me a grin. "Jerboas then. Total freaks of nature, surprisingly cute."

"Is that the one that looks like a cross between a kangaroo and a mouse?"

"And a rabbit."

"Okay, I'll take it." I smile. "They are pretty cute."

"See? You're my smart, kind, beautiful jerboa, and there's no way in hell you should exist. But you do, and I've hit the jackpot in knowing you."

I cling to him, letting my fingertips toy with the hairline at the back of his neck, not wanting to muss his hair too badly. He is impossibly gorgeous. A dream when he's casually disheveled, and a full-on hallucination when he's dressed up like this.

Casual or dressed up, he looks at me the same way. Like I'm something important. Like he can't believe his luck. Which is crazy because I can barely believe mine.

"This didn't make you want to call it off? Being with me?"

"Not even a little. It'll take a major catastrophe to get rid of me now, Jenna." He beams at me. "You called me your boyfriend back there."

"Oh." I bite my lip. "I know we haven't talked about it, but... it's what you feel like. Is it too fast?"

"I fucking loved it." He smiles into a kiss so sweet and gentle, it's like he's trying to lick at my wounds. To soothe the sting not just from tonight, but from all the years before, when I never had an ally.

A burst of laughter breaks our peace, and we both swivel toward the archway of our little haven.

"Wait here, okay?" He makes it halfway across the room before coming back to give me another kiss. "Needed to do that." He grins, backing away from me. "Give me three minutes."

He's back in two, with a corked bottle of champagne tucked under an arm and two heaping plates in his hands. He tips his head back the way he came.

"Come on. This way."

Catching up, I see the plates are piled high with desserts. Bite-sized tarts and beautifully iced cookies, and the colorful profiteroles Ronnie's been raving about since her food tasting.

"What is all this?"

"Our dinner," he says with a wink over his shoulder. He leads me toward the oversized French doors leading to the parking lot.

"Grab the bottle for me," he says when we reach his car.

I slip the bottle from under his arm and take one of the plates too. Finn opens the trunk and hops up to sit on the bed, feet dangling over the end of the car, and helps me up next.

I gather up the skirt of my dress, needing to feel the summer breeze on my skin. Wincing, I kick off the towering heels my sister mandated as part of our uniform. They've been badly pinching my toes all night, even while I sat through dinner, and that's saying something considering I rarely leave the house in a pair of shoes that doesn't add at least a few inches to my height.

As his first order of business, Finn neatly uncorks the bottle of champagne, letting the mist float from its neck before passing it to me. I take a long swig.

"How'd you convince them to give this to you?" I ask, passing it back. "They're not even serving dessert yet."

He gives me a sheepish shrug before sipping from the bottle.

"Look at you blush! Did you steal this?"

"I would *never* steal," he says in mock-outrage, handing me a heart-shaped cookie coated in shiny rose-gold frosting. "It was completely above the belt."

"Then tell me," I say with a laugh. "How'd you pull this off?"

He makes a face, pushing a loose strand of hair off his forehead. "You know. It was just..." He gives me a wide, crooked grin, the one that lights him up all the way to his eyes. My stomach flips reflexively.

CHAPTER 22

I snort. "Say no more. The King of England would throw his crown at your feet if you flashed that thing."

He shrugs again, biting into a tart with purple filling and handing me the champagne. "And yet, I couldn't finagle us champagne glasses. What a wake-up call."

"Yeah, your charm's really wearing off. It's as though you weren't just subjected to my middle-aged aunt making sexual advances while my uncle sat right next to her."

Finn shakes his head. "That was... Your mom is a piece of work."

"I warned you."

"And I believed you, but... I'm not sure anything could have prepared me for that. She's so frigid. And then she looks at your sister and it's like she's seeing the stars for the first time."

"Did I ever tell you she sent me off with our driver and my dad's credit card to buy my first bra as a kid?"

He sighs deeply. "I wish I could undo it all for you."

"I wish I'd been able to meet your mom. Do you think she would have liked me?"

Finn props himself up with his arms behind him. "She'd be madly in love with you. She'd listen to you talk about your childhood and run herself ragged trying to make it up to you."

I smile. "Would she take me to Chuck E. Cheese?"

"You've never been to Chuck E. Cheese?"

"Never."

"She'd take you there and feed you all the pizza you wanted. She'd jump into the ball pit with you, and mess around until they kicked you both out. She'd split some wine with you in the parking lot, and you'd both get so buzzed you'd have to call me to pick you up."

Balancing the plate of sweets on my lap, I lean back and tip my head to look at the darkening sky through the open top of the car.

"That sounds lovely. Is it totally weird if I pretend it's a real memory?"

He kisses my shoulder. "I'll pretend with you."

It feels impossible to have found someone like him. Someone who indulges me when I feel on top of the world just as much as when I feel rundown and insecure. And what I feel for him... I've been hurling toward the edge of this cliff since the second I met him. Since the moment I realized he'd been the one Jude had tried to set me up with.

"Why didn't you ever call me?"

Finn lolls his head to the side, brows furrowing at the question. The light from the setting sun brightens his eyes and deepens the tan he's built over the summer.

"When Jude first gave you my number," I explain. "You told her you had your reasons for not asking me out."

Finn rests his head on the back of the seat behind him. "It's hard to explain."

"Try."

He drags his thumb through the condensation coating the bottle of champagne sitting between us.

"In hindsight, it was stupid. I'd just met Jude, and I thought she was great. She really talked you up, and I thought... Okay. I'm not prepared to change my tune with relationships. And there's a real chance I meet you and you're exactly as good for me as she says. That you're exactly what I made you out to be in my head. And then I'd be in trouble. So, I never called."

"Was I? Exactly what you made me out to be?"

He shakes his head, eyes so soft when they meet mine. "You're so much better. You don't know how bad I want to go back to the night we met, just to shake myself. To tell myself to knock off the bullshit. To open my eyes. To pay attention, because that was it: *the* moment. The one people are only so lucky to have. I'd just found my person. My... my Jenna. And that meant from there on out, everything would be okay."

My nose burns, so badly I know I only have a moment to gather myself before the feeling engulfs me. I close my eyes. Willing myself to hold back the tears, not because I'm afraid of crying in front of him. But because I feel so unbelievably happy and full in this moment that tears feel out of place. I want to bask in Finn and the way he looks at me, those crooked smiles, and the way he constantly makes me laugh.

CHAPTER 22

I feel him shuffle around beside me. His lips meet my skin, the sensitive spot under my jaw, the hollow of my cheek, the tip of my nose. Bracing the back of my head with a strong hand and parting my lips with his. He tastes so sweet, like champagne and vanilla frosting. I chase more of it, a total sugar craving as I deepen the kiss, find his tongue with mine.

God, he was so worth the wait.

Finn groans with abandon, like it's the best he's ever had. If I ever learn that he kissed like this with the women before me I'll be crushed.

"Should we go home?" I whisper when he breaks for air.

He shakes his head, mumbles an *uh-uh* before coming back in for more, nibbling on my lip and taking it between his to soothe the sting.

"You want to stay?" I ask when we break apart next.

He shakes his head again. "We left your purse and my jacket at the table."

I lick at his neck. "We get them and go home?"

He grunts, tipping his head and offering me more skin to kiss, to graze with my tongue. "We need to pump the brakes, baby, or I'm gonna make a real fool of myself."

I nip his jaw. "Then you should probably let go of me."

He looks completely pained but he untangles himself anyway and shifts around, adjusting the distorted front of his dress pants. The bulge is obscene and there's just no hiding it.

I've made a mess of him. His hair has escaped confinement, spilling onto his forehead, and he's got shiny gloss on and around his mouth. He sits patiently as I clean him up. Pushing back his hair and rubbing off my lip gloss.

"You too," he says when I finish, and he combs through the strands of hair around my face, carefully running the tips of his fingers around my lip line.

"How bad is it?"

"I love you like this. Wild hair, lips all red. The way your cheeks go pink. You look like a dream."

"And what kind of dreams are these, Finn?"

"I'll show you," he says with a smirk, and a hot flash goes off in my stomach. He slides off the bed of the trunk. "Let's get the fuck out of here, yeah?"

Kneeling at my feet, he slides one of my shoes on, stretching the front strap as wide as he can when I wince.

"Shoes off? You've got nasty blisters over your toes."

"Can't. My mom would have my head."

He sets his jaw in a way that tells me he isn't happy with my answer. But, very carefully, he slides on my other heel and helps me to my feet. I shift uncomfortably.

"It's okay," I say when he looks at my feet uneasily, though they're now covered by my dress. "We'll be in and out of there. Should we bring back the rest of our desserts?"

"Nah. Consider it payment for your troubles."

Without warning, he scoops me into his arms and carries me across the parking lot back to the main building. He takes me all the way through to the door leading back to the gazebo, before setting me down and holding my arm until I've steadied on my feet.

"Gotta run to the washroom," he tells me. "Wait here, okay? We'll go in together."

Through the paneled doors I see that we've missed the rest of dinner. Most of the tables are vacant now, and the lights over the dance floor have dimmed. I catch glimpses of Ronnie's white ball gown out in the crowd dancing to the live band.

Standing here with the glass doors separating me from the party and my family, I've never felt more like a coward.

Why should I hide?

Finn's right. I've done nothing wrong, and if anyone should feel embarrassed by their performance at dinner, it should be my mother, closely followed by her sister.

The girl Finn dreams about doesn't hide.

I slip off my heels and tiptoe down the stone path to the gazebo. The guests seem to have split almost evenly between the dancefloor and the bar. The band finishes off the last notes of a song and flows seamlessly into the next.

Oh, I *love* this song.

CHAPTER 22

I slip into the gazebo, walking the perimeter to make it back to our vacant table. Dad is over by the bar, speaking to someone who's name I don't remember but who I'm fairly certain lives next door to my parents' beach house. I scan the space for my mom, shimmying to the music on the spot.

"Hey." Finn's voice is in my ear. "You wanna dance?"

My gaze drifts back to the dance floor. Ronnie is all smiles, twirling with her new husband, sending her dress spinning around her.

"We probably shouldn't."

"Jenna Bear. You're dancing in a corner."

"Really, it's fine—"

"There's nothing fine about it." He brings my hand up to his lips. "You belong in the middle of a crowd. Come on."

It's not quite the middle of the crowd. I stop us at the edge of the dance floor, giving Ronnie a wide enough berth. Finn spins me once before taking me by the waist, grinning wide when I start to let go, standing on the tips of my toes to give him a quick kiss. A thank you for coaxing me out here because I really do love this song. Without my shoes on, my dress is painfully long. So I gather the skirt in one hand and let Finn hold me tight to him. We fall into a comfortable hug where we sway together to the upbeat music.

Before long I'm giggling, a full goofy giggle because I can barely believe how much he's managed to turn this night around for me. I lift my chin to kiss him again. But Finn's gaze has drifted, and he looks suddenly drenched in dread.

"Fuck."

He moves quickly. Tucking me behind him, a shield against an incoming threat. And then I hear it.

"Genevieve."

My mother's voice is a hiss, barely audible over the band, but the fury in her eyes can't be diluted. She stops just short of Finn, trying to round him to get closer to me. But he shifts too, blocking her path, and so she settles for glaring at me over his shoulder.

"Hi, Mom," I say nervously. "Is everything okay?"

"Where in God's name are your shoes?"

"What?"

"Your shoes, Genevieve. How dare you come in here like some sort of classless—"

"What's going on?"

Ronnie materializes at my mother's shoulder. She eyes Finn, sizing him up for the first time all day. I drop the skirt of my dress, letting it cover my bare feet.

"Your sister has decided to forgo footwear. And to make out with her flavor of the month right in the middle of your reception."

Ronnie purses her lips, looking like Mom in a way I never could. "Mom, I think the words you're looking for are *flavor of the day*." She gives Finn a sickly-sweet smile. "She'll be spreading her legs for the next one by the time the sun comes up. Sorry to break the news. It's how she's always operated."

My soul is quietly shriveling in humiliation. I should grab Finn and get us out of here, but I can't for the life of me get my feet to move. Finn stands perfectly still. A few people on the outskirts of the dance floor have stopped to eavesdrop.

Why did I bring him here? Why did I think it was a good idea, exposing him to this? Why—

"I can guarantee you I've fucked more people than you lay eyes on in a month."

I choke on my inhale. Finn has drawn himself to his full height, and when I finally force myself to take a step out from behind him, he looks as pissed off as I've ever seen him, worse than the night he picked me up off the sidewalk. Frankly, I wasn't sure he was *built* to reach this level of fury.

But there's so much raw contempt in his face as he glares at my sister, all hard eyes and snarled mouth. "Let me make something real clear to you. I could be her flavor of the minute and I'd still have more respect for her than for the both of you, who can't even go one happy family event that *has nothing to do with her* without managing to make it about her anyway, and how badly you keep failing her as her family."

"What in God's name is going on here?" Dad appears at my shoulder and takes in our scene. To an outsider not immediately within earshot, it could

CHAPTER 22

pass for a casual family conversation were it not for the raw venom in Finn's face. Ronnie is still smiling wide, disguising her disapproval, and Mom is as stone-faced as ever.

Finn takes a long, steadying breath. "With all due respect, Gord, I thought my family was messed up. But this takes the fucking cake." I'm not quite sure how his eyes manage to soften when he turns to me, but they do. "How you turned out so kind and selfless, and utterly perfect around all this is nothing short of a goddamn miracle. Are you about done trying to fit in with this bullshit?"

"Yeah," my voice is shaky and a little bit gravelly, but it's clear above the music. "I'm done."

"Now hold on a minute, Peanut," Dad says, taking my arm. "You're part of this family. You should be here with us—"

"What part of this is family, Dad? Two of you can't stand me, and you can't ever back me up to their faces. I'm done being the only one to try and smooth things over. To change my hair color just to make someone else happy." I ignore Dad's sputtering and turn to my mother. "A few weeks ago, I'd never have been able to come up with a reason to quit trying so hard to get you to love me. Or act like you love me. Now? I have no idea what I was thinking. You and I are a lost cause, aren't we?" I rip my gaze from the way she purses her lips, refusing to engage me, and settle them on Ronnie instead. "I'm just sorry I tried so hard. I'm better than what you've put me through. And if by some miracle one day you wake up realizing how badly you fucked up, how horrible you've been to me, let me be clear: you'll have to work damn hard to make it up to me." I turn to Finn. "Take me home."

He grins, big and crooked and genuine.

"Let's get the hell out of here."

Chapter 23

Finn

I'm a happy guy.

Mom used to love telling stories about me like it was some mythic thing, where I started smiling and laughing sooner than babies usually do.

I wouldn't know. But growing up I do remember, and my mood would run high about ten out of ten times. Even these days. Yeah, I tend to hide behind comedy or play up the dopey thing to deflect, but I am mostly happy to be here, alive. I still have my dad and Hayls. Have a great job, great friends, and my perfect girl. What do I have to complain about?

I can count on a single hand the number of times I've lost my mind. The last time, I sent half a chicken flying through the air. This time, I confessed to my girlfriend's mother that I've fucked my way through my adult life. Not my proudest moment. But the pride I felt watching Jenna march out of that reception without a single look back at that joke of a family... There's no better feeling.

I don't know where we're going. With a hand on my arm, Jenna told me to miss the freeway exit leading home, and from the passenger seat she's quietly directed our route for the past couple of hours.

I watch her closely on the drive. She's quiet, barely cracking a smile with the wind in her hair. But she also doesn't look upset. Not a single tear in

CHAPTER 23

sight, no frown, nothing but calm control.

She catches me looking and leans over to kiss me on the cheek.

And that's the second I figure it out.

I understand how much of a goner I am. How much I've lost my head for her, how going back to the life I knew when I wasn't in love with Jenna Carling is as impossible as denying the moon landing.

And I'm hungry for more of her. To feel her and know her, inside and out, to learn everything that makes her tick. To give her back every ounce of the joy she's ever given me, multiplied by a thousand. To make her feel as wanted, and important, and alive as she's made me feel.

We pull into a long, sequestered drive and when we stop at a gate Jenna leans over me in the driver's seat to punch in a code through the window. And then we curve around a tree-lined bend, and a colossal house comes into view. Even in the dark I can tell it's the definition of old money. Bricks, spotless white columns and railings. I park us right in front of the door, and even without cutting the engine I hear waves on the other side of the house. It must sit on a lake.

Jenna holds my hand all the way inside, and I gather up the hem of her bridesmaid dress when she almost trips over it. She's still shoe-less, in the socks I pulled off my own feet so hers wouldn't get dirty walking around.

"My parents' beach house," she says, and her voice is heavy.

We stand in the foyer at the foot of a large, curving staircase, and Jenna takes in the place almost like she's never seen it before. The massively high ceilings, the all-white furniture I'm afraid to sit on because I'd probably stain them just by breathing nearby. The wall of windows beyond the staircase, framing what's probably a private beach. It's a level of filthy rich I couldn't have wrapped my head around unless I saw it for myself.

"This place is insane."

"That's the perfect way of putting it," she says. "I felt like I was going insane every time I stayed here."

"When was the last time you came?"

"Two Christmases ago. I was supposed to stick around a couple of days, but only lasted a night before needing a breather. To put a whole two hours between me and Veronica."

I nod, gazing up at the landing at the top of the stairs. "You want me to burn the place down?"

I smile at the sound of her soft laugh. "You'd do that for me?"

"Definitely. I'd Bonnie and Clyde the hell out of life with you, Jenna. It's not even a question."

She moves closer, touching her head to my shoulder. "I don't even know why I brought us here. I feel like a trespasser and I have a key to the front door."

"Wanna know my theory?" She nods. "Maybe you wanted to know what it feels like to be here with someone in your corner. Maybe you've realized you deserve to have something good happen to you here."

"I think you're onto something." She turns those perfect eyes on me. "The place is empty. They're all at the wedding."

There's something thick and pressing whirling in the air between us, and when I notice her fingers shaking a little, I know she feels it too. It feels like a moment. We're at the precipice of something important, me and her, and we stare at each other silently, letting the air between us sizzle.

I thread our fingers together. "I haven't felt this nervous since my first time."

Jenna presses my hand to her chest, letting me feel the wild pace of her heart. "Me, too. Finn, I'm so glad we held out."

"So am I."

She gets me into the most lusciously slow kiss before leading me up the stairs, down a long hallway, passing bathrooms and near-identical bedrooms. Through the last door, another white bedroom with a big four poster bed facing the windows to its own balcony. The room looks like it could be featured in one of those interior design magazines I've seen Jude read. It *smells* expensive in here. But there's also something uncomfortably cold about it.

Jenna sits on the end of the bed. "My room."

"When did you live here last?" I ask, looking around at the blank walls.

"It's been a while. But it looks exactly the same. My mom was very specific about the decor."

She hops off the bed and goes to a floor-length mirror on the opposite wall. I watch her move around a little weird as she looks at herself in the glass. Cocking her hip. Sweeping her hair off her shoulders. Bending at the knees.

"This was Ronnie's favorite game," she says without looking around. "The *you'd be so much more pretty if* game."

What the fuck?

Jenna takes hold of her hair and coils it on top of her head. "You'd be so much more pretty if you put your hair up. Yours is too messy." She drops her hair and bends her knees. "You'd be so much more pretty if you were five inches shorter. All the boys like girls smaller than they are." She pinches the sides of her bridesmaid dress. "You'd be so much more pretty if you wore dresses like mine. You can borrow the ones I wore last year."

A thick, hard lump rises in my throat, and my eyes start to burn. She doesn't look sad, looking into this mirror. She's completely deadpan, immune to the words she must have heard over and over growing up. It's the lack of emotion that gets me the worst.

I rub the tears out of my eyes with the back of my arm and go to her. She meets my gaze in the mirror. I love this woman so much it's painful. Like there's a tight fist wrapped around my heart, squeezing hard whenever I look at her. A sore, burning lump in my throat I never want to get rid of.

"I'm obsessed with you," I say, and my voice comes out gravelly from holding back tears. "Every bit of you."

Her eyebrows shoot up and she gives a surprised chuckle. "I don't know what to say to that."

I take her chin, turn her head, kiss her over her shoulder.

"That's okay. I'll do the talking."

Chapter 24

Jenna

I feel it.
 The exact moment this kiss turns different from the others, the minute the intent changes, expands. Loses its boundaries. If before he decided he wasn't going to go there, not yet, this time Finn's not looking back.
 He kisses my cheek. Behind my ear. Soft kisses on my neck. My shoulders are rising and falling quick, building speed as he brushes over my upper back, finding the zipper of my dress, fingering the straps before he brushes them off my shoulders, and lets it fall to my feet. The fabric was so fine I couldn't get away with underwear, and right now I'm grateful.
 "I love your body," Finn tells me, feasting on his view in the mirror, running his fingertips along my waist. "God, look at you. All the curves and long limbs. I've already got each one of your freckles memorized." He traces them along my back. "I could place them like a constellation."
 With his eyes on me like this, it's impossible to feel self-conscious. Even here, in this spot where I've been made to feel insignificant so many times.
 He trails a hand along my hip, down the crease of my leg. I bite my lip. So hard it pillows around my teeth. He changes direction. Strokes my cheek, my jaw.
 "I'm crazy about your smile. I'd make a fool of myself ten times over just

to see that dimple once." He pinches my chin and I give him a small smile in the mirror. "Your tits are the perfect handful." He takes them in his palms.

"They're too big for your hands."

"Like I said: perfect."

He slides his hands down. One stopping at my hip, the other trailing further, fingers spreading me as he strokes my clit. My eyes fall shut on a moan, but Finn presses his lips to my ear.

"Eyes open." He waits until I look back at our reflections. "Look at how beautiful you are. How pink your cheeks get when you're turned on. Your perfect mouth; how I can't stop picturing the way it looked around my cock. The way your hips are rocking, greedy for my fingers."

I mumble something unintelligible as his fingers slide inside me, just for a second. He brings them up to my mouth.

"Lick." With my heart in my ears, I do what he says. He lets me have a taste, then sinks his fingers into his own mouth. "You're so fucking flawless, you even taste good. So flawless that I panic every time I wake up, thinking I must have dreamed you up. That there's no way you're real. No way I'm the one lucky enough to have you."

I've got jitters. My body is pulsing as he gets hands on my hips. Spins me around to face him. Cups my ass and lifts me up. I wrap my legs around his waist, the urgency suddenly dialed up to a hundred. Get my fingers in his hair, bringing his mouth to mine, dropping my hands down between us the second he starts moaning against my lips. I attack the buttons of his dress shirt, shoving it off his shoulders.

The second it's gone he lurches forward, bracing me to him. Making sure we don't lose an inch of contact when he lies me down on the plush white carpet. The surge of anticipation is like no other. Not just a little pang of excitement. I'm aching to feel him on me, in me, desperate to touch him everywhere.

The second I'm flat on my back he pulls my hands over my head. "Hands stay up here. Don't move."

"But—"

With a hand he digs mine into the carpet above my head, using the other to lift my chin.

"Don't move." His grin is teasing. "Tell me you get it. Nod your head yes."

I nod and his smile deepens. "That's my good girl."

I whimper, and I can't tell whether it's for the words or the kisses he's trailing down my neck and across my collar bone.

"I'm so not a good girl."

"I know. But you will be for now."

Finn licks a path down my chest, kissing between my breasts, teasing bites inches from my nipples. And God it takes everything in me not to grip him by the hair and pull him there, missing the feel of his mouth since the last time he gave it to me. The anticipation is unbearable.

"I'll let you play eventually," he murmurs, kissing under my breast. "This? This is how bad I've needed you. This is what happens when I hold out for a year because, deep down, I knew no one would compare to you."

"It's been a *year?*"

Still kneeling over me, Finn rubs a thumb over my nipple. I tip my head all the way back and whimper like it's the first time I've been touched.

"A year," he says, brushing his lips over the other breast. "And next time I'll go as fast as you want. But I'm gonna take my time with you now."

And he takes my nipple into his mouth, rewarding me with a firm nip when I cry out his name. Sucking and licking, and it doesn't satiate me, not even a little. The pulsing ache between my legs deepens, thickens, breath picks up at a brutal pace the longer he teases me.

I might pass out.

It feels like I could pass out from want and I grip desperately to reality so that I don't miss a second of it. The way his mouth and fingers toy with me. How, after a last hungry tug his teeth leave my nipple in favor of lips trailing down my stomach. Covering as much skin as he can on the way down. Kisses across my stomach, the edges of my waist. Making me more and more delirious and my hands are fists, shaking fists above my head. I need to touch him so badly.

Need him to touch me, *really* touch me, so badly as he licks an easy path along the crease of my hip, and when he continues straight down with kisses along my leg, I cry out in frustration.

"I don't know what we had to be nervous about," he says from somewhere down by my knee. His hand trails up and I feel his fingers slip on the damp inside of my thigh. "This pussy has been calling my name since the second we met, hasn't it?"

"Don't pretend you haven't wanted it just as bad."

The world spins. Finn turns me around flat on my stomach, coming up to kiss the back of my neck. "There's no pretending," he says against my spine. "Tell me you see how crazy I am about you, Jenna. *You.* Every little bit of you."

And with a lick down the length of my back, with fingers skimming the line of my ass, he pulls my lower body up by the hips and drops me down on my knees so that I'm laying with my forehead against the carpet, hands still above my head.

Oh God, oh God, oh God—

More kisses down the back of my thigh. "You're shaking, Jenna."

"You're not being very nice—"

"No? What is it you want?"

"I want you to fuck me."

He hums against my calf. "We're not quite there yet."

I meet his gaze in the mirror. He's goading me. "Please." It bursts out of my mouth. "Please, Finn. *Please* fuck me—"

And the next sound out of me is a moan thick with relief. Finn's tongue gives my pussy one long, slow stroke, wrenching a desperate cry out of me when his tongue continues all the way up, ending on his own groan as though he's missed the way I taste. His fingers make the next contact, brushing over my clit, dipping just inside me, cupping me, feeling every part of me.

"How do you want it?" He's up by my ear and in another flash I'm on my back again, taking in the naked hunger on his face. He bites my neck and soothes the skin with a kiss. "How do you wanna come, the first time? Tell me quick, baby. I'm about a second away from fucking us into oblivion, just like this."

He's not kidding. His arms are shaking under the strain of his weight and the minute I realize it, the second I realize his game is over I have a hand gripping his cock through his pants. He groans into my neck.

"*Jenna. How do you want it?*"

He's frustrated. He's as desperate for me as I am for him, and God that's so *hot*. I want to see what he looks like completely unraveled. Stripped free of all bravado, control. Drowning in need. I want to see what he looks like when it gets so bad he becomes unhinged.

"I want your mouth."

Finn lets out a harsh breath and bites my neck. "Look who's not being nice, now."

I run a hand up his stomach. "I told you. I'm not a good girl."

But he wipes the smile clean off my face when he pulls away completely, throwing himself down on the ground next to me. I soak him in. The sheen of sweat over his chest, the ridges over his stomach, the dress pants straining from the weight of his cock as it tries to escape confinement. I want it to escape confinement. I want to hold it and kiss it and adore it, better than I did last time. I want to taste every inch of his body, like he just did with mine.

"Get on," he urges me.

He's breathing hard as he brushes a hand over his cock. He's not showing me where to go, I realize. The move looks absent-minded, like he's giving in to a raging urge. I watch him go for a moment. Loving how hot he is, how there's a barely-there shake to his hand as he strokes himself through his pants, and how his eyes glide over me. Darting from my face to my breasts, down my torso.

"Jenna." With a frustrated huff he pulls me on top of him so that I straddle his hips, bracing myself with palms open on his chest. "Get up here."

I'm a little disappointed at the sudden change of pace, because—I'm not going to lie—I was really dying to feel the slip of his tongue on me. But I bend down to offer him a nipple anyway. Immediately, it's clear that's not what he was asking for. His eyes widen in surprise but with a little laugh he takes the offering, nibbling at me a while until he gently pries away.

"Not what I meant, but it's almost a good substitute." He gives me his

CHAPTER 24

lopsided grin and drags me by the hips, up his body. "Get that pussy up here, Jenna."

Fuck.

Like he can't help himself, Finn lifts to gently suck at my clit. Eyes closing blissfully for a second like it's so good, *so good,* for him too. When they open again, there's something dark in them. Something goading, and I know exactly what it's about. We've talked the talk. He could easily lay me down, eat me out until I lose my mind. But he wants to see me take the reins. See how far I'm willing to go.

"Fuck my tongue," Finn orders. "Don't stop 'til you come."

"And if I don't?" I taunt.

Finn looks up at me with greed and a touch of irritation. He wrenches me down, gently licking my clit, moving me by the hips so that I'm riding his face, and—

I reach out, bracing myself with palms against the mounted mirror and he drops his hands to give me the control. I cry out at the first grind against his hot, stiff tongue. Hands trembling, legs shaking, barely able to keep up a smooth rhythm once I notice he keeps his eyes on me. The furrow in his brows deepens every minute I go, every press of my clit against his tongue, every scrape of his scruff on my skin.

I catch movement in my peripheral vision and it's me, in this mirror, looking feral and powerful and blissed out, fucking this perfect man's face. Finn reaches up to cup my breast in one hand, and I feel—*watch*—the way his fingers toy with me. Watch his other arm flex and rock as he rubs his cock behind me. And oh, that is *so fucking hot,* I'd almost rather turn around and watch that instead. But I've hit my stride now, and I couldn't pull myself off him even if I wanted to. Grinding even harder, the way I need it. And if I'm pushing his jaw past its limit, he doesn't show it.

It's his sounds that really get me going, though. The hungry noises he makes against my pussy, the tight little groans. They get my pace up notch by notch until I'm barely breathing. The only thing I can muster is the grind against his mouth. I reach for my other breast, the one he isn't teasing, and play with my nipple. Finn's eyes shut for a second, like he's fighting off delirium.

I missed this. Missed this, I missed this—and oh God—

"Oh, fuck. Finn—"

He nods frantically against me, urging me to let go until I do. I'm a tight string, stretching thin until finally I'm snapping apart, crying out, trembling over him, rubbing into his mouth for as long as I can. Collapsing forward onto this mirror when I can't anymore. Finn takes over for me, letting me ride my orgasm with gentle, soothing licks until my legs steady out.

"God, Finn." I lift off him. "I've definitely never done that in this mirror before."

He lays soft kisses on the insides of my thighs as I work to regain my breath. Licks his lips, running a hand over his glistening stubble, then sucking at his fingers.

"You're incredible," he says. There's adoration over every bit of his face. "So perfect, I can't take it."

He lifts me, switching our positions so that I'm flat on the carpet. At some point he managed to pull his cock free from his pants and they hang there, low on his hips. He takes my hand when I reach for him, lacing our fingers instead. Gazing down with heavy lids, hazy eyes, but also like he's determined to get words out before he can't anymore.

"Jenna, I... I want you to know that the way you look... What's inside you is even better. I adore every part of you. All the good bits, and I'm pretty sure that if I ever found a bad bit I'd adore it too." He pauses, brows crinkling almost like he's chastising himself. "I'd *love* it too. I'm in love with you."

This is better than the orgasm. God help me, it is. My eyes start to burn, nose prickles, and I swear, if Finn weren't pressed on top of me, I'd levitate off the ground.

Finn dots his finger under my eye, catching a tear. I run my fingers through his hair. "I love you, too. So much, Finn."

His smile beats the orgasm, too. "I wish I didn't tell you that for the first time with my dick sticking out of my pants."

I breathe out a laugh and he kisses my forehead. I'm still made of jelly, riding a high from the orgasm and the words and the smile, and he arranges

CHAPTER 24

me underneath him, spreading my legs.

"I need to fuck you now," he says, with hands waiting at his waistband. "Still up for it?"

"Is that a serious question? I might die if we don't." I nudge his hands out of the way, tugging down his pants myself. He helps me get them down to his knees, shuffles to kick them off and stills completely when I wrap my fingers around his cock.

He chuckles. "Did you just sigh?"

"I totally sighed," I tell him, stroking him gently. "It's been a year for me too."

Finn's chest heaves as he soaks in the revelation. That whatever this has been between us, he's never been in it alone. He lays a hand on top of mine, tightening my grip and upping my pace. Letting out his own sigh. We watch our hands for a moment, working together to get him off.

"Jenna, please tell me you have condoms in your childhood bedroom."

I laugh and it's the first time he's ever looked distraught at the sound of it. "I'm on the pill."

He swallows. "I'm clean. I know you only have my word to show for it, but I promise you I've been checked."

"I trust you. I'm okay, too."

It's incredible how a year off from sex can make you wonder: did it always feel this way?

Did I always get that rush of goose bumps up my torso, or is it only because it's Finn gripping my knees and pulling my legs up high around his waist? I guide his cock down where I need it. A whimper catches halfway up my throat, and nothing's even happened yet. It's only that first touch, the first nudge.

He's only a little inside me now, and then just an inch, and another one, and I can't keep my eyes off him because he's deeper than anyone's ever been. Finn holds the nape of my neck, looking down with crinkled brows, a slacked jaw, eyes a little out of focus as his cock slowly disappears inside me. And then, with a burst of momentum, he fills me completely.

"Oh my God." My moan is pure sexual relief, even though we've barely started.

"I knew it," Finn breathes as he pulls away and eases back in. His arms shake under his weight. "I knew it would be like this. I knew we'd fit so good."

I press my heels into his ass, pulling him in all the way again. "Stay there for a bit," I whisper, holding him still. I need to soak in the way it feels when he's deep, the way he presses into me from all sides and angles. "You feel amazing like this."

With dazed eyes and a lick of his lips, Finn kisses me. Pulls back to bite my lip, tilts his head to give me more. I can feel his hips vibrate, straining to move, but he stays still, fitting his hips flush against mine and keeping every inch of his cock inside me.

"You just wrecked me, you know that?" he says, with wet kisses down my neck. Still, he doesn't move his hips. "I don't know how to recover from this. Every second we're not fucking is a second wasted, from here on out."

"Quit your job. Quit everything but me."

"Fuck yeah," he breathes, awed like I've just given him the secret of the universe.

With my fingers in his hair I moan into the kiss because suddenly it's a sensation overload, feeling his lips and the hard, perfect throb of him inside me.

"Jenna. Let me move now," he begs me. "I need to move."

I drop my legs. "Fuck me."

With a grunt he starts to slide his body in and out of mine. Every push shoves a wave of heat down my body, so powerful and perfect and everything I need, and my eyes struggle to stay open. I can't let myself close them, though. I'm captivated by the way his mouth shapes around a groan, how his forehead slicks with sweat from the effort of holding steady at a soft rhythm. Because I can feel it, him holding back. Every few pushes his hips drive forward with aggression, like they're protesting the gentle pace, trying to break through into something more feral.

But he seems hellbent on taking me like this. Kissing me between my moans and his pants. Holding my face, stroking my cheek with his thumb like I'm something precious to him, watching me melt and whimper under him as he fucks me slow.

He groans against my lips. "Jenna, it's so good. I've fucking peaked. This is it. Nothing will ever feel better than this."

I nod, eyes out of focus, unable to get the words out but I'm right there with him. I hold him by the hips, and even *that* feels good. Feeling his body sway over mine.

He gives me another hard drive and it leaves me reeling this time, echoes all the way through me, unleashing something in me. I don't want him to hold back. I want him frenzied; I want him fucking me until it's lights out. Until I can't see, can't move.

I force him steady, gripping the pulsing muscles in his ass, and start fucking up into him. "Harder, Finn."

He grunts. "I'm trying to last for you. It's been a while—"

"You will last." I pull him in with a fistful of hair, slick his tongue with mine. "You'll last because I'm asking you to. And you'll do it fucking me harder than this."

I push into him faster until, with a groan, he meets me halfway with sharp, punishing thrusts. I'm sliding up the carpet and reach above me to brace my hands against the mirror, keeping me in place. His hand lands above mine for leverage as he roughly snaps his hips. Driving his cock in and out of me until he's sweating, really sweating, and a drop of it hits my cheek and I moan like he's just given me something amazing. I can't moan anymore, can't even suck in a breath as my head raps against the mirror behind me.

"*Fuck.*" The word bursts from his mouth. His eyes are wild and he barely looks in control of himself anymore. "I need you to come again. Now, Jenna. I need to feel it—"

And he runs a hand down my body, rubbing my clit with the same firm pressure I'd applied against his tongue. We're a tangle of limbs and sweat. His hips moving in a blur, my breasts bouncing fast and it's blissful, watching him give up his control. But in the end, it's the noises he makes deep in his throat that get me there. These sexy, hard grunts over the sounds of lake water crashing outside. He fucks me so hard I come quietly this time, mouth open to a silent cry, hanging onto him tightly as I shudder, sinking my nails into his hips.

He's a lot less quiet than I am. His face crumbles, feeling me come apart around him, and he groans so desperately for a moment I think he's just come too. But he stays blissfully hard and thank God because I don't want this to end. I want to stay here on my back, pinned down by his weight and rocking with the gentle sway of his hips as he slows down to give me room to breathe.

"That feels unbelievable," he says, kissing me on the forehead, then my cheek, my neck. He runs a hand down my side, squeezes my ass. Flips us around so that I straddle him, holding me up by the waist when I sway unsteadily above him. "Again. Give me another one."

"I—" God, I want that. But it seems that year off really fucked with my system, because I can barely sit up without trembling.

"Yes, you can," he tells me and he reaches down to rub the tip of his cock along my pussy. "Give me another one. Fuck me."

When I still don't move he darts up to crash his mouth over mine, kissing me hard and fast like he's trying to revive me from my sex coma. He grips my jaw and forces my eyes on him. "Destroy me. Ruin my life. Make me regret waiting so long to fuck you. Show me what this pussy can do."

With a whimper I brace one hand on his chest, sinking my nails into his skin, and reach down between us. Finn settles back into the carpet. I play with him a little, rubbing his cock over my clit, feeling consciousness return to my body with every stroke. Finn lifts his head to watch the way he moves over me, breaths coming out in harsh, impatient bursts. He licks his lips when I move him down, fit him in an inch, and when I take him right out he clamps his jaw.

I smile and do it again, and again, watching frustration overtake the anticipation in his face every time his cock slips free from me. When I bring him to my entrance again, Finn takes me by the hips, so rough I'm convinced I'll wake up with fingertip bruises as he tries to tug me down.

"No," I say, lifting off him. His eyes hit me with a look of naked impatience. "Hands over your head, Finn. Let's see how you like it."

CHAPTER 24

With a smirk he complies, and his groan echoes around us when I sink down and start rocking on his cock. His eyes glide up and down my body, from my face to the place where we meet. I swivel my hips, circling them as I sink him in deep.

"*Fuck*. I like that. Do that again," he groans. His eyes settle on my hips as I move over him. "You're so fucking sexy, you know that? Look at you riding me like a fucking pro. You put in the work so one day you could take me this good, huh?"

I've never felt so powerful. So wanted. I've never had a man look up at me with so much awe, like he's in his own personal heaven. Praising how good I look. How wet I am. How perfect I feel.

"I'm gonna come quickly if you keep talking like that," I pant, grinding into him. Rocking my hips faster and slowing down again. His eyes lose focus. "Do you want this to last or not?"

"I asked for another one, didn't I?" He licks his lips, watching my breasts bounce. "You want me to stop talking, you're gonna have to put my mouth to good use."

"You want these?"

Finn's hands curl into tight fists when I pinch my nipples. "Don't tease me like that."

"Or what, Finn?"

With a harsh breath he jerks up, wrenches my hands off my body and takes a nipple in his mouth, dropping his hands to my hips to still me as he starts to roughly fuck up into me. At this angle my clit rubs blissfully against his body, and I feel it happening again. Start panting hard at the heat pooling between my thighs, spreading and spreading until I collapse against him. In the mirror behind him, I watch the way he throws back his head at the feeling, the way his muscles strain with effort as he pumps into me.

He winds his arms tight around my waist, holding me to him as he fucks me. And thank God because I couldn't stay upright if I tried. "Tell me this isn't over, Jenna." His voice is thick, thrusts a little sloppy now, and I know he's working hard not to come "Tell me I get to have you again. Tonight. Until we can't anymore."

"Tonight." I pull him in for a kiss. "Tomorrow." And another. "Whenever you want."

And that's all it takes. He drops me flat on my back, fucks me fast and hard and a little bit painful. His abs contracting with every thrust, fingers holding my hips in place so tight. Not letting up until—

"Oh, *f-fuck*. Jenna—Jenna, Jenna, Jenna—"

I could watch Finn come for the rest of my life. The way his face twists, brow furrows, the way he desperately calls my name like it's a mantra, like I'm the only one who can make him come this hard. I could do it forever. He hunches over me, regaining himself, and I pull his weight down on me. Scraping my nails up and down his back as he pants into my neck.

"I haven't—it hasn't been—" He swallows. "I don't think I've ever fucked like that—"

I smile into his shoulder. "Like you wanted to break me in half?"

"Like I wanted to—like I wanted to become part of you." He lifts onto his elbows and kisses the growing smile off my face. "Is that a weird thing to say?"

I shake my head, eyes falling shut. God, I am so in love with him.

"Are you sore?" He shifts, trying to slide out of me, but I wrap my legs around him to stop him.

"Little bit," I admit with a breathless laugh. "But there's no way to describe how good I feel."

With a rumbling groan Finn scoops me up against him and stands, my legs locked around his waist. Somehow he's still inside me when he spins to collapse backwards on the bed, with me on top of him. He reaches out and pulls up the comforter from the side, bundling us underneath it.

"You did so good, baby. I'm so fucking lucky," he mumbles against my lips. "Let's just lay like this for a minute, okay? Then we go again."

The way he's slurring his words tells me it'll be longer than a minute. I stroke his hair, his cheek, and he grips his elbows with his arms around me. I lay little kisses along his neck until his breathing slows, my eyes close, and I fall asleep with him.

Chapter 25

Finn

Finn.

It's the best dream. Hearing my name in Jenna's voice is the kind of euphoria I'd feel if I walked straight into the sun and came out on the other side without a single burn. I'm weighed down, pressed into soft bedding, lungs constricted in the best way. And everything feels good. Every inch of my skin, that tightening sensation down my spine, the heat down my legs.

Open your eyes.

Something wet drags up my neck and I won't ever open my eyes. It smells like roses and honey, and this dream is my life now. Fingers run through my hair and my entire body bucks. So good.

God, Finn.

Please open your eyes.

"Wake up," Jenna's voice is a quiet whisper, and then a whimper.

Something shifts along my body, just a tiny movement before stilling again, and *fuck* that feels good. A little moan in my ear and my eyes wrench open.

Yes. This dream is my life now. Jenna gazes down at me, eyebrows twisting, teeth sinking into her lip. I'm groggy, looking around us. The lights are on, but it's still pitch black through the windows and there's nothing but the sounds of water crashing onto the beach outside.

"Did we sleep?" I mumble.

She kisses under my ear. "We slept."

"Are we awake?"

A little giggle against my neck. "You woke me up. Finn, you're still inside me."

Oh?

I test the theory. Shift my hips. I'm *hard* inside her. "This is..." I moan when she grinds down into me. "I'm a fucking genius."

Another giggle and it sets me off. I roll us onto our sides, face-to-face, get her knee up and punch my hips. I can't get much deeper at this angle, not as much as I want, but it's good. Really fucking good, because Jenna's face is right there, eyes on mine, lips close enough to taste, our harsh breaths mixing together.

"I missed sex," I tell her.

"Me too," she whispers.

She tilts her hips to give me a better angle and I'm in a little more. Like this, it isn't hard or fast. I stay inside her as far as I can get and we're rocking, grinding into each other and goddamn, it's amazing.

Jenna's eyes fall shut. "Oh my God."

"You like it like this?" I ask, combing the hair off her cheek.

She whispers a *yeah* with her mouth on mine and it's not amazing—it's *bliss* having her this close. It's more than I ever thought I could get out of sex. It's the way I should have been doing it all along, except that it would have been impossible because I haven't known Jenna all along.

"Tell me," I say against her lips. I'm not even sure what the rest of that sentence is, but she's Jenna, my Jenna, and she knows me. She knows everything.

"It's never been like this." She cups my face and she means it. "Finn, it's never been like this."

I moan. "Not for me, either."

Sex in love. What a fucking concept. I don't regret anything up to this point, not one bit. But fuck, it's nice to know this was out there just waiting

CHAPTER 25

for me.

I'm overheating. We're so close, sharing body heat, skin sticking together. I'm struggling to breathe with the force of the way we're kissing, and after a while it all starts to peak so high I can't do more than press my mouth against hers. Move my body against hers. I can feel her grind her clit on me every time we touch, hear how good it feels in each of her little moans. And it makes everything so much better.

I smooth a hand down her side, her waist, her hip, take a handful of her ass. She's perfection. A goddamn miracle. She's holding my cheek, eyes on mine and she doesn't need to tell me how much she likes it, *this*, being close to me too, but she does anyway.

She whispers a stream of *yeses* and *it's incredible* and *I want to stay like this*. She's talking like she's me, almost compulsively, like it's the kind of moment that needs to be filled with words and breathy moans and desperate groans and sheets rustling around us. Jenna comes with her mouth against mine and a sweet, quiet whimper, and I'm the one who's loud now, filling the room with a hard grunt when I go off a second later.

After a while, when I regain use of my own body, she follows my gaze to the white bed spread around us. It's a mess of distorted sheets.

"Think your parents will know we were here?"

She strokes my hair. "I don't care."

~

In the morning, Jenna doesn't have to ask.

I hop into the Wrangler on the passenger side, and with a happy squeak she runs around to the driver's seat. She blasts the music and we take off toward home. I've been stupid not letting her behind the wheel before now. I've missed out on that smile. The one that grows bigger when she really gets us going and her hair whips around her head.

I take one of her hands and bring it to my lips.

Jenna turns and smiles at me. And after a moment's hesitation she says: "I leave in a couple days."

There's hope over every bit of that perfect face. She wants me to ask her to stay. This is about the trip, sure. She wants me to ask her to cancel Europe, and I want her to, but there's another question in there. She's asking about the apartment.

It's the one thing we've never talked about, though if she's anything like me, the thought of her move-out date has popped into her head more than a few times this summer.

I'm torn. There's nothing that makes more sense than having her live there. We've already proven we can pull it off. But...

"You don't think that's too soon?" I ask. I can't tell if I want her to convince me it's a good idea or to tell me she was kidding.

"It's definitely crazy," she confirms. Her eyes linger on the road. "Living together this soon is crazy. But I'd like to stay."

My stomach sinks. That... wasn't helpful.

But I don't think she meant it to be helpful. The way she's firmly focused on the road ahead of her, I sense she needs me to arrive at the decision on my own.

I don't even know where this hesitation is coming from. I've told her I love her and given her every bit of me. I *feel* all in with her. Am I not? Is this the emergency exit I've been keeping in place, without even realizing it? All this has happened so fast. One second I'm pumping all the brakes on this thing with her. Now we're living together permanently?

Suddenly I wish I could snap my fingers and have the top come on this damn car. I need a second to think without the wind rushing in my ears. I think I might be panicking. My throat feels like it's constricting.

"Finn, forget I asked. It's crazy." She smiles over at me and she's trying not to be disappointed, but I know I've hurt her.

In my gut, I know that I'm spiraling over something that makes no sense. It'll feel like nothing the second we pull into the parking spot at home and settle into that sofa together. Me, Jenna, and Eddie. She belongs there. There's no question about it.

Yeah.

Jenna and her salty lamps, fuzzy blankets, and so many cupcakes that I could probably figure out this recipe down to the gram. Jenna, my little spoon—with her dimple and that tiny towel I can give back now that I'm

CHAPTER 25

allowed to see her naked. My Jenna Bear, wearing a t-shirt with my name scrawled across the back.

Hell, yeah.

That fist around my throat eases up. The relief—the want—almost drowns me. I twist around in my seat to look at her. "Jenna—"

Beyond her, I see headlights coming at us fast.

And then the world goes black.

Chapter 26

Finn

There are voices mixing in with the beeping.

They're low, slow, and too distorted to make out. I can't focus on them, anyway. Don't even bother focusing on them because it's the beeping that matters.

Beep. One second, two seconds. *Beep.* One second, two seconds. *Beep.* One second—

I feel something on my shoulder, gently shaking me. I don't look up. I keep my head buried in the scratchy blanket tucked over her, inhaling its sterile scent. Hand holding hers underneath it, pulsing my fingers along with the beeping, making sure I don't lose count.

"Finn."

Jude's voice comes into focus. She's speaking softly, and vaguely I feel stroking back and forth along my shoulders.

"Finn, honey," I hear her say. It's like she's speaking to me from the other side of a tunnel. "They need to take her for another round of tests."

More tests? My heart kicks into overdrive. I don't know how much more of this I can take.

The last time they took her away, they forgot to turn off the machine after they unplugged her and it was the sound of a flatline that greeted me when I returned from my own tests. It had me dry heaving until a nurse rushed in

CHAPTER 26

to tell me they'd just taken her away to reset her shoulder.

No. No more tests. She stays here where I can keep an eye on her. I shrug off Jude's hand.

The hand I'm holding squeezes mine tight. "Finn."

My joints are so stiff I feel like a stone sculpture coming to life. I haven't moved in what's probably been a week or a month or a year. Who the fuck knows. But I lift my head, make myself look at her. The purple bruising covering the side of her face. The cut slashing across her forehead. The dried-up flecks of blood at her hairline I couldn't get off without rubbing her skin raw. I'm told I don't look much better, but I haven't cared enough to check. The only proof is the searing pain I feel whenever I move too abruptly.

Every time I look at her I wish I'll see her healed up. But we've only been here a day.

"Finn, please stop looking at me like that," Jenna says softly. "I'm fine."

Jude's hand comes down on my shoulder again, and I see her through a kind of fog. "Come on, the nurses are waiting. Maybe you can get some air while we wait."

Air? Would that help?

I don't feel right. Haven't felt right since that split second before the accident. Even after Jenna's doctor came in to say that, besides the concussion, she was okay.

How do I ever feel right again after what happened? Watching that car come for us, stupidly trying to move her out of the way as though she wasn't strapped in place by a seatbelt. Coming to and seeing her limp body out on the sidewalk where the motherfucker who ran us over put her down as he called for help, until finally she opened her eyes as the ambulance pulled up.

Eleven years. I spent eleven years working to avoid this. And here I am anyway, in a hospital. With the image of the woman I love passed out on the fucking sidewalk burned into my brain. Why did I do this to myself?

Jenna pries her hand out of my deathgrip. "I'll be back in a bit, okay? They need to check on my concussion again." She tries to smile, flinching as it aggravates the bruises on her cheek. If I'd had anything to eat today, it would be halfway up my throat by now.

The nurse decides to take matters into her own hands. She moves between my chair and the bed, forcing me to stand. Jenna gives me a last anxious look as they wheel her bed out of the room. She stops the nurse long enough to whisper something to Theo, who's leaning against the wall by the door. He gives her a nod, and he eyes me without giving anything away.

"What, are you conspiring against me, now?" I say sullenly once she's gone.

Theo stays impassive as ever. "Sit down. Take it easy on your knee."

But I can't sit here another goddamn second. Can't take any more of Jude's sympathetic looks. The way everyone, Jenna included, has been tiptoeing around me like I'm that fucking transparent. Like they can all tell exactly what I'm thinking.

Theo throws out a hand, blocking my path when I reach the door. "Where are you going?"

"To get some air. Your girl seems to think I need some."

His jaw pulses at the contempt in my voice, and I know that in any other state he'd put me in my own hospital bed for using that tone while referencing Jude. But he must see a real fucking mess when he looks at me because he lets it slide.

Theo comes off the wall. "I'll come with you."

"And why's that?"

"Because you're a flight risk, that's why," he tells me, looking at me like he can see into my brain. "You've got *meltdown* written all over you—"

"I'm not melting down—"

"Telling yourself that this is exactly what you've been trying to avoid since your mom died and your dad couldn't recover. And the moment you go all in with Jenna the worst happens—"

Something mean and ugly snaps inside me. "It did, though, didn't it? One second into it. It took *one fucking second*, and look where I ended up—"

"And that if you end it with her now, you can try to salvage that wall you lived behind before her—"

I swat his arm out of my way with a whole lot more force than necessary. "I'll be back in a couple minutes. But thanks for the vote of confidence."

CHAPTER 26

I don't wait for a reply. I pace down the hospital hallway, past rooms of people probably going through a hell of a lot worse than what we did. We're awake, after all. We're bruised and a little concussed, but we're alright. Still, I haven't been able to muster more than biting sarcasm, blank stares, and intermittent fury in the day since the accident.

A nurse eyes me over the digital chart in her hand as I march down the hall. I can't remember whether she was the one who handed me the vomit tray during the flatline incident or the one who tried to tell me to give my aching knee time to heal.

The outdoor air hits me in the face before I even realize I've made it outside. The sun is actually out, like it just doesn't understand what's going on, and it singes my eyes. I blink, trying to understand how I got here, out front of this hospital. Next to a bench overrun by pigeons, wolfing down someone's discarded sandwich.

I try to figure out my next move. Because maybe it pisses me off to no end that he's got my number like that, but Theo saw right through me.

I could stick around. As much time as she needs to get better, fully recover. And then... A wave of nausea hits me. And then I'd have to find a way to get the words out.

She could have the apartment, because fuck knows I couldn't keep living there after everything that's happened between us. Nina would let me stay with her. She'd judge the hell out of me for breaking it off with Jenna, and I'd deserve every bit of her disgust. But at least I'd never end up here. Again.

I rub my face roughly. Fuck.

I wish Jenna were out here. She'd help make sense of what's in my head.

"Finley."

It takes me a second to register who called my name. That it can't possibly be Jenna. Or Nina for that matter because I'm still in the process of pulling out my phone to call her for advice instead, and I don't think I've developed telepathy in the last twenty-four hours.

Dad's voice catches me especially off-guard because I don't think I've seen him outside the walls of our childhood home since Mom's funeral. Also, because I didn't call him here. Yet he's standing right in front of me, looking completely out of place as he takes me in.

"Dad. What are you doing here?"

"Hayley called me," he says. "Apparently she's the one you've got down as your emergency contact. I know it makes no sense that I'd feel sorry for myself about that, given the past few years. But it still didn't feel great to hear."

I don't say anything. There's a long list of things I'd rather be doing than having a heart-to-heart right now, starting with walking right through this parking lot and not slowing down until I find out for sure if it's possible to walk off the edge of the earth. The love of my life almost died yesterday. I'm not sure I can take any more.

Dad digs a tissue from his pocket and holds it out to me. I don't realize why until I taste blood from the split in my lip, which seems to open at ten-minute intervals.

"How is she?"

"She took the worst of it. Cuts, bruises. Her shoulder dislocated. She was knocked out for a few minutes."

"But she's alright?"

I shrug. It hurts. I do it again. "Mostly."

"And you? Are you okay?"

"I'm fine. My knee is messed up and I have a bit of a headache but that's it."

"Good." Dad nods slowly. "But that's not the only *okay* I was talking about. I know I'm not the poster child for talking through feelings. But the last time we were here—"

"Trust me, there's no need to get into that. I'm not about to forget where it is Mom died."

He flinches, but he doesn't lose eye contact. "And this time it's where they brought Jenna, and the next time it'll be—"

"There won't be a next time. There shouldn't have been a *this time*. I told myself I'd never do this. That I'd never let myself end up here, like you did." I jab a thumb over my shoulder, at the hospital. "And now look. I was right."

I knew something like this would happen. I tempted fate, anyway.

CHAPTER 26

"But she's fine. You're both fine—"

"*So what?* What if she's not the next time? I lose her, and then what, huh? I spend the next decade of my life haunting our apartment, waiting for someone to come and knock me out of it the way she did with you? I can't handle that, Dad."

I feel a twinge of guilt somewhere deep in my gut, the part apparently not yet covered in barbed wire and resentment. I shouldn't be lashing out like this.

After a painfully heavy pause in which I try to dig up the right words for an apology, Dad clears his throat. "That's fair."

I sigh. "No, it's not—"

"I wasn't done. I should have been the one to look after you after Mom died. I should have done something, anything, after you dropped out of school. Should have been able to be there for Hayley through her pregnancy. I failed you both, there's no doubt about that. But if you don't think you've got a responsibility to that girl you're thinking about quitting on... Well, I'm glad I caught you before you went and decided to do something stupid. Something you might never be able to undo, once you smarten up enough to realize your mistake."

Is it written on my damn forehead, or something?

I glare over the top of Dad's head, suddenly incapable of eye contact. "You've been a mess since the day Mom died. I have to have a little more self-preservation than that."

"And if you asked me whether I'd have done anything differently, even knowing how it ends between me and your mom, even knowing I'd be a mess for a decade after, I wouldn't change a thing. I'd have soaked in even more of her, leading up to the moment she went away. I'd have memorized every detail so that I'd still have them years after she was gone." He loses steam.

After a quiet moment I make myself look at him. He's staring at a spot beyond me, face screwed up. "She had this scar on her back shaped like an anchor. I've been trying to find it in old photos for years. And still, I can't remember which shoulder it was on."

I remember the scar. She told us her dog scraped her when she was

285

seventeen.

"It was on her left shoulder," I say. "A bit closer to the middle."

Dad nods thoughtfully. "The left shoulder. I think that's probably right."

My knee throbs. My limbs feel so goddamn heavy. I'm exhausted. Missing Mom is exhausting. She'd know what to do. She'd know the words to say to help me get my head right.

"I'd bring her back for you in a second if I could." Dad sighs like he knows what I'm thinking. "And I'd never have willingly gone without her. Playing it safe the way you have—the way you're trying to do now? If Mom knew you were planning to walk out on that girl of yours…"

"She'd kick my ass."

He nods his agreement. "And then she'd make you turn right around and undo it."

I meet his eye at last, and there's something so alive in them. Like he's fondly picturing it, the way Mom would glower at me until I got it together. I feel it all over again: the guilt at how badly I let Dad down over the years. About how I'd hidden from the loss of Mom at his expense.

"I never did sneak out again, by the way," I tell him. "After the night I busted my nose."

I don't remember the last time his face lit up like this. "Your Mom was a genius." Somehow, my face remembers how to smile. It's not big. But it's there. "You want to know her secret? She let me in on it, once."

I resent the optimism that perks up in my chest. Like Dad's about to offer me a silver bullet. The one that'll get me to stop being like this. To let go of what happened with Mom, and then with Dad, and just let myself savor the fact that, somehow, I got a woman like Jenna to love me.

"No parent wants to watch their kids get hurt, make mistakes, especially not when we could see some of the ones you and your sister were making from a mile away. But Mom believed in letting you win and lose. There was a lesson in there about feeling the lows, so that you'd know to appreciate the highs when you had them. So that you *wouldn't throw them away.*"

I sigh deeply. "Subtle."

"I'm not shooting for subtlety, Finley. Unless you think there's better for you out there—"

"There isn't," I say, recoiling in disgust. What a ridiculous concept. I knew from the start that, for me, falling in love would be a one-time event. That if it wasn't with Jenna, it wouldn't be with anyone.

"I know I'm not one to talk. I was drowning when we lost Mom, and I didn't try very hard to come up for air. Even now, it's still a fight. But I'm willing to give it a try. Hayley set me up with her therapist. It may be a good idea for you to see her as well."

There's a terrible joke in there somewhere, about a man they've called Good Time Finn needing therapy. Other than Dad and Hayley, there are only a handful of people in this world who have seen me any other way. I'm thinking about walking away from one of them. And I'll probably lose two more when I do.

Therapy, huh?

"Don't do it, Finley," Dad says. "Turn around. Go back inside."

Chapter 27

Jenna

They bring me back into the hospital room in a wheelchair, just in time to catch the look Jude exchanges with Theo. I don't need to ask what it's about. But I sweep every angle and corner of the room anyway, checking the space under every bit of furniture. I start looking for my phone until I remember it got destroyed in the crash.

"Where is he?" I turn to Theo, heart beating painfully fast. "I asked you to look after him. He's having a hard time with all this—where'd you let him wander off to alone?"

"He wanted to be alone." Theo runs an uncomfortable hand through his hair. "We haven't seen him since you left. I went to look for him, tried calling him, and…"

"Jenna, I'm so sorry," Jude says quietly. "He didn't look good. We think he left."

I grip the arm of my wheelchair with my good hand, just so it'll stop shaking. "Left to get some air, or left me?" Jude stares at me grimly.

Did you really think he'd change for you? Imaginary Ronnie's words claw through my insides. *He left you in a hospital. You were never special enough to keep him. You see that now, don't you?*

Honestly? I don't. What I see is that last look he gave me right before he saw the other car heading for us.

CHAPTER 27

Finn was going to tell me yes. To stay with him, to move in for real. I was sure of it. I heard it in his voice when he called my name. I saw the way he looked at me like he was coming out of an epiphany.

I've spent the entire summer believing there was more to him than the way people saw him. All the wide smiles, the deflections, the women, the scorecard. He spent the entire summer proving me right. He spent the entire summer convincing me that I *was* special, showing me what I deserve out of the people who are supposed to love me.

I *know* him. He's worried and scared. He's traumatized, after what he's been through. But Finn's never let me down. I don't believe he'd start today.

"Look again," I tell Theo. "Find him. Make sure he's okay."

The man leaves the room so fast you'd think it was on fire.

Jude comes to crouch in front of my chair. "It'll be alright, Jenna. No matter what happens. You could always stay with us—"

"He told me he loves me."

After a shocked moment, Jude closes her eyes. "He did?"

"Yeah. Before the accident. Jude, he wouldn't do this to me. He wouldn't leave like this."

Suddenly the woman looks like she's fighting a difficult battle with a squeal. I get it. It's hard not to melt into the floor, remembering the way he looked as he told me he loved me. He meant it.

Jude collects herself, and when she opens her eyes again they're round. Hopeful. She's practically vibrating with optimism, and I let it feed my own hope.

"I don't know what happened," I tell her. "I don't know where he is. But we'll be fine."

She squeezes both my knees so hard her nails dig into my skin. "I'm so happy for you."

I let out a weak laugh. "Well, there's still a good chance I'm eating my words in a second. But thanks, Juju."

We whip around at the sound of a knock on the door, and my heart lodges itself in my throat the second I catch sight of Theo in the doorway. I hate the look he gives me. It's the kind of look you give someone when you know you're about to crush them, but you don't have the guts to do it. To say the words.

I'm hopped up on enough painkillers to dull the ache from all my bumps and bruises. But that look hurts.

"I... I'm still not sure where he went," Theo says slowly. "But I didn't come back empty-handed."

He steps aside.

It's Dad. And, tucked behind him, looking so stiff she might think she's on her way to her own grave, is my mother.

"Peanut."

The nickname almost breaks me. So does the way Dad looks at me, taking in the bruising on my face with pained eyes. But I refuse to let it, sticking to the guns I held onto at the wedding. I'm not willing to give anything a go unless they are, too.

"What are you doing here?"

My mom stares fixedly at a point above my head. Dad shuffles uncomfortably from foot to foot. "Your young man called us, Peanut. We got here as fast as we could."

Finn called him?

Gripping the arm of my wheelchair, I gingerly lift myself out of it. Jude takes my good arm to steady me. I'm a little wobbly, but after a second I'm firm on my feet. It was mostly my upper body that took the hit.

"Do you want me to stay?" Jude whispers. I shake my head. I need to handle this on my own. With a glance at my parents she adds, at full volume: "We'll be right outside, okay Jenna? Call us in if you need anything."

Mom looks thoroughly unimpressed by Jude's ominous words, watching Theo follow her out of the room.

"How are you, Peanut?" Dad asks after a silent moment.

I shrug my good shoulder. "I have a minor concussion and they had to reset my shoulder. But they discharged me after my last round of tests." I watch him stare at my sling. "I have a very hard time believing Finn told you to come here. He wouldn't do that, with the way we left things at the wedding."

CHAPTER 27

"Well, you're right." Dad shifts on his feet. "He didn't strictly invite us."

"So why are you here?"

"We want to make amends, Peanut. To fix things."

My gaze drifts to Mom. "And you? Why are you here?"

It feels criminal, speaking to her that way. Uncomfortable. But so was the way she treated me. After a lengthy breath, my mother makes eye contact.

"As your father said, we've come to make... amends."

"And you sound just thrilled about that."

Her eyes narrow. "You've asked for an effort to be made. I've come here. Are you going to turn me away without listening to what we have to say?"

My charming mother, ladies and gentlemen.

But, despite the acidic tone and the way she looks like she'd rather be doing just about anything than grovel at my feet, she's right. I owe it to myself to hear them out. I sink into the armchair in the corner of the room.

Dad clears his throat. "Peanut. I can't even begin to adequately apologize for what happened at the wedding. You didn't deserve to be treated or spoken to that way. Your mom had a word with Aunt Marian, and it's all been resolved on that pesky end—"

"And what did you say to Aunt Marian?" I ask my mom.

She purses her lips. "Her behavior was, admittedly, downright appalling. I told her so."

Goose bumps crawl up my arms. If she used half the words she's used on me to convey her displeasure over the years, Aunt Marian must have been in for a nasty treat.

"Which behavior?" I push. I need to hear the words. That she understands why it was wrong.

She sighs impatiently. "She was inappropriate with your guest. She said things to you which she shouldn't have said—"

"Like what?"

"She should not have intimated that you weren't worthy of your partner—"

"How's that any different than what you said to me that night? What you've said to me in the past?"

Dad fidgets next to Mom. I don't have it in me to back down. "You've consistently told me that I need to be someone different to earn people's affection. People's respect. And why? Because I'm different from you? From Ronnie, your proper, golden child?"

"I am your mother. If I don't tell you these things, who on earth will?"

"You *didn't* tell me these things. You carved them into my heart, Mom. You turned me into someone who couldn't figure out what the hell she was worth."

"Language, Peanut—"

"And *you*," I say, rounding on Dad. "Where have you been? You've listened to her tell me these things for years. Veronica, too."

Dad looks like he's sucked on a lemon. He's shame-faced and shrinking into himself. It seems my mother has turned to stone. She hasn't moved an inch since the last time she spoke and looks like she's on the verge of a neat and poised walk out. Elodie Carling storms out of nowhere.

I stand. "You both need to go. I don't see the point of you coming all the way here, just for this—"

"You're right," Dad says at last. He stares at me grimly. "Every word of that was right, Peanut. But you have to know I would have done more if I understood. I didn't know just how bad it really was with Veronica. I didn't realize the extent of it."

"What do you mean?"

"We recently learned some very disturbing information."

The words hang in the air. Finally, Mom brings herself to look at me, though she's still as stone-faced as ever. "About your sister. My so-called golden child."

I frown. "What happened to her?"

Mom drops her gaze, examining her immaculate manicure. "Not a thing. She's on her honeymoon, blissfully happy. For now."

"And do you plan on clueing me in on what you're talking about, or am I going to have to dance for it?"

I can tell she's struggling with the words. Whatever it is that's tormenting her about her golden child, she's fighting with denial.

CHAPTER 27

Dad beats her to it: "Did she start a rumor about you in school, Peanut?"

My stomach bottoms out. I sink back into my seat. "Which rumor?"

Dad's eyes flash with something a little terrifying. "I hope you're not telling me there was more than one."

"Did Finn tell you this?"

"Answer the question, Genevieve."

I force a steadying breath into my body, willing away the humiliation. Why should I feel embarrassed, anyway? She was the one in the wrong. "It wasn't a rumor. She told my entire class about the first time I had sex."

My mother, Elodie Carling of all people, starts grinding her teeth. Dad sags into himself. "What happened at her bachelorette celebration?"

I will not cry about this again. I don't speak until I know the words will come out steady. "She and her friends left me behind at a cocktail lounge. I suspect they planned it all along to avoid spending the rest of the night with me."

I think Mom's teeth might fall out the second she releases her jaw. "Why didn't you inform us?"

I chuckle in disbelief. "Why would I? You and I never had that kind of relationship. And Dad never bothered to stick up for me before."

She clutches her hands so tight they start to pale. "Yes, but this—these were egregious things, Genevieve."

"Jenna. My name is Jenna."

She lets a breath rattle through her teeth. I've never seen my mother a step below composed. I may be imagining it, but her hair seems to be frizzing as the fury rolls off her. "Did she or did she not make you stand in front of a mirror—"

"She did. That was her favorite thing to do."

Mom marches straight for the window next to my chair, staring out with her usual perfect posture. But when she speaks again, it's in a voice I barely recognize. It's raw. Livid. Nothing like soft dulcet tones she'd tried to instill in me as a kid.

"The trust fund goes, Gord."

Dad nods grimly. "It goes. Not that it will matter much, given who she married."

"It'll matter. Because we know what she is now. Veronica revels in other people's approval. Our approval. She'll know she no longer has it, and it'll kill her."

Surreptitiously, I pinch the side of my thigh with my good arm. It seems I am awake.

I don't know what any of this does for me. Ronnie losing a trust fund she no longer needs, my parents' approval. It doesn't fix the damage she's done over the years. But I feel intense satisfaction. Relief. Whatever Mom wishes I was, it's not who Ronnie turned out to be. However much she resents me for being different, she doesn't think I was deserving of what I got at the hands of my sister.

Slowly, Mom turns on the spot, steadying herself on the window behind her, leaving a handprint she'd normally abhor.

"What was done to you was unacceptable. What was said to you was unacceptable. From all parties involved, me included. We are twenty-nine years in, and I'm not certain I can undo any of that. But I would like to attempt it."

"Do I sense an apology?"

She takes in a long breath, squaring her shoulders. "I apologize."

"Me too, Peanut. I'm sorry I didn't pay closer attention to what was going on."

I'm locked in a standoff with my mother. I can see she loathes what's happening. Admitting fault. Realizing she was wrong.

"I'm dyeing my hair pink again," I inform her.

My mother swallows, gaze cutting to the blonde top of my head. "Very well."

"And my name is—"

"Jenna," she finishes with a brisk nod. "So you said."

I snort. This moment is ridiculous. My mom is ridiculous. It's the most heart-felt conversation we've ever had, and we're doing it with several feet between us, and no urge to close that gap. Still, though—

I return her nod. "It's a start."

CHAPTER 27

Dad rises to his feet, beckoning me into his arms as Mom heads for the door. "You've turned out so well in spite of all this, Jenna." I nod into his shoulder. I don't need him to tell me that. I already know it. But it's nice to hear, anyway. "Would you consider joining us for dinner on Sunday?"

"I can't, Dad. I fly to Portugal after tomorrow."

"Even after the accident? Is that wise?"

I shrug. "The doctor cleared me for it. But if the invitation for dinner still stands when I'm back, I'd consider it."

"It will." I watch Dad join Mom at the door. "And bring your young man with you, Peanut. I had my doubts about the whole thing at first but after all this business with your sister, it's clear he cares for you very deeply."

I think he does, too. And I really hope I'm not wrong.

Chapter 28

Jenna

Finn's apartment is rarely silent, at least when he's in it. So I'm not sure why I expected to hear a pin drop when I came through the front door, dropping my key on the kitchen counter.

"Hi, Eddie," I whisper as I cross the living room. "How's our guy doing? Does it look promising?"

Eddie doesn't seem particularly concerned with our affairs. The turtle slips off a rock and into the water in his tank. He may be begging us to get our act together, already. But I can't be sure.

"Why do I have so many pairs of goddamn sneakers?"

Sneakers? He left to mess with his collection of sneakers?

I follow the sounds of his muttering and rummaging toward the bedrooms, slamming the breaks so hard when I reach the hallway that I have to steady myself on the wall.

"What the..."

The hall is a mess.

There are piles of clothes thrown all over the place, mismatched shoes everywhere. When I freeze in the space between our bedrooms to take in the way mine has been stripped clear of nearly everything, I almost get hit in the head by a shoe flying out of Finn's open door.

"When was the last time I wore these, even?"

CHAPTER 28

The matching sneaker comes flying at me following his words.

I take a proper look at his room. It's been turned upside down.

Half his dresser drawers are open and empty, and piles of his clothes dot the hardwood. His bed is covered in pale pink sheets. My fuzzy throw blanket is hanging over his headboard. And what looks like the entire content of my closet is piled high on his mattress.

I try. I try so hard to hang onto that last sliver of skepticism just in case I'm misinterpreting the whole thing. But it's nearly impossible to keep those raging butterflies in check at the sight of my sheets on his bed.

Clearing my throat loudly, I say: "Okay, you're going to have to talk me through this one, kid."

A yelp comes from somewhere along the far wall, and when I look around his bed I find Finn on hands and knees, his upper body buried inside the closet. He scrambles out fast, hair whipping around as he follows the sound of my voice.

He looks awful, somehow worse than when I saw him a couple of hours ago. The split in his bottom lip seems to have recently reopened, and I've never seen him so disheveled. I want to hold him, and clean him up, and fuss over him, and standing an arm's length away without immediately melting into him feels like a sin.

But I need to hear him say it. I need him to tell me I was right to believe he didn't leave me. That he isn't going to try to leave me. *Leave me*, leave me.

"What are you doing here?" Finn barks.

Okay. Not the words I was hoping for.

"They discharged me after my tests," I tell him, wincing as I shrug my bad shoulder.

From his knees, Finn sweeps me from head to toe, as though triple checking me for injuries he didn't notice since the last time he scanned me. When he doesn't find anything out of place, he looks around the room like it'll offer him clues as to my arrival, then stands to dig through the pile of clothes on his bed until he produces his phone.

"Fuck. I had it on silent." He pales and meets my eye looking so pained. "I'm so sorry. The nurse said she'd call me when you were back from your tests. I didn't think they'd discharge you today. I thought I had enough time to pull this off before going back."

"You... you didn't leave me?"

His entire body deflates at the words, and then he charges. Beelines straight for me, so fixated on my face he nearly trips over a pile of clothes on the ground between us.

"No. I didn't leave you." His shaking fingers meet my cheek, touching me gently, and I realize he's brushing over my bruises. "I mean, technically I did, in the physical sense. And... And I can't lie to you, Jenna. I did consider leaving in the metaphorical way, too. But it would have been a huge mistake."

His wide eyes plead me to believe him, to forgive him, to focus on the part where he stayed. And then he seems to think better of what he's asking me to do. He marches back to his closet and rips a shirt off its hanger. Tosses it over his shoulder and replaces it with one of the skirts lying on his bed.

"I don't want you to go," he says, ripping out another one of his shirts.

"To Portugal?"

He raises an arm, and in a single swipe clears off the shelf at the top of his closet, clothes dropping to the ground. "I don't want you to move out. I know I panicked when you brought it up. I think I was still hanging on to the thought that I had an emergency exit out of this in case something went wrong. That I could point to it and think... There. We weren't real anyway. It wasn't serious. I'll be fine."

"Finn, we don't have to live together. You were honest about needing to take things slow—"

He turns, grabbing a dress off his bed. "I was wrong. Slow isn't what I want. I want everything that means you're mine. I want everything that means I get you, from now until... For as long as I can have you. Okay? I want everything you said you wanted. I want to be the hot stud you come home to, who gets to give you that shiny ring. And I know that's probably conceited, calling myself a hot stud. But—"

Finn narrows his eyes at the dress he's picked up. It's black, the one Ronnie bought me, and he launches it across the room like it's a live grenade.

"I want to live together." He looks so frenzied now, tossing a pair of his

CHAPTER 28

jeans out of the closet, and then another. "I'm so in love with you it's painful. A *good* kind of pain I realized... And I'm sorry you got stuck with someone so emotionally obtuse, but I..." He reaches into his closet and rips out a whole armful of clothes that he dumps at his feet. "You were right, Jenna. It's crazy, living with someone this early into a relationship. But it's the kind of crazy I want."

He starts pulling free heels buried under the pile of clothes on his bed and turns back to his closet cradling armfuls of my shoes like he's holding twin newborns. Finn drops to his knees and lays them out inside his closet, tossing out a couple more pairs of sneakers when he runs out of room.

A warm laugh starts bubbling up my throat. I dodge past a pair of sweats he throws over his shoulder. "Finn, sharing a closet kind of requires you to keep some of your stuff in it, too."

He doesn't seem to hear me. He continues rummaging inside. "And there *is* no emergency exit for me, okay? I mean, you're the one who should keep an emergency exit if we're being honest here. You're dealing with a bit of an idiot, and I'm probably gonna go and screw this up with you about a thousand times over our lives, but—"

"Finn." I cross the room and sink to my knees beside him.

"You almost died, Jenna. Like... Like actually *died* and what the hell was I doing this whole time, huh? Wasting the seconds I could have had with you. You almost died. You almost *died*—"

"Finn, stop." I reach for him, tangling my fingers in his shirt and tugging until he finally withdraws from his closet.

His eyes are wide and agitated, and there's a deep flush covering him from the neckline of his t-shirt up to his hair, sticking out all over the place. "I'm so sorry I left you there. I swear, I was coming back for you."

"I know. I believe you." Finn closes his eyes, shoulders dropping in relief. "You told my parents about Veronica."

He winces, shoving the hair off his face. "Yeah, that... didn't go over well. I found an RSVP from her wedding when I cleared out your room, and I called the number on it and... I didn't mean to get into it all, but the second I started talking—well, you know how I get. You deserved to have them know how close they were to losing you. How wrong they are about you. How important it is for them to try to make it up to you. Did your dad call? He promised me he would."

Oh, Finn.

I touch my lips to his, meaning for it to be sweet and quick, aware of the state we're in. Bruised and exhausted and smelling like a hospital. But there's just no hope for it. The moment I feel him I'm working for more, kissing him deeply, meeting his tongue.

Finn breaks away abruptly. "I also—I forgot to say I bought a flight to Europe. In case you wanted me to come."

My sweet Finn.

"You've been very busy." I get my fingers in his hair and he groans, leaning into the touch. "I definitely want you to come. What's your seat number? I'll try to swap to the one beside you."

"Oh. Ah..." He makes a face. "Actually, I'm not going to Portugal. I'm going to Romania."

"*Romania?*"

"Yeah, ever been?" I shake my head, and he lets his hands roam over my body, down my waist. "They didn't have any spots left on your flight. Or... really any other flight remotely close to Portugal around your departure time. Maybe you change your flight? I hear Romania's great this time of year—the internet really talked it up."

I snort, dissolving into laughter. Finn grips my face and with a playful growl he nips near my chin, over my dimple like he wants to swallow it whole. "I can come meet you in Portugal."

"No. Romania sounds great."

I find his lips again, and it seems we're on the same page. Finn moves me gently, cradling my bad shoulder as he lays me down on top of the mess of clothes surrounding us. I pull him close, the bruises along my side screaming in protest, but the desperation to have him against me, every bit of him touching every bit of me, overshadows the pain.

"Ow—*shit.*" Finn pulls away and dabs his mouth with the back of his hand. "Stupid cut won't heal. We might have to put a pin in this. Take it easy for a

CHAPTER 28

while."

I wriggle underneath him, my body already uncomfortably tight with need. The scab on his lip is still intact, but the skin around it is starting to look angry. I touch it gently. "Poor thing. Why don't we take a nice, naked bath and then have cuddles with Eddie instead?"

He groans, this long, rumbling one from deep inside his throat as though I just pushed my hands into his sweats. His eyes squeeze shut. "I'm immune. *I'm immune*, Jenna."

"And we can make steaming hot Bagel Bites and put on whichever documentary you want—"

In a second he has my shorts around my knees. "You are way too damn good at that."

Epilogue

Three weeks later

Impulse control has never been my strong suit.

Sometimes it works out in my favor, like the time I agreed to live with a basic stranger for the summer. Other times, like when I decided I wanted to try jumping my horse as a kid, without any practice... Well, I probably shouldn't have done that.

The horse was fine. I was not.

I've realized a helpful trick is to fall for someone with their head on straight, who's able to tame your impulses when you start getting a little over the top. One day, I might take my own advice. Although, it might be a little late for that.

"How are we explaining this again?"

I follow Finn through the lounge of Sunset Landing. It's that awkward time between lunch and dinner, quiet except for a couple of occupied tables. Nina is chatting up the bartender ahead. As we pass she gives us an amused shake of her head, and then dissolves into a loud laugh that effectively confuses everyone around her.

I nudge Finn. "Looks like she took it well."

He suppresses a grin. "Of course, she did," he says, leading us to the back office. "The story's simple: we're in love. We were on an amazing trip, sitting on the beach at sunset, and I had one of my usual strokes of brilliance.

These things, they just come to me."

"It sounds so nice when you put it that way. Not at all crazy."

"Hey." He tugs me back when my hand hits the office door, gathering my face in his hands. "I have no regrets. I didn't yesterday either, and I won't tomorrow. We would have ended up this way, regardless. We just cut to the chase, didn't we?"

I try to keep my smile in check. I'm not totally sure feeling this happy is particularly legal. "Yeah. No regrets."

He drops a kiss on my forehead. "Let's do this."

The office door swings open. And instead of the deafening squeal and crushing hug I played in my mind when I imagined this reunion, we're greeted by a sight not unlike the moment we just had on the other side of the door. Jude is bundled up in Theo's lap as they sit behind the desk, grinning faces huddled close together.

Their heads snap in our direction at the sound of Finn's clearing throat, with identical giddy, if not slightly guilty expressions.

"Missed us?" Finn asks, throwing an arm over my shoulders.

"A lot," Jude answers, getting slowly to her feet. "It's been a crazy few weeks."

Theo rises, too. "Actually, we have something to tell you."

"So do we," I tell them. I squeeze Finn around the middle. "Over to you, kid."

Finn clears his throat. "So, as you know, we're in love. We were just on an amazing trip, sitting on the beach at sunset. And then I had one of my usual strokes of brilliance—"

Theo snorts.

"These things, they just come to me sometimes," Finn continues, undeterred.

"Do they?" Theo pipes in.

Finn eyes him, totally deadpan. "Have I ever told you guys the story of how Theo launched his career? It was a little *stroke of brilliance* I like to call tarragon—"

Theo groans, dragging a hand down his face as Jude and I lapse into quiet laughter. "Get on with it, Palmer. You're not the only one with something to say."

"Wait," I say, narrowing my eyes at Jude. These two are being shifty. "What's your news?"

She and Theo exchange a grinning glance. And then I see it. A thin, sparkling band on her left ring finger, and a silver one on Theo's.

"Oh my God." A compulsive giggle of disbelief leaks out of my mouth. "Did you actually—you *actually*—"

"*Wait*," Jude gasps, gripping Theo's arm, and from here I can see the way her nails dig into his skin. Her gaze bounces from my left hand to Finn's, a slow smile spreading across her face. "Are you serious?"

"Totally serious."

"Holy crap."

Cue the squealing. Jude practically leaps over the desk to wrap herself around my neck, and when I pick her up and swing her, legs flailing in the air and almost whacking Finn in the process, he throws Theo a look.

"What the hell just happened?" he calls over Jude's loud refrain of *holy crap, holy crap!*

Theo gives an exasperated sigh. "I don't even try to keep up with these two anymore. Should we go get a drink? Wait them out?"

"You're sanctioning drinking during work?" Finn claps him on the back as they head for the door. "You are the *very bestest boss*—"

"I swear to God, Palmer."

With a last amused look in our direction they leave us to our squealing, bickering their way to the bar.

Sunset Landing Series

Want more Finn and Jenna? Receive a bonus epilogue set five years after the end of The No-Judgment Zone. Visit: https://BookHip.com/SWJWAZQ

The Sixty/Forty Rule (book 1) — Theo and Jude

Restaurant designer Jude Holland butts heads with grumpy chef Theo Jordan, as they work together to open Sunset Landing. Includes a bonus chapter featuring the night Finn met Jenna!

Available today on Amazon and Kindle Unlimited.

The No-Judgment Zone (book 2) — Finn and Jenna

Join Ellie K. Wilde's newsletter for bonus content and updates on future book releases! Visit: subscribepage.io/elliekwilde

Acknowledgments

There's a good chance all of this is just a dream I'll wake up from any minute, but I'll write this out anyway: one second I'm publishing my first novel just for fun, a pure labour of love that—for better or worse—I tackled on my own. Next second, there's another novel out there with an honest-to-god team behind it.

Thank you to beta readers Kinzey, Shruthi and Becky whose advice and encouragement helped make TNJZ the story it turned out to be. You also unknowingly talked me off a ledge, when I genuinely couldn't tell whether I'd written something decent or something that I should immediately set on fire.

Thank you to Jenn, my saint of an editor who saved me from a multitude of perilous run-on sentences. I don't claim to be cured from the need to stuff every English word into a single sentence, but TNJZ is much better off because of you.

Thank you to Ashley, whose cover designs for both TNJZ and The Sixty/Forty Rule truly leveled-up these books, rescuing them from the makeshift versions I created when I thought they'd only exist in a sad, dusty corner of the internet. (Jenn, how bad did that sentence make you cringe?)

To my husband, still the only person in my life who knows about this side-gig. Thank you for letting me prance around the house pretending I'm a real-life author. Also for all the pep talks in the lead-up to this release. And all the pep talks to come, if I manage to write another one of these.

ACKNOWLEDGMENTS

To everyone who read, reviewed and recommended The Sixty/Forty Rule: thank you. One of these days I'll be able to wrap my head around the fact that people actually read and *enjoyed* (what the actual f***?!) this brain child of mine.

And last, but not least, to Kathleen: ARC reader for The Sixty/Forty Rule and certified dream-maker. I cannot thank you enough for getting the book in front of readers.

Printed in Great Britain
by Amazon